# ANOTHER LIFE

# ANOTHER LIFE

A NOVEL

## ROBERT HALLER

BLACK
STONE
PUBLISHING

Copyright © 2019 by Robert Haller
Published in 2019 by Blackstone Publishing
Cover and book design by Alenka Vdovič Linaschke

Printed in the United States of America

First edition: 2019
ISBN 978-1-9825-2606-1
Fiction / Literary

1 3 5 7 9 10 8 6 4 2

CIP data for this book is available
from the Library of Congress

Blackstone Publishing
31 Mistletoe Rd.
Ashland, OR 97520

www.BlackstonePublishing.com

*For the parents. For the kids.*

My beloved spake, and said unto me,
Rise up, my love, my fair one, and come away.
For lo, the winter is past, the rain is over and gone;
The flowers appear on the earth;
The time of the singing of birds is come,
And the voice of the turtle is heard in our land;
The fig tree putteth forth her green figs,
and the vines with the tender grape give a good smell.
Arise, my love, my fair one, and come away.

—Song of Songs

Everybody's got a hungry heart.

—Bruce Springsteen

# PART 1

# I

## LAURA

I wasn't a bad girl. None of it had been my idea. Under the gazebo in the park, it was Bethany who started up about the bath salts and how snorting them was supposedly like taking acid. But she didn't know for sure, it was just what she'd heard some of the senior girls saying in the locker room last week. And, of course, Ian wanted proof. So we piled into his car and headed to Walmart, the only store that sold bath salts in our town, the only store still open at this time of night. It was Friday, the first night of summer vacation, and I was fifteen.

In the back seat, pressed up against the door handle and Bethany's left side, I looked up "snorting bath salts" on my phone and scrolled through the results. I didn't love the idea of running around town naked, out of my mind, ripping people's faces off with my teeth. It just didn't seem the best way to start the summer. But at fifteen, you can't always afford to be a conscientious objector, or even a conscientious observer. You are a willing participant or you are alone.

"Ian, why are we taking these side streets?" Nola asked, sitting on the other side of Bethany. "It's faster just to go down Main."

"I just want to see something real quick," said Ian.

I watched the town roll slowly by—blue television light streaming out from the windows of some houses while others sat dark, toys lying dormant on front lawns, Little Tikes cars and inflatable swimming pools, a lone cat prowling the sidewalk. I could feel Bethany breathing beside me, her rib cage rising and falling in steady rhythm. I didn't look at her. As Nola argued with Ian and Joey up front, demanding they change the music, I resisted the urge to grab Bethany by the arm, open the car door, and leap out, taking my best friend with me. We would hit the pavement and roll onto the curb, bruised but safe. She'd yell at me first, call me crazy, but much later—years from now, even—she would see that I'd been right.

On Linwood Street, Ian slowed the car to a crawl. Nola began to laugh. "Really, Ian? *This* is what you wanted to see?"

Ian didn't answer, just looked across the street at the house we had stopped in front of. We all looked.

There was nothing especially strange about the plain white house. The windows were dark, and the grass in front was maybe a little longer than it should have been, but not by much.

"I've heard he hasn't been out since he came back," Nola said after a moment. "Just sits in there doing nothing."

"How do you know, though?" said Ian, staring at the house. "He could be doing anything in there: writing songs, recording. It's only his mom with him, so we don't know."

Suddenly, I understood. They were talking about Paul Frazier.

Four years ago, Paul had fronted a high school band called the Seizures. The story goes that on the band's first gig at Mullen's, a restaurant downtown, people half a dozen blocks away had called the cops about the noise. Although the band had been together only a year, kids still talked about their shows. If you were one of the few lucky enough to have seen them play, you held a certain authority. At school this past year, I had overheard many arguments between juniors and seniors claiming to have gone to one of their shows, and the doubters and detractors who hadn't. Sometimes, walking through town I would see RIP SEIZURES spray-painted in the alleyways between vacant buildings.

I hadn't heard of the Seizures until this year, my first year of high school. By the time I'd been "enlightened to the noise," the band was long defunct. Paul Frazier had left for college in New York City, and all that was left of the band were the stories and the memories and a six-song EP, still available for download on their Myspace page. But earlier in May, the word was that Paul had returned. He'd moved back into his mother's house and had hardly been seen or heard from since. He stayed in his room, holed away from the rest of the town, like a monk or a sleeping vampire.

"I think it's over, man." Nola ran her hands through her short dark hair. "He's never going to play again."

Ian shook his head. "I don't know."

I'd learned quickly that this was the group's favorite topic of debate: Paul Frazier. Nola and Joey were skeptics, but Ian still clung to a slim but dogged hope. Out of all of us, Ian was his biggest fan. Although he was in our grade, Ian was a year older and the only one of us who could drive. He was also the only one of us who had seen Paul's band, sneaking out with his older brother to one of the Seizures' shows when he was only twelve—or so he claimed. During these arguments, Bethany and I stayed silent. We were the newcomers. I couldn't speak for Bethany, but in this group's presence I evaluated every word before I said it, mentally proofing future sentences in my head.

I was in this car because of Bethany, my best friend since first grade. Wherever she went, I went, too. I hardly knew these other kids. But if clever, pretty Bethany wanted to hang out with them, then I was coming along, like a dog dragged on a leash. Just a dumb, anxious dog, with nothing clear to contribute. Just Laura: sort of cute but not pretty, with a cluster of freckles splattered across my nose, and thick, unruly red hair. I was good at making myself invisible.

In the Walmart parking lot, Ian pulled into a space as far away from the entrance as possible, although there were hundreds of free spaces closer. We climbed out of his old Saturn. It was one of the first warm nights of the year, and it felt strange to be out this late with bare arms, not chilled by the breeze. While everyone else headed for the entrance, I grabbed Bethany's arm and held her back. She raised her eyebrows, impatient. I tried not to show that this look hurt. "Hey," I said, "do you know what bath salts are supposed to do to you? I just looked it up."

Bethany looked at my phone in disdain, as if phones were now beneath her. "You know, just because it's online doesn't make it true, Laura."

"It doesn't make it false, either," I said.

She glanced at Ian and Nola and Joey, who had stopped a few yards ahead and were looking back at us, waiting.

"Apparently, they make you do weird stuff," I said. "Really weird stuff."

For a second, I could see her almost caving to me; then she shook her head. "Don't be so lame, Laura. I want to actually *do things* this summer." She turned and headed toward the store, and I had no choice but to follow.

Inside Walmart, we drifted down the aisles, past mad, grinning animal faces on the fronts of cereal boxes, past women's underwear and kiddie T-shirts graced with the latest Disney starlet, everything lit in a cold fluorescent glow. This was where I went with my mom and little brother for laundry detergent or school supplies, but tonight, it didn't feel familiar. Tonight, we were on the verge of something strange and dangerous.

It turned people into zombies, one article on my phone had said, blood-hungry zombies. Ian led us to the health and beauty section and, after a minute of scanning the aisle, pointed to a small tub with the words "Soothing Bath Salts" on the front. The second he picked it up, my dumb heart began to pound. None of us spoke on the way to the checkout line.

Only one register was open, and the large, scowling cashier raised her eyebrows when she saw us. "Before I ring you up," she said, "can you tell me what five kids are doing buying *bath salts* at eleven o'clock at night?"

Ian replied without hesitation. "It's a gift for my mom. Her birthday's tomorrow."

Eyebrows still raised, the woman made no move to ring up our purchase. "These ain't gonna get you high, you know," she said.

I clenched my fist and glanced at Ian. "Excuse me?" he managed.

"The salts that get you high, you can't get at a Walmart—or anywhere in Grover Falls. Trust me, you aren't the first bunch of kids I've seen try to do this." A bemused, almost evil grin spread across her face. "Just thought I'd save you some time."

We all looked at Ian. It was a full ten seconds before he mumbled, "It's a gift for my mom," and pushed the salts closer to the register. The cashier rang it up. "Twenty-two fifty, please," she said.

THE BATH SALTS LAY BETWEEN MY FEET on the floor of the car, and as we pulled out of the Walmart parking lot and onto the road, I wondered what Ian would do with them now. Maybe he would give them to his mother after all.

"I have some of that weed left in my bag," said Nola, now in the front passenger seat, as Ian began to drive back the way we'd come. "The stuff we had last weekend."

Ian nodded. From my spot in the back seat, I could see his profile, lit intermittently by passing traffic. He looked sad and disappointed.

"Are we really going back to your basement to smoke?" Joey asked, sitting next to me. It was the first time I'd heard him speak without being spoken to first.

Nola looked at him the rearview mirror. "You have any better suggestions?"

Joey sighed but didn't say anything. I felt my body begin to tense. I had never smoked weed before, and the idea of doing it for the first time around kids I was trying to impress sent my heart into overdrive. We had just tried to buy bath salts to use as narcotics, but at least then we'd all been equally clueless. Nola talked about weed the way Bethany and I might talk about going to the mall—it was something they did all the time. She had it in her bag, and we were going to her house to smoke it. No Walmart cashier was going to stop *us*.

"It's just so cold in your basement," Joey burst out again, "and we go there all the time."

"Well, we could go to your house, except that your parents are fucking Nazis," Nola snapped, turning around in her seat to look at Joey. "Or, Ian, what about your house?"

Ian shook his head. "Not happening."

"Guess that leaves my basement." Nola gave Joey a triumphant jerk of her head.

"I have the keys to the church," Bethany said in a rush.

For a moment, everyone was silent. Bethany's father was a pastor. Our town was small enough that they all surely knew this already, but during the past few weeks, whenever Bethany was around her new friends during lunch or study hall, she had gone out of her way to avoid the topic. I couldn't understand why she suddenly wanted to remind them.

Nola looked at Bethany. "So?"

"So we could smoke the weed there … if you wanted," Bethany said timidly.

Nola was looking at her with raised eyebrows, and I could almost physically feel the skepticism in the car. Then Ian broke it. "Hey, your dad's church is the one that used to be a school, right?"

Bethany nodded. "Yeah."

"We could smoke on the roof and watch the stars."

"How romantic," Nola muttered.

New Life Center was in a brick school building that had been closed since the eighties, after a new, larger school was built on the other side of town. It sat in a field on the outskirts of Grover Falls, with a long drive that spilled into a giant parking lot. New Life had bought the property about ten years ago, after our old church building burned down in a fire. In the years between the school's closing and our church's buying it, the town had turned the giant surrounding field into a twelve-hole golf course. Our church had decided not to anger the town by shutting down the popular golf course, so instead, we ran it ourselves. Some people in the congregation didn't think it was right for the course to stay open on Sunday mornings, but since that was when it got most of its business, it didn't make sense to close it. Sometimes, during Bethany's father's sermons, you could hear a golfer yelling "Fore!" out on the green.

It had been easy enough to find a way out onto the roof. Bethany led us through the door, and we sneaked through the dark hallway and up the stairs. I'd been in the building countless times, but never this late at night. The empty darkness had a menacing feel that our whispers and giggles didn't seem to relieve. One of the third-floor classrooms had a closet with a steel ladder that led up to an unlocked trapdoor, bringing us out onto the roof. By the time we were on top, I had pretty much forgotten about the weed. It seemed thrilling enough to have broken and entered, to be out here, the night breeze wafting across my face and through my hair, the lights of Grover Falls visible in the distance.

But Nola wasted no time. She knelt down, dug the weed out of her backpack, and quickly rolled a joint. After it went around the circle that ended with me, I had no choice. When the smoke hit my lungs and I started to cough, I panicked.

"Come here, son." Nola placed a hand on my shoulder and gently took the joint from me. "Let me show you how it's done." I watched her pale face pull in and grow thin as she inhaled, and then the bloom of her dark lips as she breathed out the smoke, talking in a pinched voice as she did. "You have to *invite* it into your lungs. This weed is a friend; make it feel welcome." She brushed a strand of hair from her face and handed me back the joint.

One minute I wanted to kiss someone, the next I was dying to talk about extraterrestrial life. I settled for spreading myself out on the cold roof deck and staring up at the stars. If I squinted, I could make them all come together and form a giant ball of light, like how I imagined things had been at the beginning of the universe, before God decided that his own divine presence wasn't enough.

As the others laughed and fooled around with some irons and golf balls Ian had taken from the supply shed, I pulled my phone out of my pocket and held it above my face. A new message was waiting for me on my MatchUp app: Martin. Though I wanted to, I resisted opening the app and reading the message. Someone might see. Also, my phone battery was almost dead. Instead, I looked back up at the sky and wondered, not for the first time, what Martin would say if he could see me now.

Our online conversations had grown longer and more intimate in the past few weeks. Only the night before, we'd landed on the subject of death. Michael Jackson had just died, and Martin was upset. On chat, I did my best to appear upset, too, but in truth, the King of Pop's death hadn't fazed me much. I didn't listen to his music, so for me he was just a sad old R&B star. To cover myself, I tried to steer the conversation away from Jackson by talking about death in general. I mentioned how death scared me because it was the one thing in life everybody had to confront, but the one thing we knew absolutely nothing about. I talked about how

I'd been raised to believe in an afterlife, though usually the idea of *not being* seemed more convincing to me, but also more terrifying. I'd begun writing all this to Martin as a way of deflection, but as I typed, I realized it was all true: I was afraid of death. If I thought about it at night, it was hard to fall asleep. I was scared I would never again wake up.

I had worried that my fears would sound dumb and immature to Martin, that he would think me childish. But, as usual, he understood. He told me he used to feel the same way, but he had come to the conclusion that the idea of not being, of nothingness, was comforting. Death was no different from before we were born, when not being had meant no pain or fear. I'd never thought about it that way before, and Martin was right, the idea was comforting.

Bethany's face filled up my vision. She lay down beside me on the roof. "How ya doing?"

"Just stargazing." I let my anger at her go. I could always get it back if I wanted to.

I turned to look at her, and it hit me. "You like Ian, don't you?" I said. I had already been suspicious but hadn't known how deep it went. If she was willing to snort bath salts for this boy, if she was willing to break into church and risk getting caught by her dad, then it must be serious.

We both looked over to where Ian stood, hitting golf balls off the side of the roof. Nola was beside him, drawling in a voice I recognized but couldn't place—"Ah say, ah say, boy, ya gotta put more energy into yer drive there, son. Really put yer back into it!"—while Joey looked on and laughed.

Bethany looked back up at the sky. "No, Laura, I don't like Ian."

It was standard practice, of course, to deny any allegation of a crush the first time it was made—even one made by your best friend. Still, her lie hurt a little. "Bullshit," I said, trying to keep my voice light.

"No, seriously …" she began, but then stopped.

A bright floodlight had come on in the church parking lot. Then a man's voice: "Whoever is up on that roof, you are trespassing on private property. Do not move! I'm coming up."

Of course we all moved. We moved in every direction, scrambling to find a way off the roof that wasn't the way we had come. My head felt weightless, like a balloon filled with helium. It felt as if there were hundreds of us up there, searching for an escape route. We kept bumping into different versions of ourselves. Finally, out of the confusion, I heard Joey shout, "Over here!"

He was at the far corner of the roof, looking down. When we reached him, we saw the ladder leading down to the jutting wing of the first story. From there, it was only about ten feet to the ground. I followed Ian down the ladder, the others behind me, and soon we all were looking out over the edge of the first-story roof.

Ian was the first to jump. Without hesitation, he launched himself off the roof and into the air. We heard a dull thud at his body hit the grass, and then his voice: "It's okay. It doesn't hurt. Jump!"

I found myself jumping. For a moment, I was airborne, falling through the night. A second later, I was standing on the wet dew of the lawn next to Ian, waiting for the others. I felt a sharp pain in my right ankle, but when Ian asked whether I was okay, I said I was.

Nola jumped next, then Bethany and Joey. For a second, we all stood there in the grass, slightly dazed. Then there was a shout; it sounded as if it were coming from heaven. I thought it was God. We looked up to the third-story roof. A figure stood where we had been five minutes before. "You kids, I see you. Stay where you are! You're only going to make things worse for yourselves if you run."

Beside me, Bethany let out a small gasp. "Shit, that's my dad!"

"There's no way he can tell who we are," said Ian, and since I couldn't tell who was up there—Bethany had recognized her father only by the sound of his voice—I guessed he was right.

Ian took off across the green, and we followed. Instead of heading back toward the road, where his car was parked on the curb, he led us toward the woods behind the church. After the golf course was a wall of pine, and after that a small marsh. We would have to wade through the marsh to get to the other side of town. I wondered whether Ian knew this as I struggled to keep up with the rest of them. Sharp pain flared in my ankle every time my foot hit the ground. I tried to ignore it and keep running. Warm summer air whipped across my face, and I heard crickets singing in the night. Stars fell down on me.

By the time I reached the pine grove, it was becoming harder and harder for me to run. The others were getting farther ahead. I called for them to wait but was so out of breath, I could manage only a weak gasp. The next second, my foot caught on something—a protruding rock or an exposed root—and I fell face-first onto the ground.

The wind was knocked out of me, but the forest floor was soft. When I picked myself up, I couldn't see the others. They hadn't noticed me falling behind, or maybe they had but decided not to stop. I felt like crying. I considered turning around, going back to the church and finding Bethany's dad, ratting us all out. I'd get in trouble, but they would be in a lot more, especially Bethany. But loyalty won out, and I continued through the woods alone. Limping along, I thought of all the things I would say to Bethany when I saw her again, all the wonderfully cutting things, trying to keep other feelings at bay—feelings I couldn't let get the better of me. I was alone in the woods at night. *Alone. Woods. Night.* Three things that didn't go together well.

After what felt like forever, although it couldn't have been more than five minutes, I came to the edge of the grove. The marsh spread out before me. Now the deep, jugging calls of bullfrogs mingled with the chirr of crickets. Mosquitoes were already buzzing around my head. "Fuck my life," I muttered as I took my first step into the water.

When I made it to the other side of the marsh ten minutes later, I must have looked like something out of a horror movie. Muddy water was splattered all the way up to my waist, and my right elbow was wet from when I caught myself falling. My hair had come out of its ponytail and was a frizzy, tangled mess. My face and arms were now peppered with bug bites that would stick out above the freckles, and my skin was damp with sweat.

I climbed up the steep embankment that met the road, flopped down on the shoulder, and took off my shoes to check my feet for leeches. Relieved to find that my feet were clean, I looked around and tried to get some idea of where I was. I'd never had a good sense of direction, and although Grover Falls was a small town, I could see no markers to help me find my way. On one side of the street, the marsh stretched out as far as I could see. On the other, a few unfamiliar houses were visible in the darkness. It must have been close to two or three in the morning, although

I couldn't be sure, since my phone was now dead. I wobbled to my feet and winced. My ankle still hurt. I knew that walking on it wasn't helping, but I had no choice. I turned left and started out, barefoot, holding my shoes by their strings in my hand, feeling the hard pavement against my soles. The night had cooled down, and I was wet and a little cold.

I saw the headlights approaching slowly. Panic gripped me. What if a serial killer was in that car, or a rapist? Or someone who didn't normally rape but would if they saw a young girl alone on the road at night? I had the insane urge to scramble down the embankment, back into the marsh.

The car lights came closer; I had to squint. Then the high beams shut off, and the car slowed to a halt next to where I stood on the shoulder. The driver poked his head out the window and looked at me with wide eyes. "Hey, are you okay?" he asked.

I knew right away who he was. I had never seen him in person, but I'd seen photos online and in old high school yearbooks. The world knew the faces of John Lennon, Jimi Hendrix, and Kurt Cobain. And Grover Falls knew his. I knew who it was, I just couldn't believe it. Now his face was looking at me as if I were the weirdest thing it had ever seen. "Kid," he said, "are you all right? Can you hear me?"

"Yeah," I breathed, "I'm okay."

Paul Frazier had just asked me if I was okay. *Paul Frazier.* He looked around the road, as if searching for clues to explain my being here, looking like this. "Were you in an accident or something?"

I shook my head. "No, I'm just walking." I realized how dumb that sounded as soon as I said it—just limping down the side of the road at three in the morning, soaking wet, barefoot—and I felt my face grow red. "I'm heading back now," I added stupidly, "back home."

Some realization dawned in his eyes. "You're April Swanson's daughter, aren't you?"

Greater than my surprise at this unlikely meeting was that he, Paul Frazier, knew who I, Laura Swanson, was. Or at least, who my mother was. "Yeah," I exclaimed, "I am!"

Paul shook his head, but now he was smiling. "What are you doing out here in the middle of the night? Why aren't you wearing any shoes?"

"I … sort of got lost."

Paul nodded, as if this answer didn't surprise him. "Where do you live?"

"Grant Street."

"You're heading in the wrong direction. Get in. I'll take you home."

He didn't ask any questions once I got into the car. In fact, he didn't say anything. I should have come up with some explanation for myself, but I was nervous and still a little high. I sat rigid in my seat, hands on my knees, staring straight ahead. I was painfully aware of how awful I smelled and that I was getting muddy water all over the seat of his old Toyota. Maybe it wasn't such a good thing that he knew who I was. After tonight, he wasn't going to forget.

Still, I couldn't help but sneak sideways glances at him as he drove, his face illuminated every now and then by a passing streetlight. He was beautiful. Photos didn't do him justice. His dark hair hung down, partly obscuring his eyes—sea blue, and under them I could see dark circles. There was a sadness to him that only made him more magnetic, and I resisted another urge: to grab him by the hand and tell him that I loved him and that everything was going to be okay. I dug my nails into my knees until it hurt.

I wished that drive could have gone on forever, but it was only a few minutes before we reached my house. He pulled up into the drive. I saw the light in my mother's room flip on.

Paul saw it, too. "Sorry, should have killed the headlights for you," he said.

I felt goose bumps rise on my arms and the back of my neck; we were complicit. I shook my head. "It's okay. I don't think I could have snuck past her anyway—she's a very light sleeper."

He gave me a smile. My heart raced. "Good luck, kid," he said.

"Thanks for the ride, Paul," I said. He looked surprised when I said his name, but before he had time to say anything, I leaned forward and kissed him, quickly but forcefully, on the lips. Then I opened the door, leaped out of the car, and half-ran, half-limped up the driveway to the door of my house, without looking back.

# 2

## PAUL

As on every other morning for the past few weeks, first he heard the kitchen door downstairs open and close, then her soft footsteps as she came up the stairs, then the water running in the bathroom as she took her shower. Every morning, she tried her hardest not to wake him, and every morning, he was already awake.

Four years ago, the idea of Sharon Frazier waking up before dawn would have sounded ridiculous to Paul. Now, back home for more than a month already, he still hadn't grown used to the sounds of his mother up and about before 6 a.m., back from her morning jog. It still felt wrong.

When Paul Frazier returned home to Grover Falls after four years of school in New York City—four years of nights spent barhopping in Williamsburg and the East Village; four years of waking up on floors in strangers' apartments, with a head that felt like one of those giant cartoon anvils; four years of chasing Jameson with Red Bull backstage a minute before his band was to go on (it gave him wings); four years of friending on Facebook the saddest-looking girl in class and proceeding to have her take notes for him for the rest of the semester; four years of letting caffeine, alcohol, cocaine, and nicotine compete for his affections before the inevitable collapse—he found that his mother had been born again, again.

Sharon had been born again once before, when Paul was twelve. That was after Ron—the fourth one since Paul's father—left her. Instead of opting for another man clad in wifebeater and cutoffs, with tattoos stamped across his burly arms and neck, Sharon Frazier had opted for Jesus.

It was an early-September afternoon. Paul had come home from school to find a woman he'd never seen before, sitting with his mother at the kitchen table, drinking coffee. He'd been startled. His mother didn't usually entertain female guests. With her perfect hair and autumn-colored outfit, the woman looked as though she had stepped out of a fabric-softener commercial. Paul couldn't think of any reason why a woman like this would be here.

Sharon's cheeks were flushed as she introduced her son to Linda. She told him she had some great news: she had decided to give her heart to Jesus.

"Does this mean we have to go to church now?" he asked.

His mom looked annoyed, but Linda laughed. "Our church is a little different," she said. "I think you'll like it."

Paul hadn't. All the adults seemed overly happy (Paul didn't trust overly happy adults), and none of his friends were there. He hadn't wanted to leave his mom for children's church, so she let him sit with her during the sermon. It had been over an hour, Paul sitting hot and bored, his neck itching from the button-up shirt his mom had forced him to wear.

What followed was Paul's one brief yet thorough encounter with religion. He was dragged to church every Sunday, and then again for prayer meeting on Wednesday nights. His mother started reading the Bible, listening to Christian radio, saying a prayer before dinner every night. But even more surprising to Paul were the things she *stopped* doing. There were no men around the house anymore. Sharon quit drinking and cut back on the cigarettes. It went on like this for months, long enough that Paul began to grow used to his new, though not completely attractive, life. Then something happened. Paul wasn't quite sure what. Jesus let his mother down just as all the men before him had. He didn't cheat on her or hit her or call her a bitch in front of her friends, but he did *something*. He must have. Because as quickly as Sharon had picked Jesus up, she dropped him.

Paul had been relieved. Although he hadn't liked any of the other boyfriends—even the nice ones had been annoying, always inviting him to take rides on their snowmobiles or trying to teach him how to load a shotgun—Jesus had been worse. The obsessive way he dominated Sharon's life, keeping tabs on how she dressed and what words she used; the vague but pointed references she made about Paul letting the guy into his own heart—an idea he didn't understand but found thoroughly creepy. And as with all her breakups, after Jesus' departure Sharon found solace in spending time with her son, the only man in her life who ever stayed. When she had parted ways with yet another useless bastard, Sharon would stay up late with Paul, watching horror movies they'd picked out together at the video store, she bingeing on wine and he on ice cream and junk food. After Jesus left their lives, a glorious week followed that included *Rosemary's Baby, The Exorcist,* and Paul eating so many Oreos he got sick.

At eighteen, Paul's biggest hesitation about leaving for school in New York hadn't been the cost of tuition (which was high) or the cost of living in the city (even higher), but the nagging sense that leaving his mother in this lonely house in this forsaken town meant he was deserting her. During his first few weeks in the city, Paul had called her often to ask how she was doing. "You don't have to worry about me, Paul," she had told him, her voice a mix of irritation and affection. "Concentrate on yourself. You're in New York City, go make bad decisions."

So Paul had. And when he returned with a useless liberal arts degree, a mountain of debt, and no career prospects to speak of, he was a little shocked at the change his mother had undergone in his absence. Sharon Frazier had really gotten her life together. There were no cigarettes hidden in the drawers below the sink, no bottles of wine in the cabinets above the fridge. There were no men, either. She was working two jobs: waiting tables at the diner and working the floor at the hardware store. She went for a jog every morning and was eating a healthy, balanced diet. Sharon had found Jesus again, and this time Jesus had been good to her.

IT WAS THAT UGLY TIME OF MORNING, just before the sun rises but after the birds have started singing. Paul had been up most of the night, lying in bed thinking dark thoughts, and then driving around the empty sleeping town, thinking darker ones. But he wasn't tired. Yes, he would probably stay in bed until late in the day, with the window shades pulled down and the lights off, but not because he felt like sleeping—he just didn't feel like doing anything else.

Someone let out a soft murmur beside him on the bed, and for a moment, Paul allowed himself to believe that he was back in his apartment in Brooklyn, and the girl asleep beside him was Sasha, and Sasha was still his girlfriend. It would be late summer, and when she woke up, stretching her long white arms and blinking her big brown eyes, their day would begin with her smoking a cigarette out on the fire escape, clad in nothing but one of his old T-shirts, while he put a record on the turntable, lay on the bed, and watched her. But as he examined the girl's profile in the gathering dawn light that seeped in through the window shades, he had to come to terms with the fact that this girl, a blond, thin wisp of a thing, was not Sasha, was not his girlfriend. This was just some girl he'd met at the all-night Sunoco and brought back here and fucked.

Paul had been about to come home after another late-night drive. He had just dropped the Swanson girl off at her house, which had left him agitated. The girl had kissed him, on the lips, before he could do anything about it. Paul wasn't sure how old she was, but she hadn't looked more than sixteen. And the fact that some teenage girl covered in swamp water could in two seconds awaken things inside Paul that had been sleeping for months was a little alarming. At the time, he had thought going home and jerking off to porn was his best option—his only option, actually—and he'd planned on doing just that after filling up his empty gas tank and buying a candy bar at the gas station.

A girl was sitting on the steps outside the Sunoco, smoking a cigarette. There was something in a brown paper bag beside her, but Paul hadn't needed this evidence to know she'd been drinking. She gave him a wide, inviting smile when he passed her to go pay for the gas; it stayed with him inside the store. At the register, he had to put back the Snickers when he found he had only enough cash to pay for his ten dollars in gas. When he came out of the store, she was still there, and he hadn't been able to resist asking to bum a smoke.

She offered him her pack and lighter. "Thanks," Paul said, taking a cigarette and lighting up.

"Anything for the great Paul Frazier," she said.

It had been the second time in as many hours that someone he didn't know called him by name. Being back in this town was disorienting.

She saw the look of surprise on his face. "You probably don't remember me," she said. "I was a few years behind you in school. Nicki Chambers." She stood up and he handed her back the cigarettes.

"I think I remember seeing you around," Paul lied.

Nicki nodded. "I went to all your shows. You guys were the shit. I still listen to that EP."

He took a deep drag of his cigarette. "You were a few years behind me? So that would make you …?"

She looked at him evenly. "Twenty. I'm twenty years old," she said. There it was: perfectly legal.

Now, looking at her sleeping beside him on the bed, Paul wished he hadn't done it. Hopefully, she would understand that it hadn't meant anything, that it wasn't going to go anywhere. Nothing meant anything to Paul anymore. Nothing was going to go anywhere. All the same, he couldn't help admiring her blond hair, falling down in tresses on the pillow and around her face. He had stolen a cigarette from the pack in her bag and smoked it while he watched her sleep. She let out another soft murmur, and this time her eyes opened with a flutter. There was only one moment of sleepy confusion on her face before it bloomed into a smile at the sight of him.

Paul did his best to smile back. "Good morning."

"Hmmm … morning." She stretched out her arms, winced, and squinted. "What time is it?"

Paul glanced at the alarm clock sitting on the table beside the bed. "Nearly six."

Nicki sat up, blinked and nodded, then motioned for the cigarettes beside the clock on the table. He handed her the pack and the lighter, and after she had taken a few drags she looked at him. "For a rock star, you get up early on a Saturday."

Paul snorted. "Maybe that means I'm not a rock star."

Nicki jerked her head in challenge. "Well, you're definitely the closest thing Grover Falls has to one."

He shook his head but didn't say anything. It was too early to talk about this—not that any other time of day would be better.

Her big blue eyes studied him curiously. "I saw some stuff online, of your band in the city. You guys were good. What happened?"

Paul tried to keep his voice light. "Oh, you know, the usual bullshit: creative differences, financial troubles, too much drugs and alcohol."

"It's a shame."

He nodded. "A tragedy." He meant it as a joke, but maybe it hadn't come out that way.

Nicki's eyes suddenly brightened. "You should start another band. Here in Grover! Are you looking for any musicians? My little brother plays drums. He's only eighteen but he's decent. He would just *die* to play with you."

"Thanks, but I'm sort of enjoying lying low right now."

Nicki looked around the room, and the disgust was clear on her face. Paul couldn't blame her. Dirty clothes were strewn across the floor and sat in mounds along the walls. His guitars (the only two he hadn't yet sold) were gathering dust in the corner of the room. He decided he would throw a blanket over them later so he wouldn't have to look at them any longer.

"Well," said Nicki, "if you ever decide to come out of retirement, let me know. I've got connections."

Before Paul could say anything, a voice called from downstairs. "Paul, are you up? Coffee's ready."

He cleared his throat and called back. "Just getting dressed, Mom."

"Jesus, have you guys not heard of sleeping in on the weekend?" Nicki asked, lowering her voice.

"My mom goes out for a jog at five thirty every morning. I've just been getting up early lately."

Nicki looked at him for a moment. "You don't sleep much, do you?"

Paul shook his head. "Not really."

"Will your mom mind an extra person for coffee? I'm not complicated; black is fine."

"I was actually going to ask if you wouldn't mind leaving out the window so my mom doesn't see you."

She laughed, then saw the look on Paul's face and stopped short. "Seriously?"

"That big maple tree has an overhanging branch that's easy to grab. I got a lot of use out of it as a teenager."

"Paul Frazier, twenty-two years old and still sneaking his one-night stands out his childhood bedroom window."

Paul shrugged. *One-night stand*—she had said it, not he. "Sorry to spoil your image."

Nicki looked at him as if trying to decide something. "It's kind of cute, actually," she said at last. She gave him a quick peck on the lips, then hopped out of bed and began gathering up her clothes off the floor.

Watching her slender naked body as she shimmied back into her underwear, then her jeans and shirt, Paul almost wished for a moment that he could tell her to come back to bed and he would bring her coffee and scrambled eggs. But then she was dressed, looking expectantly at him, and he got up and went over to the window and pulled up the shades. The sunlight was dazzling, and he squinted as he opened the window. Nicki looked out at the thick tree branch sitting almost level with the window.

"I *am* sorry about this," Paul said.

"You owe me," was all she said. She gave him another kiss—a longer one, one he had to return. Then she climbed out the window with surprising nimbleness, and a few seconds later, she was standing in the backyard. She gave him a goofy salute, then turned and headed around the house and out of sight.

PAUL WENT INTO THE BATHROOM. He let the water run in the sink for a moment before he took some in his cupped hands and splashed it on his face. Then he opened the cabinet above the sink and took down two plastic vials. He took a pill out of each and swallowed them, washing them down with a Slurpee cup full of water.

When he went downstairs into the kitchen, his mom, showered and dressed, her cheeks flushed from her jog, poured him a cup of coffee. "How'd you sleep?" she asked, handing him his mug.

Paul shrugged. "A few hours at least."

"We need to talk to Dr. Schumer about adjusting your medication."

He leaned against the counter and yawned. "Yeah, maybe."

"I thought I heard you talking to someone earlier, when I got out of the shower."

"I had talk radio on," Paul said, and sipped his coffee. It was a weak alibi—he had never listened to talk radio in his life—but his mother accepted it without comment.

She took a seat at the table. "So," she said, staring at him until he met her eyes, "are you ready for your interview?"

Paul's chest tightened and his heartbeat quickened. He had almost forgotten. He had a job interview today, although whether you could really call it a "job" was up for debate. And the feeling of dread it inspired in him said less about the position than about his ever-growing anxiety when faced with any structured social interaction.

A week after moving home Paul had seen a rare NOW HIRING sign at the Starbucks in the local mall and told the barista he was interested. She'd handed him an application and called for the next customer. Looking at the form with its cookie-cutter questions and spaces for him to sum up his life in a few words, Paul had begun to feel sick. He tossed the application in the trash on his way out the door.

Later, he had decided it was the uniform—that black baseball cap and green apron. He just couldn't work anywhere that told him how to dress. But the thing was, despite a diploma that would seem to suggest otherwise, Paul realized he wasn't qualified for any job that trusted you to choose your own clothing every morning. In the paper, he'd come across a classified ad for a construction company looking for carpenters. The rugged, physical nature of the work had appealed to him in an abstract way. He pictured himself tan and glistening, arms corded with muscle, wielding a circular saw. But farther down the ad, the words EXPERIENCE REQUIRED practically jumped off the page at him, and he threw the paper aside. Nobody had even taught him how to hammer a nail.

And the longer Paul put off finding a job, the harder it became even to think about. Thoughts of résumés, interviews, and cover letters filled him with anxiety and sent acid rising up from his stomach. He couldn't face it. But soon he would have to.

On Monday he had received his first loan statement from Sallie Mae. Two days went by before he got around to opening it, and when he did, it felt like a death threat. The numbers looked positively unreal—the digits just kept coming. He had tossed the piece of paper onto the floor and collapsed on the bed. An hour later, shaken from a fitful half-sleep, he had woken to find his mother standing over him. She had news: the person who ran the sound department at her church was moving. New Life was looking for someone to work the sound board for Sunday-morning service, mix the music for the worship band, and handle and take care of all the equipment for the daily vacation Bible school that started up in a week. She thought it was the perfect opportunity for him.

Paul had laughed. She couldn't be serious. But Sharon had frozen him with a sharp glare. "Now, Paul," she had said, "I know you think my church is some kind of nuthouse, and I'm a nut, too, now, but come off your high horse for a second. A job is a job. A paycheck is a paycheck. And it's not the kind of thing where you'd have to submit a résumé and go through five rounds of interviews. I would tell Pastor Eric you're interested, and he would meet with you to decide if you're right for the position. Easy-peasy. It's the kind of work you're good at, and if you let yourself, you might even enjoy it."

As his mother talked, Paul had come up with a hundred lines of dispute to take, but suddenly, he couldn't think of one. All he could think about were the digits that haunted his dreams only minutes earlier.

Were it up to him, he probably would have gone on jobless, defaulting on his loans as long as he possibly could. But there was his mom. Sharon tried her best not to put any pressure on him to find work. She was fond of reminding him that the country was in a giant recession. But it didn't matter—living in her house, eating her food, drinking her coffee, without contributing anything or even working toward anything, made Paul feel like some sort of parasite. The money from selling his instruments and equipment had almost run out, which meant that soon he would have to ask his mom for cash to buy a pack of cigarettes or fund his late-night drives. He needed a job, if only to avoid losing whatever scrap of dignity he had left. So, reluctantly, Paul had agreed: he would at least meet with her pastor.

But since giving his mom the okay at the beginning of the week, Paul had dealt with the issue the way he dealt with all issues now: by ignoring it. He did his best to forget that he had agreed to talk to his mom's pastor about getting a job he didn't want. But now, here was his mother, reminding him, asking whether he was ready.

"I can't wait," he answered.

# 3

## APRIL

April Swanson stood out on the church green, thinking about Florida.

It happened at the beginning of every summer: her mind began to drift down south, to Melbourne, where her sister lived. Maybe it had something to do with the heat or with the fact that school was over and she was through marking up papers and submitting final grades. But for the past few years, setting up for her church's vacation Bible school was consistently haunted by visions of the blue-green Atlantic Ocean from Palm Beach, and the feel of thick, wet sand rising between her toes, the smell of the sea breeze, and the sight of her children charging headlong into the surf.

*That's where you should be right now,* whispered a woman in April's head, who was not quite April, not quite her sister, and not quite her mother, but some strange combination of all three: *Florida. Relaxing. Taking a* vacation. *Not spending your Saturday standing on your church's lawn organizing a program you don't even care about anymore.* And, as she did whenever this voice sounded in her head, April did her best to ignore it, even though she couldn't say she completely disagreed.

She had been heading up her church's vacation Bible school since President Clinton and the Monica Lewinsky thing. She remembered because, while everybody else had been talking about obstruction of justice and private versus public morality and whether a blow job really counted as sex, April had been thinking about ways to make the Ark of the Covenant out of papier-mâché, and whether the story of Samson and Delilah was too mature for ten-year-olds, and whether there was a simple way to explain the concept of the Trinity. She had been twenty-eight years old, a fierce young mother who had just moved to Grover Falls with her husband and two small children. Mortgage on a four-bedroom house in town, the obligatory minivan, new recipes jotted down and attempted. The obvious next step was to settle into her local church, and taking over the VBS had seemed a good way to start. A three-week program every July, open to all kids seven to fourteen—how hard could it be? She didn't realize what she was getting into until Helen Walters, who had overseen the program for seven years and was stepping down only because her doctor had pretty much ordered her to, had invited her over for a tutorial. Chatting over iced tea on her porch, Helen's face had been drawn and anxious as she talked about how much the VBS meant to the folks at New Life, how it was widely regarded as *the* vacation Bible school in the Saratoga area (giving herself most of the credit for this with a practiced subtlety), how unique and exciting and enriching it was in a way no other church could touch. April had left Helen's house determined not to let anyone down.

She could finally let out a breath of relief at the end of July, when the feedback started coming in: "My son had such a great time at the VBS this year! He fought tooth and nail not to go, but now he can't wait till next summer!" "I was amazed when Erin came home with so many verses of scripture memorized, and she's been reading the Bible on her own ever since. Thanks for keeping the focus where it should be, April!"

The only thing that threatened to spoil April's happiness over the universal praise she received was her suspicion that it was a rather pathetic thing to be happy about. Never in her wildest dreams would she have seen herself as the sort of person who could derive so much pleasure and satisfaction from a vacation Bible school. But she couldn't help it. Since she quit teaching high school math after her daughter was born, it had been four years of dirty diapers and *Sesame Street*, Cheerios in Ziploc bags, applesauce, laundromats, and exhausted sex. The world of motherhood seemed to have rendered her invisible, a hidden moon stuck in ceaseless orbit. The VBS was the first thing she had done outside its gravitational pull, and she had a done a good job. She had "kept the focus where it should be," and that made her proud.

That had been in 1998. In 2001, she was divorced, with full custody of the kids, and a mortgage to pay. She began teaching again—a new era of carting her children off to preschool and kindergarten in the morning before work, balancing the checkbook on her lunch break, lesson planning at the kitchen table well into the night, after her kids had gone to bed. Suddenly, the VBS didn't seem such a big deal anymore. Still, years had passed and she never quit heading up the program, although her sister, Sarah, had done her best to persuade her.

Sarah was the assistant director at a large nonprofit in Melbourne that helped at-risk youth graduate from high school and prepare for college. For a long while now, whenever April and the kids came down to visit, Sarah spent half the time trying to get April to move down to Florida permanently and take a job at the program. Sitting on the beach watching their kids play in the ocean in the afternoon, or eating dinner out on the dock as the sun set, Sarah went on and on about how much meaning and satisfaction the job would give April, how great it would be if the kids could live near each other, how it would be so convenient to find Mom a nice little condo down here, too, and how April must be so bored up there out in the country and how she needed a change.

"Sarah, I'm perfectly happy with my life, trust me," April would always tell her. "Besides, I'm almost forty—too old to be moving to the other end of the country and starting a new life."

"I know you," Sarah would counter. "You can do anything if you put your mind to it. And as for believing that you're happy, I have my doubts."

April resented this allegation. Shouldn't she be the best judge whether she was happy? Just because Sarah had a career she loved and had lucked out with a husband who had stuck around, was a good dad, and made killer grilled salmon to boot didn't give her the authority to measure other people's happiness. Anyway, it was such an abstract word: *happiness*—so vague as to be almost meaningless.

Out on the church lawn, April tried to focus on the matter at hand, and looking back down at her notepad, she came to the odd but familiar realization that the matter at hand was absurd. Nevertheless, she studied her list, then looked up at the large green field spreading out until it met the golf course. Today the field was empty, but on Monday it would be filled with brightly colored tents and aswarm with children—running, shouting, laughing, crying children. The VBS had become a monster. The games and activities grew in number and extravagance every year, culminating, at the end of the program, with a weekend camping trip for the older children in the Adirondack Mountains.

April had initiated this event her third year as supervisor. As a younger woman, she had always looked forward to the trip, giving all these kids a chance to experience the wilderness. She would wake up early and go down to the lake to listen to the call of the loons. But as the program grew, the trip had soon become a logistic and administrative nightmare, and she wondered why she had even started it. The sun beat against the back of April's neck. She could hear the call of a lone crow. "If we put Zebulun's tribe on the north end of the church," she said after a moment of thinking, "we could still squeeze in Issachar and Levi."

Lydia Newman, standing beside her, nodded and scribbled something down in her own notebook. "That takes care of all Leah's tribes. Now we just have Rachel's and the Maidservant's."

Five years ago, April had had the bright idea of dividing all the kids in the VBS into twelve different teams, or "tribes": the Twelve Tribes of Israel. Each tribe got its own tent and team leaders, and all the tribes competed in games and contests throughout the summer, collectively earning points. The tribe with the most points at the end of the program was declared King of Israel—April didn't mind admitting she had gotten the idea while watching one of the Harry Potter movies with her kids. "*Ten points to Gryffindor!*"

When she first came up with the idea for the tribes, April had hoped it would promote friendly competition and a sense of unity, but it had grown into its own sort of monster. Loyalty to your tribe was a must, and hostility toward other tribes could be at once petty and extreme. Rivalries flourished; treaties were made and broken; resentments festered. This summer, April was trying to temper some of the contention by moving the tribes' locations, as a way of keeping tabs on the factions. She hoped she was cooling the pot rather than stirring it.

"And Simeon and Asher don't get along," Lydia was saying, "so maybe we should put them on opposite ends of the camp."

April cocked her head to one side. "I thought they were on good terms."

Lydia shook her head. "Not since the end of last year, when the Simeon kids accused Asher of cheating in the relay race. Remember later, some of the kids from Simeon raided Asher's tent with water balloons?"

April nodded wearily. "Oh, yes, I remember now. Yeah, let's put them as far away from each other as possible."

Lydia began scribbling in her notebook again. April glanced at her from behind her sunglasses. For years now, ever since Lydia "graduated" from the VBS herself, she had been April's right-hand girl when it came to planning, setting up, and running the thing. April dreaded the day when Lydia finally got tired of helping or decided to actually do something with her life (go to college, maybe?), leaving April to manage such delicate tasks as positioning all twelve tribes by herself. *But this is my last year,* she reminded herself. *I won't be doing this next summer.* And then came the voice again: *Then why haven't you said anything? Why haven't you let Pastor Eric know that after this summer, you're done?*

Again, Florida. The sun rising over the ocean, the steady sound of waves hitting the shore. April blinked, squinted out at the golf course. From where she stood, she could see Laura and Bethany on the other side of the field, setting up the poles for the portable fence that, once completed, would wrap around the church property and mark where the VBS ended and the golf course began. She'd had to implement the fence a few summers ago, after repeated incidents of kids straying away from camp and onto the fairways and greens, much to the golfers' chagrin.

Last night, April's daughter, Laura, who was supposed to be spending the night at Bethany's house, had come home at three in the morning, wet, dirty, reeking of pond water and marijuana, and refusing to tell April where she'd been.

"It's not important," Laura had said, looking at the floor as April stood in her pajamas in front of the stairwell, blocking the path up to her daughter's room.

"*Not important?*" April had repeated. "Since when do you decide what's important in this house and what isn't? I cannot *believe* you right now."

"I'm home, aren't I?" Laura had snapped. "I'm here in one piece! What else do you want?"

"What I want is a responsible daughter with a good head on her shoulders, which I thought I had, but I guess I was mistaken. Would you just *look* at yourself? Where were you?"

The argument had escalated from there, and looking back on it, April felt regret. Nothing good ever came of arguments at three in the morning—she could attest to this from those months before her divorce. The last thing Laura said before running up to her room was "I hate you!" and April had gone back to bed trying to convince herself that her daughter hadn't meant it.

When she got up that morning, April had resolved to keep her cool. After she showered, dressed, and made her son breakfast and Laura still hadn't stirred, April had filled a glass of water and gone up to her daughter's bedroom. She still slept the way she had as a baby: eyes closed tight, face almost clenched, as if even sleeping was something that filled her with anxiety. April coughed, and Laura stirred and opened her eyes, blinking at her mother in confusion. "Your throat's going to be dry," April said, handing her the glass of water as she sat up. "Drink this and get dressed. You're coming with me today."

For the first few minutes of the drive to church, they sat in uncomfortable silence, April paying more attention to the road than was necessary. Then Laura suddenly blurted, "I only took one puff, and I didn't even like it. I knew it was wrong, so I stopped. I'm sorry."

Since their argument last night, the muscles around April's neck had been tense. She felt something release inside her. Now she could ask in a perfectly calm voice, "Are you ready to tell me where you were last night?"

Laura explained that she and Bethany had hung out with some kids from school, who had started smoking. "But we didn't feel comfortable with the situation," she said, "so we left."

"Bethany went home?"

Laura nodded quickly.

If only April could believe her daughter. If only she could leave the matter there. "Who was that who dropped you off, then?"

"What?"

April tried to keep her voice level as she stopped the car at a red light. "The car I saw that dropped you off at the house, who was that?"

"I cut across the park on the way home—that's how I got wet; I tripped in a puddle—and Paul Frazier was driving by and he offered me a ride."

"Paul Frazier?" It took April a moment to place the name: Sharon Frazier's son. He had been in April's twelfth-grade algebra class maybe three or four years ago. She remembered him as a bright but lazy student who never applied himself. Last she'd heard, though, he had moved to New York City after graduating. "I thought he went away for college."

"He's back. Graduated."

April was quiet as she waited for the green light. Her daughter's story was strange enough to be almost believable. Why else would she mention the Frazier boy?

"Are you going to tell Bethany's parents?" Laura asked.

April bit her lip and hit the gas as the light turned green. Eric and Linda wouldn't take the news that their daughter had been out smoking weed with strange kids as calmly as she had. It would result in a long, tedious meeting with parents and daughters, leaving no stone unturned, and then another meeting with just her and Eric and Linda, to discuss consequences and motives and what needed to be done, topped off with a long and fervent prayer session. The mere thought of it was exhausting. "Text Bethany," she said at last. "Tell her to get her butt to church for VBS setup ASAP, if she knows what's good for her."

So there they were: two girls setting up for vacation Bible school to atone for their sins. April wasn't sure it had been the right decision. Maybe harsher punishment was called for. Part of her wanted to let the matter go. She worried about her daughter. Laura was an anxious girl, concerned about her looks, and April had the suspicion that the only reason her daughter had been hanging out with these other kids in the first place was because one of the boys was the object of her affections.

April thought Laura was beautiful, but then, every good mother thought her own daughter was beautiful. And as a high school teacher, April didn't have the luxury of forgetting the savage nature of a teenage girl's life, the Darwinian struggle to survive in the social biome of lip gloss and miniskirts, texting battles and boys. These days, the girls seemed to grow up faster. By the time they'd reached April's class, they were like miniature twenty-two-year-olds, perfect little projections of their future selves. Her daughter wasn't overweight, but she had a certain roundness about her. Her face had a generous scattering of freckles, and the red hair she'd inherited from April was thick and often frizzy. And although Laura didn't talk about boys, they must surely be on her mind. What fifteen-year-old girl wasn't thinking about boys at the beginning of summer?

April made it a point to stay in shape and had miraculously been able to preserve the petite, athletic build she'd developed running track in high school. Aging had been kind to her skin as well as her figure, and she had only faint stress lines around her eyes and forehead. Not that it mattered—April hadn't been with a man, or so much as been on a date with one, for years. There had been the initial push a year or so after her divorce, when, with sister Sarah's encouragement, she had gone on as many as two dates a week. "Anything to get your mind off that asshole ex-husband," Sarah had said.

Most of the men she'd gone out with had been nice, and more than a few had wanted to see her again. But every night, after they parted ways in some restaurant parking lot (at her age, it just seemed silly to have them pick her up), and she had gone back to the safety of her own bathroom, she immediately crumbled into a hot, wet ball of anxiety. Sometimes, her lungs would constrict and she would struggle just to breathe, or her stomach would churn and she would spend half the night gazing at her toilet bowl, wondering whether she would vomit up the dinner she'd had on the date, without ever actually doing so. And sometimes, she would just cry. Sob and sob until her eyes were red and her cheeks bloated and puffy.

It wasn't long before she decided that these dates, however pleasant, weren't worth this sort of trade-off. It was like taking medication for migraines when the side effects included blindness or heart failure. If she were to go on a date now, April didn't know whether the same delayed attacks of anxiety would befall her. But she was too busy these days to find out, and didn't really see the point, anyway.

"April!" a man's voice called out. She turned around to see Pastor Eric approaching her from the church. He smiled when he reached her. "And so it begins again."

April nodded. "It does."

"Excited?" Eric asked, still beaming. For a moment, April wondered whether he was being sarcastic, but Pastor Eric didn't really do sarcasm.

"Definitely." She nodded again, smiling and trying to match his eager tone, then feeling that maybe she had overdone it. She hoped he didn't think she was mocking him.

But her pastor only blinked mildly. With his silver-streaked hair and stubbled chin, Eric was the sort of man who had eased into his forties as if middle age were a warm bath that one gently lowered oneself into. "Well," he said after studying April for a moment, "I just came over to let you know Jon will be training our new recruit today." He nodded back toward the building. April could see Jon Newman—Lydia's brother and the church's worship leader—standing with someone she didn't recognize. "Sharon Frazier's son, Paul—do you know him?"

For a second, April didn't answer. Paul Frazier, her daughter's late-night ride. But it was just a strange coincidence, maybe not even all that strange. In a town as small as Grover Falls, where everyone knew everyone else, such happenstances hardly even rose to the level of coincidence. "I taught him math in twelfth grade," she said, "but that was years ago."

"Well, I just had a nice conversation with him, and I believe it's going to work out great. He knows his stuff, and I think working here will be good for him. I can call him over so you two can say hi."

April shook her head a little too quickly. "Oh, no, that's fine. Still have a lot to do here."

Eric stifled a yawn. "I think I'll head home, then, maybe even take a nap. Had a late night. We had some uninvited guests here around two in the morning. On the roof. Kids, I think, though I didn't get a good look at any of them."

"Really?" Lydia's voice blurted beside April, who had almost forgotten she was there.

Eric nodded. "The weird thing was, I couldn't find any sign of a break-in: no unlocked door or open windows. But they weren't there just for the view. They left their joint behind."

"Their what?" Lydia said.

"Marijuana," April said. She had a sinking feeling inside her chest.

It took April only a minute to decide what to do. Then she marched out across the field to where the girls were setting up the fence, and said quite calmly, "Both of you will be helping out every day at the VBS for the entire session—no arguments, no exceptions." They had looked up at her, wide-eyed but not protesting. They knew that she knew, and neither dared question how or argue against the stiff sentence she had just imposed.

That was that, April thought as she headed back toward the church. She wouldn't tell Pastor Eric what she knew, and Laura and Bethany were obliged to be here, where she could keep an eye on them, every weekday until August. Blackmail? Maybe, but it was the best solution April could come up with.

Still, something was bothering her. It took her a moment to remember about Paul Frazier. This morning, Laura had told her it was Paul who gave her a ride last night, and now here he was, working at the church. Coincidence or not, she wondered how much Paul knew about her daughter's little escapade and whether he was the sort of guy who would keep something like that to himself. She tried to remember him from her class years ago. He had been quiet but popular, definitely no Boy Scout. All the girls' eyes had strayed off the whiteboard whenever he entered or left the classroom. It struck April as both funny and a little sad that now she was worried about this boy ratting her out to her pastor. It wasn't just that, though. She didn't like the idea of Paul—or anyone, for that matter—thinking she was your typical oblivious mom, with no clue what her children were up to. Call it vanity, though she preferred to think of it as image management. She decided it wouldn't hurt to say hello to Paul Frazier, see what sort of person he had turned into.

She found him on the plywood stage that three of the dads had erected on the lawn just outside the church building. He had his back to her, kneeling in front of an amplifier. She knew it was him. Jon had told her where to find him, and she still recognized that unruly mop of dark hair from back in algebra class. He had to know there was someone standing behind him, must have heard her coming up onto the stage, but he didn't turn around—just kept fiddling with the wires connected to the amp.

After a few seconds, April cleared her throat. "Paul?"

He turned his head slowly, squinting, with one hand shielding his eyes from the late-morning sun that blazed down from behind her head. "Yeah?"

"Hi, it's April. April Swanson. Do you remember me?" she asked, feeling foolish but also a little indignant—kids never remembered their teachers anymore.

But then Paul stood up. The hand dropped to his side, and the blank look disappeared, replaced with a smile. "Oh, hey! How are you? Sorry, I couldn't see you with that sun in my eyes."

Should she believe him? Was this really the reason he hadn't recognized her until she introduced herself? She decided, seeing that smile on the boy's face, that she was too old not to accept his excuse or to hold anything against him. "How have you been?" she asked as they shook hands.

"Okay."

"I hear you're taking over running the sound here."

"That's the way it appears."

Young people could never just give you a straight answer. "You were in the city, weren't you, for school?"

Paul nodded.

"How was that?"

He didn't say anything, just looked at her.

April smiled uncomfortably. "Sorry, I guess you're sick of people asking you that, huh?"

"Asking me what?"

"How school was."

Paul shook his head. "You're the first, actually."

Was he being sarcastic? She cleared her throat again. "So I just came over to welcome you aboard. I run the Bible school, so we'll probably be seeing a lot of each other this summer."

Paul wiped sweat from his brow and nodded.

"All right, then," April said. She stuck her hands in the back pockets of her shorts and half turned away, then twirled back around on the balls of her feet to face him. "So I heard you gave my daughter a ride last night," she said.

"Yeah, I did." He smiled. "She's an interesting girl."

"I just wanted to let you know that I did become aware that she was out that late. Her behavior was dealt with. There were consequences."

"Okay."

"I just didn't want you to think, like, that I'm an irresponsible mother, or anything—that I'm not on top of things."

"I would never be dumb enough to think that, believe me."

Was he making fun of her? He was making fun of her. April didn't know what to say, so she just stood there smiling stupidly from behind her sunglasses.

"Although, if I were you," Paul said, "I'd be careful with those consequences."

"What do you mean?"

"I just think it has a way of fanning the flames. Like, if you tell your kid over and over not to do something, then odds are, when they get the chance, that'll be the first thing they do. It's teenage nature."

April crossed her arms. "So you're saying I should have kept my mouth shut, just let my daughter roam the streets till all hours without any repercussions?"

"Not necessarily. I'm speaking hypothetically."

"Well, at my age you can't really afford to be hypothetical anymore. Everything's pretty real."

Paul shrugged. "Just my opinion."

April was suddenly infuriated, by his little half shrug and half smile, by his smug opinions, vague answers, and the way he just stood there looking at her, sweat glistening on his forehead. "Yeah, well," she almost snapped, "you let me know how that works out for you when you have your own kids, okay?"

She was surprised when he laughed. It sounded like genuine laughter. "I'll do that," he said. "We can get together and compare notes."

April didn't know whether she should laugh along at her unintended joke. She settled for giving him a faint smile and then taking a step back. "Well, I'd better get back to work. It was nice to see you again, Paul." Turning and heading off the stage, she could feel his eyes on the back of her neck, watching her go.

# 4

LAURA

There were times I thought my mom was psychic. Just when I thought I had gotten one over on her, I would find her one step ahead of me. The morning after my swamp adventure, on the ride to church, I gave her my version of events. Though untrue, it had contained just enough truth that I thought she might buy it. So I was surprised later in the morning, as Bethany and I were setting up that stupid fence for VBS, to see my mom come marching across the green toward us. I could tell by her resolute stride that it wasn't going to be good. And sure enough, she told us that we would be expected to help out at Bible school *every day* until it ended. She had found out more about the night before—how, I had no idea. I was stunned.

And the day only got worse from there. While we worked on the fence, safely out of earshot of the adults, Bethany told me the rest of the story. While I was wading through the swamp, she, Nola, Ian, and Joey had merely waited in the woods until they were sure the coast was clear, then doubled back to Ian's car, which was parked up the road from church. How simple! While I was getting eaten alive by mosquitoes and obsessing about leeches, they had gone back to Nola's house and had a sleepover in her basement.

"Where did you sleep?" I asked Bethany while hammering a plastic fence stake into the soft earth and trying to keep my tone casual.

"On a couch."

"Where did Ian sleep?"

"On a couch."

"The *same* couch?"

Bethany had picked up the next stake but stopped long enough to fix me with an irritated glare. "Laura, I already told you, I don't like Ian."

Oh, puh-*lease*! I thought, giving the next stake a good swat with the mallet. Then why else were we hanging out with those potheads? Also, she hadn't answered my question. Mostly, though, I was miffed at myself. Last night had been my chance, my trial, and I had botched it gloriously. Running off into a swamp and acting like an idiot while they watched horror movies and made microwave popcorn—okay, I added the popcorn part, but still. There was only one good thing about that night: what happened to me after I got through the swamp. I hadn't told Bethany about my encounter with Paul Frazier. Besides my mother, I hadn't told anyone. I thought of it as my ace in the hole, the secret weapon to make myself relevant again. Even Ian and Nola would be dying to talk to me when they found out I'd gotten a ride from the great Paul Frazier. But something kept me from saying anything just yet. I felt that the longer I kept the secret, the more powerful—almost sacred—it became.

But only twenty minutes later, walking back from the field to the church for a water break, there he was. For a second, I thought maybe the heat had gotten to me and I was hallucinating. But it was him, in the flesh and only a few feet away from us, walking by with Jon Newman. Jon smiled and said hi, but we only gawked and kept moving.

"Was that who I think it was?" Bethany murmured.

I nodded. "It's him, I'm sure."

"What the hell is going on?" Bethany asked. But I could hardly speak. I was thinking of the kiss I gave him last night—that awful, wonderful kiss—and the way he had smiled faintly at me just now. A smile of recognition … and something else. Amusement? Disdain? Fondness? I couldn't tell. But I was painfully aware of the sweat soaking through my shirt and dripping from my forehead. How rumpled and burned out I looked! Twice in a row now, I had managed to look my worst for Paul Frazier.

AROUND FOUR O'CLOCK ON SATURDAY, after Bethany and I finished setting up that stupid fence, my mom took us to get dinner—pizza, despite my very vocal and very valid objections. (It's unhealthy. It's greasy. It's gross.) We still didn't know how she found out what we'd done, but she had cooled off since that morning. We sat down at a booth, and when my mom asked us what kind of pizza we wanted, I muttered that I'd just get a salad.

She gave me her exasperated cocking-of-the-head, raising-of-the-eyebrows look. "What about you, Bethany?" she asked. "Are you hungry from working out in the hot sun all day, or are you with my daughter?"

Bethany smiled. "I could really go for a slice of buffalo chicken."

"Buffalo chicken it is," said my mom.

While my mom and my best friend shared a small pizza, I picked half-heartedly at my salad (iceberg lettuce with other watery, tasteless vegetables thrown on top) and tried not to envy either the hot, greasy meal they were enjoying or the fact that both of them could enjoy it without worrying about the food's effect on their bodies. God had granted them the priceless gift of being able to eat whatever they wanted without gaining weight. No such gift for Laura.

Bethany and my mom chatted about school and Bethany's plan to travel overseas after she turned eighteen and before she started college, but I refused to be drawn into their talk. I was still angry at my mother for enslaving us for half the summer. The sentence was much too harsh. A one-night mistake did not call for endless weeks of misery. Bethany, however, considered it a bargain. "Trust me," she'd said to me earlier, "this is much better than what my parents would do to me." She had texted her parents that she was "volunteering" to help out at the VBS, and they were ecstatic. So, as usual, Bethany remained untainted, perfect, the daughter any pastor would want. I hated it, though. Only last summer, we had been *attending* vacation Bible school, and now that we were finally too old for the stupid thing, I'd been looking forward to a summer of freedom. Being forced to help felt like a giant step backward.

Bethany laughed loudly at something my mom said, and I shot her an annoyed look. Bethany got along well with my mother, who, she always said, was the coolest mom at church. I never had the energy to dispute this. I think Bethany was also under the false impression that if she really sucked up to my mom during the next few days, we might get time off for good behavior. But I knew this to be a lost cause. Once my mom had settled on something, that was that.

"So, Ms. Swanson," Bethany said after finishing her first piece of pizza and moving on to the next, "how's the VBS staff looking this year? Any promising new recruits?"

My mom smirked and took a piece of chicken off her slice and popped it into her mouth. She always did this, picked a thing apart and ate the component bits separately instead of as a whole, the way it was intended to be eaten. "If you're fishing for a compliment," she said, "I'll say that yes, you girls did a good job today. Not having to worry about putting up that fence is a big load off my mind."

Bethany shook her head, "I wasn't talking about *us*, actually. I noticed that Paul Frazier was there today. What's the deal with that?"

My mom shrugged. "He's taking over running sound from Mr. Cornish, because the Cornishes are moving. It's my understanding that he'll also be helping out at the VBS a lot."

"Crazy," Bethany said, and gave me a look that I didn't return. I kept my eyes on my almost untouched salad. Bethany seemed to think it was okay to share our secrets in front of my mom, but I knew better.

"What?" my mom asked, looking from Bethany to me. "You girls know something about him that I don't?"

Bethany took a drink of her soda before replying. "We just think he's cute, that's all. Don't you think he's cute, Ms. Swanson?"

"Just because a boy is cute doesn't mean he's good news; you girls should know that. And he's a little old for you, don't you think?"

Bethany nodded and sighed. "Alas, he is. The price of being young."

My mom gave a short, hollow laugh. "You enjoy being young while it lasts, Bethany Moyer. Things only get harder from here on."

That was bullshit, I thought. There was nothing harder than being a fifteen-year-old girl in early summer, without a boyfriend. Nothing in the whole world.

SUNDAY MORNING I STOOD IN THE CHURCH service, fighting to stay awake.

New Life's sanctuary had a basketball hoop at either end. The old school had been small enough that one room served as both gymnasium and auditorium. About five hundred folding chairs had been set up on the finished hardwood floor. When the church first bought the building, the hoops stuck out like a punk band at the opera. Now no one but newcomers gave them a second look.

Up onstage, the worship band had just ended one of the current favorites—an upbeat tune whose chorus had a hook that would replay in your head for hours afterward—and were shifting to a slower number. The worship leader, Jon Newman, strummed on his guitar while breathing heavily into the microphone. These transitions were always a chance for us in the congregation to sway back and forth with our eyes half-closed, maybe shouting out a few "Amens!" or "Yes, Lords!" here and there.

Standing in our row in the congregation, my mom on one side of me, my brother on the other, I stifled a yawn. I was often tired on Sundays, because I would stay up till long after midnight the night before, talking online with Martin. Sitting on my bed in the dark with my laptop, headphones in my ears, I would e-chat with him for hours. We talked about all sorts of random topics, though I was always careful to keep it on familiar terrain, steering our conversations back to subjects I understood whenever they began to veer into the unfamiliar.

I remember one particularly late night—it must have been close to three in the morning—when I told Martin I'd better log off since I had church the next day.

"You go to *church*?" he asked.

For a few seconds, I had stared at the blinking cursor, contemplating my answer. For some reason, in that moment, I wanted to be honest: *Yes,* I typed back. *I run my church's vacation Bible school.*

Martin had been surprised. He told me he would never have taken me for a churchgoer. And although I wasn't sure how I felt about church anymore, I felt insulted. I asked him what he meant by that. Martin could sense my anger and quickly apologized—said he was projecting, relying on stereotypes. I typed back that it was okay; my ex-husband was the reason I started going in the first place, and now I'd just been going for so long, it was more habit than anything else. Martin said he completely understood; we do a lot of things not because we want to but because we feel we should.

Another yawn. My mom shot me an irritated look, and I covered my mouth—I couldn't risk her investigating what was making me so tired on Sunday mornings.

Pastor Eric had taken the stage as the last worship song ended in a flurry of cymbal rolls and synthesizer runs. "Good," he said, looking around the room at us all with a proud smile, as if he were a coach in the locker room and we were his team. "It always blesses my spirit to see so many of you gathered here, ready to worship the Lord. Take a few minutes to greet a few folks this morning." Everyone began milling around the room to shake hands, give hugs, and exchange pleasantries, and the sounds of laughter and small talk filled the gym. I made my way across the room, to the front hallway, where Bethany and I always met.

Someone grabbed my arm from behind, and I turned and saw Bethany, her eyes wide. "We have a problem," she said.

I winced under the pressure of her grip. "What?" I asked, pulling my arm free.

"So I was texting Nola earlier, telling her about … you know who, and she said she wants to see for herself. She's coming *here*, Laura. Any minute now."

*You know who.* She was talking about Paul Frazier. I hadn't completely believed my mom when she told us the other day that Paul was now a church employee, but this morning Bethany and I had spotted him manning the sound booth, looking a little put out but otherwise perfectly normal. I didn't understand. Had he lost some kind of bet?

Bethany was anxiously awaiting my response. As if there were anything I could do about Nola coming here, though it did feel good to have my best friend so desperate for my help. But I played dumb.

I shrugged. "So?"

Bethany gaped at me. "Laura, are you crazy? I don't want her to see …" She gestured around us at all the parents talking inside the gym, at the banners displaying Bible verses on the wall. "All *this*."

Tom Walker had just taken the stage, inviting everyone back to their seats so he could share church announcements. Bethany and I sat in a back row, close to the entrance. "She already knows you're a pastor's daughter," I said.

Mr. Walker was talking about a men's retreat next month. (What were they retreating *from*?) Bethany shook her head quickly. "It's too much, too soon," she said, and even though I knew she was self-conscious about this place in front of her new friends, I was a little taken aback by her concerned, almost frantic look. I started to feel bad.

"At least it's not Ian who's coming," I said, but before Bethany could respond, I felt a hand on my shoulder. There was Nola, in her usual attire: black jeans, black sneakers, black hooded sweatshirt—in midsummer.

"'Sup?" she said, smiling.

"Nola!" Bethany whispered. "You didn't have to come all the way here. I could have sent a pic or something."

Nola shrugged. "The sign said 'everyone welcome.'"

"Oh, yeah, it's just that"—Bethany gestured around her—"this is a little embarrassing."

Nola shrugged again. "Whatever gets you off, I guess." Then she took the free seat next to mine.

Up front, Mr. Walker had finished the announcements, and Pastor Eric was taking the stage to the congregation's applause. (At New Life, just about anything was cause for applause). "Good," Pastor Eric said, holding the microphone and looking at all of us, "It's a great day to be alive, Amen? Let's give it up for Jesus!"

As the room exploded in applause once again, Nola leaned over to me: "That's Bethany's dad, right?"

I nodded grimly. And on the other side of me, Bethany's face had turned a deep shade of pink.

# 5

## BEN

They called it a "vacation" Bible school. But what kind of vacation is it if you spend the whole day baking in the hot sun and getting bossed around by a bunch of stupid, stuck-up teenagers? What kind of vacation is it if you're forced into seriously lame activities? *Ben, come join the relay race! Ben, it's time for the pottery lesson! Ben, we're doing papier-mâché!* What kind of vacation is it if you're always in a bad mood, hot, sweaty, and bored, counting down the hours until it's time to go home, just so you can do it all again the next day?

Monday morning, the first day of VBS. My mom dropped me off in the church parking lot like I was some hitchhiker she'd picked up on the highway. And as I watched her pull back onto the road and speed away from the church a lot faster than she usually drove, I wondered if maybe the "vacation" part never was about us kids.

Another summer stuck in hell. Four years in a row, and because of the Weight, I knew this one would be the worst. "The Weight" is what I called the kid standing beside me in the parking lot, because that's exactly what he felt like: a weight hanging from my neck. DeShawn Vinson, my foster brother and my responsibility at VBS. DeShawn was eleven, two years younger than me and from New York City, and even though I'd lived with him for half a year now, that was all I knew about him. You *felt*

DeShawn more than anything. I felt his presence beside me in the parking lot even though he wasn't saying anything. I felt his presence at home even when he wasn't in the room. When I heard him through the wall, moving around in his bedroom, I wouldn't be able to concentrate on my Xbox. When he came down for dinner every night, I'd feel something heavy fall over the dinner table. Nobody else seemed to notice, or if they did, they pretended it wasn't there.

A year ago, when my parents first told me we were taking in a foster kid from the city, I'd been excited. I pictured a miniature Chris Rock, swearing up a storm at the breakfast table and cracking dirty jokes. I imagined him downloading all the best gangsta rap onto my phone (*"I'ma hook you up."*), maybe even giving me some tips on basketball. But as soon as DeShawn moved in, I knew it wouldn't be like that. The Weight didn't talk about hip-hop or basketball. He didn't talk much at all, just glared at you with his angry eyes. Even my parents, who were clued in on his life story, didn't seem totally sure about what he liked or didn't, what he was thinking. "So far, he's something of an enigma," my dad said about a month ago. "But that's okay, eventually he'll open up. Just don't push him." So I didn't—actually, I did my best to ignore the Weight, even as I felt him always dragging me down.

The parking lot was a traffic jam of parents dropping off their spawn. The giant green in front of church was already swarming with kids. I started over across the green to the big open tent where you signed in, making sure the Weight followed. All around us were brightly colored tents, cones, and flags marking off different games and contests, Christian hip-hop blaring from giant speakers set up on either side of the field. If you didn't know any better, this might even look fun.

Lydia Newman was sitting at a folding table under the sign-in tent. In front of her was a clipboard, and under the table was a plastic tub filled with colorful pieces of cloth. She smiled when she saw us.

"Hi, Benjamin! Excited for another amazing summer?"

I nodded and tried to smile back. With people like Lydia, so simple and happy, it felt almost wrong to be real with them.

She asked me what tribe I belonged to, and I couldn't help feeling a little proud when I told her Levi. We were respectable. Maybe not as cool as Judah, but not totally lame like Zebulun.

Lydia checked my name off on her clipboard and then dug an orange cloth out of the tub and handed it to me. I looked at it sadly for a second before tying it around my head.

"And you're DeShawn, right?" Lydia said, giving my foster brother a sunny smile. "We're so happy to have you this year! You'll be in the same tribe as Ben."

I stopped messing with my turban. "What? You didn't even check your list."

Lydia didn't look at me when she answered. "Yep. He's in Levi, too."

*Shit.* It was my mom, had to be. She'd called Ms. Swanson and asked her to put DeShawn in my tribe, even though there was a rule against parents doing that anymore. This place was getting so corrupt.

Lydia offered DeShawn a cloth the same color as mine, but he just stared at the thing, so she gave it to me. "Ben, can you show him how to put it on?"

DeShawn shook his head. "Nope, not wearing that."

"It's how we tell our tribes apart, DeShawn," Lydia said. "If you don't want to put it on your head, some kids tie it around their waists."

"Not wearing it like a dress, either."

"I'm sorry, DeShawn," Lydia said, looking almost scared, "but that's the rule."

And then DeShawn did what he always did when faced with something he didn't like, he walked away. "Wandering," my parents called it—like in school this past year, when he'd "wander" around the halls instead of going to class, until one of the teachers spotted him. Or that time at the grocery store a few weeks ago, when he "wandered" away from Mom and me and we spent ten minutes looking for him. Today, I was tempted just to let him go. Let him "wander" down the road to wherever the hell he wanted, see if I cared. But I knew my parents would kill me. So I started after him, back toward the parking lot. "DeShawn, get back here now!" I shouted. Then I froze. Pastor Eric's car was pulling into the parking lot, and a second later, she was getting out of the passenger seat, dressed in hot-pink shorts and a white T-shirt, her hair pulled back in a ponytail. Seeing her unexpectedly was like getting a brain freeze from eating ice cream too fast—so sweet it almost hurt. She glided across the parking lot, over to DeShawn, and laid a hand on his shoulder. The next second, Bethany Moyer was walking DeShawn back toward me and the tent. My palms were sweating.

"What's the problem?" Bethany asked, when she and DeShawn reached the tent.

"I'm not wearing that gay-ass thing on my head," DeShawn said, pointing at my turban. "I don't care what she says."

I could have strangled him for using me as the example, but Bethany hardly even glanced at me. She took the piece of cloth from Lydia and examined it. "I don't blame you." She thought for a few seconds. "Although …" She turned to the table and grabbed a pair of scissors from a jar next to Lydia. "I may have an idea." She cut the piece of cloth in half, then in half again, so that it was basically a long orange ribbon; then she motioned for DeShawn to hold out his hand. She knelt and tied the cloth around his wrist. "There," she said. "That's not so bad, is it?"

"That's not how it's supposed to be worn," Lydia said, frowning.

"It's fine, Lydia," Bethany murmured without looking at her.

DeShawn studied his wrist skeptically.

"*I* think it looks cool," Bethany declared as she stood up. "Actually, I kind of want one." She took the other half of the cloth she'd cut and tied it around her wrist. "Now we match, DeShawn. Because, guess what? I'm going to be one of Levi's team leaders this summer. We're in the same tribe, man!" She raised her hand for a high five, and when he gave her one, he did something I'd never seen him do before—he grinned.

FIVE MINUTES LATER, I was sitting on the ground in the middle of the field in front of the stage, waiting for the usual welcome spiel. There were maybe a hundred others like me, all of us in our colored turbans, listening to my friend Jason's mom, Ms. Swanson, go over the rules and daily schedule. I wondered if it ever got boring for her, repeating the same speech summer after summer. At least, one day I would be too old for this camp, but Ms. Swanson—when did *she* get to quit?

My hot, itchy turban was already giving me a headache. I tried to ignore DeShawn, sitting next to me and admiring his new bracelet. To the left of the stage, I could see the team leaders, about fifteen or so teenagers I recognized from church. Bethany sat next to her best friend, Laura Swanson, and even from there I could make out Bethany's expression—the far-off one, the one that was somewhere else. I always wondered where. I still couldn't believe she was going to be one of Levi's team leaders. It meant I would see her every day, and she would see me, pay attention to me. It would be her *job*. I couldn't decide if this was an amazing stroke of luck, or a looming disaster.

I wanted to be alone with Bethany Moyer, but under the right circumstances. Like in a zombie apocalypse, for example, holed up in my room, after all our friends and family had been devoured. At first, she'd be sad. I would take care of her, braving the zombies outside and making trips to the abandoned grocery store, bringing back canned soup and her favorite candy (Swedish Fish, I heard her say once). We'd watch funny movies on my TV, and she would lean against my shoulder and giggle sadly. And at night, when we heard the screams and snarls outside our window, I'd hold her close, but I wouldn't try anything. We'd kiss for the first time after a few zombies finally broke into the house and I'd taken them out with a baseball bat. Bethany would step over their lifeless carcasses sprawled out on the floor, careful not to get brains on her shoes, and throw her arms around me. "I'm so lucky to have you, Ben," she'd whisper. "I don't know why I never noticed you before." And suddenly, it wouldn't matter that she was a popular teenager and I was just a snot-nosed kid. It wouldn't matter that she was tall and tan and gorgeous and I was big and pale and pasty, that her skin was smooth and clear and mine was dotted with volcano-size zits. She'd lean in, and I would taste her cherry lip balm.

And that's when the zombies would attack, growling and slobbering as they broke through the doors and into our hiding spot. Except that they weren't growling and slobbering—they were laughing and shouting and saying things like, "Wait, which tribe am I in again?" and, "Has anyone seen my water bottle?" I looked around the church green. Announcements were over, and kids were rushing in every direction to find their tribe's tent.

On the way to Levi's tent, I was quickly sandwiched by Jason and Dylan. Jason slapped a hand on my shoulder. "So, do you think you'll be able to handle it, Ben?" he asked.

"Handle what?"

"Bethany as our team leader, of course."

"We don't want you to have a heart attack, or anything," Dylan added.

My love for Bethany Moyer might have been sacred to me, but for my two best friends, it was just material for endless teasing.

"I think Ben will be able to deal," Jason continued. "I'm not sure about his dick, though."

"Fuck off, will you?" I snapped. My friends and I had only recently started swearing, but we were naturals. Now the curses sat like jungle cats on our tongues, just waiting for a chance to spring. We swore whenever we could, even in a crowded field of kids on the first day of vacation Bible school.

"Where's DeShawn?" Dylan asked now that they had grown bored of teasing me.

I looked around. He'd been sitting beside me during the announcements, but I must have lost him in the rush after. "Not my problem." Though it *was* my problem.

"This has gotta be so lame for him," Jason said.

Because DeShawn was black and from the city, my friends were in awe of him. It didn't matter that when they asked his opinions on hip-hop, he just shrugged. It didn't matter that when they told a joke, he barely cracked a smile. It was like he didn't have to earn being cool. I didn't understand it, but then, according to my friends, that was because I was a racist. They'd been ribbing on me for that even before the Weight showed up, ever since I'd made the stupid mistake of admitting I wasn't attracted to Beyoncé.

We'd been watching YouTube videos at Jason's house on his mom's computer, playing a sort of impromptu who-would-you-do with visual aids. "I'm not saying she's not hot!" I cried after Jason clicked on another of her music videos, trying to get his point across. "I'm just *personally* not that into her."

Jason looked at Beyoncé dancing in a leotard on the screen, then back at me. "Dude, you're a fucking racist," he had declared before closing out the window and erasing the browsing history.

They made fun of me because my favorite rapper was Eminem. They even made fun of me when Obama got elected last November, acting like I had such a hard time with it even though I didn't give a rat's ass about politics. When DeShawn moved in later in January, the minute I expressed any dislike for the kid, they were ready to attack. "Just because I don't like one black person does not make me a racist!" I shouted at one point. "It might if he's the only black person you know," Dylan had snapped back, and for a moment it didn't sound like he was joking, and we all got quiet. After that, they cooled off about it.

But my dislike for DeShawn had nothing to do with Obama or Beyoncé. It had to do with the fact that he was a rotten little kid, and if I was the only one who could see that, oh, well.

"Look, there he is," I heard Dylan say beside me, and when I saw where he was pointing, I felt a little sick. There was my foster brother, walking with Bethany Moyer, the only girl I had ever wanted to impress and to make laugh, and he was saying something, and she was laughing like it was the funniest thing she'd ever heard.

By Friday, I was beginning to wonder if maybe my friends were right: having Bethany as our team leader might give me a heart attack. Each day was a new opportunity, all right—a new opportunity for me to thoroughly embarrass myself. If I missed an easy catch in a game of Frisbee, I prayed she hadn't seen. If I felt myself starting to sweat when she was nearby, I was terrified she'd smell my BO. The saddest part was, she didn't even notice. It turned out Bethany could be my team leader and still ignore my existence. Each tribe had at least two team leaders. Bethany mostly looked after the girls while Jon Newman watched the boys. To her, I was just another dumb, pimple-faced kid. Any way I could think of to set myself apart—disobeying the rules, starting a fight, having an asthma attack—felt counterproductive to my cause.

The only boy Bethany paid any attention to was my foster brother. Every morning, when we walked across the green to Levi's tent, she said hi to him in this sweet voice, giving him a smile she didn't use on anyone else, all without even looking at me. If DeShawn was in one of his moods, she'd put a hand on his shoulder and ask if he was okay. If he didn't want to participate in an activity, she'd tell him he didn't have to. On Wednesday, while I was forced into the bobbing-for-apples competition, I pulled my head out of the freezing tub of water, an apple the size of a melon lodged in my mouth, and there were Bethany and DeShawn, sitting on a blanket under one of the maple trees, laughing.

It wasn't right. *I* could be quiet and moody all the time, *I* could spend the day glaring at everyone for no good reason, but no one would give me special treatment. Tell me who's really racist.

On Friday morning, I heard DeShawn say the N-word. We were in the kitchen, eating breakfast before going to VBS. DeShawn was filling his bowl to overflowing with Honey Nut Cheerios, and I was worried there wouldn't be any left for me.

"You wanna save me some, maybe?" I said.

He ignored me and kept pouring.

"DeShawn."

No answer.

"DeShawn."

He slammed the box down on the table. "Nigga, will you get off my back?"

My mom was right there in the room. I saw her stop buttering her toast at the counter, her back to us. Then she started again and said in an almost normal voice, "Ben, there's more cereal in the cabinet."

"That's the last of the Honey Nut, though."

"Then eat the regular!" she snapped.

By the time we got to VBS, I was in a bad mood. And when I saw my cousin Becca coming across the green, calling out my name, it got even worse. I wanted to pretend I hadn't seen her, but we'd already locked eyes.

"Guess what?" Becca said when she reached me. "Zombies *do* have souls!"

"What?" I acted confused, though I knew exactly what she was talking about.

My aunt Janine and her family had moved to Grover Falls a few weeks ago, after my dad got her husband, Owen, a custodial job at the glass-and-ceramic plant where my dad was an engineer. They were from Pennsylvania but had been out of the country for a while, doing missionary work somewhere. When my mom told me they were moving up, I hadn't been thrilled. They were a weird family. My uncle always had this sour look on his face, like he had permanent constipation or something, and my aunt was this quiet woman who winced anytime she laughed. The girls, Rachel and Rebecca, wore long skirts down to their ankles, and dorky, out-of-date sweaters. Also, they were homeschooled. You'd think they would have it made, getting to sleep in every day and do homework in their pajamas, but you could tell it wasn't like that. They knew all the state capitals and could recite the periodic table. I would have felt stupid around them, only they were clueless when it came to real things: they didn't know who Lil Wayne or Lady Gaga were. They probably didn't even know how to use the internet.

A week ago, my parents invited them over for a welcome dinner. I guess DeShawn had sensed something, because he pretended to have a headache, and my mom let him stay up in his room when they arrived. I had to sit there at the dinner table, eating my meatloaf in silence, listening to my dad and uncle talk about the new job and avoiding looking up at my cousin Becca, sitting across from me.

It was my aunt who finally asked me a question when there was a short break in the men's conversation: "So, Benjamin, what would you like to do when you're older?"

When I answered that I wanted to go to school to design video games, Aunt Janine nodded with this blank expression on her face, then quickly looked down at her food. My uncle then decided to bring up an article he'd read, on the violent effects of video games on today's youth. My parents listened politely, but I wanted to stand up and leave the room. My uncle had never played a video game, so what did he know? He didn't know how it feels when you're angry or upset or embarrassed and the only thing that helps, the only thing that can calm you down, is the weight of your Xbox controller in your hands. In the old days, guys might go out and hunt a bear or chop down a tree, but all we had now were our game consoles. I couldn't make anyone understand this, though, so I just waited for dinner to be over.

After dinner, my mom asked me to show the girls around, and I did my best to let her know I wasn't happy about this, without being so obvious I'd get in trouble later. I led the girls into the den. "So there's a TV here," I said lamely, like a Realtor showing people around a shitty house, "and some board games."

Rachel, who was older, just nodded. She looked almost as bored as I was. But Becca went over to the bookshelf where the board games sat. "Do you want to play something? Which is your favorite, Ben?"

I hadn't played a board game in years. I shrugged. "I actually forgot to do something important—I'll be back."

Soon I was in my room with the door closed, sitting in my beanbag chair in front of my TV, a controller in my hands, blowing zombies' heads off. Eminem playing on my iHome. Nobody could touch me here. I was safe. Until there was a knock on my door. I knew it was my mom.

"Yeah?" I snapped without pausing the game.

Becca stood in the doorway. "*This* is the important thing you had to do?"

For a second I felt guilty, but I tried not to show it. I wished I could tell her to piss off. I wished I could be meaner. I kept my eyes on the screen and shot another zombie in the face, pressing harder than I needed to on the trigger of my controller. "I just have to beat this level real quick," I mumbled.

I waited for my cousin to go, but she just stood in the doorway. Eminem rapped quietly about killing his mom.

"What do you have to do?" she asked after a while.

"Um, just kill zombies, basically."

At the moment, I was defending an abandoned McDonald's from a ravening horde of the undead. I was behind the counter with an AK-47, mowing them down as they climbed through the broken windows, their heads exploding and bits of blood and brains splattering onto the TV screen. I glanced at Becca's disgusted face. "You can sit down if you want."

"There's so much violence," she said.

"Yeah."

"Do you like playing games with so much violence?"

It was a weird question, different from what her dad had been saying downstairs. Not *did I think it was good for me*, not *did I think it was right*, but *did I* like *it*. I hesitated a second. "Well, I'm fighting to save the world. I'm killing the *bad guys*."

Becca shook her head. "Jesus said love your enemies, pray for those who persecute you."

"What about, like, David and Goliath, then?" I asked. I couldn't quote verses, but I was pretty sure there was a lot of killing in the Bible.

"That was in the Old Testament. We're under a new covenant now."

I decided this conversation was hopeless and turned back to my game. "I don't even know what you're talking about," I muttered.

Becca thought I was asking for an explanation. "Jesus fulfilled the Old Law when he died on the cross and rose again. Now we follow his commandments. And one of his commandments is to turn the other cheek, repay evil with good."

"They're just zombies!" I almost shouted. "Is there anything in the Bible against killing zombies? Because I'm pretty sure there isn't. I'm pretty sure Jesus doesn't care. It's not like they have *souls*, or anything."

"Zombies don't have souls?" Becca asked, sounding curious, like she really wanted to know.

I shrugged. "I don't think so." It wasn't something I'd ever thought about before.

"Oh," Becca said. "I guess it's not so bad, then."

We didn't say anything for a bit, and soon I was overpowered by a giant zombie boss. The screen filled up with blood. You could hear my tortured screams.

I turned to Becca. "Wanna play?"

Ten minutes later, Becca was sitting next to me on the beanbag chair, and I was teaching her how to aim her gun. "No, no!" I shouted, laughing.

"Remember, this one controls your body and *this* one controls your gun."
I took her hands in mine and showed her.

"I don't get it! I don't get it!" she cried.

It was a new way to play video games. With the guys, we were always
shouting at each other and making mean jokes and teabagging each other's
dead bodies on the screen. With Becca, I was laughing until my face got
red and tears came down my cheeks. She died about every ten seconds,
and every time, she would let out this little shriek and throw her controller
down and bury her head in her hands. And then she would pick it back up
and say, "Okay, this time for real," with this hard look in her eyes.

We stayed up in my room for the rest of the evening. When Rachel
came in around nine o'clock, she looked with shock at the controller in
her sister's hands. "Becca, I don't think Dad would want you playing that."

Becca tried to smile up at her sister, but I could see she was nervous.
"No, it's okay, Rachel. They don't have souls."

"What?"

"They're just zombies," I said, trying to help. "So it's okay to shoot
them."

Rachel looked at us both and frowned. "It's time to go," was all she said.

Watching them leave, I wondered if Rachel would rat on her sister,
and I wondered what her father would do if she did. He wasn't someone
I'd want angry at me. I went back into my room and started playing again,
but I felt weird inside, lonely almost. I tried to forget about how much
fun I'd just had.

Now here was Becca, standing in front of me on the church green, her
head wrapped in a blue turban, grinning. She held the book in her hands
up for me to see. "I checked this out at the library the other day," she said.

I read the cover: *Rise of the Undead: Slavery, Colonialism, and Zombies
in 18th-Century Haiti*, by Robert F. Whitehead, PhD. On the cover, a very
thin, very old black man stared at me with huge white eyes. I wished she
would put the book down.

"In this book," Becca said, "he talks about the African slaves that
were brought over to Haiti in the seventeen hundreds to work the sugar
plantations. This was where the zombie myth originally came from:

African folklore. Some of the slaves believed that when they died, their souls would return to their home country—unless they killed themselves, or a witch doctor cast a spell, and then their souls would be trapped in an undead form, forever in the New World, and they could never go back to their homeland. Forced to remain on the plantations for eternity. Zombies." She smiled at me. "So you were wrong: zombies *do* have souls."

I wanted to smile back, but the black man on the book cover was still staring at me with those giant eyes, and DeShawn was right beside me, listening. I just said, "Cool," and tried to keep my voice disinterested.

Becca looked disappointed and lowered the book that I hadn't accepted from her. She turned to my foster brother, who was still staring at the book. "You must be DeShawn. I was at your house the other day, but you weren't feeling well." She noticed DeShawn's interest in the book and offered it to him. "Here, maybe you'd like to read this. It's real interesting. I found it while doing research on Haiti. We lived there for a while. I'm moving back when I turn eighteen."

This surprised me. I wasn't exactly sure where Haiti was, but it didn't seem like any place I could picture Becca living. I had a quick vision of my cousin in her ankle-length jean skirt and orange long-sleeved T-shirt, sitting under a palm tree, a fruity drink in her hand. I figured DeShawn would just stare at her and make her feel stupid, the way he could do so easily to anyone, but instead, he took the book and said, "That's where my grandma was from." It was the most I'd ever heard him say about his life.

"It's a library book," Becca said, "but you can borrow it for a while."

DeShawn glanced up at her for a second and then opened the book.

"I didn't know you were coming to this," I said to Becca.

She grinned. "My mom convinced my dad to sign me up late. I'm so excited!"

I wanted to warn her, grab her by the shoulders and tell her to leave while she still had the chance, but then Jason and Dylan had found us and were looking at Becca, waiting for an explanation.

I looked at the ground while introducing the guys to my cousin. She smiled and said hi, but Jason just nodded at her blue turban. "You're in the tribe of Judah."

Becca nodded.

"So that means we can't talk to you," said Jason. "Levi is archenemies with Judah."

Becca's smile faded. "Oh …"

"Yeah," Jason said, "so you'd better get to your tribe now."

I knew that Becca was looking at me, but I kept my eyes on the ground until she had turned and walked away. Jason shook his head. "Newbies."

DURING THE FIRST WEEK OF VBS, every camper was supposed to choose a verse in the Bible to memorize. Once they could recite it perfectly to a team leader by memory, they went on to the verse after it. The more verses you learned, the more points you earned. Whoever had the longest passage memorized by the end of the program won a thousand points for their tribe.

That afternoon, Jon Newman had the whole tribe of Levi gather around our tent so we could each tell him the verses we had picked. I didn't like Jon—he was always trying to give me high fives and telling me that Jesus had great things planned for me. How the hell would he know that? Also, I knew he had a thing for Bethany, which was weird since he was a few years older than her. And yeah, I was a few years *younger*, but somehow that didn't seem as creepy.

"Remember," Jon said to us as the whole tribe of Levi sat down in a semicircle outside the tent, "no John eleven, forty-five" (the shortest verse in the Bible: "Jesus Wept." You couldn't earn points for two words, three syllables). "And, of course, no Song of Songs." (Every year some smart-ass kid tried to pick a verse from the "Book of the Bible for Married People," as my mom called it.)

While I waited for Jon to get to me, I flipped through the thin pages of the Bible till I found Song of Songs. Everybody made jokes about the book, but I'd never actually thought to look it up. *Let him kiss me with the kisses of his mouth. For your love is more delightful than wine, your anointing oils are fragrant, your name is perfume poured out …* I scanned farther down the page. *Your hair is like a flock of goats descending from Mount Gilead. Your teeth are like a flock of sheep just shorn … Your lips are like scarlet ribbon; your mouth is lovely … Your two breasts are like two fawns, like twin fawns of a gazelle, that browse among the lilies.*

It was weird and a little gay, but reading the words, I felt something moving inside me. I looked up at Bethany, standing on the edge of the circle, scrolling through her phone.

The breeze was ruffling her hair, and she was smiling a little, like she had a secret, and she didn't even look up until Jon said her name three times. "Can you help me out?" he asked, trying to smile. I knew that Jon got annoyed with how Bethany didn't seem to care about being a team leader, but he would never say anything.

Jon went around the tribe and asked each of us what verse we were starting with, and then checked it in his Bible, and Bethany recorded it in her notebook. "Okay, Molly, how about you?" he asked Molly Thompson, sitting next to me. But Molly wasn't paying attention; she was looking at the girl who had just appeared on the edge of our circle. We all were. She was dressed all in black—black eyeliner, black hooded sweatshirt, tight black jeans full of holes—and she had a lip ring.

"Nola!" Bethany rushed over. "What are you doing here?"

"Just came to see what's kicking," the girl said, and when she saw the look of surprise on Bethany's face, she raised her eyebrows. "Is that a problem?"

"No!" Bethany shook her head quickly. "It's just …" She stopped. She seemed to realize for the first time that we all were looking at them.

"Do we have a visitor, Bethany?" Jon asked.

"Um, yeah. Everybody, this is Nola. Nola, this is … everybody."

Nola nodded. "'Sup?" Then she turned to Bethany and smiled. "What's with the turbans?"

"Oh, that's just so we know what tribe they're in."

"A little racist, don't you think?"

Before Bethany could answer, Jon said loudly, "We're just in the middle of something, Nola. You're welcome to come join us."

"Actually," Bethany said, "I'm gonna show Nola around first."

Jon looked annoyed but he nodded, and Bethany grabbed Nola by the arm and basically pulled her away. I watched as they headed across the field, talking and laughing. I stared after them until I heard Jon call on my foster brother. "Okay, DeShawn, your turn."

I was surprised to see that DeShawn was reading the zombie book Becca had given him, and he didn't even look up at Jon as he answered. "I'm not doing a verse."

"Come on, DeShawn," Jon said, "you need to try."

DeShawn shook his head. "Bethany said I didn't have to."

"Well, she shouldn't have told you that. The rule is, everyone tries to memorize at least one verse."

DeShawn kept his eyes on the book and didn't say anything.

"What's that you're reading?" Jon asked, holding out his hand. "Let me see."

DeShawn hesitated a second and then handed the book over. Jon flipped through it, frowning. "I'm not sure this is something you should be bringing to VBS, DeShawn. There's stuff about black magic in here." He closed the book and stuffed it under his arm.

"Hey!" DeShawn cried.

"You'll get it back after program," Jon said. He put his Bible down in front of DeShawn. "For now, I want you to look through *this* book, and choose a verse." He smiled. "Okay, man?" Jon reached out to give him a pat on the shoulder, but DeShawn jerked away so fast, Jon's hand just hit empty air. He kept smiling and moved on.

Five minutes later, after Jon had gotten around to everybody, he told us to divide up into pairs and start practicing our verses. I teamed up with Dylan. "Where's DeShawn?" Jason asked me. We looked around our tribe but didn't see him anywhere. He'd wandered again.

# 6

PAUL

There used to be cigarettes everywhere. In the kitchen cabinet above the sink and in the drawers where she kept the silverware. Stuffed between the cushions of the living room sofa and perched above the light fixture in the garage. They were stashed away all over the Frazier home, always within arm's reach. But that was before. Before Jesus, before New Life. When Paul first came home from New York, he had raided his mother's favorite hiding spots after she told him she had finally quit for good, and found them empty.

But after two days of working at the church, Paul searched the house again. This time, he wasn't looking for cigarettes to disprove his mother's claim. This time, he'd been looking for cigarettes because he badly needed one. His first paycheck wouldn't come for another week, and Paul was desperate. There must have been one hiding spot his mom had missed when throwing out her stash, one place she'd passed over. He finally got lucky in the basement, when he thrust his arm into the crack of space between the old chest freezer and the wall and felt victorious glee as his hand closed around a soft package. Marlboro Reds—his mom's brand—and by the look of them they were years old. Paul didn't care. They were cigarettes.

Now, in the church basement, in what used to be the boys' locker room, Paul lay on his back on a bench and counted the remaining cigarettes in the pack. These had to last until his paycheck came. He had already smoked one since coming down here. He should save the rest. But the morning had gotten to him. His muscles were sharp and tense, and he could feel a headache lurking at the back of his temples. He pulled another out of the pack and lit up.

In a few minutes, he must face them again. Parent pickup time was always the worst. Ten-year-old kids who believed in Jesus and thought they were going to heaven when they died were one thing; adults who did were something else. When they arrived in their minivans and SUVs, when they waved and smiled at him in the parking lot, Paul would marvel at how normal they looked—just your average American citizen. If you saw them at the grocery store or a baseball game, you wouldn't notice anything different about them, they blended in so perfectly. But now Paul knew better. He had seen their true form, had been let in on the secret, and it was terrifying.

Sunday had been Paul's first full day on the job. And on the drive over, sipping his stale drive-through Dunkin' Donuts coffee, he'd had to remind himself: *I am not going to church because of any existential or spiritual crisis on my part. I am going because someone offered me a job, and I badly need one. I understand that any questions I might have about the meaning of life or finding inner peace cannot be answered here. On the contrary, places like this only add to the turmoil and confusion in the world. This is about work and nothing else.*

But within the first five minutes of the worship service, Paul had already begun to second-guess himself. Jon Newman had set him up in the sound booth, erected at the back of the gym, above everyone's head. It gave Paul a bird's-eye view of the sanctuary, and although his job was to pay attention to the sound of the band, it was hard not to focus on the congregation. Wide-eyed, he watched a woman in the back row, who looked at least forty, jumping up and down in wild euphoria to the music. She had her arms outstretched, reaching toward the ceiling, her body shaking and moving in a dance that was utterly unrestrained yet somehow devoid of even the faintest hint of sexuality. Her eyes were closed as she belted out the words to the song in a voice that was decidedly off-key, oblivious of how ridiculous she looked. They all were. No one in the room, whether they were jumping up and down, clapping to the beat, or just swaying back and forth in place, ever betrayed a hint of embarrassment or self-consciousness that Paul could see. As far as they were concerned, it was perfectly normal for a bunch of otherwise rational, functioning adults—adults who held down jobs, raised children, voted in elections—to gather once a week in a gymnasium and sing love songs to a being in the heavens whose very existence was in serious doubt.

Even Paul's mother, standing near the outside aisle, not jumping around (thank God), but still holding one arm up and singing along with eyes closed, appeared completely comfortable with this scene. And watching her face, so fervent, elated but also somehow serene, it came as a shock to Paul that this wasn't at all an act for Sharon Frazier. She really believed this stuff. He had to look away.

Paul didn't believe in God, but had he been on the fence concerning the existence of the divine, coming to a church like this would have been a very efficient way to push him over the edge from casual agnosticism to militant atheism. Modern evangelicals had probably done more to swell the ranks of atheists than a thousand Carl Sagans could ever have dreamed of doing.

As the worship band ended one song and dived straight into another, Paul adjusted the bass and wondered what Sasha would say if she could see him now. Ever since the breakup, he had found himself doing this: imagining his ex's reaction to the ever-worsening situations he found himself in. In a dive bar in the Village, being kicked out at 3 a.m. because he couldn't pay his tab—what would Sasha say? At his apartment in Brooklyn, drinking the last of the peach schnapps that had for some reason been in the freezer and then watching hours of porn on his phone because he couldn't sleep, clicking numbly on one video after another, barely even aroused—how disgusted would she be? Back home in Grover Falls, listening to another lecture from his mom about the importance of vitamin D and getting enough sunlight—would Sasha take his mother's side, or tell him it was okay, he could go back to bed? But here, looking out at this basketball court with a bunch of religious fanatics, mixing the music that made it possible for their cult to function, Paul felt he had reached an all-time low. What would Sasha do? Laugh? Take pity?

Or would she firmly and in no uncertain terms remind him of what he already knew: "*Paul, baby, I know you're crazy, but you're not* this *crazy. You're desperate, but you're not* this *desperate. You absolutely, positively are not allowed to work here. I forbid it.*"

Well, if his ex-girlfriend forbade it in his imagination, that was that. He couldn't work here. So there was no point in staying here any longer, was there? He should just leave. But then Paul remembered he couldn't leave. He'd ridden here with his mom, because his mom had a job and could afford gas, whereas Paul did not have a job and therefore could not afford gas. This was his dilemma.

So Paul hardened his resolve. He tried to banish all thoughts of Sasha, all thoughts of God or religion, and concentrate only on the reasons here was here: the mixing board before him and the band on stage. Jon Newman, the worship leader, was a short, wide-faced guy Paul had known in high school. His mild appearance did not match his singing voice, which was deep and rough and sounded uncannily like the guy from the nineties band Creed. Jon had been the one to show him around yesterday, and Paul had found him even more annoying than he'd remembered. The guy went on and on about how the Lord was doing amazing things at New Life, and how happy he was with his choice not to go to college but to stay and help out at the church, without once asking Paul about what was going on in *his* life—not that he would have obliged Jon with an answer.

It did allow Paul to make the sad observation that while he had gone to school and accumulated a degree and a mountain of debt, Jon had no degree and no debt—and now Paul was essentially the sound technician and roadie for Jon's band. The rest of the worship team—electric guitar, bass, keyboards, and drums—were also kids who looked no older than Paul. They weren't half bad, really, it was just the music they chose to play that was terrible. Mixing was second nature to Paul, and he spent the rest of the worship service watching the cute girl on keyboards, who also provided backing vocals, and trying to decide whether she was a virgin.

WHEN WORSHIP ENDED, a man wearing a white button-down and a robin's-egg blue tie had gone up on stage and declared that God was good, and then invited everyone to greet someone around them. Paul had thought it a safe moment to duck out to the bathroom, but on the way back to the sound booth, he had been accosted. Faces—faces he'd never seen before, coming up to him, welcoming him with big smiles, saying his name and telling him how happy they were to see him here. "So good to see you, Paul!" "Paul, I've heard so much about you from your mom. Wonderful to finally meet you!" It took all his self-restraint not to walk out of the building and head down the road toward his house, car or no car. "I tried, Mom," he would tell her when she came home and found him in his bedroom, under the blankets. "I tried, but it's just not going to work." But he managed to escape back to his sound booth, and after the announcements, it was time for Pastor Eric's sermon.

Paul had been ready to detest the patriarch of this pseudocult his mom had fallen into, when he met him yesterday. His mother had introduced them in the church parking lot. Eric Moyer was a good-looking middle-aged man with a warm smile and a gravelly voice that pleasantly offset his clean-cut appearance. When he had told Paul it was so great to finally meet him, it was hard to believe that he didn't mean it. He had invited Paul to come inside to his office. He didn't know what he'd been expecting, but he was surprised by the room's stately elegance, with an oak desk and an Indian rug on the floor. It was surprisingly … *normal.*

The interview didn't last long. Pastor Eric sat behind his desk and asked him a few questions about school and the city, which Paul was able to deflect with vague responses, and a few more about his proficiency with sound equipment and instruments, which Paul could be a lot more direct and specific about. Eric laid out the responsibilities of the job, which ranged from sound technician to roadie to all-around handyman at the church and VBS. He would also be expected to accompany the VBS on its end-of-program weekend camping trip in the Adirondack Mountains (a small detail that Paul's mother had failed to mention). After making sure Paul was comfortable with the duties involved, Eric paused and then said, "Well, Paul, I'd love to give you the job. If anything, it appears you're *over*qualified, and we'd love to have you here. But I do have to be honest and tell you that we've never had anyone work at New Life who hasn't made a firm commitment to Christ and the church."

Paul didn't say anything. It seemed the wisest thing to do at the moment.

"Usually," Pastor Eric continued, "we prefer them to be members as well. That being said, I know you've been going through a tough time recently"—Paul tried not to wince. How much had his mom told this guy?—"and I firmly believe that the scripture teaches to give everyone a chance. But I'm just curious to know where you are right now, spiritually speaking. What are your thoughts on what we believe here?"

Paul wasn't sure what to say. He could remember only one thing close to a spiritual encounter in his life. It had to do with heckling a street preacher in Union Square one late drunken night.

His second summer in the city, the latest manifestation of the Seizures had opened for a group in the East Village. It would be the biggest act the band ever opened for. Cross Breeze was a five-piece from Bushwick, described by a prominent blogger as a "dreamy synth-pop act with close boy/girl harmonies and a hint of 1960s revivalism." A few weeks ago their single, "Forever Summer," had been included in *The Brooklyn Regulator's* monthly, "Songs You NEED to Hear Now." Paul had listened to the song after they got the gig and had found it both catchy and utterly insufferable. He had proposed to the rest of the band that they do a cover.

Niles, his bass player, apartment mate, and frequent voice of reason, was skeptical: "What? Why would we cover the biggest song of the group we're opening for?" It was Niles who had gotten them the gig with Cross Breeze. He was reasonably well connected.

"It would be ironic," Paul replied.

So they had closed out their set with a raging and bitingly scornful version of "Forever Summer." When the crowd caught on, there were jeers and boos. And Paul, who had snorted two lines of coke before the set, raised a middle finger to the crowd, knocked over the mike, and walked off stage.

Ten minutes later, he and the rest of the Seizures were packing their instruments and equipment into their van as fast as they could. Paul was handing his guitar up to Colin in the back of the van when Niles had appeared beside him.

"Yo, I've got a friend inside who wants to meet the idiot responsible for this disaster."

Paul groaned. "Let's just get out of here."

"Trust me, man," Niles said, "you're going to want me to introduce you."

Paul followed Niles back into the club, to the far end of the bar, where a girl sat with a mixed drink in front of her. Her name was Sasha. Inside a minute, Paul was in love, or else just high and drunk and wanting to fuck and was there a difference?

Sasha had told him she liked their cover, that it improved on the original, and Paul had said thank you and that she was probably the only person in here with that opinion.

"Drink with me," Sasha commanded.

"I'm pretty sure I've worn out my welcome at this particular establishment," Paul said, looking around the club. So far, no one seemed to have noticed him.

Sasha placed an arm on his shoulder, guiding him to the empty stool beside her. "Don't worry, I'll protect you."

Paul ordered a beer. Sasha observed that he had looked pretty angry up onstage. She wondered where all that rage came from. Paul assured her it was all a facade, that he was really a quiet, well-adjusted boy from a small town upstate. He asked whether she was a Cross Breeze fan. Sasha shook her head, told him she'd gone to high school on Long Island with one of the singers—her boyfriend was the fan. Where was her boyfriend? Somewhere around. Paul met him after doing a line of coke with Sasha in the bathroom. Funnily enough, it wasn't the boyfriend he pushed, but one of the boyfriend's friends. They were thrown out by a bouncer before it could turn into any sort of brawl.

Out on the street, they stood dazed. "I'm dizzy," Sasha told him. "Carry me." She leaped onto his back and wrapped her legs around his waist, and they wandered down Fourteenth Street, a laughing, looping mess.

When they reached Union Square, they stopped at a gaggle of people crowded around an old man standing on a box. He had a shirt wrapped around his head and was telling everyone to repent, for Jesus was coming back soon to separate the sheep from the goats.

"Is that a literal soapbox he's on?" Sasha asked, still on Paul's back.

Paul wondered aloud whether he was a sheep or a goat.

"I'd rather be a goat," said Sasha. "Sheep are too ... white."

And then someone—maybe it was Sasha, maybe someone else—began to chant, "Goats! Goats! Goats!"

The man on the box looked out at the crowd chanting for goats and shouted, "And they were cast into the outer darkness, where there is weeping and gnashing of teeth!"

Paul would like to remember his first time with Sasha as a night of tenderness, two people newly in love and in awe of each other's body, rather than as the cocaine-and-alcohol-fueled haze of grappling, fumbling flesh that it had actually been. He remembered only fragmented images of them groping at each other on his mattress on the floor. And he remembered, near the end, trying to come, and Sasha breathing in his ear, "Is Jesus coming back tonight?"

Paul had let out a moan.

"Is Jesus coming back tonight?"

"Jesus is coming back."

"Should I repent?"

"You should repent."

"Father, forgive me for my sins. Hallelujah. Hallelujah. Hallelujah."

IN HIS OFFICE, Pastor Eric cleared his throat. Paul blinked and realized his mind had gone somewhere else. Did he have to speak now? Spoken words from him now seemed necessary. He opened his mouth, but it was dry. He coughed. "Yeah, no, okay ... I, um, I guess ... I've never been really spiritual or anything. I've always kinda put that on the back burner of my life, I guess you could say. But now I have a lot of questions, like about God and the afterlife and all that. And I think working here would help me, you know, start to sort those questions out and maybe find some direction for my life."

He stopped. Pastor Eric was nodding and smiling, as if this was exactly what he had wanted to hear.

IT HAD BEEN A WEEK NOW, and though Paul had yet to grow used to this place, he was beginning to understand the appeal it had for his mother. For anyone alone in life, anyone lost, afraid, or struggling, it must be a relief to find a group of people who didn't know you but were nevertheless ready to welcome you with open arms into their family. The only problem was the stipulations. You couldn't be part of the family if you didn't believe the world was created in seven days by a being in the sky. You couldn't be part of the family if you had sex with people of your gender. But was there *any* group of people who came together and accepted everyone without any conditions or expectations? Paul didn't think so, it was just that these people's conditions and expectations happened to be particularly stupid.

Paul was on his back, cigarette between his fingers, staring up at the locker-room ceiling, when he heard the door creak open. *Fuck,* he almost said out loud, without looking up. It would be the janitor, or one of the teenagers, and they would tell Pastor Eric he'd been smoking down here, and that would be the end of yet another failed episode of his life. Briefly, Paul contemplated what sort of person couldn't even hold down a job at a church. But after a few seconds, when no words of reprimand came, he propped himself up on his elbows and looked at the boy standing in the doorway.

For a second, the boy seemed to consider turning and leaving the room, but something about Paul—maybe it was the cigarette—kept him there. He shut the door, came into the room, and leaned against the lockers.

Paul sat upright. "Hey, are you supposed to be down here?"

The boy nodded at the cigarette. "You supposed to be smoking that cig?"

Paul looked sadly at it. "I'll put it out."

"You don't gotta do that. I like the smell." The boy sank to the floor, his head against the lockers and his knees pulled up to his chest. He closed his eyes and took a breath.

Paul couldn't help smiling. "What's your name?" he asked, taking a drag.

The boy opened his eyes. "You gonna rat on me?"

"Wasn't planning on it."

The boy studied him for a moment. "DeShawn," he said at last.

"You're living with the Waid family, aren't you?" Paul asked. It was hard not to notice when a white family suddenly acquired an adolescent black son.

"Don't remind me," said DeShawn.

"Where are you from?"

"Brooklyn."

"Yeah?" said Paul. "I lived down there for a few years. Just got back, actually. What part of Brooklyn?"

"Brownsville," DeShawn answered with disdain in his eyes, and Paul suddenly felt stupid. He nodded. He had lived in Williamsburg, and all he knew about Brownsville was that when he first moved to New York, it was one of the places his friends had warned him never to go.

"So why are you here?" Paul asked. Then, realizing how that sounded, he added, "I mean, here in the locker rooms. Why aren't you up with everyone else?"

"Why aren't *you* up with everyone else?" said DeShawn.

Paul shrugged. "This is my break before I have to start tearing down."

DeShawn nodded and closed his eyes again. "This is my break, too, then."

Paul took another drag and watched him. DeShawn looked as if he might fall asleep right there. He was trying to think of something more to ask him when the door burst open and April Swanson stood in the doorway. She looked from Paul to DeShawn, back to Paul, searching for an explanation that wasn't presenting itself. DeShawn stood up. "Yeah, yeah," he muttered, "I gotta get back to my tribe."

He tried to push past April, but she placed a hand on his shoulder. "DeShawn, this can't happen. You cannot just leave your group whenever you want without telling anyone. We were all looking for you and were very worried."

"Yo, get your hands off me!" DeShawn snapped. He pulled away from

April as if she were a hot iron and rushed out of the room. April gave Paul a look, somewhere between angry and pleading, before turning around and following DeShawn. Paul stubbed the last of his cigarette out on the bench and tossed the butt in the trash can on his way out the door. He followed the two through the basement hall, up the stairs, and back into the brightness outside.

AFTER DESHAWN HAD BEEN SAFELY RETURNED to the rest of his tribe, April turned to Paul, as he knew she would, and asked if she could speak to him in private. And following her across the parking lot to the other side of the green, Paul had a sharp flash of déjà vu: twelfth-grade math, 2004. Ms. Swanson had been the teacher. And though he hadn't been much of a student, Paul had still been a little bit sad when his mother told him it was the same woman who had taught him how to solve for $x$ who was responsible for the vacation Bible school monstrosity.

It was a little destabilizing. Back in high school, Paul had liked April (or Ms. Swanson) more than he would ever have admitted to his friends, the stoners and future dropouts of Grover High, who called her things behind her back, reciting the paraphrased line, *"April is the cruelest bitch,"* after being forced to read *The Waste Land* in English class. Maybe it was only that he was a confused, horny teenage boy and she was the only one of his female teachers under the age of forty, but for Paul there had always been something enticing about her. Looking back, he thought it had been a frank and unsparing self-awareness, a hard-earned knowledge about the world that made everything she did and said feel just short of knowingly ironic. She was in on the joke. And as a teenager, Paul had wanted her to see that he was in on it, too, that they shared an existential understanding that, were it ever to be plainly articulated, would have boiled down to something like *none of this really matters.*

Probably, though, she never gave him a second thought. He had kept a passing grade, but only because school came easier to him than to most of his friends. He didn't need to try very hard to keep from failing. He did remember one instance, though, when he had forced his math teacher to give him her undivided attention. It was after he'd missed his final precalculus test, which counted for more of his grade than he could afford to throw away. He had approached her later that day, when his hangover wasn't quite so debilitating. "I don't have a good excuse, Ms. Swanson," he told her in the hallway outside her classroom, "other than that I made a really bad decision and I wish I could take it back."

She had looked at him evenly with her arms crossed, frowning slightly. He had to avert his eyes to the floor. Finally, she said, "Well, Paul, I don't normally do this, but in your case …" She trailed off with a sigh, and he never found out why she had made an exception just for him, why he was different. She just told him to come to her classroom, final period.

During the makeup exam, alone in her classroom, he had tried to focus on the problems, but he kept glancing up at her, sitting at her desk, grading papers. She had taken off her cardigan, and her bare arms were swathed in afternoon light slanting in through the window. He had the stupid urge to say something to break the silence and kept biting his tongue.

When he finished, Paul went up to her desk and handed her the test. "Thank you for this, Ms. Swanson. I was lucky to have you for a teacher this year."

She laughed. "Don't lay it on too thick, Mr. Frazier. You already got your makeup exam."

"No, I mean it, I—"

But she cut him short. "Have a good summer, Paul."

He turned to go. And just as he was about to leave the room, she said his name. She looked at him over her reading glasses.

"Take care of yourself, okay?"

He nodded. "Yeah, I will." Out in the hallway, Paul was surprised to find that his heart was beating fast.

It was this memory that always came to him when he thought of April Swanson, and now, following her across the lot, he found his heart was beating in much the same way. She stopped under the shade of a small red maple, away from the joyful clamor and chaos of the camp. Paul could see golfers, getting through the hole before the light went.

April massaged her temples with her forefingers. "Okay, I'm trying to figure out what exactly was going through your head down there, and I just can't come up with anything. You wanna help me out?" She put her hands on her hips and looked at Paul.

"What do you mean?"

"Like, help me understand what made you think it was okay to be down in the locker room, smoking cigarettes with a eleven-year-old boy."

"You make it sound like we were passing it back and forth."

April held up her hands. "For all I know, you could have been!"

Paul laughed and shook his head. "Look, I was down there by myself, taking a break, and the kid just showed up. He was only there for, like, five minutes before you found us. Don't worry, I didn't offer him a smoke."

"Did it occur to you that he probably shouldn't have been down there, that there were probably people looking for him—people who were concerned and worried?"

Five minutes ago, while following her across the field, Paul had been preparing an apology for April. But now all he could find inside him was anger and defensiveness. "Hey, I'm sorry, but it's not like the kid is really my responsibility. I'm just the sound guy."

"That's a great way to look at it. Very mature of you. But not all that surprising, I have to say."

Paul felt an unsummoned smirk rising to his face. "Let's make sure we're sticking to the matter at hand, how about."

"This isn't a joke, not when a child goes missing. Sure, it turned out fine this time, but that's only *this* time. How was I to know that he hadn't run off, or gotten … *abducted,* or anything? And really, how was I to know what *you* were doing with him down there?"

It was an unfortunate trait of Paul's to smile wider the more uncomfortable he got. "Jesus *Christ,*" he said, now grinning stupidly and feeling his face go red.

"I'm not saying that. All I'm saying is, how was I to know? You could have been anybody." She stopped, sighed, and then shrugged. "But I guess, really, you're right: it's my responsibility, not yours. So looks like you're off the hook," she finished with a rueful grin.

He avoided her eyes. She was looking at him, it seemed, partly with exasperation, partly with hope. He looked away, across the parking lot, where parents were beginning to arrive for pickup. Paul cleared his throat. "I gotta go tear down." He pointed dumbly.

April nodded. "Sorry," Paul muttered. He turned away and left her in the shade of the little maple tree.

ANOTHER WEEK WENT BY, and at eight o'clock on a Friday night, Paul parked in the driveway of his mother's house. When he shut off his car's engine and the blare of Hüsker Dü died along with it, the sudden silence was jarring. He was done with work for the week. He had received his first paycheck, and a small but by no means negligible sum of money now sat in his bank account.

He went into the house and stood in the dark kitchen. His mom was working a late shift at the diner. White shadows played against the floor and the walls. He pulled the old cell phone his mom had given him out of his pocket and placed it on the counter. The local phone book sat uselessly on the counter next to the toaster, where his mom stubbornly kept it. Paul opened it and started flipping idly through the pages, slowly at first, then picking up speed until he found the name he realized he'd been looking for all along.

Chambers.

Was there a Nicki available?

# 7

## LAURA

I didn't want to go to our church's abortion protest.

For the past three years, at the beginning of September, the church youth group took a van down to Albany to demonstrate in front of the clinic there. I had gone last year, and when it was over, I promised myself I'd never do it again. But on Saturday evening, I was sitting on the bed in Bethany's room, and she was begging me to go on the trip with her in two months.

"Please, Laura," she said, grabbing my wrists with her hands and swinging them back and forth. "For me?" And then, "P-p-*please!*" in her Roger Rabbit voice—the one she used whenever I was being particularly stubborn about something, the one that made me smile and eventually cave.

Last year in Albany, I had stood in front of the clinic with everyone else, holding my sign, but in only fifteen minutes I began to feel nauseated. People passing by looked at us as if we were monsters or lunatics, or both. One woman, driving by with her children in the back seat, had rolled down her window and, looking right at me, shouted, "You people represent everything that's wrong with this country right now!" That was when I had to put down my sign and escape to a McDonald's across the street. I had knelt in the bathroom and stared down at the toilet bowl for half an hour, breathing in the smell of grease and fries and grilling meat. When I came back, the others at the rally told me it was just nerves and not to worry about it.

In church, they had shown us videos of inside the abortion clinics, of the blood and dismembered limbs. I had tried to keep those images in my head to remind myself that what we were doing that day was right, that we were fighting for the defenseless unborn, but for some reason, I couldn't make the connection. What we were doing out on that gray rainy day in the state capital seemed to have nothing to do with those videos I'd been shown.

But sitting there on the bed, Bethany was giving me her big puppy-dog eyes, her lower lip protruding. "I don't want to go alone," she said. "And you know I *have* to go. My parents expect me to."

I sighed. "Okay, okay, I'll go."

"Oh, fank you, fank you, fank you!" Bethany cried, and collapsed onto me. I fell back on her bed and she lay on top of me, laughing.

"Ugh," I said between giggles. "Your hair's in my mouth!"

She sat up and, taking a hair tie from her wrist, pulled her hair back in a ponytail. "I shall buy you dinner in Albany, my dear. A reward for your pain."

I sat up. "Like I'll be able to eat after that!"

"Hmm, you're probably right." She turned her body and sat next to me on the bed. With her hair back and her cheeks flushed from laughing, she was a different kind of beautiful. It always amazed me how many kinds of beautiful she could be. "Plus, we'll have to drive down to Albany in that *van*." She stuck her finger in her mouth and mock gagged. "Those rides always make me sick."

I didn't respond. The mention of Albany had made me think of Martin, and the thought of going down to that city in a month made my heart beat a little faster. Of course, there was really nothing to worry about. Our chances of running into each other were low, and even if we did, he wouldn't know who I was. Still, the thought made me nervous.

If anyone had seen what I was doing with Martin, had viewed our relationship—or whatever you want to call it—from the outside, they would probably say I was foolish, or stupid, or maybe just crazy. I wouldn't have been able to argue. But I do think, if I could take them back to the beginning of Martin, back to the origins of our connection, and show them how it all began, then maybe they might … if not understand, at least judge me a little less harshly. I think a lot of things in life are like that.

It began with the photo. Last summer, we'd had a family reunion at my grandmother's house down in Troy. My aunt and my cousins came up from Florida. Bethany tagged along with us because her parents would be out of town for a church conference.

Bethany and I had been up in my grandma's attic, instructed to look for a certain casserole dish, when we stumbled across the cardboard box stuffed with old family photographs. They were mostly pictures of my mom and my aunt, going back to their childhood and up until their twenties. Bethany and I knelt on the hard attic floor and giggled over their seventies and eighties hairstyles and outfits, arguing over which decade had worse fashions, which haircut we would least rather have.

Then we came across the pictures of the vacation at Myrtle Beach. My mother was in a blue one-piece bathing suit. Her hair was long and her body brown, and she wore an expression on her face I'd never seen before. We gaped. Bethany said, "I always thought your mom was pretty, but *seriously?*" I turned the photo over. Handwritten on the back was the date: July 1990. She'd been only twenty years old. Four years later, I would be born. I didn't want to look at the picture anymore, didn't want to think about it, but Bethany wouldn't let it go. She held on to the photo and continued to study it, as if it held some secret, which, if she looked long and hard enough, would enable her to look the way my mom had at that age.

"We have to show this to your mom," she said.

I grimaced. "Do we?"

"Definitely! She'll get a huge kick out of it."

I knew I didn't have a good reason to dissuade her, so I suggested we bring the whole box down, hoping that might take the focus off that one photo.

My mom, my aunt, and my grandmother pored over the pictures, with all the predictable commentary. "*Do you remember this?*" and "*Ooh, look at that awful hairdo! What was I thinking!*" When Bethany showed my mom the swimsuit photo, she smiled, blushed just a little, and said, "Whatever happened to *that* girl?" before tossing the picture aside.

Later, my mom and her sister tried to divide the photos between them but kept arguing over who got what. It was Bethany who suggested they take the lot and scan them onto a computer; that way, they both would have access to them all. My mom had turned to me and asked if I still wanted to make some extra money. She said she would pay me to take all the photos and commit them to digital permanence. I could use the scanner at the church.

MAYBE A WEEK LATER, on a Friday night, Bethany and I were hanging out in my room, waiting for her parents to come pick her up because, for some reason I can't remember, she wasn't sleeping over that night. I remember Bethany was lying on her back scrolling through her phone, with her legs stretched up against the wall, and her long hair spilling over the side of the bed. I was at my desk on my laptop, going through the hundreds of photos I had scanned earlier that day, sorting them into the folders I was then going to email to my aunt Sarah. The job had been something of a pain, but my mom was paying me well for it and I was glad for the extra money.

As I went through the photos, Bethany read me an article on her phone, about a woman who had dated a man online for two years before she found out the truth about him. He had told her he was a US Marine, twenty-nine and single, living in Texas. Actually, he'd been closer to fifty, an accountant in Michigan, married for twenty years with three kids.

"Can you imagine that?" Bethany asked, rolling over onto her stomach and looking at me. "You date a guy for two years to find out you don't know anything about him."

I had nodded, a little distracted by my task. I didn't really see the look in her eyes until after I heard her say, "Let's make a profile on one of those online dating sites."

I turned around in my chair to look at her. As soon as I did, I knew that she was serious. Throughout our friendship, Bethany would sometimes suggest that we do something completely wild or strange, accompanied by this hard, gleaming look in her eyes, which was how I knew when she wasn't joking, when she was for real. And I knew she wouldn't let it go.

"Why?" I asked. "You just said that stuff is weird."

Bethany stood up off the bed. "I just want to see how it works."

I grimaced. "I don't know."

But Bethany was already by my side at the desk. "Oh, come on, I'm not saying we actually *meet* anyone on it, but it would be kinda fun, wouldn't it, to make up a person online?"

I gave her a look of my own. "Would it?"

"Anyway, I'm bored," said Bethany, and thus ended the debate.

So, with Bethany sitting on my lap and controlling the laptop while I offered comments and advice, we made a profile on MatchUp.com.

We gave the site my email and our zip code. We named our person Kim Moore (I had just discovered Sonic Youth online, and while I found their barrage of noise and distortion hard to listen to, I thought they were cool beyond words). We answered random questions about her: she was a vegetarian, she liked dogs better than cats, she didn't smoke.

"We need a profile pic," Bethany said.

"Why?" I asked.

"Seriously, Laura, nobody's gonna believe our Kim is real if there's no photo of her."

"I thought we weren't actually gonna do anything with this."

"It's the *principle* of the thing."

I was about to ask what kind of photo she wanted to use, when Bethany suddenly shrieked and squirmed excitedly in my lap. "Oh, my god, I have an idea!"

I watched as she opened the folder that contained all the family photos, and before she had even found the photo, I was protesting.

"No, you're not serious!"

She opened the photo of my mother on the beach and paused. I thought that maybe she was thinking better of it, but then I realized she was just transfixed by the picture. "I wish I had legs like that," she said.

I rolled my eyes. I hated when she complained about her body in front of me; it was just insensitive. But now I was staring at the picture, too, the bronze skin, the hazy look in her eyes. "She doesn't even look like the same person," I murmured.

Bethany broke the spell by clicking on the photo and uploading it onto Kim's profile. Now our Kim had a face: my mom's.

BETHANY QUICKLY FORGOT ABOUT OUR KIM. Almost immediately after we uploaded the profile picture, my mom knocked on my door to tell us Bethany's parents were here to pick her up, and we quickly closed out the web browser. I didn't see Bethany again until Sunday, and by then she had forgotten about our creation or, at least, didn't care to mention it.

I felt strange that night after we'd made the profile, knowing that a picture of my mom was floating around out there on an online dating site, like a lifeboat drifting on a dark ocean. In bed, trying to sleep, I kept imagining my mother, in the bathing suit but sitting at her desk, on the computer, talking to strangers. I told myself that the next day I would delete the account first thing.

I didn't, and I'm still not sure why. Maybe I really did forget to, or maybe I just didn't feel like going through the task of opening the website and logging in, having to face the idiocy of what we had done. Either way, the profile stayed active, but by the end of the week, I had completely forgotten about it. And I didn't think about it again until two weeks later, when I checked my email account to find a message from MatchUp.com, notifying me that a certain BradyTom66 had messaged me.

I couldn't read the message through the email. I would have to log back in to my account to see it.

For a long time, I just looked at the email. Just some lonely creep messaging every woman he comes across, I thought. That's all. Still, it might be funny to see what he said. I could show it to Bethany; she'd get a laugh out of it.

It was a Wednesday afternoon. The house was quiet. Jason was in his room playing video games, and my mom was probably napping downstairs, the way she did sometimes after school. I put on music and logged on to MatchUp.com.

"*Hi sexy*" was all the message said. And clicking on BradyTom66, I found a fat, balding middle-aged man who appeared to be obsessed with the New England Patriots football team. I began to giggle. It was just too ridiculous. My giggling stopped short. My message box had blinked. Someone else had messaged me.

This one was a little less direct: "*Hey how's it goin*"

WallaceJoseph22 was younger, black, and not bad looking. After a moment of hesitation, I messaged him back a tentative greeting. We talked for maybe two minutes before I had to stop. Not because I was frightened or because my common sense kicked in, or anything, but because I just didn't know what to say. I was speaking for a person I didn't know anything about. Kim Moore was a stranger to me. Bethany and I had come up with only the most basic details: her sex, her age—we put her birthday as August 1985, which would make her twenty-four—and the town she lived in (only because we'd had to put in our zip code). Other than that, she was a blank slate. After closing out the chat bar, I decided to fill out her profile properly, figure out exactly who she was. I grabbed a pen and one of my notebooks from my backpack and opened it up.

Kim Moore was a writer and freelance journalist. She also dabbled in photography. She traveled a lot. Her parents had died when she was young, and she had lived for a long time in New York City and then California. She was in Grover Falls only temporarily, working on a story (what story she could possibly be working on *here,* I had no idea, but that didn't matter). She had a golden retriever named Sam that went everywhere with her. I was allergic to dogs and didn't like them all that much, but I thought it was a nice touch. She loved music, hiking, politics, espressos, old movies, surfing, snowboarding, books, Mexican food. She'd been in a long-term relationship for the past few years but had to end it because the guy had become overbearing and possessive. The breakup had been painful, but in the end, it had made her a better person with a clearer idea of who she was. She was adventurous. She spoke her mind. She didn't take crap from people. She had lots of friends.

The last thing I did was change her photo. If I was going to do this, I couldn't have her in a swimsuit as my profile picture. I sifted through the old photos of my mother and found one that I really liked—pretty, but just of her face so that the eighties and nineties fashions didn't give it away.

It really was a joke to begin with, or maybe just something to pass the time because I was bored. I wanted to see whether I could get away with it, just for a little while, and anytime I wanted, all I had to do was delete the account and I would be rid of it all.

All that changed with Martin.

MartinBanner messaged me one night last September, just after school started. I was in my room, doing homework and playing music on my laptop, when I got the email notification. Men messaged me now pretty frequently, and though Kim rarely responded, I always logged in and read the message and visited the man's profile.

Martin was different from most of the other men I had found on MatchUp. After reading his innocuous greeting—*Hey, how are you?*—I viewed his profile. His pic showed a reasonably attractive, somewhat scruffy middle-aged man. His birthday was July 11, 1969, making him just a year older than my actual mom. Under "occupation," he had put "Writer, with past work as a professor," without mentioning where he had taught. His interests included literature, art, films, travel, and music. He lived in Albany. I clicked through the few other pictures of him. In a strange way, I found him attractive. I messaged him back.

Our correspondence began casually. Martin wasn't aggressive. He didn't come on strong. He wanted to get to know Kim, which complicated things because, aside from the basics, I didn't know much about Kim myself. Every time he asked her a question about her life, I had to stop and think. What sort of journalism did she do? Where in California had she lived? Every question was a potential trap, and I had to work hard and stay focused not to get caught out. As much as I could, I kept the attention on him. At first, it was just a strategy of diverting attention away from Kim, but soon I found Martin actually interesting.

I began to enjoy our online chats. He was smart and witty and had done a lot. Back when he was an undergraduate, he'd seen the Who and the Rolling Stones. He'd been to Europe—told me Paris was overrated but everyone should see Florence before they died. And he knew so much about books. I had always done well in English, completing all the extra-credit reading assignments and scoring high on my essays, but I couldn't even pretend to keep up with Martin, who had a master's degree in English literature. He talked about writers I'd never heard of. Had I read this book or that book? And I couldn't say that I had.

It wasn't just books. Kim was supposed to be a journalist, and I didn't know enough about politics or current events. I'd never traveled *anywhere.* After a few days of conversations with Martin, I knew I would have to end it. There was no way I could continue to lie believably. What did it really matter, anyway? It wasn't as if I would ever meet the man. It wasn't as if his relationship with Kim could go anywhere. I could delete my account, and that would be that. No one would ever know. But still I didn't want to. For one thing, I didn't want to hurt him. Martin seemed genuinely nice, unlike most of the other guys I'd met on this site, and it felt wrong to play with him just to disappear afterward. I felt I owed him an explanation. For another thing, I had started to look forward to our evening online chats. They had become the highlight of my otherwise dull September.

But since I couldn't keep up this deception any longer, I had to make a choice. So the next time he messaged me, in my room one evening after dinner, I didn't hesitate. I wrote, *Martin, I have been lying to you.*

What about?

I stared at my blinking cursor for a long while, then typed, *I'm not who I say I am. I'm not a twenty-five-year-old journalist. I'm almost forty. I'm a mom. Divorced. Two kids. I'm a high school math teacher. That is my picture, but it's old. I don't look like that anymore.*

I held my breath and waited, my heart thumping away.

Martin wrote, *Okay.*

Then, *How old are your kids?*


HE DIDN'T END IT WITH ME. If anything, he became more interested. I continued to lie about my identity. But now the lies came easier because I knew what I was talking about. All I had to do was draw from my mom's life, which I did liberally though without giving away too many specifics. My mom didn't read novels. Except for Canada, she had never been in another country. It was much easier to lie when the lies were true. I told Martin the reason I'd been dishonest on my profile was that since my divorce, I'd become terrified of meeting people. I had created this profile to try to ease myself back into the dating scene, but as soon as I began talking to Martin, I knew I couldn't continue in the lie. I would understand if he was angry with me and wanted to stop corresponding. I told him I wasn't ready for a real relationship. I wasn't ready to actually meet anyone, and I knew this wasn't fair to him. But he told me he understood. He told me it was okay if we put off meeting for a while, but he would like to continue talking to me. We could just be friends. Friends who never saw each other. Friends who had never met.

So we were. We continued to talk, and more and more, Kim became a real person to me. She wasn't my mom, although I'd based her life on my mom's. She was more like a rogue extension of myself. It was almost as if I had another life. And sometimes, even when I wasn't online talking to Martin, I caught myself thinking like Kim.

More than once, I'd tried to tell Bethany about Martin, but I could never bring myself to do it. It was too complicated. I was scared she wouldn't understand. Why would she? Why would anybody? I knew that the moment I said out loud what I was doing online, I would have to stop doing it, because there was no way to defend or justify the thing. So I kept silent.

But now it was July. Almost an entire year had gone by since I first began talking to Martin. It wasn't completely regular. There would be breaks. He would be offline for a few weeks, saying he'd be traveling, or I would say I was taking some time off, and not log in for a while. But always, we returned to each other. And now, as was inevitable, Martin was beginning to talk about meeting. I told myself this was a sign that enough was enough. I had to get rid of the profile. But I kept putting it off. I hadn't logged on in over a week, and with the VBS and Paul Frazier and everything else, I'd been able to keep Martin shoved to the back of my mind. But now, with the prospect of going next month to Albany, where he lived, I couldn't help but think about him and what I was going to do.

Beside me on the bed, Bethany snapped her fingers in my face. "Hey, girl, you okay?"

I shook myself. "Yeah, sorry."

"Thinking about Paul again?"

I shook my head. "No, I'm over that guy."

We both laughed at this—how could you be over Paul Frazier? More than anything, it was Paul who kept thoughts of Martin at bay. It was Paul—the possibility that he might look at me, smile at me, maybe even speak to me—who made working at the VBS halfway bearable. I was still in love with him, and unlike Martin, he was real. I saw him almost every day. Every morning, getting ready for "work" (that was how I thought of the VBS, although I wasn't getting paid), I would agonize over what to wear, whether my hair looked okay, whether my face was too round.

Paul's presence at New Life was intermittent. He wasn't there all day, and when he was, he usually had some task to keep him busy. And although he didn't really talk to anyone and seemed disinterested in everything except doing his job, still, every morning, I hoped that today would be the day something happened between us, that some sequence of events would push us together, like that first night of summer, and that we would find ourselves alone again. This prospect both excited and terrified me, and I would stay up at night concocting possible scenarios. Always, I would think back to that kiss, which was becoming harder and harder to remember in all its brilliance with every day that went by. Lying in bed on my stomach, I would press my lips against my pillow and think of his face, one hand clutching the edge of the pillowcase and the other resting between my legs.

It had been two weeks since the beginning of VBS. There was only one week left, and so far, I'd had only one interaction with Paul. This consisted of his asking me to plug a wire into an amplifier while he fiddled with something on the mixing board. "Laura," he had called to me as I walked past, "could you do me a favor?" And afterward, he'd smiled and thanked me, and that was it. Nothing really. But also something. He had remembered my name, and he asked *me*, out of everyone, to help him. And he had smiled at me. He smiled so beautifully.

"Do you think he's sleeping with anyone right now?" I blurted.

Bethany shrugged. "Don't know. You'd think we would have heard about it. This town is so small." She looked at the wall. "I need to paint this room," she said after a moment.

Bethany's bedroom walls were a light Easter-egg yellow and had been as long as I'd known her. "I'll help," I said.

She gave me a side hug, squeezing my shoulder. Then her mother's voice called up from downstairs. "Girls? Come on down! Dinner's almost ready."

"Okay, Mom," Bethany called back, and we sat there on her bed for just one more moment, our feet dangling off the sides but not quite reaching the floor.

AFTER MY MOM LIFTED MY GROUNDING SENTENCE, I was so eager to get out of the house that even somewhere as familiar as the Moyers' felt almost exciting. Bethany's house was like my second home. Every Saturday night, I went to her house for dinner and spent the night, or she came to mine. It was a tradition as set in stone as presents on Christmas and fireworks on the Fourth of July.

When we came downstairs, Pastor Eric was sitting with Jon Newman at the dining room table, discussing Jon's idea for creating a permanent recording studio in the church.

"We could record Christian artists," John was saying. "Get local talent. It would be a really great way to spread the gospel."

Pastor Eric nodded. "I think it's a really interesting idea, Jon. Let me think and pray about it, and we'll see." He turned and smiled as Bethany and I came into the room. "Hello, girls."

"Hi, Laura." Jon glanced at me for a second before shifting his eyes to Bethany and leaving them there. "Hi, Bethany."

Bethany gave him a quick smile and wave. "Girls," Mrs. Moyer called from the kitchen, "would you two be angels and help set the table?"

As we went into the kitchen, I whispered in Bethany's ear, "Jon was looking at you like you were a piece of ripening fruit."

"So creepy," Bethany muttered. "It's bad enough I have to spend all day with him at church. Does he really have to be over here on Saturday?"

Jon was good friends with Bethany's older brother, Daniel. But with Daniel off on a mission trip in Uganda this summer, and away most of the year at Messiah College in Pennsylvania, we didn't understand why he still hung around the Moyers' house so much. We had begun to suspect that Jon had an interest in Bethany that wasn't strictly pastoral. Anyone (except maybe Bethany's parents) could see it in the way he looked at her.

In the kitchen, Mrs. Moyer was pulling a dish out of the oven. Bethany sniffed the air. "Lasagna?" she asked her mom.

Mrs. Moyer put the pot on the counter and said, "You don't sound too excited."

Bethany went to the cupboard above the counter to get the plates. "I didn't say that."

Bethany and I both agreed that her mother's lasagna left a lot to be desired, but we would never tell her this. I don't know that she would have cared too much, though. With no job, Linda Moyer proudly called herself a "homemaker," but she was away from home almost as much as a working woman. Whether it was directing a women's retreat, attending a bridal shower, or leading a book study group, she was quite a busy person. And the quality of her lasagna probably didn't rank high on her list of priorities.

Mrs. Moyer looked at me. She was the sort of person I couldn't imagine ever having been young. Not that she wasn't pretty, but it was the sort of stately, elegant beauty that seemed suited for an older woman. I couldn't see how it would work on a young person. She raised her eyebrows and tilted her head at her daughter, whose back was turned. "You like my lasagna, don't you, Laura?"

I nodded. "That's why I'm here, Mrs. Moyer. You think I come over all the time to hang out with *Bethany*?"

Mrs. Moyer threw back her head and laughed as if my joke had been legitimately funny. I could never tell whether she was merely humoring me when she did this or was just that easily given to laughter.

"Laura, you're hysterical," she said, taking off her oven mitts. "Has your mom given any more thought to my offer?"

There was a long-standing joke that the Moyers would buy me from my mom. I had yet to pass the joke on to her, though. I shook my head. "No, she's still bent on subjecting me to her tyranny for at least another few years."

Mrs. Moyer howled again. "Oh, but you must be such a blessing to her right now, with Bible school and everything. I tell Eric all the time, I don't know how that woman does it. The VBS gets better every year, and it's all because of her. Your mom's an extraordinary woman."

I nodded and began gathering up the silverware to bring out to the dining room. Ladies at church were always saying things like that to me about my mom, but I couldn't help but notice that none of them really talked to her—not for any extended period, anyway. I was never sure whose fault this was. It was true that in public my mom had this way of giving off an aura of coldness that could make her feel unapproachable, but I also suspected that most women in church were more comfortable around other married women like themselves, who they didn't have to feel sorry for. Even Mrs. Moyer, while always friendly around my mom, never went much further than the usual pleasantries.

Bethany had a stack of plates in her hands, and I was about to bring out the silverware when the front doorbell rang. "Oh, Laura, would you mind getting that?" Mrs. Moyer said. "I don't know who would be coming over right now."

I walked down the hall to the front door. My smile died the moment I opened the door and saw who was standing on the Moyers' porch.

"Laura" she said, looking surprised to see me. How dare Nola Sternson, who had known Bethany for just a few months, be surprised to see me at Bethany's house! We'd been best friends since we were five!

Last Sunday, Nola had shown up unannounced at church after Bethany texted her about Paul. But then, on Friday afternoon, while I was at my tent going over what verses everyone in my tribe was going to memorize (in that moment, telling some smart-ass he couldn't do Song of Songs), I had looked up across the field to see Nola, heading over to where Bethany sat with her tribe. She stayed the entire day, doing nothing in particular from what I could tell, just hanging around with Bethany and helping out when she could.

On Monday, she was there again, and every other day of the week. I didn't understand it. Why would someone like Nola, who smoked weed and drove around with boys at night listening to punk rock, choose to spend her summer days loafing around a church green filled with wild children in robes and togas, helping with pottery projects or refereeing a kick-ball game? I was there only because I was forced to be, and my mom *ran* the dumb thing. And since I had to oversee my tribe all day, I could only watch from a distance while this interloper and my best friend spent the week together, talking, laughing, throwing water balloons at each other. During lunch or after dismissal, when I was free of my responsibilities, they would always find me, but by then they would have so many inside jokes and stories I hadn't been a part of that I felt annoyed and displaced. By Wednesday, I started heading straight to the car after dismissal. But I wasn't sure the girls even noticed my snub; they were too busy enjoying each other's company.

Yesterday, Friday, Bethany had texted me in the morning and said she and Nola were going to see a movie that night, and she asked whether I wanted to come. It was a movie I wanted to see, but I was so annoyed that Bethany had made plans with Nola before inviting me, I told her I didn't feel like it.

"You sure you don't want to come?" Bethany asked me that evening after dismissal, when she and Nola caught up with me in the parking lot of the church.

I had thought Bethany would have picked up on the latent resentment in my texts, but she seemed completely oblivious. I felt stupid then but stuck to my decision. I planned on spending the rest of the night online, listening to music and talking to Martin. "Yeah, I'm tired," I said.

Bethany gave a mock pout, but I could tell she wasn't overly disappointed.

I was waiting by the car for my mom when I looked up to see a familiar car pull into the church lot—Ian. I hadn't seen him or Joey since the bath-salts night. I watched as Ian stopped at the church's front steps, and Bethany and Nola climbed into the back seat. Then the car pulled around the lot toward me, and I felt my familiar and paradoxical desires to be invisible, but also not to be ignored. The car sped past, and relief and disappointment washed over me in equal measure. A second later, I heard the chirp of tires on pavement, and the car gunned in reverse and skidded to a halt right in front of me. Ian poked his head out the driver's-side window. I could see Joey beside him in the passenger seat, and the girls in the back, laughing and berating Ian for his manic driving.

He ignored them and pointed at me. "Hey," he said, "why isn't *she* coming?"

"*She* is being lame," said Bethany from the back seat, "but why don't you ask her yourself?"

Ian grinned at me. "Seriously, Laura, you should come. I promise, no Walmart tonight."

I felt myself blushing, but at the same time I was shaking my head and saying, "No thanks, not tonight." I didn't think my mother, who knew I'd been with these three the night I came home at three in the morning, would be keen on letting me go out with them again, but even if she had, I think I still would have declined—not because I wanted to, but because it was easier.

I was surprised when Ian looked genuinely disappointed and gave me a sad smile and wave before hitting the gas and pulling away. Immediately, I felt lonely and sad, standing there by myself in the parking lot as the sun started to set. And with a logic not completely clear to me, I blamed it all on Nola.

Now here she was, standing in front of me on the Moyers' doorstep.

"How's it going?" she asked.

I shrugged. "Fine." Although it was a warm evening, she was wearing her usual black hooded sweatshirt, unzipped to display a black T-shirt graced with a giant face of Kurt Cobain. It didn't look like those new shirts you could get at one of the trendy stores at the mall; it looked straight out of 1994. I wondered where she found these things.

"I was just looking for Bethany," she said after five seconds or so of me glaring at her.

"She's busy. We're eating dinner."

"Wait—do you live here?" Nola asked, and I couldn't tell whether she was joking. Before I could answer, I heard Mrs. Moyer's voice behind me. "Who's there, Laura?" And then "Oh! You're Bethany's friend! You've been helping at VBS! Nola, right?"

Nola nodded.

Ten minutes later, I was sitting next to Jon at the dinner table. I glared at Nola, sitting across from me, next to Bethany, while Pastor Eric said grace.

"In Jesus' name, amen," he said at last, and as we picked up our forks and began eating, Pastor Eric looked at Nola. "So, Nola," he said, taking a bite of lasagna, "I've been meaning to thank you for helping out at VBS so much this past week. It's very generous of you."

Nola smiled awkwardly. "Oh, right. Thanks. I mean, welcome." Her voice trembled a little. This was the first time I had ever seen her nervous. Bethany looked nervous, too, keeping her eyes fixed on her plate. I knew she was just praying we could get through the meal without anything happening and with no one revealing any incriminating information.

"We'd love to see you at church more," said Pastor Eric. "Or does your family attend another church?"

"Uh …" Nola glanced at Bethany, but Bethany wasn't about to meet her eyes.

Pastor Eric waved his hand. "It's okay. You can be honest here. I'm not trying to interrogate you, or anything."

"We're not out to get you, dear," Mrs. Moyer said with a smile. "You can relax." She and Eric both chuckled.

Nola forced out an embarrassed laugh. "Yeah, no. Well, I live with my mom. But she doesn't really go to church, or anything."

Pastor Eric nodded. "Well, just remember, you and your mother are always welcome at New Life, okay?"

Nola nodded, and I watched her take a long drink of water. She wasn't so tough now, without her boyfriends to boss around, without her weed and her punk rock to hide behind. She was nervous and frightened, and eager to please this pastor and his family.

"Who is that man, honey?" Mrs. Moyer asked, nodding at Nola's shirt. "I know I've seen that face before."

"It's Kurt Cobain, Mom," Bethany muttered without looking up from her plate.

"Who?"

"Kurt Cobain." Nola put down her glass. "He was the front man for the band Nirvana."

"Oh," Mrs. Moyer said, still staring at Nola's shirt. "You know, there's something about him that reminds me of Vincent van Gogh, in a way. I think it's the eyes."

"That's kinda funny," Nola said with a sheepish grin, "because they both shot themselves."

Mrs. Moyer gave a little gasp and put a hand to her mouth. "Really?

Oh, that's so sad!" From her expression, you would have thought she'd known Kurt personally.

"Yeah." Nola's voice had lost most of its tremble. "He couldn't handle the pressure of fame and success. Plus, he was depressed."

Mrs. Moyer nodded. "It just shows that everyone's looking for something to fill that hole in their heart, and it's so sad when people give up before finding the one thing that truly satisfies."

"Right," Nola said. Beside her, Bethany was studying her untouched lasagna.

"Some people think he was murdered," I blurted.

Everyone looked at me in surprise. Mrs. Moyer looked as though she was about to respond, and then thought better of it and turned back to her food. It was Jon who finally ended the uncomfortable silence. "That's one of the reasons I think the studio at New Life would be such a great thing," he said to Pastor Eric. "It would be an opportunity to get more positive music with uplifting messages out there."

"Jon has a vision to set up a recording studio in the church," Eric said.

"Oh, I think that's a really great idea, Jon," said Mrs. Moyer. "Eric, don't you think so?"

I was surprised to see that Pastor Eric looked almost annoyed. "We'd have to think about it, honey. It wouldn't be cheap. And you'd need to be sure you were using it enough to justify the expense."

"If you decide to," said Nola, "you should totally record Paul Frazier."

Who *was* this girl who thought she could talk to my best friend's parents as if she were part of their family?

"Paul Frazier?" said Mrs. Moyer. "Sharon's son, who's running sound? He's a musician?"

Pastor Eric nodded. "Apparently very talented. Doing a great job with sound, anyway."

"He's, like, a genius," said Nola.

"Oh, Eric," said Mrs. Moyer, "I didn't know that. Why doesn't he ever lead worship?"

"I don't think he'd be interested in doing that," Jon said sharply. Then, seeming to realize his tone, he quickly began picking at his salad.

Mrs. Moyer looked crestfallen and a little confused, but only for a moment. She turned to Nola again. "So, any big plans for this evening?"

Nola shook her head. "Not really. My mom's working late, so I just kinda came over to see what Bethany was—"

"You mean you're all alone tonight?" Mrs. Moyer cut her off. "Well, if it's okay with your mom, you're more than welcome to stay over tonight. Laura is, too. You girls could have a *slumber party*." She tried to say the phrase with irony, but irony didn't suit Mrs. Moyer very well. She gave me a smile and I did my best to return it, but I probably just looked sick.

"And no pressure, of course, but if you're interested, tomorrow is a very special Sunday at New Life. Dr. Sheldon Langston will be speaking, and later on this week, Thursday evening, we'll be having a special service of prophetic ministry."

"What's that?" Nola asked.

"Dr. Langston will be prophesying over certain members of the congregation," said Mrs. Moyer. "It's a really incredible time."

"Prophesying?" Nola repeated. "Like he tells the future, or something?"

Pastor Eric shook his head and smiled with easy patience. "We believe in giving the Holy Spirit room in our lives to speak to us, Nola. I know it probably sounds weird to you, but the Bible teaches us people are blessed with certain gifts—wisdom, healing, even miracles. The apostle Paul's first letter to the Corinthians tells us all about it. Dr. Langston is blessed with the gift of prophecy. Now, that doesn't mean he can see the future or gets crazy visions or anything like that. It just means the Lord has given him the gift of being able to hear the Holy Spirit's voice and discern what it's saying to the individual, with more clarity and focus than most of us have. It's still up to the individual to take the Holy Spirit's word and apply it to their lives." Pastor Eric stopped abruptly and looked around the table and grinned. "Sorry, didn't realize I'd started preaching."

Mrs. Moyer placed a hand on Nola's shoulder. "You'll have to excuse my husband. Once he gets started, it's hard for him to stop—force of habit."

Everybody laughed. We were all one big, happy family. I put down my fork to keep from reaching across the table and lodging it in Nola's arm.

## APRIL

About a year ago, Laura had asked her mother why she didn't seem to have any friends. At the time, the question had surprised April. Of course she had friends. She was around people constantly. If anything, what she needed was *less* social interaction, more time for herself. She remembered giving her daughter a sarcastic and not altogether fair reply—something about being too busy paying Laura's phone bill to worry about her social status. But that night, thinking about it in bed, April had realized that her daughter was right. She didn't have any friends. There was her older sister, Sarah, in Florida. They made it a point to get together at least once a year and called each other on a regular basis, but it wasn't the same as having her there across the street. And if the only friend she could name was a sister who lived over a thousand miles away, maybe that wasn't a very good sign.

When April had first started attending New Life, over ten years ago, dozens of women at church befriended her. They had brought her to all the events—the Bible studies, the game nights, the prayer meetings—and almost instantly she felt completely accepted. Never had she so swiftly or so thoroughly been thrust into a social circle. And most of those women who had made friends with her back in the late nineties were still there today, but things were different now. April no longer took part in most of the ladies' meetings, and her conversations with them at church, while always friendly, were usually brief and limited, never daring to scratch below the surface.

April hadn't noticed exactly when this change started, but now she traced it back to her separation from her husband, Ray. Given the circumstances surrounding the demise of her marriage, there was no way to keep it private from her friends at New Life. And although everyone at church inevitably took her side in the divorce, she began to sense a subtle shift in how the congregation viewed her, starting not long after her marriage ended. Maybe it wasn't so much the divorce itself that changed the way the women at church interacted with her, but how April had handled it. In the weeks and months after she and Ray separated, whenever she was forced to discuss the ordeal, April had assumed a resigned, what-are-you-gonna-do attitude toward it all.

She remembered, in the June following her divorce, meeting with Pastor Eric in his office. He asked whether she still wanted to head up the VBS. He made clear that the question had nothing to do with her divorce, but with the fact that she was now raising two kids on her own, working a full-time job, and managing a household all by herself. Maybe it was a little too much?

April had listened quietly, hands on her knees, until he was finished and waiting for her response. Then she smiled and said, "Well, Ray never really helped around the house, anyway. So there's that." Pastor Eric never again asked about her quitting the VBS.

It wasn't until much later that April realized her flippant attitude toward the divorce must have struck many at church as disconcertingly blasé—even heartless. The irony, of course, was that if April had betrayed even a fraction of the pain, confusion, and fear she was feeling in those initial months following her separation, she would have collapsed into the unsuspecting arms of those busybodies and forced them to hold her, forced them to tell her everything was going to be okay.

When time passed and April showed no signs of looking for a new relationship, it seemed to her that the members of New Life had a harder and harder time knowing where to place her in their social context, and she herself had a harder time knowing where to go. Working single mothers, while abundant everywhere else in the country, were rare at New Life. And April acted so confident in her new position, so at ease with her singleness, that she denied the congregation the satisfaction of even feeling sorry for her. In social situations, she displayed a glib cynicism, a knowledge of the unfairness of the world that many people there had never been forced to confront. Women, especially those her age, seemed to find April's jadedness off-putting and distressing. April discovered that she got along easier with men, but at church, a middle-aged woman couldn't just be friends with a middle-aged man, especially if that middle-aged man happened to be married.

While April continued to attend church without fail, her conversations with the other mothers at New Life became more and more limited to a few safe go-to subjects, usually the VBS. "So, April," they would say when they felt they needed to say something, "any big ideas for the vacation Bible school this summer?" She got questions like this so often that it felt almost like the script for a bad play: *We both know we have nothing to say to each other, so I'll just ask you about the one thing I can think of.* She found it more than a little irritating that after ten years, her one defining characteristic at church was a vacation Bible school. She wondered what would happen when she stopped heading up the program and they were forced to come up with something new to ask her. *So, April, are you excited for summer now that you don't have Bible school to worry about?*

She found it was easier outside church. She got along well with most of her fellow teachers, and for a year or so now—since not long after the time Laura had accused her of not having any friends—she had taken to going out with a few of her coworkers at least once a month. Always on Saturdays, always when her children were over at a friend's house or away with their dad for the weekend. That way, if their mom came home a little tipsier than might be appropriate for the director of a vacation Bible school, she could be sure that at least her children wouldn't see.

The two women she usually went out with were Angie Walters, the social studies teacher, and Karan Manning, who taught English—both fellow veterans who'd been teaching at Grover Falls High as long as or longer than April. The assistant coach, Joe Cornish, a balding red-faced man whose bad back forced him to walk as if he were perpetually looking for something he had dropped on the ground, sometimes joined them. And when he did, he became the reluctant defender of the entire male gender whenever their conversations veered toward critiques of their husbands—or, in April's case, ex-husband.

He was with them now, at their usual spot, Maxy's, a bar and grill that would become more "bar" and less "grill" as the night wore on and bars came into higher demand. Tonight, April was going through her wine a little faster than usual, watching Angie tease Joe in the battle of the sexes.

"All I'm saying, Joe, is that a lot of men have a hard time with the concept of responsibility. It's just a fact."

Joe shook his head. "And all *I'm* saying is, you can't say things about all men just based on your experience. That's what's called a ..." He snapped his fingers in the air to try to summon the right phrase.

"Gross generalization?" April offered, putting down her glass.

"Gross generalization!" Joe seized on the phrase with triumph and relief. "Thank you, April."

Karan slapped her on the arm. "*April!* Don't help him out!"

"See that?" said Angie. "Men rely on us even to make their arguments for them." The women laughed while Joe shook his head and took a drink of his beer.

They continued to argue, and April continued to laugh, but her mind kept drifting. She'd had a light dinner and felt drunk already—drunker than she'd been in a long time. She felt she deserved it, though. This past week had been a long one. Her mind and body had been tense and wound up for days, like a coiled spring pressed between two rocks, and this wine was the first thing that had done anything to help her relax.

Since Friday, April had been chanting in her head, *only one week left, only one week left,* like some sort of mantra. But the end of next week was the camping trip, and she was dreading that Friday-through-Sunday ordeal in the Adirondacks. She knew she had no one but herself to blame for that. It had been her bright idea to implement a weekend in the mountains for all children ten and older. *"Oh, April, what WILL you think of next?"* And she had this groundless but uncomfortably persistent feeling that something bad was going to happen on those last three days of the program this year, and there was nothing she could do about it. This summer had already had its low points. Yesterday, Friday, an actual fight had almost broken out. She couldn't remember anything like that happening since '03 and the "slingshot incident."

Yesterday afternoon, April had been in the church greeting room, sitting with seven-year-old Michael Sanders. Lydia had caught the boy mooning the tribe of Asher again. It was the third time in two days. April had sat him down to give him a talk about how some things were private and not meant to be shared with others. When she had finished, the boy looked at her with a vacant expression on his face, his mouth hanging open and one hand stuck halfway down his pants. (She knew she should tell him to remove his hand, but at that point she just didn't have the energy.)

"Does that make sense to you, Michael?" she asked him at last.

It was a full five seconds before he decided to nod his head.

"Good," she said, unconvinced.

That was when Lydia rushed into the room, her face red with sweat, and her eyes wide. "Ms. Swanson, you'd better get out here. Something's going on at the Cross of Repentance."

"Now what?" April groaned and stood up. She grabbed Michael by the hand that wasn't down his pants and followed Lydia quickly out of the church.

The seven-foot-tall plywood Cross of Repentance had been erected at the very edge of the church grounds. Throughout the program, kids were encouraged to write down on red or white slips of paper anything they felt guilty or ashamed about—all their sins and fears—fold it in half, and nail it to the cross. At the end of the program, these pieces of paper were taken off the now paper-covered cross and gathered up to be burned in the giant bonfire on the last night of the camping trip. The idea was that Jesus had taken away these sins and now you were free of them. It had been one of April's first ideas when taking over the VBS, and Pastor Eric loved it.

At first, the brilliant summer sun was blinding. But as April crossed the field at a fast walk, with Michael holding her hand and trotting to keep up, she could see a cluster of kids gathered around the Cross of Repentance. As she got closer, she saw that they were circled around two kids in the middle: Benjamin Waid and his foster brother, DeShawn. They were standing inches away from each other, shouting. Jon Newman was trying to get them apart, approaching them timidly and talking quietly into their shouts, only to retreat a few steps when they ignored him.

With Michael still in tow, April made her way through the circle of kids. Jon rushed over to her, looking relieved. "I'm really not sure what happened," he said. "We were all nailing one of our sins to the cross, and suddenly these two were going at it."

"Jesus, DeShawn," April heard Benjamin say, standing across from his foster brother, fists clenched, "you're such a little shit. I don't know why my parents took you in. You don't deserve it."

April heard something like a collective gasp from the rest of the kids. She bit her lip. Ben was one of her son's closest friends, and she knew him well. He got angry easily and said things he probably didn't mean. Right now his face was red and wet, from sweat or tears or both. April cleared her throat and spoke loudly. "Okay, people, back to your tents. Team leaders, let's get started on the next activity."

There was a slow, reluctant migration from the Cross of Repentance as team leaders shepherded their tribes back to the tents. Finally, only Ben, DeShawn, Jon, and April remained—and Michael, who had not yet let go of her hand. Ben and DeShawn were still glaring at each other, not moving, but at least they had stopped shouting. "Okay, boys," April said when it felt safe to speak, "how about we sit down, get a drink of water. We can lose our heads in this heat."

They remained standing, staring at each other in the summer haze. The cross cast its foreshortened shadow on the grass behind them. April turned to Jon, who had his hands in his pockets and looked uncomfortable. "Jon, you wanna run over to the coolers and get some water bottles?"

He nodded, eager to have something clear and simple to do. "Right, sure!"

"Oh, and, Jon," she said as he turned to go. She lifted the wrist that still had Michael's hand attached to it. "Could you take this guy with you?"

When they were gone, April put her hands on her hips and looked at the two boys, who still hadn't moved. "So does either of you want to tell me what happened?"

Neither of them spoke.

"Ben?" she asked.

DeShawn snorted.

April turned to him. "DeShawn, do you have something you'd like to say?"

DeShawn squinted up at the sky. "Could think of a couple of things."

"Look, I don't know what happened between you two," April said, "but you guys should know, if you have a problem, you need to come to a counselor or me about it. So we can work it out together, okay?"

"This is bullshit," said DeShawn, kicking at a tuft of grass.

"What is, DeShawn?"

He looked at her as if surprised by the question, then gestured around them. "All of this."

April wasn't clear whether he was referring merely to the vacation Bible school or to life in general, but she didn't ask him to clarify. "Let's try to work this out," she said. "Whatever happened, there's no reason for you two to stay angry at each other."

"I'm not apologizing to him," said Ben. It was the first time he'd spoken since all the shouting, and his voice sounded wet and hoarse.

"Good. 'Cause I don't want your apology," said DeShawn, kneeling down now and examining the grass.

April pulled her phone out of the back pocket of her shorts. "All right, well, if you guys aren't calm enough to have this discussion now, I'm just going to call your parents to see if they can pick you up. We can sort this out tomorrow." She realized that tomorrow was Saturday, but decided to let it go.

DeShawn had pulled up a dandelion and was picking the yellow petals off with his fingernails, swaying back and forth on one foot. "She's gonna call my parents," he muttered. "She says she's gonna call *my* parents."

"You know what she meant, DeShawn," Ben snapped, "so shut up."

"Make me, nigga," DeShawn said calmly, without looking up from his flower. "You're not the boss of me."

"Maybe I will!"

"Boys!" April barked, putting her phone back in her pocket. She realized she had handled this all wrong. She should have separated them at once, before there was any chance of escalation. Now here she was, alone with two boys who were just about ready to come to blows.

"Hey, DeShawn!" a voice called from behind April, and she turned to see Paul Frazier standing on the other side of the field, a coil of wires slung across his shoulder, and two music stands in one hand. He held the other hand to his forehead, shielding his eyes from the sun. He was looking at the three of them from maybe forty yards away, and April could see that he was smiling slightly. "DeShawn," he said again.

"What?" DeShawn kept looking at his flower.

Paul moved his hand away from his eyes to beckon DeShawn over. "Could you do me a favor and help me bring this stuff over to the stage and set up?"

The stage was on the other side of the field, and April realized that Paul must have seen them from a long way off while bringing the equipment out of the church and came all this way to investigate.

She didn't think DeShawn would go for it—it was too easy and too simple, and kids his age seldom wanted to take the easy or simple solution. But April watched as DeShawn dropped the dandelion, crushed it under his shoe, and moped his way over to where Paul stood, muttering as he passed, "Better than being with these two." Paul handed DeShawn one of the music stands, and they headed off in the opposite direction. Paul didn't look at her once.

April stood in the grass, the sun beating down on her, and Ben sighed and plopped down on the ground. "I want to go home," he muttered.

"Yeah," said April, watching Jon return with the water bottles no one needed. "Yeah, me, too."

AT MAXY'S BAR AND GRILL, the atmosphere was turning decidedly "bar." April saw the young people beginning to arrive, crowding the bar and taking command of the pool table and jukebox in the next room. April checked her watch: nearly ten o'clock. Soon it would be time to go. She felt warm and relaxed now. The muscles in her arms and back and neck had unwound, like knots being loosened. She laughed at her friends' talk, although she hadn't really been listening.

Angie was leaning forward across the table to get right in Joe's face, imperiling her own margarita. "Joe, I'd really like to know, what was your mother like? Were you breastfed as a child?"

April stood up to use the bathroom and, for a moment, had to steady herself. The wine was getting to her more than she had realized. She felt it rise to the top of her head and swirl around up there, making her a little dizzy. Then she shook herself and began making her way across the room.

She was standing by the door of the women's room, waiting, when she saw him.

He was at the bar, leaning forward and talking loudly at the somewhat annoyed-looking bartender. There was something manic in his face—he looked angry, although he was laughing. A small blond girl sat on the bar stool next to him. She had her hand on his shoulder and was talking in his ear.

April had not actually spoken to Paul Frazier for two weeks, since the first DeShawn incident. Ever since they argued under the tree and she inadvertently made a reference to his touching an eleven-year-old boy in the locker room, they both had made it a point to stay out of each other's way. She wanted to thank him for helping her out yesterday, but something had kept her from approaching him. Now here he was. The woman came out of the bathroom, and April was free to go inside, but she hesitated, watching Paul laugh. He looked very drunk. She wondered whether the girl beside him was his girlfriend, or just some girl he had met and planned to sleep with. Then the bartender handed Paul his beer, and before April could do anything, Paul had turned in his stool and was looking right at her. He smiled. "Ms. Swanson!" he cried, beckoning to her as he might to one of his friends. "April! April Swanson!"

She felt herself redden. She didn't know what to do. After a slow second, she turned and went into the bathroom, pretending not to have noticed him, although she knew there was no way he would believe that—they'd been staring right at each other.

*So embarrassing*, she thought as she used the bathroom, washed her hands, and then looked at herself in the mirror. *So, so embarrassing*. It was all she could think about. She couldn't think about *why* it was so embarrassing, only that it was. Embarrassing. *I'll just go home*, she told herself. *It's time to go home*. She gave herself one last glance in the mirror and then opened the door.

"Omigod," she said, all in one breath, before she could stop herself.

Paul was leaning on the wall opposite her, quite close, in the narrow passageway to the restrooms. He pointed dumbly at the men's room to the right. "Just waiting for the bathroom," he mumbled.

"Paul," she said, when she'd recovered her breath, "how are you?"

"Fine," he said, and smiled. "I'm—what do you people say?—'filled with the spirit,' or whatever."

April had distant memories of being as drunk as Paul was now, when she'd been a different person, before her world had shifted itself into clear definition. His head was drooping toward the floor as if pulled there by a magnetic force; his hair was in his eyes. "Paul, are you okay?" she couldn't help asking.

He swung his head back up to look at her. "Don'tchu worry 'bout me, Ms. Swanson. I'm keeping out of trouble. Haven't been molesting any kids in the church locker rooms, or anything."

"Oh, Paul, I didn't … When I said that, you know I …" She gave up, seeing that it was useless. Anything she said to him now, he wouldn't remember tomorrow.

The song on the jukebox had changed. April didn't really pay attention to music; she wouldn't even have noticed except that it was a song she used to love and hadn't heard in ages. It seemed to her that she hadn't heard it since she'd been as drunk as Paul was now, in her college dorm room or in the passenger seat of some boy's car. Stevie Nicks, but not that really famous one, the one about the dove. Another one, April's favorite. She had even owned the record. But she couldn't remember what it was called. She waited for the chorus: *Stand back, stand back.* For a second, she could taste the cigarette in her mouth, feel the night wind whipping across her face.

"Take care of yourself, Paul," she said. "Make sure you get some sleep."

"I don't believe in sleep," Paul muttered, now craning his neck up, looking at the ceiling. Then his head swung down again, and he was looking in her eyes. "You know, I used to have a crush on you," he said. "I always thought you were very pretty."

April swallowed, felt her hair stand on end. "Get some rest, Paul."

The next moment, the blond who had been at the bar was at Paul's side and apologizing to April as she led Paul away. "So sorry, ma'am. He's just really drunk. We're gonna take him home."

*Don't call me "ma'am,"* April wanted to say, but she only nodded. She stood for a long moment, against the wall. She listened to Stevie. Then she rubbed her face, took a breath, and returned to her table and her friends. "Well, I'm about ready to call it a night," she said, standing over them. "I think I've had enough."

## PAUL

Paul woke up to his stomach announcing its refusal to hold its contents any longer. He shot up into blackness, feeling the prespasm rumble. He leaped up off whatever he'd been lying on and waited for his immediate surroundings to make themselves visible. They didn't.

A thin, pale light came from somewhere to his right—seeping in from under a closed door, he supposed—and he moved toward it with his hands outstretched, like a blind man feeling his way through the emptiness in front of him. Something caught his left knee, and a sharp pain shot through him. He cursed and half stumbled, half crawled the rest of the way to the light. He pushed against the door, and it swung open.

The toilet sat partially illuminated by a green night-light plugged into the wall, and when Paul felt the next rumble, he knew he wouldn't be able to keep it down. He charged into the room and knelt at the toilet like a penitent kneeling before an altar, just as the vomit spewed out of his mouth in a heavy brown gush.

At last, he wiped his face and fell back against the wall, breathing heavily, sweating. He sat in that position for what felt like an hour, although it could not have been more than a minute before he felt the next surge and knelt once more before the bowl.

When his stomach was so empty it felt weightless, Paul stood up and went over to the sink and splashed water on his face. He found a bottle of mouthwash in the cabinet behind the mirror and gargled some of it.

He turned on the light in the bathroom and opened the door, so that the light spread across the room he had been sleeping in. The room was large, with a low drop ceiling. There was a couch against the far wall, and in front of it, the reason for his now throbbing left knee: a coffee table littered with empty beer bottles and Chinese takeout containers. Looking at the room began to bring back the memories, which were only half defined, like the objects in the dim room. This was Tommy's apartment—Nicki's little brother's. Paul had come here yesterday evening, after he called Nicki to hang out. And that had been when the drinking began, yesterday evening—that is, if it was still Saturday. How long had he slept? The last thing he remembered was being in a bar with Nicki and Tommy, and then …

Paul made his way back to the sofa and searched for his (mom's) phone. He found it wedged in a crevice between the sofa cushions. He checked the time: half past midnight and, technically, Sunday. There was a text from Nicki: *Hey, u were pretty out of it so we brought u back here. Sleep. We'll be back later.*

The text, with its lack of smiley faces or exclamation points, felt cold and slightly hostile. Either Nicki was the rare sort of girl who texted with great detachment, or he'd done something in his drunken state over the past two nights to piss her off. The latter explanation seemed the more likely, but he couldn't say for sure. His memory was hazy and full of holes.

He went into the kitchen, where more beer cans and half-full bottles of liquor sat on the grimy table, and got a glass of water from the tap. He drank and tried to remember.

He remembered calling Nicki on Friday night, and her surprised, excited voice when she answered. She told him to come here to her little brother's apartment and gave him directions. He remembered sitting around in the living room, drinking and smoking pot with Nicki, Tommy, Tommy's housemate Seth, and Seth's girlfriend, Krista. Paul couldn't say he didn't enjoy the almost reverential way the kids treated him. Tommy (the drummer Nicki had told him about) seemed especially in awe. He kept asking Paul if there was a specific kind of beer he wanted and if the music was okay.

But it was Krista whose attention Paul particularly appreciated—the way she laughed at everything he said, and kept staring at him with her big, just-graduated-from-high-school brown eyes, even as her boyfriend sat with his arm around her. As the evening wore on, Paul could see Seth getting more and more annoyed with his girlfriend's blatant flirting, and Paul actually considered taking him into the other room and telling him, Don't worry, I've already decided I'm not going to sleep with your girlfriend. But he found it entertaining just to watch poor Seth wallow in jealousy.

He remembered, around midnight, heading to a bar downtown. He remembered sitting at the bar with Tommy, doing shots of Southern Comfort and lime. He remembered complaining loudly about the music—Top 40 country and heavy metal. He remembered taking control of the jukebox, and when some dumb hick with a John Deere cap and a half-assed goatee complained about the Bruce Springsteen, Paul remembered putting another five-dollar bill in the jukebox and playing "I'm Goin' Down" over and over, until the bartender switched it after it started up for the fourth play. He remembered swearing at the bartender, demanding that he put back on the song Paul had paid good money for. "I was trying to compromise here, asshole!" Paul shouted. "It's fucking Springsteen! I thought even Republican fucking rednecks like you were cool with Springsteen!"

He remembered Nicki talking in his ear and rubbing his back, telling him to calm down. He remembered being led out of that bar (or maybe they were kicked out) and wandering down Main Street. Then they were at some house party. He remembered beer pong. He remembered more shots. He was in the bathroom, and Krista was there, giving him something to slip under his tongue. He remembered laughing when Seth burst into the bathroom, yelling at Krista and yanking her away. He remembered being alone in the bathroom, staring at himself in the mirror sweating, and wanting to put a fist through the glass.

Then he didn't really remember any more from Friday night. They had come back here. He had a vague memory of sleeping with Nicki, but he couldn't recall whether they'd had sex—not a good sign, in his experience. On Saturday, by one in the afternoon, the drinking had begun again. They had driven into the country for a bonfire with a bunch of Nicki's friends. They sat around the fire in lawn chairs, drinking and smoking and watching the flames. More kids had shown up, pulling into the clearing in an assortment of jeeps and pickup trucks. Boys in muscle shirts and backward hats, girls in summer dresses or shorts and tank tops.

It was summer, and everyone was tan and happy, and Paul felt irritated that it was summer and everyone was tan and happy. He kept thinking about Sasha. That was when he started to really drink. He remembered being really drunk and watching the flames. He remembered being really drunk and riding back to town in the back of some guy's pickup with Nicki as the sun set. Then he was in a bar again. He was drinking again. He was talking to ... He was talking to April Swanson. *Jesus.* She'd been there at the bar. He was sure of it, although he couldn't quite remember what he had said. All he remembered was her shocked expression as he made a fool of himself. That was the last thing he remembered.

Paul put the empty glass on the counter and ran his hands through his hair. Although he had consumed enough alcohol in the past forty-eight hours to kill a large dog, and although he knew that legally he should be nowhere near the keys to a car, Paul now felt completely sober. This was basically how his last months in New York had gone: for a few days he would drink himself into a stupor, and then there would be that moment of collapse, followed by the vomiting that left him feeling new and empty, weightless. And now came the restlessness, the urge to be doing something. The drunkenness had left him, but not the adrenaline. He needed action.

In the city, after stumbling out of the last bar of the night, Paul would wander the streets of Manhattan or Brooklyn sometimes till dawn, passing gaggles of other drunk kids heading to the trains, and homeless men sprawled out on the sidewalk, and construction workers getting their coffee and breakfast sandwich at the bodega before starting their day. He would feel completely alone but also a part of something bigger. Wandering around drunk was what cities were made for.

For a moment, he considered calling Nicki, finding out where they all had gone, but he decided against it. He knew that if he met them, he would just start drinking again.

His car keys were still in his pocket, which meant his car was still parked out front. He would have failed a Breathalyzer test, but there were only a few cops in this town.

PAUL DROVE AIMLESSLY THROUGH GROVER FALLS. He kept off Main Street to avoid the small strip of downtown, where he knew he wouldn't be able to resist the golden light and laughter spilling from the bars out into the night. So he drove slowly down the side streets, looking at the houses lining either side, interchangeable in the night, the same square shadow repeated endlessly.

When he stopped at an intersection, Paul realized he was now on Grant, the street the Swansons lived on. He slowed when he came to the house he remembered. The light was still on in the window, illuminating a small pocket of front lawn. All the other houses on the street were dark. He drove past. Reaching the end of the street, he circled around again.

The second time he reached her house, Paul stepped on the brake. The adrenaline running through his body was augmented by a generous dose of impulsiveness. He parked across the street, killed the engine, and walked up to April Swanson's front door.

The instant he rang the doorbell, Paul regretted it. The sudden sound, so jarring in the silence, seemed to scream how crazy it was for him to be here at this hour, but he couldn't very well go back now. So he stood there, shifting his weight from one leg to the other, scratching at the back of his neck.

The door opened only an inch, enough for April to see through and not much more. When she saw who was standing on her doorstep, she did not smile and open the door wider. To the contrary, she looked a little frightened. Paul suddenly realized that he could be a terrifying image for a woman alone, when standing at her doorstep in the middle of the night. He felt instantly ashamed. April didn't say anything, just looked at him with wide, confused eyes. Paul cleared his throat. "Ms. Swanson ... April, I'm not ... I just came here to apologize for my behavior earlier."

"It's after one in the morning, Paul," she said in a voice just above a whisper. "You should go home."

Paul nodded. "Yeah, okay. Sorry, I just ... I was passing by and I saw your light on. I thought I'd come say sorry."

"Where are you going?" she asked.

"Huh? Oh, nowhere in particular." He lifted one shoulder. "I'm sorry, I shouldn't have come here now. It was a bad idea. Sorry." He gave her a stupid wave, then turned and headed back down the drive.

He was halfway down when he heard her call his name. He stopped and turned. April had come all the way out of the house and was standing on her front step. She was wearing baggy sweatpants, an old T-shirt, and slippers. A small blanket was wrapped like a shawl around her shoulders.

"Paul," she said, "are you driving?"

He nodded.

She shook her head. "You shouldn't be. You can't be sober enough to drive."

"Oh, no." He waved his hand dismissively. "I'm totally fine. Not drunk at all, I—"

"*Shh*," she hissed, cutting him off. He realized how loud he must have been talking. She looked from her left to her right, but the street remained quiet. A noise did begin to come from within April's house, though—a steadily rising squeal. Not having grown up in a house where people made tea, Paul didn't at first know what it was. April looked back into her house, then around the street, then at Paul. Then she quickly waved him inside and turned and went into the house.

The noise had stopped by the time Paul came into the kitchen. April was standing over the stove, where a red enamel kettle was steaming. "I'll drive you home," she said without looking at him. "Just let me get on some shoes." Then, after a moment: "Actually, do you want some tea before we go? I was just about to have some."

Paul stood in the kitchen, hands at his sides. "Um, okay," he said.

"Great, just give me a second." She still wasn't looking at him. She told him to take a seat and went about making the tea, moving around quickly. He sat down at the kitchen table and watched her back as she filled two mugs with steaming water.

"I've never actually had hot tea before," he said.

When she finally turned and looked at him, the two mugs in her hands, she was smiling, although the smile looked a little forced. "Really?" she said. "You've never had tea? How is that possible?"

Paul shrugged. "My mom raised me on coffee. I guess I'm a little deprived."

She took the seat across from him at the table and slid one of the mugs his way. "You've gotta let it steep for a few minutes."

He looked at the mug in front of him.

"Put your hands around it like this while you wait," April instructed. She had her fingers laced around her mug. "That's the whole point."

Paul did as he was told and felt the warmth seep into his fingers. She smiled at him. This time, the smile looked real. "So is that, like, your thing? Driving around town in the middle of the night?"

"I don't sleep much," he said. "I have to find ways to keep myself occupied."

She nodded. "Well, I guess it was a good thing you were out driving that one night, anyway, to save my wild daughter."

Paul chuckled. "Is she locked in her room now?"

April shook her head and let out a long breath. "No, both my children have flown the coop for the night, actually. Won't be back till tomorrow."

He glanced up at the clock above the refrigerator. It was now close to one thirty in the morning. "You're up pretty late yourself."

"I couldn't sleep, either."

Paul looked down at his mug. "Look, I'm sorry for whatever I might have said at the bar. I'm not a good person when I'm drunk. That's not a real excuse, I know, but anything I said back there, I didn't mean."

"Do you remember *anything* you said?" April asked after a pause.

He looked up at her and shook his head.

She looked at him for a long moment, as if deciding something. "You said that I was very pretty," she said finally. "You said that you always thought I was."

He couldn't think of anything to say, so he just stared at her. She gave him a quick, pinched smile and then stood up. "I'll go get my shoes," she said, and hurried out of the room.

He sat there watching the steam escape from his mug. A minute later, he heard her sneakers squeaking on the kitchen tiles. "Ready?" she asked, zipping up her windbreaker and avoiding his gaze.

She was taking her car keys from a hook on the wall when he got up and stood beside her at the door. "I do think you're pretty," he blurted.

April shook her head and laughed, fingering the keys. "Paul, stop. I just thought it was kind of funny and sweet, that's all."

"But I *do* think you're pretty. You are pretty."

She had to look at him because his body was there, against the door. She gave the keys in her hands a halfhearted shake and looked up at him, her eyes big and a little frightened. "Ready to go?" she asked.

He took a step toward her, and she stiffened but did not back away. He took another step, and then he placed his hands on her shoulders and kissed her. At first, she didn't respond; her lips remained closed and her shoulders were still and tense under his hands. Then she opened her mouth and wrapped her arms around his neck.

Even as he pushed her up against the refrigerator, knocking magnets and coupons and photographs to the floor in a clatter, even as she dug her fingernails into the back of his neck and he placed his hands on her thighs and lifted her up against the wall, in some part of his head he kept thinking, *Any second now she's going to realize what she's doing and who she's doing it with, and stop.*

But she didn't stop. They moved down the short space of hallway, pressing each other up against the wall, and when they got to the empty sea of living room, with no tight spaces, April took his hand and led him through the room and into her bedroom, where she closed the door and turned and looked at him, smiling slightly. Paul reached down and unzipped her windbreaker, and she arched her back so that it fell to the floor.

"Take off your shoes," April said.

Looking at her, with those searching eyes and that faint smile still playing on her face, Paul felt something leap up inside him, some sort of emotional spasm. And the most irrational and stupid things forced their way to the very edge of speech. *I love you, April. Will you marry me? Let's have kids.* He could have said any of those things in that moment, and in that moment, he would have meant them all.

Instead, he knelt and began frantically untying the laces of his Converse All Stars.

On the bed, she ran her hands through his hair. He helped free her of her sweatpants. He no longer felt any shock that this was happening. It felt like the only thing that *could* happen. There wasn't any other way it could be. It had to happen that he put his lips to her breasts. It had to happen that she laced her arms around his back, her fingernails pressing into his skin, and wrapped her legs around his waist. He was inside her, panting, her breath beating against his face, when she lifted her head and gasped into his ear, "You can't come inside me." So when he felt the rising surge, Paul rolled onto his back and lay beside her on the bed, both of them staring up at the ceiling and breathing heavily.

THE SECOND TIME PAUL WOKE UP that night was because of sweat. Sweat sticking to his body and bleeding from his skin onto the sheets. He sat up in the darkness and looked around. The place in the bed next to him was empty. There was no one else in the room. His pants and underwear lay in a heap on the floor. He got up and put them on. Shirtless, he went into the adjacent bathroom and splashed cold water on his face. He looked at himself in the mirror. His face was red and wet. Two framed Norman Rockwell prints hung on the wall behind him. The bathroom was white and cheerful.

He found her sitting out on the living room sofa, upright and erect, hands placed on her knees, staring at the far wall.

"Hey," he said, coming into the room.

April looked at him and nodded, then turned back to the wall.

Paul sat down beside her on the sofa. "Can't sleep?" he asked.

She nodded. He wanted to touch her, put an arm around her, but her stiffness suggested she might snap upon physical contact. She had changed into a new T-shirt and gym shorts. "You?" she asked after a moment.

"I don't sleep much, remember?"

She nodded. "That's right," she whispered, still gazing straight ahead.

They stayed this way for a long while: she sitting forward on the sofa, eyes ahead, motionless, like some avid member of a congregation listening to a preacher; he beside her, his body turned slightly toward her, hands placed on the sofa cushion, trying to read her inscrutable expression. Finally, when he could no longer stand the stillness, Paul took the TV remote from where it lay on the coffee table in front of them and turned on the TV.

He flipped through channels until he found a grainy black-and-white. Audrey Hepburn and Gregory Peck. "This is a good one," he said. "You ever seen it?"

April shook her head. He couldn't tell whether her eyes were on the TV or still on the wall beyond it. "I don't think so," she said.

He leaned back and stretched his arm out across the back of the sofa. Eventually, she sank into him. Eventually, she rested her head on his chest and he put his arm around her, and they watched what was left of the movie.

# 10

BEN

"Please turn with me in your Bibles to the book of Acts, chapter nine."

Dr. Sheldon Langston wore a suit the color of a rotting plum. He looked down at us from the stage, an old man with thin white hair, a stern expression on his face. We'd had guest speakers before; it was nothing new. But something about this guy was different. For half a minute, all you could hear in the gymnasium was the soft stir of pages turning as people searched their Bibles—a sound I'd always liked for some reason. Then Dr. Langston picked up the glass of water sitting on the lectern and took a long drink. The microphone hooked up to his suit collar meant we could hear him as he gulped and then wetly smacked his lips. He took a deep breath and looked at us.

"It's in the book of Acts that we first meet Saul the Pharisee, better known to us as Paul the Apostle. How many of you know that God's plans are not our plans, that his ways are higher than our ways? Think about this: Paul the Apostle, the great leader of the early church, author of over half the New Testament, one of the most recognizable figures in scripture—when we first meet him, he's on his way to Damascus to terrorize and imprison followers of Christ. Verse one: 'Saul was breathing *murderous threats* against the Lord's disciples …' Verse nine: 'If he found any there who belonged to the Way, he'd take them as *prisoners.*'"

Dr. Langston had only just started his sermon, and already he was getting red in the face, his voice booming through the huge, echoey room. Usually, this was my cue to zone out—Bethany and me, zombie survivors in California, building a cabin on the beach, watching the sunset every night. But today my imagination wasn't working. These days, it was getting harder and harder to drift away—where I was in real time and space wouldn't always let me go. It was warm and stuffy in the sanctuary, and my ass was stiff from sitting on the hard chair. I was starting to get a wedgie, too, but there wasn't enough room to readjust my crotch without looking like I was playing with myself. My mom was on one side of me, DeShawn on the other.

"How many of you ever wished for a fresh start, a clean slate? How many of you have thought at one point in your life, 'If I could just take everything back, start over, if I could have a new name, I'd do it all differently'? Well, brothers and sisters, let me tell you something: if the Lord Jesus Christ can do it for this miserable man who at one point was dead set on destroying forever the very *message* of Christ and his church, then he can do it for *every single one of us*. It wasn't just Paul's *name* that was changed; it was his *life*."

The Bible my parents had given me as a birthday present a few years ago sat under my chair. I bent over, picked it up, and began flipping through it for something to do. I liked how thin the pages were—more like silk than paper—and I liked the rough feel of the leather binding. I didn't like reading the Bible, but I did like to hold it. I wondered if, for some men, that was the reason they became preachers.

"Now, when I was a young man, I might not have been persecuting Christians like our friend Saul here, but let me tell you, brothers and sisters, I was on the express train to *destruction*. I thought I was smarter than God, folks. I thought I could *outrun* him. How many of you know that the Lord sometimes lets us learn the hard way, amen? Every day, we get on our own private road to Damascus, don't we, brothers and sisters? You see, I believe that in his heart, Saul knew—he *knew*—the truth, but he just wouldn't let himself believe it. The Lord had to appear to him *in broad daylight* before he got the message, just as the Lord appears to us every day, in our hearts, when we know the truth but won't let ourselves *understand* it. How many of you are on the road to Damascus this very morning? How many of you have something that the Lord is speaking to you about, convicting you about, and you're not sure if you want to listen? Let me urge you, brothers and sisters, to *stop*. Stop and listen. You can't outrun the Lord. Believe me, I've tried."

I looked up from my Bible. Dr. Langston was pacing back and forth on the stage, holding his Bible tightly in his hand. Of course, he wasn't looking at me. Of course, he didn't know what I was thinking—so why did it feel like he was talking to me? Why did it feel like any second now, he might stop pacing, turn and look me straight in the eyes, then slowly lift one of his wrinkled white fingers, point straight at me, and, in front of the entire congregation, expose all my secrets?

"You see, names mean something in the Bible. When Saul's name is changed to Paul, we know that his heart and soul have been transformed as well. God cares about our actions, but how many of you know that our actions are dictated by our hearts, amen? Before we do anything, we must change our hearts, and how do we do that? By *listening*, brothers and sisters. By *listening* to the voice of the Lord and letting ourselves *understand.*"

It felt like the sermon would never end, and when it finally did, I felt relieved, like I had been holding my breath the entire time. It was something I'd never felt before with any of Pastor Eric's sermons.

I was hot and sweaty and needed to take a dump. I pushed through the crowded sanctuary to the back hallway where the bathrooms were. Nothing beats the feel of smooth molded plastic against your bare ass, in an empty bathroom, when you've been holding it for a long time. I let myself just sit there and breathe, staring at the floor tiles.

When I heard the steady trickle of someone pissing in the nearest urinal, I started. I'd thought I was alone and hadn't heard anyone come in through the door.

The trickle continued. "And in the last days, God said, 'I will pour out my spirit on all people. Your sons and daughters will prophesy, your young men will see visions, your old men will dream dreams.' The sun will be turned to darkness, and the moon to blood, before the coming of the great and glorious days of the Lord."

It was Dr. Langston, I was sure, but how had he gotten back here so fast, and why was he quoting verses in the bathroom?

He didn't say anything more, and I waited in the stall with my hair standing on end and my breath coming sharp until I heard him zip up his pants, wash and dry his hands, and go out the door. I was sweating again.

It took me a while to finish my business after that, and when I finally did, I found Jason, Dylan, and DeShawn waiting for me in the hallway. We were going to see a movie, they told me—they'd already checked it with my parents. I nodded, not looking at DeShawn.

"What's wrong with you?" Jason asked me, looking more annoyed than concerned. "You look weird."

I wiped my forehead and told him I was fine. Jason shrugged, and I followed them out of the church. I told myself I wasn't bothered that they'd invited the Weight to the movie before talking to me—I was in the bathroom; it made sense—but as we piled into Dylan's parents' van and I was forced to sit in the back with Dylan's little sister, the other guys up front, I felt something crawling inside me. My friends never even mentioned the fight between DeShawn and me, pretending like it never happened, but somehow it felt like they were secretly taking my foster brother's side. As for DeShawn and me, we hadn't spoken to each other since Friday.

It had started on Friday morning, in my bedroom, when I woke up suddenly to a horribly loud screeching. I'd been dreaming of Bethany— the kind of dream so good, it's like winning the subconscious lottery—and then I was sitting bolt upright in my bed, breathing hard. The noise was beating against the far wall and rumbling through the floorboards. The next thing I knew, my chest was tightening and I couldn't breathe.

My inhaler was sitting on my dresser on the other side of the room. I jumped out of bed, tripped over the sheets my feet were tangled up in, and stumbled over to the dresser.

As I got my breath under control, I realized what the noise was: music—really loud music. It was coming from DeShawn's room. It wasn't even eight o'clock.

I went down the hall in my pajamas. DeShawn's door was wide open. "Hey, what the hell is …" I stepped into the room and stopped short.

My dad and DeShawn were sitting on the floor, going through a big cardboard box of vinyl records. The music was coming from a record player sitting on DeShawn's dresser, hooked up to two giant old speakers set up on either side of the room.

"Benjamin!" My dad looked up at me and smiled. He was still in his sweatpants and an old T-shirt. Usually by now, he had already left for work. He almost had to shout over the music. "What do you think? We set up my old sound system."

I nodded. I could feel the bass rumble under my feet.

"I dug these out of the attic," he said. "What's left of my collection." He pulled a record out of the box. "Check it out: *Led Zeppelin Four*."

"Is that what woke me up just now?" I asked.

DeShawn shook his head and held another record up. "Jimi Hendrix."

"'Purple Haze,'" my dad said. "One of the all-time great guitar riffs."

I nodded and slowly backed out of the room.

Downstairs, I found my mom in her office, typing furiously on her laptop. She barely looked up at me. "Good morning, Ben."

"I'm not the one playing that music; it's DeShawn."

She kept typing. "I know. Your father took the morning off and got out all his old records. I think they're having fun up there."

"Well, they woke me up."

"I'm sorry, honey," my mom said. She didn't look it. "You should probably start getting ready for Bible school, anyway."

"Don't you think it's a little early to be blaring music, though?"

My mom stopped typing, sighed, and turned in her chair and looked at me. "Are you upset about something, Ben?"

My mom had this way of throwing me off guard with her attention and the lack of it—one second, she'd be ignoring me, and the next, I'd be under intense focus. "No," I said, "I just think it's a little inconsiderate, that's all." Talking to my parents, I tried to use their words back at them whenever I could: *inconsiderate, disappointed, concerned*—squeezing in words like these gave your arguments more power.

"Ben," said my mom in her slow, almost-annoyed-but-I'm-giving-you-one-last-shot voice, "as you're well aware, DeShawn hasn't had the easiest time adjusting to life up here. And your dad and I have felt a little lost about what to do. I'd like to say you've been helping us on that front, but ... well, you can speak for yourself on that."

I tried to, but she held up her hand. "Anyway, last night while you were upstairs playing your games, your dad and I sat down with DeShawn to see if there was anything we could do to make his time up here a little easier. You know he isn't the biggest talker, but we finally got it out of him that he's interested in music. Who knew, right? He thinks he'd like to learn guitar, so we're going to look into lessons for him. And your dad had the idea of giving DeShawn his old records. I didn't think he'd go for this, but when he heard it was rock and roll, he actually seemed interested. It was the first time I'd ever seen a look like that on DeShawn's face. Now they're going through them, and it seems to be a success. So, Ben, unless you have any other complaints, I think you should go upstairs and get ready for vacation Bible school."

I turned to leave the room. "Don't call it a vacation," I muttered.

I DIDN'T ESCAPE JIMI HENDRIX even when we got in the car. Apparently, my dad had also found his old CD collection, and driving DeShawn and me to the church, he popped in a CD. "Purple Haze" blasted from the car's speakers.

In the back seat, I stuffed my earphones into my ears and leaned forward in my seat. "Dad, can you turn that down a little?"

My dad shook his head. "Sorry, bud, Jimi doesn't work on low volume." He glanced at me in the rearview mirror. "Take those things out of your ears! It doesn't get any better than Hendrix."

"I'm okay," I said, and sank back in my seat.

"You'd really rather listen to that horrible *M-and-M* over this?"

No matter how many times I told him it was "Eminem," my dad never corrected himself—he thought his pronunciation was so hysterical. In the front seat, my dad laughed and DeShawn even cracked a smile. I looked down at the floor. The book Becca had let DeShawn borrow sat at my feet. The old black man with hollow eyes stared up at me from the darkness. I grabbed the book and shoved it into my backpack. Then I closed my eyes and turned Slim Shady up so loud it hurt my ears, but I still couldn't completely drown out the sound of that guitar.

When my dad pulled up to the church green, I jumped out of the back seat and slammed the door. I was halfway across the field, heading toward Levi's tent, when I stopped. All of a sudden, I was so tired. I couldn't take Jason and Dylan's stupid jokes, couldn't watch Bethany giving DeShawn another one of her pretty smiles, couldn't listen to Jon Newman tell me to put on my turban. I looked around. Kids were hurrying across the field in every direction, rushing to their tribes. There were so many of us. Ryan Fletcher with his gelled hair, wearing a tank top to show off his preteen muscles. Nine-year-old Katie Tupper, still with a blue nose and cat whiskers lining her cheeks from yesterday's face painting. If we all rose up together as one army, one voice, we could start a revolution. We could end this tyranny! I saw Ryan tying his turban to a spear, turning it into a flag, and leading his tribe against our oppressors. Katie transformed into some wild cat-girl, hissing and growling as she clawed at some counselor's face.

I was standing there, caught up in my vision, when my cousin walked right past me. No smile. No hello. I paused for a second, then followed Becca across the green.

"Hey," I said when I had caught up with her. She was walking fast, bending over with the weight of her backpack, which looked like it was stuffed almost to bursting.

She looked at me with suspicion for a second, like she thought I was going to play a trick on her. That's when I remembered how I had treated her last week. I tried to smile in a way that said I was sorry. "That bag looks heavy," I said. "What do you got in there?"

"It's *my* bag," she almost snapped. "I have every right to put whatever I want in it."

I hadn't realized how much I must have hurt her when I snubbed her in front of my friends. I wished I could just shrug and walk away without caring. I wished I could be meaner. We had reached Judah's tent, and Becca had tossed her bag on the ground with a thud and stood glaring at me. For a second, my mouth just hung open stupidly and I couldn't think of anything to say. Then I put down my own bag and opened it. "I just wanted to give you this," I mumbled, pulling out the book and handing it to her. "Thought it might be due back soon."

"Thanks," she said without looking at me.

As I turned to go, I had the feeling inside me of falling faster than my stomach, though I didn't know why. What did I care what my lame cousin thought about me? I should be glad to be rid of her.

Then I heard Becca call my name. I turned back around. She was kneeling in front of her bag and looking at me. "Do you want a protein bar?"

She unzipped the bag. It was stuffed so full of bars in blue wrappers that a few spilled out onto the grass. They said "FUEL" on the package and weren't a brand I recognized.

"Where'd you get all those?"

"It's an initiative I'm taking part in." Becca began picking the spilled bars up off the ground. "To raise money for orphans in Haiti. For every bar I sell, all the proceeds go to a charity that offers housing for orphans and unwanted children. It's run by Michael Keegan—do you know him?"

I shook my head as I helped her pick up the last of the protein bars. Becca unzipped another compartment of her bag and pulled out a flyer, handing it to me. On the front was a good-looking white dude with blond hair and tan skin, surrounded by a bunch of cute, smiling black kids. "A better tomorrow for Haiti," it said. On the back was another picture of the man (without the kids), and some information:

Since 2006, Michael Keegan's organization has provided food, housing, education, and health care for over five hundred Haitian children in need. In addition to physical nourishment, the children are also given the spiritual tools and guidance they need to prosper in this life and the next. Along with his charity work,

Keegan is a bestselling author and motivational speaker on the topics of spirituality, health, fitness, and achieving your goals. Visit his website at www.KeeganMinistries.com and follow him on Facebook.

I looked up at Becca. "Isn't that great?" she said. "I want to work for his organization one day." She held out a protein bar. "They're four dollars each."

I felt a little like I'd been trapped. I wasn't hungry, and four dollars seemed high for something that would probably taste like crap. But I thought it would be nice to help the orphans, and I still felt guilty about how I had treated Becca earlier. I took out my wallet and handed her the money. She smiled and handed me the bar. "Tell all your friends," she said. "I'll be selling these things all summer."

"Does Ms. Swanson know you're doing this?" I asked.

She shrugged. "Why should she care? It's for a good cause."

I didn't know, except that adults always seemed to have weird rules when it came to money. The whistle blew in the middle of the field. Everyone had to be at their tent for the beginning of the program.

I thanked Becca for the bar and headed toward Levi's tent. As I walked across the field, I unwrapped the FUEL bar and took a bite. I was right: it tasted like a stale glob of sawdust and wax. But I thought about the smiling kids on the flyer and made myself swallow.

A FEW HOURS LATER, I was sitting in the grass under the Cross of Repentance, listening to Jon Newman talk about sin and grace and feeling like I might throw up. I wasn't sure if it was the protein bar or the sloppy joes we'd had for lunch. You know how they tell you to wait two hours after you eat before swimming? I think the same should go for stuff like this. As Jon had our tribe gather in a semicircle around the cross, the sun glaring down on us, my stomach felt weird and queasy.

"Today I want to tell you the story behind a song," Jon said, standing in front of the cross. "How many of you guys know the hymn 'Amazing Grace'?"

We all raised our hands except for DeShawn—maybe because he really didn't know the song, maybe because he just didn't care. Jon seemed happy for the excuse to sing.

"*Amazing grace, how sweet the sound, that saved a wretch like me. I once was lost but now am found, was blind but now I see.* Pretty familiar words, right? But I think most of you will be surprised to find out the story behind that song, behind the man who wrote it, John Newton. I know, the name sounds a little bit like somebody else you know, right?" He clicked his tongue and winked, and some of the girls giggled weakly.

Jon smiled, looking satisfied. He probably wished Bethany were here to see him in his glory. But she and Nola were manning the face-painting station at the other end of the field. Ever since that Nola girl started coming around, they found reasons to leave the rest of the tribe and do things together. I had noticed them earlier, giggling as they gave each other cats' eyes and bunny noses.

"So," Jon was saying, "John Newton lived in the seventeen hundreds, and guess what? He wasn't a good man. He did bad things. *Really* bad things. John was a slave trader. He sailed on a big ship from England to Africa, where he took African people that had been captured and imprisoned, and brought them to Europe or the Americas, to be sold as slaves.

"Now, we probably all know from history class how bad the conditions on the slave ships were. How they were packed tight together in the ship's hold, and it was hot and awful down there and they got only a few spoonfuls of slop every day."

Jon stopped. DeShawn had raised his hand. I'd never seen him do this before, and Jon looked a little nervous.

"Yes, DeShawn?"

"Yeah," DeShawn said, "they actually let a lot of them starve if they didn't think they'd get enough money for them. They'd let them starve and then throw them overboard. Sometimes even before they were dead, so they'd drown because they were still tied together with chains."

Everybody was quiet. I saw a lot of the girls looking at DeShawn sadly. Most of the boys looked down at the grass or out across the field, embarrassed.

Jon nodded slowly. "DeShawn is right. It really was one of the most terrible times in man's history. Once the ships finally reached Europe or the New World, families were split apart, the younger, stronger slaves usually sold to plantations, and others were taken to work inside the houses and mansions of their owners, as servants."

DeShawn had his hand up again. "They weren't just servants there. Most of the plantation owners picked the young, hot slave girls so they could have sex with them."

Jon raised up his hands. "Okay, DeShawn, thank you, but we don't have a lot of time left, so we can't get into all the specifics. But you're totally right; a lot of horrible things were done."

I looked at DeShawn, who was nodding, and that was when I realized he must've gotten all this from that book Becca had given him.

"So, this was John Newton's job," Jon was saying, "making it possible for all these horrible things to happen to thousands of innocent people. And he didn't feel bad about it. He didn't question it. It was just how he made his living. Now, one night, crossing the Atlantic, John's ship runs into a terrible storm. High winds, thunder and lightning, waves that tower over the sails—there doesn't seem to be any chance that anyone on board will survive. John's scared. He thinks he's going to die, and suddenly all his life catches up with him. He understands that there's a creator out there, he understands he's going to be judged for all the countless sins and horrible things he's done, and you know what he does? In desperation, John calls out to Jesus to save him. This man, who spent his whole life in sin, calls out to the Lord. And you know what happened? The Lord hears his prayer. The Lord answers. The ship doesn't capsize, the storm dies away, and the crew survives. And right then and there, John Newton gives his life to Jesus Christ. And he writes this song, 'Amazing Grace.' John Newton becomes an abolitionist, somebody who devoted their life to ending slavery." Jon paused. DeShawn had raised his hand again.

"So what happened to the people on the boat—the slaves?" DeShawn asked. "Did he let them go?"

Jon smiled and nodded, then stopped nodding and frowned. "Well, actually, I'm not sure of the exact time frame, but yeah, soon after that storm, he stopped slave trading and joined the abolitionist movement."

"Yeah, but the people on *that* ship—he didn't set them free?"

"I'll have to look that up for you later, DeShawn. It's a good question."

Jason was sitting next to DeShawn. He pulled out his phone. "I can google it."

Jon smiled. "I don't know if we need to do that now, Jason. The point is, after John called out to the Lord, he had a heart transformation. He found Christ's love and grace, and his entire life was changed because of it."

Jason had his eyes on his phone. "It says on Wikipedia that the storm happened in 1748, and John Newton didn't stop slave trading till 1754. So … six more years."

DeShawn's mouth fell open. Kids started whispering.

"Okay, guys," Jon held up his hand again, "we don't have to analyze this too much. Maybe there was a more gradual conversion. Maybe the storm started something in his heart that didn't completely take effect until later on. What I want you to take away from this is the idea of Christ's grace—how we all need it, how we are all wretches like the ones in Newton's song."

DeShawn snorted. "Not me."

Jon looked like he would just as soon ignore DeShawn and continue, but we all had heard him, so that wasn't an option. "What's that, DeShawn?"

"I said I'm not a wretch like him. I never done anything that bad, like straight-up *evil*."

Jon smiled. "Well, no, of course none of us here have done anything like *that*, but the Bible tells us we all have sinned and fallen short, DeShawn, so in one sense, we need Christ's grace just as much as John Newton does."

DeShawn looked confused. "Why would I need it as much as he does? What that guy did to all those people was off the chain, and then he gets scared he's gonna die and go to hell, so he just prays and writes a song and God forgives him? Musta' been a pretty kick-ass song, for God to forgive him for *that*."

A few kids laughed, and Jon looked around quickly. "It's not about the song, DeShawn. It's about—"

"And he didn't even let those slaves go free! Even though you said he was the captain! God saved him, but *he* didn't save *them*. Why wouldn't he set them free if he could?"

DeShawn was almost shouting now, angrier than I had ever seen him. I looked around me. Half the kids looked uncomfortable. The other half, Jason and Dylan included, were smiling.

"We're running out of time," Jon snapped. He stopped and took a deep breath. "Look, these are very important questions, DeShawn, and I'm happy to keep talking to you about it later, but right now we have to move on."

DeShawn looked at the ground and didn't say anything.

"Okay." Jon took a deep breath. "I want everybody to bow their heads and close their eyes."

We did as we were told, but it was obvious by now Jon's lesson had been ruined. And even though I didn't like Jon, I felt a little bad for him. All he'd wanted to do was tell a nice story with a moral, and DeShawn wrecked it. I wondered how DeShawn could get away with something like that when none of the rest of us could. Was it just because he was the only black kid in VBS? I thought it must be more complicated, because these things usually were. I thought it must have something to do with how little we knew about him. All I knew was that his mom had died, but I didn't know how, and my parents wouldn't tell me. They said it was up to DeShawn to decide how much he wanted to share with other people about his life. And I realized now why he didn't share anything: the less that people knew about his life, the more power he had. He could use everything we didn't know—his past, where he came from—like a weapon.

"Now," Jon said after all our heads were bowed and our eyes closed, "what I want you to do is think of something Jesus has been convicting you about, something that has been separating you from the grace of God. It might be a grudge you're holding against a friend; it might be a lie you told your parents. You aren't going to share this with anyone, so be completely honest. Once you have your sin, I want you to open your eyes and write it down on the piece of paper I gave you earlier, fold it up, ask Jesus to forgive you, then come pin your sin to the cross."

With my eyes closed, I tried to think of something quick and easy to write down on my paper, but nothing was coming. My stomach still felt weird, and the sun beating down on me was giving me a headache. Behind my eyelids, the darkness was starting to move. Finally, I opened my eyes and blinked. Most everyone else was writing something down. A few kids were already at the cross, pinning up their sins.

I looked down at the piece of paper in my lap. I wished I had something clear and obvious to write: *I shoplifted at the mall* or *I stole one of my dad's beers*, or even something better.

Beside me, Jason stood up and walked over to the cross. Dylan was already back from putting up his. The more kids around me who got up, the more I felt I needed to write something down, the less I could think.

I kicked a stray dog and tied firecrackers to his tail.

I slashed Jon Newman's car tires and spray-painted curse words on the windshield.

I installed a hidden camera in the girls' locker room and watched them get undressed.

When Jason came back and sat down next to us, he looked satisfied with himself, like he'd taken a massive dump or something. "Come on, Ben," he said to me, low enough that Jon couldn't hear, "just write something down so this can be over."

"I'm thinking," I muttered, staring at my paper.

I had sex with a hooker.

I killed someone.

"Saw you talking to your cousin earlier," Jason said after a while. "You guys real close?"

"Shut up," I said, still looking at the blank piece of paper. I could feel my face get red, though.

"You guys seem like you hit it off. Too bad she's your cousin."

I tried to ignore him. That was usually the best way to get Jason to drop something.

Then I heard DeShawn: "They were up in his room forever last week, playing video games."

I looked up at my foster brother. "Knock it off, DeShawn."

Jason was grinning. "Really? How did we not hear about this?"

"Yeah." DeShawn smiled. "I heard them giggling all night."

I couldn't take it anymore. I leaned forward and shoved DeShawn hard. "I told you to shut *up*."

DeShawn fell back on his hands, and for a second he just looked surprised. Then something in his face turned hard and he lunged at me. I had to duck, and Jason grabbed DeShawn by the arm. "Whoa, guys, calm down." But DeShawn shrugged him off and came at me again. The next second, we were both on our feet and DeShawn was trying to push me and I was grabbing him at the wrists and trying to hold him back. It was a weird time to be thinking it, but with my hands tight around his wrists, I realized this was the first time I had ever actually touched him. As soon as I could, I broke free of him and took a step back, breathing hard. I could feel the whole tribe's eyes on us, but I couldn't just sit back down now. I had to say something.

"Next time, stop when I tell you to stop," I said.

DeShawn still had his fists clenched. "I don't have to listen to you. You're not the boss of me."

Then Jon Newman was between us. "Boys! What's going on here?"

Out of the corner of my eye, I saw everyone looking at us wide-eyed. I saw a group of girls who'd been over near the cross, practicing an interpretive dance, rush over to see what the shouting was about. *Everyone* was going to hear about this. And instead of this calming me down, it only made me angrier at my foster brother. He always messed up everything. I clenched my fists.

Pretty soon, Ms. Swanson showed up and made everyone else go away. I was glad for that, because by then I was so mad and embarrassed and almost sick, I felt like I might do anything, even cry. I sat there on the grass with my head throbbing and my stomach tight, wishing I had never gotten up that morning, wishing I was still in my bed, caught in that amazing dream.

When my mom came to pick us up, I could tell from the look on her face that she was more upset than angry, which meant my punishment wouldn't be that bad. It was funny, but when I did something just a little bad—like say a curse word where my parents could hear—my consequence usually sucked, like no internet for a week. But when I did something that really concerned them—like getting in a fight with my foster brother in front of everyone—my parents just sat us down to discuss it, like that would fix everything.

That evening, my mom and dad sat us down in the living room and tried to find out what the fight had been about. I didn't know how to answer, and DeShawn didn't try, so we both just looked at the floor and shrugged. My dad started talking about respect, about self-control, about using words, but I wasn't really listening. I was wondering if Bethany had heard about the fight yet or, worse, if she had actually seen it.

When I finally got upstairs to my room to be alone, it was only seven thirty in the evening. My parents hadn't even told me I had to stay up there, but I felt so bad and sick of everything that all I wanted was to just be asleep, even though light was still coming in through my windows, and I could hear birds singing. I emptied out my pockets. Two things: the crumpled-up protein bar wrapper and the blank piece of paper where I'd never written my sin. I tossed them both in my trash basket and fell on my bed.

Now, IN THE VAN, I was sitting next to Dylan's little sister, who kept trying to show me the picture she'd drawn in Sunday school. In the seat in front of me, the guys were cracking jokes that I couldn't hear.

Dylan's parents dropped us off in front of the movie theater. We got tickets for the PG-13 action movie, but once we were past the lobby, there was nothing stopping us from sneaking down the long hall to theater three, where the R-rated horror movie was playing. When we reached the entrance, we stopped short. I felt something in my stomach flutter. Bethany, Nola, and Laura were standing by the entrance, about to go in. They looked at us with raised eyebrows.

"Jason, what are you guys doing here?" Laura asked.

"What's it look like?" said Jason. "Going to see a movie."

"I don't think Mom would want you to see this."

"I don't think Mom would be especially thrilled about *you* seeing this.

But Mom's home sick. If we both keep our mouth shut, we're good."

Laura looked like she was about to say something but then decided it wasn't worth it. She sighed and shrugged. We stood there awkwardly for a few seconds. Although we all saw each other almost every day, it was usually at church or someone's house, where things were safe and contained. Here, each group had caught the other breaking the rules, wanting to do the same thing, and something in the air between us changed. No one knew what to say. I tried not to look at Bethany, who was really pretty in a blue summer dress. It was Nola who finally spoke. "What's up, DeShawn?" she asked, smiling at my foster brother.

DeShawn nodded.

"Excited for our camping trip next week?" Bethany asked.

"I can't wait," DeShawn said.

The two girls laughed like he'd said something hysterical, like he was the first person who ever used sarcasm. By now everyone had heard about our fight, and they'd also heard about DeShawn's argument with Jon Newman. The girls looked at him like he was Jay-Z.

When we went into the theater, I thought for sure the girls would sit in a different row. That was just how our world worked. The older girls never hung out with us unless they were forced to. So I was shocked when they followed us deep into the row we had chosen, near the back of the theater— Bethany, then Nola, then Laura. We were all sitting in the theater together. I was second to the end of my friends, so the only thing that separated me from Bethany was DeShawn. She and Nola were asking him more questions about how much he hated Bible school, and even though he kept giving them short, sarcastic answers, they laughed like he was doing a stand-up routine. I realized then, *he* was why they had chosen to sit with us.

It felt like no matter where I went, no matter what I did, the Weight would always be there, stealing the show. I crossed my arms and looked down at the floor, waiting for the day to be over. Then I felt DeShawn tap my shoulder. "Can we switch seats?" he asked. "I like to be more in the middle." For a second, I just stared at him. He raised his eyebrows and gave me a look. Was this some kind of trick? Finally, I nodded, and DeShawn and I switched seats.

I was sitting next to Bethany Moyer in a dark theater, about to watch a horror movie. I couldn't have planned it better if I tried. I could smell the sweetness of her perfume, and I hoped I didn't smell bad. I was worried I was breathing too loud. I couldn't even think about eating my popcorn, so it just sat there on my lap, hot and untouched.

The first twenty minutes of the movie, before the screaming, Bethany giggled and whispered to Nola, sitting on the other side of her. I waited for my chance. I was set on not flinching during the scary parts, not even moving. How I would do this was just by not paying attention to the movie at all. That way, I wouldn't be startled when the shit went down. And then maybe, just maybe, when Bethany got scared she would reach out for that solid, unshakable body there beside her and hold on and not let go. It would only be after the movie was over that she realized it had been me, Benjamin Waid, sitting right there all along, making her feel safe. The movie was hard to ignore, though, and I tried hard not to get drawn in. I was worried I would flinch or, worse, scream.

When the first character bit the dust—the blond, of course—Bethany let out a shriek and grabbed the arm of the person next to her, but it wasn't me; it was Nola. She looped her arm around Nola's and rested her head on her shoulder, laughing nervously. I felt cheated.

A few seconds later, Laura stood up. "I'm going home," she said in a flat voice. "I feel sick." In the dark of the theater, we couldn't see her face.

"Great," I heard Jason mutter beside me. "First my mom, then my sister. I bet I'm next."

## APRIL

April woke up to the smell of butter frying. She heard the soft spit and crackle. She was lying on the sofa in the living room, tangled up in a blanket. She had a crick in her neck, and her back hurt. But for a long while, she didn't move. Lying completely still, she stared up at the ceiling. As long as she didn't move, she wouldn't have to confront what had happened last night, or face what was happening now.

He was out there in the kitchen. She could hear him moving around. The butter frying, the clatter of dishes being moved. He must be making her breakfast. How sweet! April felt as if she were about to throw up. Her kids! Where were her kids? It was Sunday, so they'd be at church. What time was it?

When she came into the kitchen, the blanket wrapped around her shoulders, she saw him standing over the stove, a spatula in his hand, making eggs. He looked up and smiled. Watching that smile spread across his face was like watching dawn light spread across a valley. "Good morning," Paul said. It sounded almost profound.

April swallowed. She tried to answer, but all that came out was a weak croak. She cleared her throat and tried again. "Good morning. What time is it?" she asked, looking at the clock above the refrigerator.

"Quarter after eleven," Paul said, confirming what she already knew.

"I never sleep this late."

"Well, you didn't get much sleep last night."

April turned from the clock and looked at him. He was wearing the jeans he'd slept in and his flannel shirt, unbuttoned with the sleeves rolled up, revealing the brown of his chest and arms. His hair was tousled and his face unshaven.

April felt her chest tighten. She went over to the table and grabbed her phone from where she had left it last night. A text from Laura at 10:40: *Where are u?*

Church service started at 10:30. Without hesitating, April texted back: *Not feeling well. Staying home today.* It was almost alarming how easily the lie came to her, although, she could argue, it wasn't exactly a lie—she really didn't feel very well at the moment.

"You okay?" Paul asked. He was pouring her a cup of coffee.

April glanced out the window. The street outside was empty. Thoughts crowded her head, pushing and shoving to be first in line. "We should close the curtains," she said, going over to the window. "How long have you been out here?"

Paul walked over to her and handed her the cup of coffee. "Relax. Nobody saw me."

With the curtains closed, the kitchen was dark. Paul turned back to the stove, eyes on the frying pan. "How do you like your eggs, anyway? I'm making scrambled because I thought, everybody likes scrambled. But I can make them different if you like. When I was in New York, eggs were like the only thing I ate with any nutritional value. They're so easy. I can't cook for shit, but you literally cannot fuck up an egg, I don't think. Even if you make it wrong, it still works—it just wasn't what you intended."

April watched this boy babble on about eggs. Last night, she had kissed this boy. Last night, she massaged his naked back and chest. She had stroked his nipples and wrapped her legs around his ass.

"Paul," she said softly.

"Even more than pasta, I think eggs are like the saving grace for guys who can't cook but don't want to look like complete cavemen. 'Hey, I don't know shit about mincing garlic or how to tell when the chicken's done, but I can make you a killer omelet.'"

"Paul!" she said again, louder. He stopped, surprised, and looked at her. "I think you should go, Paul," she said. "I think that would be the best thing."

He looked at the eggs, then at her. "I wanted to make you breakfast."

"I'm not really hungry."

Paul put down the spatula and walked over to where she stood. When he put his hands on her shoulders, she flinched. "April, you don't need to worry about this."

She bit her lip. "I don't?"

"I understand how this must be for you, but everything's gonna be okay."

"I don't think you do … understand. This is a lot more complicated for me than it is for you."

"I get that."

"You can just sleep with someone. You can just sleep with someone and leave the next morning."

Paul spread his arms out. "But I *didn't* leave. It's the next morning and I'm still here. See?"

Yes, he was still here, standing in her kitchen, making her breakfast.

"Look," said Paul after a few seconds passed and she hadn't spoken, "why don't you have your coffee? I'll finish making breakfast and then we can talk. Okay?"

She couldn't think with him standing there. She couldn't focus. *They could talk.* What was there to talk about? There was nothing to say. There was nothing to salvage from this situation.

On the table, her phone buzzed. A text from Laura: *Okay. Going to a movie with Bethany after church. Won't be back till evening. Hope you feel better.* April remembered that Jason also planned to spend the afternoon with his friends.

"I'm gonna go take a shower," she said to Paul, and walked quickly out of the room.

She couldn't think in the shower and didn't try. She turned the water up as hot as she could, and let it nearly scald her. After her shower, a towel wrapped around her, April stood looking at the unmade bed. It was the first time her bed had been used for sex since her divorce, ten years ago. April hadn't had sex in *ten years*. And, gee, when put like that it made her sound pathetic, like an old spinster. She'd been busy! She'd had kids to raise, a family to support, a goddamn vacation Bible school to run.

It wasn't as if she'd made a conscious decision about it, it had just happened. Since Ray, she simply hadn't met a man she was interested in having a relationship with. That was that. April remembered, a few years back, when a mechanic at a car garage told her she really needed to get laid. It was after she'd given him a piece of her mind regarding the bill he gave her. He'd said it as an insult, but also with an expression implying that if she decided to take his advice, he could make himself available. Of course, at the time, she'd been furious, storming out of the garage and never going back. But there had been nights afterward when she wondered whether maybe that mechanic had been onto something.

Certainly now, in her bedroom, her having sex last night did not somehow make her problems disappear. It hadn't eased the tension in her back and shoulders or erased the headache she felt coming on, and it definitely hadn't made her feel any cooler or more relaxed about her current situation.

Getting dressed (she'd finally settled on the most boring outfit possible—jeans and a cream-colored T-shirt), April decided on what she would say to him: It was a mistake. We were both in a weird place. It was a one-time thing. But here she had to check herself, because had it been? Really? *April, think back. April, be honest.*

They had fallen asleep together on the living room sofa, yes, but in that weird window of half-consciousness just before they drifted off completely, with their bodies already pressed up tight against each other, had she not pulled herself even closer to his body so that she pinned him against the back of the sofa? Had she not started to grind slowly against him, placing her hands firmly on his back and buttocks, guiding him? He had already fallen asleep, she remembered. She actually woke him up by moving against him, and she had felt him grow hard. The first time, in the bedroom, had been fast and fevered and over quickly, but on the sofa, they had gone about it leisurely, almost sleepily. They had kept their clothes on and she'd felt like a dumb teenager in love, she and her boyfriend dry-humping noiselessly in her bedroom, careful not to wake her parents. And it had been really, really good.

What must he think of her, waking him up for more? For Paul, this must all have been a lark. No doubt, she was just another notch on his already well-marked belt. She must have come off like a suppressed, sex-deprived housewife, so overeager, so ravenous. Well, it didn't matter now. Let him say what he liked to his friends. "*Yeah, bro, she totally came back for round two.*" Let him exaggerate and embellish or outright lie. "*And then she sucked me off—swallowed, and everything!*" She didn't care. But why did she get the feeling he wouldn't do that? Why did she get the feeling he would never breathe a word of this to another soul?

When she came out, Paul was in the living room sitting on the sofa, two plates of eggs and toast sitting on the coffee table in front of him. "You look pretty," he said when she came into the room.

April felt herself begin to blush and took a quick, deep breath. "Paul," she began, "what happened last night—"

"I know." Paul cut her off and stood up. "I know what you're going to say, so you don't have to say it."

"What was I going to say?"

"That what happened last night was a mistake, and we should both just try to pretend it never happened and move on."

April nodded. A bit blunter than she would have put it, but more or less accurate. "So, you agree, then?"

Paul shook his head. "No. I like you, April. I don't see why we have to pretend this was a bad thing."

"You like me? Paul, you don't *know* me. Not really. I don't know you. And you're ..." She trailed off. *You're a boy. I'm almost twice your age.*

Paul took a step closer. She realized again how good-looking he was. Better-looking than any of the boys she'd dated back in high school or college, better-looking than Ray even at his peak. None of them came close.

"April," he said, "none of that shit matters."

She swallowed and looked him in the eyes. If Paul were an animal, he'd be a dog—a big, sad, beautiful dog. A German shepherd, maybe, or a Siberian husky. Yeah, a husky because their eyes were so blue …

"April?"

"Paul, this won't work. I have kids. I have a life. I teach kids math. I taught *you* math. You have your life. You must have things you need to do, don't you?"

Paul grinned and shrugged. "Nothing comes to mind."

"Who was that girl?" April asked suddenly.

"What girl?"

"That girl who was with you at the bar last night. Who was that?"

He paused for a moment. "Oh, Nicki? Nobody. Just a girl I knew from high school."

April asked, although she wasn't sure she wanted to know the answer. "Did you sleep with her?"

"What?"

"Have you ever slept with her?"

Paul sighed. "Yeah, once—twice, maybe. I'm not completely sure, to be honest. But it didn't mean anything. It was a mistake."

April felt dizzy. She put a hand to her temple and closed her eyes. "Just as this was a mistake."

She felt a jerk and opened her eyes as Paul put his hands on her shoulders again. "*No*, April, *not* like this. That's what I'm trying to tell you—this is different. I like you. I like being around you. I always have. Being around you is good for me. Look, I haven't even taken my medication today, and I feel fine."

"Your medication?"

"I have … mild anxiety issues, nothing really."

"Oh."

"And I understand that no one can know about us. I understand that we'd have to keep it a secret, but …"

"Shh," April said. She'd heard a sound. Someone was opening the kitchen door.

Without a word, she grabbed his wrist and led him quickly back into her bedroom, closing the door softly and locking it behind her. He stood dumbly in the middle of the room, like an actor waiting for her to give him his next direction. She mouthed the words *Go out the window* and pointed frantically to the large window on the far wall, overlooking the backyard.

For a few horrible seconds, she thought he wasn't going to obey, that she would be caught in her room with this boy, by whoever had come into the house. Then he came up to her and, in a voice that was barely a whisper, said, "Think about it. Give us a chance." He kissed her. Then he turned and went over to the window, opening it wide with one giant heave. And he was gone.

APRIL BECAME AWARE OF A VOICE calling her. "Mom? Mom?"

Just like that, she was somebody's mother again.

She opened the door of her bedroom. Her daughter was standing in the living room, where Paul had been only ten minutes before. "I thought you were sick," Laura said, looking at her mother curiously.

April swallowed. "I am sick."

"It's just that ... you're all dressed and everything."

"I took a shower. I was thinking that maybe if I made myself look better, I'd feel better, too."

"Did it work?"

"Not really."

Laura gestured at the plates of eggs and toast on the coffee table. "Why are there two plates of food here?"

April looked at them dumbly. "They're for you and Jason," she answered at last.

"But we weren't supposed to be back till later this evening."

"Oh ... well, I guess I forgot."

April didn't know whether her daughter was buying this, but she couldn't say she cared all that much—her mind was still reeling from what Paul had said, her body still reeling from his kiss. She rubbed her arm and waited for Laura to stop staring at her, to go somewhere else.

"Mom, can I ask you something?"

*Give us a chance*—that was what he'd said. What did that even mean? That was what they said in the movies, where people had the luxury of second chances. She wasn't that kind of person. Her life was fixed and not going anywhere.

"Mom?"

April started. Laura was looking at her with raised eyebrows. "Hmm? Yes, honey, what is it?"

"I wanted to ask you something."

"So, go ahead, ask." She couldn't keep the irritation out of her voice. Why did her daughter have to pick today of all days to have a heart-to-heart? Usually, it was like pulling teeth trying to get this girl to open up.

Laura looked genuinely hurt. "Forget it. You obviously don't feel like talking right now."

"Laura, don't be like that. I'm listening."

"Maybe I'll call Dad."

April couldn't help it, she burst out laughing. It wasn't the first time her daughter had made such a threat when they had a disagreement about something, but at this point, both of them knew it was an empty one. Ray tried his best—or at least what he would consider his best—to stay halfway involved in the lives of his children, but that still limited the talks on the phone to little more than the kids telling him how they were doing in school and him telling them about the new pickup truck he'd bought.

April would intermittently eavesdrop on these occasional conversations, listening from the kitchen as they talked in the living room, or stopping in the hallway outside their bedroom doors, and wince at their strained, forced quality. Still, if either of her kids ever asked to talk to their dad, April would always honor that desire, even if she knew, as in Laura's case, that it was only meant to get a rise out of her. Now, however, after the night she'd had, after what she'd woken up to, it was just too much. April was doubled over in near hysterics, and when she finally got her breath back, she stood up straight and said, "Go ahead, honey. You have his number."

Laura was looking at her as if she'd lost her mind. And maybe she had. "I don't see what's so funny. What is *wrong* with you?"

"Nothing. You should call your father. Really, I insist."

"You think I'm joking? I'm not joking."

"Me either. Call him."

Laura's mouth quivered, and she blinked twice. Then she turned and walked out of the room.

"Where are you going? The phone's in here," April couldn't help calling after her. No answer, just the sound of the kitchen door opening and then slamming.

April stood alone in the living room, listening to the birds outside and the hum of the refrigerator in the next room. Then she went over to the sofa and sat down. She picked up one of the plates of breakfast Paul had made. By now the eggs were cold, but she ate them anyway.

# 12

LAURA

There's nothing worse than feeling miserable on a beautiful day.

It was one of those days where the weather was so perfect it was almost painful, the sky a clean slate of blue, and the soft, warm breeze playing on my cheeks and through my hair as if to say, *Come on, it's not* that *bad.*

I walked quickly down the street with my head down, determined to ignore all the pleasantness around me: the chirping birds on telephone lines, the kids shrieking and laughing under sprinklers on front lawns, the sun as it danced across my face.

I didn't want to talk to my dad. What the hell would I say to him? And what the hell would I have said to my mom, for that matter? But I needed to talk to someone, and as I walked down the street, only one person came to mind. I stopped at the intersection of Grant and State and turned left.

I'd never been in Ian's house, but I'd seen where he lived when we rode in his car to the park that first night of summer vacation. It seemed like so long ago now. On the far edge of town, past the apartment complex and on the other side of the river. It was a long walk, and I was hot and tired by the time I reached his place: a low-slung white house in dire need of a paint job. Someone needed to take a Weed Eater to that front lawn soon, too.

I rang the doorbell, waited, then rang again. I was about to turn away when the door opened and a guy who looked an awful lot like Ian, only a little older and with longer hair, stood in the doorway, looking at me with tired, disinterested eyes. "Yeah?" he said impatiently.

"Hi, I'm looking for Ian?"

He turned around without a word, leaving the door open. I hesitated a second, then followed him inside, closing the door behind me. After the brightness of the afternoon, my eyes had to adjust to the dim light. All the window shades were pulled down, and no lights were on. There was a stale smell in the house. The boy led me through the kitchen and into the living room, where he flopped down on the sofa in front of a TV blaring *MythBusters.*

I stood in the middle of the room, wondering what to do, until he reached for his can of Budweiser on the table and, as if surprised to see me still standing there, said, "Ian's upstairs, I think, in his room."

"Oh, okay," I said, "Where …?"

He pointed vaguely to his left and turned back to the TV. I wandered into the next room and found the stairwell.

I knew it was Ian's room by the music blaring out from behind the closed door. I had to pound on the door to be heard.

"Yeah?"

When I came in, he was lying on his bed, looking at his laptop. His room was dark and small and looked even smaller because of the dozens of posters hanging on the walls—so many it almost made me dizzy. Weird creatures, bands I'd never heard of, with names like the Cramps and the Dead Kennedys. Ian's music—a singer chanting over a heavily distorted guitar about how much he hated everything—was blaring from a set of large speakers plugged into his laptop. When he saw me standing in the doorway, he turned it down slightly and raised his eyebrows.

"Hey," I said. I felt suddenly awkward and intrusive and wondered why I had thought coming to his house without any notice was a good idea. I hardly knew Ian.

He sat up on his bed. "Come in." It was more a command than an invitation.

I took a step into the room.

"Shut the door," he said.

I shut the door.

Ian studied me from his spot on the bed, his eyes roving over my body in a mixture of curiosity, bemusement, and something else I had yet to find a name for. It was the first time a boy had ever looked at me in that way.

I felt my face grow red, and I blurted, "Nola's such a bitch."

Ian nodded. "Yeah."

I was surprised. I had expected a challenge. "I thought you two were really good friends."

"Sure. 'Really good friends' is exactly what we are."

"I just don't know why she's spending all this time at church. Does she have no life? Is she that bored, or does she just really hate me?"

Ian shook his head. "I don't think it has anything to do with you, Laura. I think it has to do with the preacher's daughter."

"Bethany? But I don't get why she wants to be around Nola so much. They're total opposites, and—"

"*Jesus*, Laura." Ian cut me off with a groan and rubbed his hands over his face. "I thought you would have figured it out by now. Nola's into your friend, okay?"

"*Into* her?" I repeated dumbly.

"She first told me she had a crush on Bethany weeks ago, before they even started hanging out."

I couldn't think of anything to say. I stood there gaping like a dying fish. Though in that moment, I wasn't thinking about Nola or about Bethany, but about how stupid and sheltered Ian must have thought me. How had I not seen this? I said slowly, "Okay, but she knows, right, that Bethany isn't into girls, that Bethany isn't into *her*?"

Ian smirked. "You sure about that?"

"She would have told me if she liked Nola that way. She wouldn't have kept something like that from me. We tell each other everything."

Ian shrugged. "Whatever you say." Then he laughed and patted the space beside him on the bed. "You look like you need to sit down, kid."

I sat down next to Ian. I felt as if I might cry. I couldn't let him see me cry. I covered my face with my hands and groaned loudly, stupidly, to push back the tears. "I'm so stupid," I said into my hands. "How was I this stupid?"

I heard Ian chuckle. "Hey, it's okay. Honestly, it took *me* longer than it should have to figure out Nola's tastes. Don't beat yourself up."

I rubbed my eyes and looked at Ian. "I don't like your friend," he said. "She's fake and self-involved." He placed a hand on my lap. "You're okay, though, Laura. You don't pretend. I like that."

I'd always imagined kissing as an out-of-body experience. You'd float above reality—the details and particulars—in some pink bubble of romance and elation. Kissing Ian, I was aware of everything: how his lips felt against mine; how I had to turn my body clumsily to the side, hurting my neck; how his breath, while not exactly bad, was also not completely fresh; the angry music as it pulsed above and around me. And then there were the incessant, maddening questions in my own head: Was I doing this right? Did *my* breath smell? Should I move my body into a better position? Did kissing Ian make me a slut? Was he kissing me only because, for some reason, he felt sorry for me?

After a few minutes, Ian pulled away from me, his face flushed and his eyes hard. Whatever my qualms, he was enjoying himself. "We should smoke some weed," he said.

I started. Why was his immediate reaction to get high after kissing me? I didn't want to smoke. It hurt my throat and reminded me of Nola, and I didn't want to think of her, especially right now. But Ian had jumped off the bed and was digging through his top drawer. He came up with a plastic bag of weed.

"Actually, do you have any alcohol?" I asked, brushing a loose strand of hair out of my eyes and trying to sound casual. "I'd rather be drunk." As if I'd been drunk so many times before.

Ian turned and looked at me. "Sure," he answered after a moment. "Just give me a second." He rushed out of the room, shutting the door behind him.

The instant I was alone, I leaped off the bed and rushed to the mirror on Ian's dresser and inspected myself. I looked better than I'd expected—the dim light of the room flattered my face, and my hair was messy but in a way that felt appropriate. I took a step back and tried to examine my body, but the mirror was too small. I settled for brushing off my shirt and jeans. Then I went back and sat down on the bed, trying to take slow, deep breaths. I studied the posters on the walls. Strung-out musicians and strange satanic creatures looked down at me as if in judgment.

When Ian returned to the room, he was holding a large squarish bottle of amber-colored liquor, a half-full two-liter of Diet Coke, and two glasses of ice. He looked excited as he sat down on the edge of the bed, put the bottles and glasses on the table, and started pouring.

"All I could find in the basement was Jim Beam," he said as he offered me a glass. "Still, better than nothing, right?"

"Right," I said, taking my drink.

"Cheers," said Ian, and we clinked our glasses. I didn't know how much to drink, and I panicked and downed it. Ian, who had taken only a sip, stared. "I didn't know I was dealing with a certified alcoholic here."

My chest burned, but I liked it. I handed him my glass. "Can I have another?"

My head felt fuzzy as Ian went through his laptop and decided what to listen to. "I'm in the mood for Sonic Youth. But what album? I think *Sister* is their best. How about you?"

I wanted him to shut up so we could start kissing again. I thought I'd be better at it now that my head felt light and my body felt warm and relaxed—or at least, I would enjoy it more. I put my hand on his arm. "Can we listen to the Seizures?" I asked. I wanted to hear Paul Frazier's voice.

Ian looked up at me. "Perfect."

As the heavy sound of Paul's guitar filled up the room, and then the rough, ragged wail of his voice joined in, I finished my third drink, and Ian began stroking my hair. When he started kissing my neck, I couldn't keep from giggling. He looked up at me. "What? You don't like that?"

"No, I do," I lied. "I guess I'm just ticklish." Then I took his face in my hands and began kissing him on the lips again, using my tongue to feel his tongue, tasting the whiskey and the Coke. *This is why people drink,* I thought. *It makes so much sense.*

I closed my eyes. Paul Frazier's voice was ringing in my ears, his music beating against my body. I pictured kissing Paul in his car that night. I pictured him kissing me back. Alone in that car, in front of my house.

Paul would be a good kisser; he had to be. And what about Martin? How would he kiss? I'd imagined kissing Martin before, in my bed after sitting up late chatting with him online, before I drifted off to sleep. I knew how he would be: attentive and gentle, but confident. He'd smell like an older man's cologne, and his cheeks would be just a bit rough from his five o'clock shadow.

On the bed, Ian pulled away from me, panting slightly. "Jesus," he said, but he was grinning.

"What's wrong?" I asked impatiently.

"Nothing."

"Good." I pulled him close. When we kissed, and only when we kissed, Martin would take off his glasses, revealing the startling blue of his eyes— or were they brown? I suddenly couldn't remember. I tried to think back to the pictures, but the color wouldn't come to me. His hand was on the back of my neck now, and then the other was over my shirt, learning the shape of my breast. I imagined Martin, then Paul. My eyes were still closed. I ran my hand through his hair. I fell back on the bed and pulled him with me. We were moving fast against each other. Breathing hard, I pressed my body even closer to his. Then suddenly, I felt it—a change, as if the air had been sucked out of him. I continued to kiss him, quickly, almost roughly, trying to pull him back to me, but it was no use. I had no choice but to open my eyes. "What?" I said, but he was looking down at himself, and suddenly I understood. We both pulled away from each other and sat up.

"Just give me ten minutes," said Ian. His face was beet red, and I suddenly didn't want to be anywhere near him. Paul and Martin were gone. It was just me and this boy I hardly even knew. I didn't know where any of it had come from, what had woken up inside my body, but it scared me. I got up off the bed and almost collapsed. My knees were so weak, I had to put a hand on the bed to steady myself. Then I knelt and began putting on my shoes.

"Where are you going?" Ian asked.

"Home," I said, tying my laces to avoid looking at him.

"Seriously? Just give me ten minutes."

"I think it's better if I just go now."

"That's not what you were saying five minutes ago."

I looked up from my shoes. His eyes were hard and ugly. "I'm aware of that," I said.

Suddenly, he was embarrassed. "It happens to a lot of guys. It's normal," he muttered, and looked down at the bed.

"I never said it wasn't."

"Maybe if you hadn't come on like a fucking maniac," he said, still not looking at me. "Maybe if you'd let me take my time."

"What?" I stood up, feeling dizzy. I had a sick, sinking feeling in the pit of my stomach: the opposite of waking up out of a nightmare into reality—the sensation that things you thought you'd done dreaming, you had, in fact, done wide awake.

Finally, he looked up at me. "I should have known all you Christian girls are repressed sex psychos. You're all just a bunch of horny sluts."

I felt water rising to my eyes. "That's really mean."

"Truth hurts."

"Go to hell."

I whirled around and went to the door, but I couldn't leave, not like that. I needed to claim at least something. I marched back over to the bed, and the expression on Ian's face was a mixture of hope and terror, then confusion, as I grabbed the quarter of a bottle of bourbon from the table. "I'll be taking this," I said, holding it up with one hand and placing the other on my hip. "Guess I'll see you around the schoolyard." I didn't know why I said this—it was an outdated expression I'd only ever heard my mom use. Before Ian could say or do anything, I walked out of the room and shut the door behind me. Then I ran down the stairs, through the living room, past the blaring TV and the guy lying on the couch, through the dirty kitchen, and out the front door into the summer evening.

I TOOK THE BACK WAY HOME. Holding the bottle by the neck, I walked fast down State Street until I came to the Green Meadows apartment complex and cut through the parking lot and past the apartments into the sprawling green field behind it. The evening air was still and warm, the sky was a deep, dark blue, and the stars were appearing as I walked through the field and took a long swig from the bottle. I coughed and wiped my mouth. After the second drink, my chest began to burn and my head regained that dizzy, weightless feeling I'd had in Ian's bedroom. The crickets sounded rhythmic and hypnotic. I lay down in the long grass in the middle of the field and tried to look up at the stars, but I gave up after the bugs began biting me.

I thought I heard a rustle behind me and turned, but there was just the empty field and the low shadows of the apartments in the distance. I started walking, and again I heard something coming up fast behind me. When I whirled around, there was nothing, not even anywhere for a pursuer to hide.

"Ian?" I whispered, but I knew that whatever it was, it wasn't Ian. I stood there, listening to myself breathe, and took another long gulp from the whiskey. I turned and began to walk again, singing one of Paul's songs to myself—the only slow one: *Went looking for you last night, got lost studying the pavement cracks, just like the Lord Jesus, I know that you're not coming back ...* After that, I sang "Jesus Loves Me." *Jesus loves me, this I know, for the Bible tells me so ...* and trailed off because I couldn't remember any more. And the thing followed me all the way through the field, and I let it. I didn't even hurry, almost daring it to catch me, but when I got to the end of the field and was back on Grant Street, I couldn't hear it anymore and told myself it had just been the alcohol.

Standing on Grant Street, I looked at the nearly empty bottle of whiskey. I looked around me. The street was quiet. I lifted the bottle over my head and hurled it. It landed on the road but didn't break. I picked it up and threw it again, harder this time. The sound it made as it shattered into pieces made me jump. I ran headlong in the opposite direction, toward my house.

THE HOUSE WAS DARK AND QUIET when I came in. All the lights were off. My footsteps sounded intrusive as I walked through the kitchen and living room and went up the stairs.

I half expected him not to be there when I knocked on the door, that the house would be empty—the rapture had happened, and I'd been left behind.

"Yeah?"

I'd never been so relieved to hear my brother's voice.

I opened the door. Jason was in front of his TV, playing a video game, an open bag of Doritos next to him on the floor.

"Where's Mom?" I asked.

"In her room," he answered without looking at me. "She's sick, remember?"

I'd been gone for hours now, but she hadn't tried to call me. She hadn't even noticed. *Nobody* had noticed.

I wanted to ask him what he'd had for dinner. I wasn't remotely hungry. I felt dizzy and sick but felt I should have the option. Whenever my mom was too sick to make dinner, she would give us money to order a pizza, or give me instructions to reheat leftovers. I didn't trust my voice, though; my tongue lay heavy and sluggish in my mouth.

"Dinner?" I managed.

Jason just held up his bag of Doritos. Then he looked at me for the first time since I opened the door. "You sound weird," he said. "Where were you, anyway? I thought you were sick."

"I *am* sick," I said, keeping it short so my brother wouldn't hear me slur, and closed the door.

I went into the bathroom, locked the door, and turned on the fan. Under its heavy roar, I vomited into the toilet. I swirled mouthwash around in my mouth. I brushed my teeth. I looked in the mirror and grinned at myself. In my room, I took off my dirty clothes, and changed into shorts and a tank top. Then I got on my bed, opened my laptop, and told Martin I wanted to meet.

# PART II

# 13

## PAUL

For the first few days after Paul Frazier's return to Grover Falls, his mother had mostly ignored his disheveled appearance, his self-imposed seclusion in his room during the day, and his propensity to answer her in monosyllables. "You must be tired," she would say almost hopefully as he passed her in the hallway from the bathroom. He would pause long enough to nod before retreating into his room. It wasn't as if he were lying.

Paul didn't remember exactly how many days it was—three? five?—before Sharon burst into his room without knocking one day around noon, marched over to the window by his bed, and pulled up the shades, flooding his world with harsh bright light.

She sat down on the end of the bed and said, "I know you're sad, but you can't go on like this forever."

He remembered wondering why he couldn't. In the city, his bouts of anxiety had felt like an unwanted visitor, an intruder who had hijacked his life and taken him places he didn't want to go and made him do things he didn't want to do. But here in his old town, in his old bedroom, the anxiety seemed to have stabilized into something that felt not only manageable but maybe even appropriate. What else was he supposed to do in this place besides sleep?

But his mom had been insistent. So he reluctantly explained to her a little bit about how he felt. He spoke of how, if he thought about certain things too long, his chest would tighten up and make even breathing difficult; how even though he was in bed for most of the day, actual sleep was more elusive than ever, a fleeting visitor who could stay no more than an hour at a time; how, even when he did sleep, he had dreams so vivid and frightening that staying awake almost felt more restful.

His mom had been adamant about taking action. Paul, already leery of his mother's return to faith, had feared a proposal involving some spiritual intervention—a prayer session at her church, or a visit from the pastor. But Sharon's proposition was much more practical. She wanted him to see a doctor.

After writing prescriptions (Klonopin for the anxiety attacks, and Cymbalta to up his serotonin levels), Dr. Schumer said that much of Paul's anxiety stemmed from "feelings of powerlessness and lack of control regarding an unknown future." Hell, he didn't need a shrink to tell him that. He had always been that way. It was one of Paul's distinguishing characteristics that the happier he was, the less time he spent thinking about the future. Or maybe it was the other way around: the more successful he was in avoiding thoughts of the future, the happier he felt. But in either case, didn't it follow that when the unknowable future no longer felt important, when instead the immediate, here-and-now reality became the focus, Paul's anxiety would then melt away like slush in the rays of a hot sun?

THERE WAS NO AIR-CONDITIONING in New Life's sanctuary, so Paul had spent the afternoon setting up giant industrial fans in the windows above the gym's bleachers. But even at seven in the evening, with eight fans blasting, the room was thick and heavy with the smell of perspiration, and he could see dark stains under the congregants' armpits.

Paul sat in his usual spot in the sound booth, high in the back of the gym. Here, he had a bird's-eye view of the congregation. During a normal service, people talked and whispered to each other, and babies and toddlers squawked and fidgeted. But tonight, as the last chords of the worship song died away and Jon Newman put down his guitar and left the stage, the room was silent. All eyes were fixed on the stage, where Pastor Eric and the prophet, Dr. Sheldon Langston, stood. Two empty chairs were set up in front of them, and in the heavy silence, Pastor Eric cleared his throat and spoke into his mike: "May I have Mary Reed come up here, please?"

A middle-aged woman Paul recognized but had never spoken to got up from her seat in the congregation and walked up onto the stage, where she sat down in one of the empty chairs and bowed her head. Pastor Eric and Dr. Langston each laid a hand on one of her shoulders, and the hush remained over the room as they closed their eyes and bowed their heads in silent prayer. After a minute of this, Paul began to wonder whether this was all the "prophetic ministry" was—a glorified prayer meeting—but then Dr. Langston began to speak.

"Lord, we thank you for this sister in Christ. We thank you for her patience, for her diligence. The word that comes to my mind for you, sister, is *long-suffering*. You are a woman who has known long suffering. Yes, Father, and the Lord would say unto you that he recognizes your faithfulness, he has not forgotten about you, praise Jesus, and now he is bringing you up into a new place of fruitfulness, a new place of victory, as you continue to serve the Lord, *praise Jesus!*"

A low rumble of assent stirred through the crowd.

"And the Lord would say unto you, *do not be afraid*, sister, as you come into this new place in your life. When the Lord calls you into his waters of grace and truth, do not be afraid to jump in with both feet, sister. Do not be afraid to dive right in, *praise Jesus!*"

"Amens" and "Praise the Lords" emerged intermittently here and there in the congregation.

Paul began to feel something in the room—a pulsing energy as palpable as it was impossible to pin down. And as the night continued and more members of the congregation came up to be prophesied over, sometimes individually, sometimes as a couple or family, he felt himself growing more and more agitated. But it wasn't because he found the idea of an old man's rambling being taken as the "Word of God" weird, which he did—weird, ludicrous, and probably dangerous. It wasn't because, as the night wore on, the mood in the room became increasingly strange and emotional. (Paul saw a woman sobbing uncontrollably in her chair, and one of the elders stand up and begin "speaking in tongues"—chanting out one long torrent of unintelligible speech, which everyone not only seemed to find perfectly normal, but actually welcomed.) It was because every one of Dr. Langston's pronouncements, although they might touch on the past, always ended up focusing on the individual's future. And Paul, who had successfully been keeping thoughts of the future at bay for a string of consecutive days now, didn't appreciate being so forcefully and repeatedly reminded of it.

As a way of keeping himself calm, Paul tried to tune out Dr. Langston's words to a low hum and scanned the congregation till he found her, sitting in her usual spot on the left side of the gym. All he could see was the back of her head, but it was enough. He kept his eyes there and struggled to keep his thoughts there, also, with her, the only safe refuge he had left.


FOUR DAYS AGO, when Paul had stumbled out of April Swanson's bedroom window and into her backyard late Sunday morning, his attention went immediately to the bird feeder dangling from a small maple in the middle of the lawn. A bright, sharp-tongued blue jay was chasing away all the smaller birds, the sparrows and finches and chickadees, not allowing them to partake in the feast. It would sit on the feeder, pecking sporadically, and whenever another bird ventured close, it would fly off its perch screeching, and chase the newcomer away. Paul was fascinated. Were all blue jays assholes, or was this guy some kind of anomaly? Paul realized he didn't know anything about birds. He would have to look up blue jays when he got home. But for now, he decided this wasn't the time or place to take up birdwatching as a hobby, and he walked quickly to the end of the yard, hopped the fence, and doubled back to Grant Street for his car.

Paul felt good. Driving through town, he drummed his fingers on the steering wheel and bobbed his head to nonexistent music. In that moment, he could have listened to the Beach Boys without a trace of irony. He felt he had been at the edge of some precipice, about to fall (or jump), and at the last possible moment, someone had yanked him back from the brink.

It was not unlike the feeling he got the morning after those nights of heavy partying, when the worst of the hangover had subsided and he crawled out of bed to find texts from friends proposing brunch. On those lazy afternoons filled with bacon and omelets, and anecdotes of the night before already being woven into mythologies, Paul always felt the most grateful to be alive. Remembering 3 a.m., when he had retreated drunkenly into the darkest caverns of himself; remembering the blistering headache he had awoken to earlier that morning, he could only feel glad that now he was here with his friends, in a Brooklyn diner, dousing his food in maple syrup, relatively unscathed. You had to get drunk to appreciate being sober.

April. April had pulled him out of the perpetual 3 a.m. inebriation that had been his life for the past few months, had brought him back to a diner sober. But there the metaphor broke down, because Paul felt better than sober. He felt *high*. High on life. High on the sun, the breeze whipping across his face from the open window, the thought of that obstreperous little jay. April had brought him back to here and now; the past and future no longer held any sway.

And yes, abstractly Paul was aware of the irony that sleeping with April had not simplified his future but, in fact, made it much more complicated. He was aware that any sort of relationship with April would have to be carried out in secret, furtively. He was aware that April had not, in fact, affirmed that there would even *be* a relationship. She hadn't given him the slightest hint that last night was anything more than a giant mistake on her part.

But all that, while not altogether irrelevant, was also no cause for alarm. All he wanted to think about was April. Not the logistics of having a relationship with her, but April as a person. That little half smile on her face when she had told him to take off his shoes before they got into bed, how big her eyes had been the moment before he kissed her. And the sex. How, despite her age—or perhaps because of it—there had been a wild, almost violent energy between them, how it all had felt so new and unadulterated. They were the first two people ever to have slept together, the first ever to have kissed, to have fit their bodies together in such a way. It was as if they had invented fucking.

And it wasn't just the sex. With April, everything felt new, full of possibility. That they were so different meant that every conversation was unpredictable, every moment they were together a potential discovery.

It had never been like that with other girls. Near the end of their relationship, Sasha had been fond of pointing out to Paul that his derision and scorn for his own generation spoke not to any superiority on his part, but to a secret and persistent self-loathing. Paul hated the hipsters and students and wannabe artists of Brooklyn, not because he was better than them, but because he was *one of them*. And now Paul was ready to concede his ex's point. He was ready to admit that yes, although discovering that both he and Sasha loved all the same bands had been a turn-on at first, it had soon become a disappointment. After all, what good was a boyfriend if he couldn't make his girlfriend a mix of songs she didn't know? But he could make a mix for April! She wouldn't know the songs. There was sure to be much they disagreed on! Politics, art, interior decorating. But instead of turning him off, the way it would had she been someone his own age, it filled him with excitement and joy. He imagined arguing with April over an election or whether a carpet was ugly, and he felt an immediate rush of pleasure.

Paul's good mood didn't leave him when he got home and came into the kitchen to find his mother sitting at the table, looking out the window with a forlorn expression on her face. It merely hiccuped. He couldn't fathom anyone not feeling as good as he did. Then he remembered that his mom hadn't slept with April Swanson last night and so had no reason to feel good. She was deprived. "Hey, beautiful!" he said, walking into the kitchen and giving her a hug that she did not return. He left off embracing her a bit awkwardly and went over to the refrigerator. "What's cookin', good-lookin'?" he asked as he opened the fridge.

"Where were you this weekend, Paul?" said his mom, not in a "just asking" voice. This was her "I have a right to know" voice.

Paul kept his head in the refrigerator, pretending to examine its contents. Sharon Frazier hadn't demanded an account of her son's whereabouts since he was sixteen, and on another day he would have resented this question. But not today. Today he was on a higher plane.

"I was just hanging out with some old friends from high school," he answered at last, pulling out a can of seltzer water. His mom had started buying seltzer in bulk since she quit drinking. This was his first time trying it—he was ready to experience new things.

"All weekend?"

Paul turned around. His mom was looking at him intently. It was impossible that she knew anything. Impossible. "Yeah," he said, looking at her evenly. "Why?"

"Do you know what day it is, Paul?"

"Sunday," he answered, and then it hit him: *Sunday,* as in Sunday-morning church. He'd skipped out on work without even realizing it. "Oh, shit," he said, and sank down into the chair across the table from his mom, trying not to show his relief that this was all she was calling him out on. "Whoops."

The can of seltzer gave a pop as he opened it. "Mom, I'm sorry. I totally forgot."

"Look, Paul, if you didn't want this job, you didn't have to take it. I wouldn't have forced you."

Paul shook his head. "No, I did, I *do.* This job is great. I'm really grateful for it." He took a long gulp of his seltzer.

"Please don't mock my church, Paul."

"No, Mom, I'm being serious. This job has been good for me, I think. I'm really getting to know people."

Sharon looked at him, searching his face for signs of the usual sarcasm, but his smile looked like the real thing. "I just wish you'd take it a little more seriously. I stuck my neck out for you."

"I just forgot, that's all." He took another drink of seltzer. This stuff was good. Why hadn't anyone ever told him?

"I called you. More than once."

"The phone died. I couldn't charge it." He decided he would drink this from now on. He was going to quit booze. Smoking, too. He was going to go for jogs in the morning, get in shape.

"Whatever. But just so you know, I had to call my pastor and lie to him this morning, tell him you were sick. That didn't feel good, Paul, lying to my pastor."

For the first time since he came into the house, Paul felt almost irritated. The way she said "pastor" with so much weight, it was close to reverential. *God forbid you lie to your* PASTOR, he wanted to exclaim, *Anyone else, fine, but not your precious* PASTOR. "I'm sorry," he said flatly. "I fucked up."

"That tone is really convincing."

Why was she trying so hard to kill his vibe? How could he make her understand that this wasn't, in any way, a big deal? "What else do you want me to say?"

She sighed. "Nothing, Paul. I don't want you to say anything."

A LONG, HOT SHOWER HELPED RESTORE PAUL to his earlier state of Zen, and when he came into his bedroom, dried himself off, and changed into a pair of shorts and a fresh T-shirt, his bed looked inviting to him in a way that it hadn't in months—not because he had nothing better to do, not because it was the best way to escape his maddening thoughts, not as any last resort, but because he was simply and amazingly exhausted. He collapsed onto his bed and let the world drift away.

He was woken up maybe ten minutes later, when his phone, which he had left charging on the table by his bed, began ringing. Paul sat up, looked at the caller ID, and yawned a hello into the phone.

"Paul?" Nicki sounded as if she couldn't quite believe she was hearing his voice.

"Yeah, it's me. What's up?"

"'What's *up?*'" Nicki repeated. "Are you serious right now? Have you checked your phone lately? The two dozen missed calls and messages I left you?"

This phone would be the end of him. "Sorry, I haven't. I got home and kinda just crashed."

"Where did you go last night?"

"Uh … home, I went home."

"Where are you now?"

"I was sleeping."

"I was really worried about you, Paul. We got back and you were gone, and your car was gone, and you were so drunk … I thought something must have happened." He could hear her voice cracking.

"I'm sorry," Paul said. Maybe he should just get those two words tattooed on his forehead and put it on his voice-mail greeting, to save time. *You have reached the voice mailbox of Paul Frazier. If you'd like to hear him apologize, press "one."*

"You know you were completely horrible this weekend. You are aware of that, right?"

"I have a vague idea. But I don't remember everything, to tell you the truth."

"Convenient for you. Convenient not to remember. Let's just say calling you a total asshole would be an understatement."

"I won't dispute the charges."

"I don't get you, Paul. When we first met up, that night back in June, I thought we hit it off, sorta. I mean, yeah, it was just a night together, but we had fun, didn't we? And you were nice. Sad but nice. Then in the morning, you make me sneak out your friggin' window, and I did, because I thought that's what you wanted, and I have this thing where I tend to do whatever boys want me to do—original, I know. But I don't hear from you forever, and then you call me out of the blue. We hang out and you're insane—not just as a figure of speech, but literally insane. And then you disappear. No explanation. I mean, you had me worried sick. I didn't know where you went, and you'd been saying some weird things. You won't answer your phone. And now, when I finally get a hold of you, you're *sleeping*? You couldn't even bother to send me one little text so I know you're not in the ER or dead in a ditch somewhere? And let's not forget, *you* called *me* to hang out. You fucking called *me*, Paul. So I think I deserve a text. I deserve at least one goddamn text."

"Nicki, I—"

She cut him off. "No, Paul, forget it. I'm not gonna be that annoying bitch you have to apologize to. I'm sure you've had enough of those. Have a nice life."

He said her name again, but he knew she had already hung up. He looked at the phone in his hands for a moment, then put it back on the table, rolled over on the bed, and went back to sleep.

THE NEXT MORNING, Monday, dawned bright and hot. By nine, the temperature had already risen above eighty, and the air was thick and heavy, as if the heat were some physical weight the air was trying, and failing, to hold up. Paul hardly noticed. He arrived at church by nine thirty, half an hour earlier than he needed to be there. Pulling into the parking lot, he scanned the area for April's silver Honda. He didn't see it.

By ten o'clock, when the VBS started, she still hadn't arrived. Paul couldn't think. He couldn't concentrate on the simple task he had given himself: putting a new blade on the church's old Weed Eater that was stored in the shed. Every ten seconds, he was looking up to the drive, hoping to see her car pull in.

At ten forty-five, having abandoned the Weed Eater in a state worse than when he'd found it, Paul went to the main pavilion, where Lydia Newman was sitting at a table, scribbling something in a notebook. Beside her was the empty chair where April usually sat. Lydia looked up at him and quickly tried to hide her initial surprise—for the first time that day, Paul noticed he was sweating profusely. His shirt was damp and clinging to his back. His forehead appeared to be leaking.

"Paul!" Lydia said brightly, "Jeez, you look hot. Do you need some water?"

"I need to speak to April," Paul croaked. His throat was dry.

"Ms. Swanson isn't coming in today. She's home sick."

Paul stared at her.

"Is there something you need help with? Technically, I'm in charge of things when Ms. Swanson's out. So I'll try my best." Lydia gave a nervous giggle, but Paul had already turned away without answering, and walked out of the shade of the tent and back into the glaring sun.

Up until now, he had been unaware of the heat. Now it seemed to enclose him in its thick, sticky embrace. The sun hammered down on him as if it wanted to drive him into the ground, and a headache throbbed in his temples, just below the skin.

He wanted to call her. He had to resist the urge. He had to resist the urge to get in his car, drive to her house, and burst through her front

door, find her where she was hiding. He would take her in his arms ...
and then what? Scream and swear at her? Break down sobbing?

All around him were kids. Laughing and screaming, running around
in seemingly random circles. He knew there were adults supervising, but
at the moment, he couldn't see them. Just kids dressed up in robes and
headdresses, throwing water balloons at each other, arguing over whose
fake gold was whose—a field of adolescent chaos. A Biblically themed
coed *Lord of the Flies*. It was terrifying.

In the Middle Ages, a citizen might run into a church and plead
sanctuary to receive temporary safe haven from pursuers.

But there was no real sanctuary at New Life. No rows of wooden
pews or giant stained-glass windows. Nowhere for a citizen to hide. As
Paul walked slowly through New Life's empty gym, the din from outside
was only barely audible. He stopped below one of the basketball hoops
and wondered whether he could still jump up and reach the rim, but
decided not to try. He wandered over to the front of the room and
leaped up onto the empty stage. Jon Newman's acoustic guitar sat on
its stand in the corner, and beside it was a chair, as if they had just been
waiting for Paul to show up.

He hadn't touched a guitar in months, not since Sasha broke up with
him, but holding it in his hands and beginning to strum absently, he
didn't feel anything, good or bad—not a sense of homecoming, nor any
sort of revulsion. It was just a guitar. And these were just chords, waves
of sound, meaningless vibrations. If he moved his fingers on the frets, the
sound waves changed.

"What song's that?"

Paul looked up to find DeShawn standing on the end of the stage,
near the curtains, his hands in his pockets.

"Jesus, DeShawn," said Paul, unslinging the guitar from around his
neck. "Are you *ever* actually where you're supposed to be?"

DeShawn walked onto the stage. "It's a free hour right now. I've still
got a little time before they notice I'm gone."

"You know, I got in a lot of trouble last time, in the locker rooms, when I didn't turn you in."

DeShawn smirked, almost smiled, and shook his head. "No, you didn't."

Paul couldn't argue. Besides the talk with April, there had been no consequence. And although at the time the conversation had been extremely uncomfortable, he now remembered it fondly, as he did any memory involving April. He had so few to choose from.

"You know Jimi Hendrix?" DeShawn asked, coming closer and inspecting the guitar Paul was now holding by the neck.

"The name founds familiar."

DeShawn looked at him quizzically, and Paul realized that his sarcasm had gone undetected.

"Yes," he said, "I know Hendrix."

"You like him?"

"Yeah, I like him."

"Is it true nobody taught him how to play guitar? He just did it?"

Paul nodded. "He was self-taught for the most part, yeah."

DeShawn smiled. "Crazy. Who taught you?"

"I never had a real teacher—just picked it up from different places. Once you master the main chords, you can teach yourself a lot."

"The main chords?"

"Yeah." Paul reslung the guitar over his shoulder. "C, D, and G are the ones to know for beginners." He placed his fingers on the strings and strummed. "This is G." Paul showed DeShawn D and C. "That chord progression is responsible for an ungodly number of pop songs." He began to play "Sweet Home Alabama."

DeShawn watched Paul's hands intently, almost hungrily—so much so that Paul stopped playing and stood up. "All right, man, take a seat," he said, offering DeShawn the guitar.

DeShawn looked at him suspiciously, as if he expecting him to yank the instrument away the moment he reached for it.

"Go on," Paul said impatiently. "I know an aspiring Hendrix when I see one."

DeShawn took the guitar and sat down in the chair. The instrument was big and awkward on the boy's lap, but his arms were long, and almost immediately he had it in the right position.

"Okay, so ..." Paul looked around and saw another chair folded up on the side of the stage. He brought it over and sat down next to DeShawn. "Let's try a G first," he said. "I'll show you where to put your fingers."

DeShawn flinched visibly when Paul put his hand on DeShawn's. "It's important that your hand be relaxed," Paul said as DeShawn adjusted and allowed him to place his fingers on the strings. "Okay, now, press down hard and strum."

Paul had gone through the motions of giving people their first guitar lessons before. Girls, mostly. He never offered, but at parties or alone in his room they always asked, their eyes big, looking up at him, *"Paul, will you teach me how to play guitar?"* It was a very efficient way to get close to someone—physically, at least. But of all the guitar lessons he'd given, Paul had never seen anyone catch on as quickly as DeShawn. In less than ten minutes, he had down the three chords Paul had shown him and was working on moving back and forth between them.

Paul laughed. "You're sure you've never played before?"

DeShawn shook his head, keeping his eyes on his fingers. "My mom never listened to music, except for church stuff."

Paul didn't say anything. He had no idea what had happened to this boy's mother and wasn't about to ask.

DeShawn looked up as if something had just occurred to him. "My dad, though ... I think my dad plays guitar or bass. He likes music. The one time I went to his apartment, he had this whole wall of records. But it's all black music—not like rap, though, or Michael Jackson, but all this weird stuff from Jamaica or somewhere."

"Reggae or ska, probably," said Paul.

DeShawn shrugged. "I don't like it. He just listens to it when he's smoking, anyway."

"So your dad's still around?" Paul ventured to ask.

The kid nodded. "Yeah." And then he paused. "But he don't want me." He looked down at the guitar.

Paul almost said, *Yeah, mine didn't, either,* but stopped himself.

After a second, DeShawn looked up. "I like Jimi Hendrix, though. Mr. Waid gave me all his old music. I like most of it, even if it is mostly by dead white guys."

"Yeah, well, rock and roll came directly from the blues. It's just another thing we stole."

DeShawn looked at him—Paul couldn't tell whether it was with curiosity or disdain—and then he stood up and carefully placed the guitar back on its stand. "I gotta go back or they gonna notice." He hopped down off the stage and walked quickly out of the gym. No *thanks for the lesson* or even a *see you later.*

AROUND FIVE THIRTY, Paul had just finished with tear-down, putting away everything that needed putting away—the cones, tables and chairs, gym equipment, water coolers—leaving the church field empty except for the tents and the stage. He was heading across the parking lot to his car when he saw her daughter, sitting on the church steps at the front entrance. Hope sprang up in his chest.

He didn't know exactly what his plan was when he turned and headed over to Laura. But at this point in his life, Paul Frazier was making it up as he went along.

Despite the still oppressive heat, Laura was wearing a sweatshirt with the hood up. Her head was buried in the phone on her lap, and when Paul reached her, she looked up at him in surprise.

"Hey, Laura," Paul said a little breathlessly.

She seemed too startled to respond. The sweatshirt, which had "A&H Construction Co." across the front, was much too big for her, and he wondered how she wasn't sweating. "Hey," she said at last.

Paul nodded. "What's up?"

"Not much," Laura answered, her voice nervous and fluttery.

"So, your mom's sick?"

She looked confused. "Yeah, she's not feeling well."

Paul looked around the empty parking lot. "Is she coming to pick you up now?"

Laura shook her head and squashed his dumb blossom of hope. "No, Pastor Eric's giving me a ride home once he finishes locking up."

Paul struggled not to show his disappointment. Laura studied him for a moment; then something in her expression changed. She leaned back against the steps, pressed out her chest, and cocked her head to the side with a smile. "Why? Are you offering me a ride, Paul?"

Through her oversize sweatshirt, Paul could make out the shape of Laura's breasts. He thought of the night he'd driven this girl home, the kiss she'd given him. He shook his head. "No, I … your mom—is it serious? Like, do you think she'll be in tomorrow or …?"

Abruptly, Laura sighed and her voice hardened. "Jeez, how should I know? I can't read her mind, thank God."

Paul tried to speak, but Laura cut him off. "Look, if you're just gonna ask questions about my mother, then I'm kinda busy, so …" She sat upright and went back to looking at her phone as if he weren't there.

Paul was stunned. He wasn't used to being spoken to this way by a fifteen-year-old girl—or any girl, for that matter. He was used to girls freezing up in front of him or babbling on nervously. He was used to little girls giving him wide-eyed stares as they passed him on the street holding their parent's hand. He was used to teenage girls calling out to him, "You're cute!" in coffee shops before hurrying away in a fit of giggles. He was used to girls his own age giving him the eye in bars and then looking pointedly at the empty stool beside them. He was used to older women working at the DMV or the doctor's office throwing him wide smiles and calling him "hon" and filling out forms for him, making his experience much faster and more efficient than it might otherwise have been. He *wasn't* used to girls blowing him off, and he certainly wasn't used to girls ignoring him. Wasn't this the same girl he had caught staring longingly at him more than once these past weeks? Wasn't this the same girl who kissed him on the lips in his car less than a month ago?

But Laura didn't look up again. And Paul, not knowing what else to do, gave her a dumb wave that she did not acknowledge, before turning and heading to his car.

PAUL'S GOOD LOOKS AND DEBAUCHED LIFESTYLE of the past few years meant that sustained periods of isolation and, therefore, sustained periods of masturbation were not something he was very familiar with. But in the first few weeks after Sasha left him, he must have rivaled his puberty-awakened twelve-year-old self for the record in jerking off. Holding his dick in his hand, and Sasha's body and face in his memory, he had made love to her in more passionate and creative ways than he ever did in real life. And then angrily, bitterly, and, at some point, callously. In his Brooklyn apartment, he had reached a place of total emptiness. His body became a shell, an arid wasteland where not only desire but all feelings seemed to have dried up and shriveled, leaving him hollow and dehydrated. To jerk off, you had to have something to hold on to and something to get rid of. He hadn't masturbated since. When Paul got home, on his childhood bed, he held April in his mind and emptied himself onto the sheets.

PAUL HADN'T KNOWN WHAT TO EXPECT on Tuesday, when he arrived for work late in the afternoon. Maybe she would be out again. Maybe she'd be there but would ignore him or tell him emphatically that it had been a mistake and to keep away from her. What he hadn't expected was, the moment he got out of his car, to see April walking across the parking lot in his direction.

He stood frozen, watching her approach. Everything about her said that nothing was out of the ordinary. She was wearing an outfit he recognized: shorts, a plain blue T-shirt, and sneakers. Her expression was neither playful nor serious, betraying nothing.

"Paul," she said when she reached him, and her voice was as blank as a new sheet of paper, "I know you just got here, but would you mind running to Walmart for some supplies for the camping trip? I would have called, but I don't have your cell."

Paul looked at her face and then around him, bewildered. There was no one in the immediate vicinity, no one who could have heard them. Had she gone crazy? Had *he*?

April cleared her throat. Paul looked back at her. She was offering

ANOTHER LIFE | 167

him a piece of notepad paper. He took it hesitantly and glanced at the handwritten list: *5 large coolers, flashlights, 8 cans of bug spray* …

Was it code? Paul looked back up at her. Her expression was mildly impatient but otherwise not telling him anything. "How many flashlights would you like?" he asked at last, his voice a dry husk.

But April shook her head. "I'm going to have to go with you. That's a lot of stuff. We can take my car. It has more trunk space."

She passed him at a brisk walk, and he turned and followed.

FOR THE FIRST FIVE MINUTES in the car, they didn't speak. April drove with both hands on the steering wheel, her eyes now hidden behind her sunglasses. In the passenger seat, Paul couldn't seem to find the correct way to sit and kept repositioning himself. He waited for her to say something, but she didn't. It wasn't until they had pulled out of the church driveway and were well down the road that he worked up the courage to ask her, with only a hint of irony, whether she was feeling better.

"What?" April glanced at him and then back at the road. "Oh, yes, thanks. Much better."

He waited a moment, but since she didn't offer anything more, he began, "April, what are we—"

She shook her head and cut him off. "Just wait. I can't talk and drive at the same time."

When they got to Walmart, April pulled the car around to the empty excess-parking lot behind the building. She shut off the car, took off her sunglasses, and turned and looked at him for the first time with some acknowledgment in her eyes. "So I thought a lot yesterday," she began. Then she closed her eyes and rubbed at her temples and looked at him again with a wry smile.

"And?"

April breathed out loudly. "And I got nothing."

Paul didn't know what that meant, so he didn't know whether he should be smiling, but April was smiling, almost smirking, so he smiled back stupidly, hopefully.

"This is dumb," she said finally, and looked out the window.

Paul wanted to grab her and kiss her. "When can I see you next?"

She turned back to look at him. "Aren't we getting a little ahead of ourselves? I haven't even decided whether to continue doing ... whatever it is we're doing."

But Paul could tell from the way she was looking at him, from the slight tone of amusement in her voice, that she had indeed already decided. "I need to see you," he said.

"Even if I wanted to," April said, "there are logistics to think about ..." She trailed her finger on the stick shift. "Despite my single status, I'm not exactly free as a bird."

"I'm not supposed to come in to work tomorrow till late in the afternoon," said Paul. "Come up with some excuse to go back to your house for an hour around one o'clock tomorrow, and I'll meet you there. Your kids will be at church. It's perfect."

April raised her eyebrows. "You thought that up pretty quick. Have you done this before?"

Paul shook his head. "No, I'm making this up as I go, believe me."

She laughed, then placed her hands on her face and groaned. "I'm turning forty this Friday, Paul. *Forty.* Did you know that?"

He grinned. "Your birthday's in two days? We have to celebrate!"

"That wasn't what I was getting at, actually."

"Do you have plans?"

She looked confused. "No, we have the camping trip this weekend, remember?"

"I'll think of something. But for now ... we're on for tomorrow?"

"You're making this sound like a date to the movies."

"Which I would be perfectly down with, but I don't think anything good's playing."

April nodded. "Okay, fine. Sure. Tomorrow. Great."

"One o'clock?"

"One o'clock."

And so, without so much as touching, they had confirmed the next rendezvous for their affair as if they were confirming a doctor's appointment. Paul found April's poker face, her almost businesslike detachment, incredibly arousing. The next second, April opened her door and got out of the car, then turned and stuck her head back in, where Paul sat looking after her. "Come on," she said. "I wasn't kidding about all those supplies. We've got some shopping to do."

PAUL WAS DRAWN BACK INTO THE MOMENT by the wave of grating feedback. The last person signed up for prophetic ministry had been called up and prophesied over, and Eric was now leading the congregation in a closing prayer, but there was something wrong with his mike; high feedback kept cutting through his words. Paul trimmed the EQ and adjusted the volume, and then, when the feedback had disappeared, he stood up, left the sound booth, and went out into the sanctuary to make sure the volume was at the right levels. He walked halfway down the side aisle, then stopped and leaned against the wall as Pastor Eric finished up the prayer with an amen. He was about to turn away when Dr. Langston, still standing on the stage, turned and, looking Paul straight in the eyes, said into his mike, "Brother, would you mind coming up here? I think the Lord has a word for you."

# 14

APRIL

Forty was a semiperfect number, equal to the sum of some (but not all) of its proper divisors. It was an octagonal number and, being the sum of the first four pentagonal numbers, also a pentagonal pyramidal number. In the Bible, the number came up a lot. During Noah's flood, rain fell for forty days and forty nights. Three separate times, Moses spent forty days and nights on Mount Sinai, waiting to hear from God. The Israelites wandered in the wilderness for forty years before reaching the Promised Land. The giant Goliath provoked the Israelites for forty days before David challenged him. King Saul, King David, and King Solomon each ruled for forty years. In the New Testament, Jesus fasted in the desert for forty days and nights before his temptation by the devil. And after his resurrection, Christ remained with us sad people for a mere forty days before ascending back to heaven.

April remembered, as a new Christian, noticing this number's persistent pattern during Bible studies, and being intrigued by it. She had always liked deciphering hidden messages. What did it *mean*? She'd done some research that left her vaguely disappointed. It was probably just a question of translation. In Hebrew tradition, the number forty was often used as shorthand to signify a large number or long period of time. So most likely, all those forties in the Bible were not actual forties—they meant only "more than a few."

In only a few hours, April would be forty years old. As she pulled off the exit ramp and merged onto 87 North, leaving Grover Falls behind, she tried to invest this fact with the weight and import it apparently deserved, but in fact, she didn't feel much about it, one way or the other. And she wondered whether she should be concerned about this indifference. Of course, she hadn't expected to feel the way she had felt turning sixteen or eighteen or twenty-one—those milestones that, however manufactured, were deep and brimming with significance. But forty was an important year in one's life, and she had expected to feel *something*, even if it was only existential dread, as she entered middle age.

She remembered her thirtieth birthday. Ray had hired a sitter and taken her out to dinner. It was just when their marriage was at its zenith, soon after which it would begin its sudden and swift decline. She remembered more than once that night saying to her husband, "I can't believe I'm thirty," and meaning it. Thirty was an age deemed by all so momentous that it had become for April too abstract to apply to her life—she couldn't fit herself inside the number.

She didn't feel the same way now, with forty, but maybe because, when she thought about it, the age was pretty much a total drag. It didn't offer the excitement and trepidation of new adulthood the way thirty did, or the respect and maturity that came with turning fifty. Forty was limbo. Forty meant you definitely weren't young anymore, but you were not so old that people had to respect you. It was the age of banality. Of backaches and migraines, menopause and midlife crises. The age when your kids ignored you, your parents now relied on you, and everything was your fault. Forty was the age to be realistic, the time to reassess your diet, try and fail at new exercise regimens, plan a better budget. It was the time to dream of vacations but never go on them. It was the time to reevaluate the choices you'd made, long after there was still time to do anything about them. And for April Swanson, apparently, it was the time to sleep with a twentysomething boy just for the hell of it.

What had happened back there? April had done her best to keep from thinking about it, at least immediately afterward. She felt she needed a little distance, both physical and emotional, from the incident. The further away she got from the church, and the more time that passed, the more dispassionate her evaluation—at least, that was the hope. But now, as she sped north up 87, with no more turns to make or lights to stop at, nothing but open highway before her, she couldn't keep herself from thinking about it.

It had been hot in the church. So hot that when Dr. Langston called Paul up on the stage, April could attribute the sweat gathering on her forehead and trickling down the back of her neck to the temperature. Her pounding heart, however, had no such alibi.

It wasn't as if she had expected God to suddenly begin speaking through Dr. Langston, outing her and Paul in front of the entire congregation. She'd been going to church most of her life, and not once had she felt that God was speaking directly to her. It would be completely absurd and ironic for him to start now. And maybe, given the way she had come to think about God over the years—constantly subverting her expectations and prone to cruel humor—completely typical.

She waited, hardly breathing, while Paul slowly took the stage and sat down in the empty chair before Dr. Langston and Pastor Eric. She tried to catch his eye, but he kept his eyes on the floor going up, and when he sat down, he closed his eyes and bowed his head. April didn't blame him. What else could he do? Sitting there on the stage as the two men laid their hands on his shoulders, he looked so confused and frightened that April felt a surge of protective emotion rise up in her. She wanted to leap up from her seat, run up onto the stage, and throw her body over his, screaming at the men and at God, "*Take me but leave the boy! If you must have someone, take me!*"

AFTER PAUL LEFT THROUGH HER BEDROOM WINDOW late Sunday morning, April had spent the rest of the day trying to go over recent events and the present situation in a calm, objective manner—and failed miserably. All she could think about was last night—not its implications or how to proceed in light of it, but how it had felt during, how it had felt to have his hands on her bare legs and breasts, how it had felt to have him inside her. She sat on her bed that evening, cross-legged, the lights off, watching the sunlight gradually fade from the window he had climbed out of. And by the time the room had grown completely dark, the one thing she knew for certain was that she wanted Paul inside her again.

But April well understood the simple, sad truth that people did not necessarily want what was best for them, that many times those two things were diametrically opposed. So the next day, she called in sick to VBS and planned to take the day determining whether her desire to have Paul inside her again was greater than, or at least equal to, the consequences that the fulfillment of that desire might bring.

Again she had been flummoxed. Instead of spending the day in a reasoned back-and-forth debate with herself, she'd spent it daydreaming about Paul and wondering what he was doing now at the VBS, whether he missed her, whether he was thinking about her. It got her nowhere. All she had by the end of the day was this bit of reasoning: For the past twenty years, April had spent her life working solely to make those closest to her happy, with varying results, and last night, she had made a big decision solely for herself. And now the world around her would have her feel that this decision had been bad, wrong even, and she just wasn't sure that was fair. So tomorrow, Tuesday, she would approach Paul. She would talk to him alone, but she would not propose anything. She would wait and see what happened. That was all she would do: wait and see what happened.

What happened was Walmart. They had gone shopping, and April tried not to wonder what it said about you if the best time you'd had in years was in a Walmart store. They strolled down the aisles, taking their time, picking up supplies for the camping trip: coolers, water balloons, bug spray, first-aid kits. They had not touched—except for when she slapped him lightly on the arm after he made a very funny but very mean joke about one of the church elders, and except for when he dragged her by the hand to the grocery aisle and tried to convince her to feed the campers nothing but Spam and saltines for the weekend.

What happened was, April felt a teenage sense of giddiness welling up inside her. And this should have alarmed her, she supposed. She shouldn't have felt this happy, not given the circumstances this happiness had sprung from.

Confusion, anxiety, confliction—these were the things she was supposed to be feeling. But she just didn't. Something must be wrong with her.

What happened was, the next afternoon, April found herself completely naked, lying next to Paul on her bed, breathing heavily.

Beside her, Paul let out a long sigh and then said, "Do we have time to go again?"

April began to giggle; she couldn't help it. She felt high—no, she was completely sober, but her world was on drugs. She turned on her side and picked up her watch from where it sat on the bedside table. It was past two o'clock. She'd been gone from church for more than an hour now. Her alibi for her absence had been her internet service. Yesterday evening, she had gone to the living room, turned off the wireless router under her desk, unplugged it, and thrown it in her bedroom closet. As if on cue, five minutes later, Laura came downstairs, complaining that she had no connection.

April had been finishing up the dishes and glanced up from the sink. "There's something wrong with the router," she said. "I'll have to call the company tomorrow to come replace it."

Laura marched over to the desk in the living room. "Where'd it go? Did you toss it already?"

April had dried off her hands with a towel and followed Laura into the living room. "Yes. It's shot."

Laura's eyes narrowed. "It was working fine literally ten minutes ago. How are you so sure it's unfixable?"

April looked at her daughter. She was wearing her dad's old hooded sweatshirt, the one with the name of the construction company he used to work for. She had been wearing it for a few days now, throwing it over her outfit every morning as if this were the middle of the winter and not the hottest time of the year. April knew that something was bothering Laura, and that wearing her father's old sweatshirt constantly was only the most visible sign. But she just hadn't found the time to sit down and talk with her, not that Laura looked especially open to a heart-to-heart. She was scowling at her mother now, her hands thrust deep inside that horrible sweatshirt.

"Aren't you hot with that thing on?" April couldn't help asking.

"I'm fine," said Laura. "Where is it, anyway? It probably just needs to be unplugged and plugged back in."

April could have kicked herself for having chosen such a contentious excuse to get out of an hour of work the next day. She could have blamed it on a leak in her bathroom, or faulty wiring. But there was no going back now, so she crossed her arms and said, "Laura, I already took the trash out. It's broken. I think I know when something in my house is broken."

"You shouldn't have thrown it out. You should have let me at least try and fix it."

"You spend too much time online anyway. You can survive a night without your precious Facebook."

Laura looked close to tears, which genuinely startled April. "I wasn't even *on* Facebook! God, Mom, you are such a jerk sometimes." Then she turned and marched out of the room and back upstairs.

April had felt a little guilty about her lie after that, but so far, it was the only thing she felt guilty about. She didn't feel guilty about lying here next to Paul after making love in an unrestrained, almost feverish way, attacking each other's body with a sense of wild urgency as if, at any moment, either of them might disappear, leaving the other alone in a tangle of sweaty sheets. That morning in her bathroom, April had shaved between her legs, and in bed she spread them open wide and let Paul move down the length of her body and put his mouth there. She had writhed under him, moaned, buried her fingers in his hair, and when he lifted his head, she sat up and kissed his mouth as her hand moved down to grab his hard sex. This time, they had been ready with a condom. When it was over, Paul lay there on top of her, and April rubbed his back, savoring the feel of his weight pressing down on her.

She did not feel guilty. And when Paul asked her if she wanted to do it again, there was no question in her mind—yes, yes, she really did. But something kept her from replying. It was the nagging thought that she couldn't let Paul grow too comfortable with all this yet, that on some level she had to keep him waiting and wanting more. She resented herself for thinking this way. It felt petty and outdated. After all, at this point they both had made it perfectly clear that they wanted to have sex with each other, would go out of their way to make it happen, so why shouldn't they have sex whenever, and however many times, they both were willing and able?

But she couldn't shake the thought that if she consented to whatever he proposed, he might find her easy and eventually lose interest. So instead of saying, *Yes, please, let's do it again*, she turned to him on the bed and said, "Better not risk it," smiled, and put her hand on his cheek. In response, he groaned, pulled the pillow over his head, and said, "April, you make me crazy."

This admission made her flush with pleasure. How long since someone had said that to her! And Paul looked as if he meant it. He *must* have been crazy—a boy like him, wasting his youth working at a church, sleeping with the vacation Bible school teacher.

April placed her hand on Paul's chest. "You're aware that we're like characters in a smutty romance novel, right?"

Paul laughed. "I know. Isn't it fantastic?"

After a moment, April continued, trying to keep her tone light. "What ends up happening to the characters in those books? Because right now I'm having trouble seeing how this ends—happily, anyway."

Paul rolled over onto his side so that he was facing her. "There's no point in thinking like that." He placed a hand on her leg. "When can I see you again?"

"I don't know, Paul. I can't have my internet on the fritz every day."

"How about tonight?" He was stroking her thigh now, moving his hand underneath the sheets.

"Tonight? My kids will be here, and I can't leave."

"Lock your bedroom door and leave your window open. We'll be quiet. Like mice."

Paul had his hand between April's thighs, and she felt a tingle of pleasure. The thought of doing it with her children oblivious upstairs made her hot and giddy, and she began to cover his neck in quick, fierce kisses. He moved his hand faster and harder against her. Then she rolled over on top of him, and they began to rock back and forth. And again that night, with the door locked and their noise masked by the giant fan on full blast, they rocked back and forth together, and when April came, she had to press her teeth against Paul's shoulder.

Paul got up, tossed the condom into the wastebasket by her bed, and lay back down beside her. She had her back to him, and he nestled against her, his body warm and slightly damp. He kissed the back of her neck, the hollow of her shoulder, her head. There was a moment of stillness. Then she felt his weight come off the mattress as he got out of the bed. She heard the rustle of his clothing and the snap of his belt buckle as he got dressed, his soft footsteps on the carpet as he walked across the room, and the faint thud as he dropped from her window to the backyard. For a while, the only sound was the steady drone of the fan, blowing summer night air in through the window, and then the muffled sound of her weeping softly into her pillow.

THE NEXT DAY, APRIL WOKE UP in a fog. She drifted through her morning routine on autopilot, taking her shower, drying her hair, getting dressed. On the drive to the church, Jason had to tell her to turn on the AC, because despite the blistering heat, she hadn't noticed it wasn't on. Distantly, as if through a wall, she could hear her son and daughter bickering in the car, but she didn't listen to what they were saying. When she got to church, she greeted Lydia and some parents dropping their children off, but she was only half aware of their presence. It was as if her body—her legs, her arms, her mouth, her voice—knew that her mind had drifted away, and it was doing its best to keep going with no conscious direction.

The cloud didn't lift until she saw his green Toyota pull into the parking lot, and him get out of the car. April sat next to Lydia at her table under the main tent and watched him approach.

When he reached them, he greeted Lydia with a smile and said to April, "Ms. Swanson, here's the receipt for the camping supplies I picked up the other day." He handed her a piece of paper. It was a receipt for fifteen dollars in gas, and scribbled across it in black ink was a note: *Boys' locker room, 20 min.*

When she came into the locker room, he jumped up, grinning, from the bench he'd been sitting on (the same one where, only two weeks ago, she had caught him smoking a cigarette with DeShawn).

"Paul," she said immediately, "I don't know if we can—"

He silenced her by running up to her and putting a finger to her lips. "Happy birthday," he said, and handed her another piece of paper.

This one looked like a printout of a web page:

You deserve a vacation! Come get away for a weekend at the All Seasons Inn, located in beautiful Lake George. Experience the natural beauty of the Adirondack Mountains, with easy access to lovely campsites, hiking trails, and scenic lakefront. Enjoy the many attractions of the historic, charming town of Lake George, with great dining, shopping, and tourist attractions all at your fingertips!

There was a photo of the inn, a sprawling chalet-style affair, with a phone number and address.

April looked up at Paul. "What is this?"

"It's your birthday present. Many happy returns."

"I don't understand."

"It's where we'll be staying tonight."

"*Tonight?*" said April. "Paul, just tell me what you're thinking, please."

"After I left you last night, I couldn't sleep. I hated leaving you. I couldn't stop thinking about you. So I tried to come up with a way we could be together, at least for a night. I went online and found this. The inn's only a twenty-minute drive from the campsite we're staying at—I checked. So here's what we do: You call Pastor Eric today, now, and tell him you've been doing a lot of thinking the past couple of days. Tell him God is speaking to you, or whatever, and you want to go up to the campsite a night early, to talk to God, to pray and commune, or however you'd put it." She tried to speak, but Paul held up his hand. "He'll totally buy it; you know he will. All you have to do is mention how the Lord is moving you, right? And plus, you deserve it. You do all this for *free*, April. They can't possibly hold it against you if you want to have a night for yourself before the camping trip.

"I'm supposed to bring all the sound equipment from here up

tomorrow morning. What I'll do is bring it up with me tonight when I meet you, and I'll call Jon in the morning and tell him I got up really early and took it, to get a head start. The kids aren't leaving here tomorrow till late in the morning, right?"

April nodded. "Eleven thirty."

"Great! So it's easily a forty-minute drive from here. Think about it, April. That means we have all night and all morning—till noon at least—to *ourselves*, in the mountains, without having to worry about anybody finding us." He placed his hand on her shoulders and squeezed.

April opened her mouth and closed it again. While he was laying out his plan, April found it full of holes, but now she couldn't see any of them. It seemed just about perfect. She was sure she could convince Pastor Eric that she needed a night for herself. The very short notice would only make it that much more convincing, and they would have more than enough time to get to the campsite before noon the next day. They might even order breakfast together. And their chances of running into anyone they knew in Lake George were indeed slim. They would be nobody special, just a couple of anonymous tourists in a town full of other anonymous tourists. But just as she was beginning to get excited for real, something occurred to her. "What about tonight's service, the prophetic ministry? Don't you have to be here to run sound for that?"

For a second, Paul looked at her without understanding. Then his eyes rolled back, and he groaned. "Damn it! *God* damn it! How did I forget about that?"

April couldn't help smiling. "You really aren't the most reliable of employees, are you?"

"And I already missed a Sunday," said Paul. Then he shook his head and shrugged. "Whatever, I'll skip it anyway. If they fire me, they fire me."

"No, Paul, don't be silly," April said. "You're *not* quitting your job." She didn't voice the thought that if he lost this job, he'd have no reason to come to church, which meant that excuses for the two of them to interact would essentially disappear. "The plan can still work," she continued. "The service starts at seven, right? It should be over by nine. So we'll just meet at the inn by ten."

"I'll ditch as soon as I can," said Paul.

April had to smile at his earnestness. She placed a hand on his cheek. "I'm sure you will."

As PAUL HAD PREDICTED, Pastor Eric bought April's claim that the Lord was telling her she needed a night to herself. He said he completely understood, though he did seem a little perplexed by her desire to spend it in the mountains. "You're sure you want to be up there all alone for the night?" he asked her on the phone.

"Well, that's kind of the point," April said, immediately regretting it because it sounded brusque.

"You know our prophetic ministry is this evening," Pastor Eric said. "Maybe it would be good for you to come. Alone time can be healthy, but it's also important to spend time with the rest of the body."

Although she knew there was no way he could suspect anything, April was still eager to be as amicable as possible, to avoid arousing any unwanted curiosity. So she said, "Of course! What I'll do is come to the service tonight and head up to the campsite after."

"Wonderful!" Eric sounded pleased. "I think that'll be good for you."

"Yes," she said. "I do, too."

THE SILENCE IN THE SANCTUARY was so total, April could hear the distant sounds of a baby crying in the nursery, far down the hall on the opposite side of the church. She could hear the bullfrogs outside in the swamp, their deep calls coming in through the open windows. And she could hear the slow, deep breathing of Dr. Langston through his microphone as he stood with head bowed, eyes closed, and his hands on Paul Frazier's shoulders.

Then he lifted his head and, with his eyes still closed, began to speak.

"Lord, it says in your word that your servant Moses wandered the desert for forty years, aimless, without a goal or destination. And it says that when you spoke to him through the burning bush, Moses was reluctant to hear your call. He did not think he was the right man for the job. He thought that you might have made a mistake. But, Lord, we know, *you do not make mistakes.* We know that your plans are bigger than our plans, that your ways are higher than ours.

"And the Lord would say unto my brother here that just like Moses, you have been wandering in your own wilderness, without goal or destination. You have felt lost; you have felt confused; you have felt alone. But the Lord would say unto you, my brother, that just as he did with Moses, he is calling you *out* of that wilderness now and into the plan that he has made for you, thanks be to God, praise Jesus!

"The Lord would have you know that he has prepared a way for you. He has made a plan for you that is greater and more amazing than you have had the faith to imagine. The Lord would say unto you, my brother, that soon, very soon, something is coming. Indeed, maybe it has already arrived but you have yet to recognize it. Something is coming, and this thing will change your life forever. The Lord would encourage you not to be afraid of this thing, not to feel that it is beyond your ability or strength to deal with, because the Lord would remind you—*he* will give you ability, *he* will give you strength, if you have faith and call out to him.

"And the Lord would say unto you, do not be afraid of this thing, though it may be frightening. Do not be confused by this thing, though it may be confusing. It has come from God. It is part of his plan, and what it will do, my brother, is help make you into the person the Lord intended you to be, praise Jesus! It will test you, yes. It will make you work, but through this thing, you will become a great man in the house of God, thank you Jesus. You will become a man of integrity, of wisdom and strength, and you will serve this house; you will serve this church and be a shining example to the body and to the world beyond, praise Jesus.

"This is the Word of the Lord. Praise God."

Dr. Langston took his hands from Paul's shoulders. Paul raised his head and opened his eyes. And this time, it was April who averted her eyes to the floor.

APRIL HAD ALWAYS LIKED TO DRIVE. She enjoyed the motion and the sense of freedom and anonymity it gave her. A long drive gave you a chance to think. But also, if you wanted to, you could empty thoughts from your head, feel the breeze whipping in through the open window, and see the sky spreading out before you like a big blue sea that you were barreling toward. But now, on the last night of her thirties, heading north up the interstate, into the mountains, to Lake George, April found she could hardly stand it. She felt alone in a way that was total and terrifying, as if she would be forced to stay in this car forever, in eternal night, driving down empty, endless stretches of highway. Although it was warm, she felt chilly. The lights from other cars were like beacons when she passed them on the road, but they offered only small comfort. Suddenly, the sense of alone-togetherness of highway driving struck her as weird, even absurd— how so many people could be heading in the same direction, on the same night on the same road, and yet be so completely separated.

She had the sudden memory of being a little girl, taking a long road trip with her family to somewhere. They were on a three-lane highway, her parents arguing in the front, her sister snoring in the back seat beside her, and April, gazing out the window, had locked eyes with a boy sitting in the back seat of a minivan passing them in the left lane. The van had sped past them, but ten minutes later the two vehicles were again side by side. And this time when she and the boy made eye contact, he smiled and she smiled; he waved and she waved. Then the boy had bowed his head for a moment, and when he looked back up he was holding a piece of paper with two words scrawled in black marker: HELP ME.

April had laughed, the boy had laughed, and then the car sped past them and was gone. She knew at the time that it was a joke; they both were laughing. But there were nights afterward when, seized by the irrational fears of preadolescence, she had convinced herself that it wasn't a joke, that the boy had been abducted by horrible people who were taking him somewhere to do horrible things to him, and he'd been trying desperately to get out a message. And April had failed him utterly. *I could have saved him,* she would think, lying in her bed and staring up at the ceiling. *I could have saved him and I didn't. So whatever happens to him, whatever those people do to him, is my fault.* And she would pray, *God forgive me, God forgive me, God forgive me.*

Now, as the dark outlines of the first low mountains loomed closer, April searched for distraction on the radio. She flipped through channels—a newsreel about suicide bombings in Iraq, a country singer claiming he was better off since you left him, and an angry man saying that since taking office in January, Barack Obama was already the worst president this nation had ever seen. When she landed on a Christian station and she heard the voice of a preacher talking in long, honeyed tones about "walking in the light of Christ," she turned off the radio in despair.

After the prophetic ministry service was over, all the congregation had crowded around Paul as if he were some sort of celebrity. "*Great word, Paul!*" they said. "*Amazing word. We're excited for you!*" as if *he* had come up with those words, as if *he* were somehow responsible for it. April had stood in the hallway for a while, a little way apart from everyone, watching him smile and nod at all who wanted to "congratulate" him. And she had noticed another woman standing on the opposite end of the hall, also watching the throng around Paul. But this woman was smiling, with tears in her eyes. The rude shock came when April realized that it was Paul's mother.

APRIL GOT TO THE INN at nine forty-five. Though it was late on a weeknight, the town of Lake George was still bustling with people on the streets, businesses still open, as if she had arrived in the downtown area of a large city and not a small Adirondack tourist town. There was obviously some sort of festival going on. Driving down the street, she had seen more than one collection of bikers on Harleys, and street vendors selling hot dogs and cotton candy.

Waiting in her car in the parking lot of the inn, she watched a family of tourists piling out of their SUV, the mother leading the pack with a toddler sleeping against her chest, and two older kids following, the father behind carrying a cooler and picnic basket. A silver Porsche pulled into the lot, and a young blond couple hopped out. April guessed they were up from the city on vacation. They waltzed into the building with their arms around each other's back, their hands in each other's hip pocket. April hated them for making love look so easy.

Five minutes after ten, and Paul still had not arrived. April drummed her fingers on the steering wheel. By ten fifteen, she didn't know whether to be annoyed or worried, and she kept checking her phone to make sure she had service. They had agreed not to text each other, but a call was permissible if absolutely necessary.

Finally, at ten twenty, she recognized the church pickup truck, pulling into a spot on the opposite end of the lot. April waited till he had parked before she dialed his number.

"April, I'm so sorry," he said when he answered. "It took me forever to get out of there. They basically surrounded me."

"I'm going to go in first and take care of everything," she said. "Once I'm in the room, I'll call and give you the number. Just wait here until then."

"I wanted to pay for the room," he said.

"Don't be silly," she said, and hung up.


Affairs, when April had imagined them, took place in dingy motel rooms with puke-colored carpeting and stains on the sheets. Their room at the inn was large and clean and comfortable and filled with all manner of rustic Adirondack kitsch—exposed beams running across the ceiling, a large stone fireplace on the wall across from the giant bed, a small wood carving of a bear roaring in a corner by the minifridge. Of course, it was preferable to that dingy motel of her imagination, but somehow less romantic.

April sat on the bed and waited, shivering. The AC was turned up too high, but she didn't bother getting up to fix it.

When Paul came in, he flicked on the lights, tossed his bag on the floor, and rushed over to her. "Hey," he said, and sat beside her on the bed and kissed her on the mouth. "You okay?" he asked, pulling away and standing back up as if to assess her.

"Yeah," she said, "I'm fine."

"I'm really sorry about the wait. It took me forever to get out of the church."

"I know," she said. "It's fine. I hardly had to wait at all."

"And I wish you hadn't paid for the room. I wanted to."

"I know you can't afford this, Paul."

"But it's your *birthday*."

April checked her watch. "Not for another hour and fifteen minutes." She reached out to him and used a word she hadn't spoken since her daughter was born: "Now, stop apologizing and fuck me before I'm forty."

AFTERWARD, LYING ON A BED much more comfortable than her own (although she wasn't crazy about the flannel bedspread), April said, "So I guess we should probably talk about what happened to you tonight, huh?"

"Do we have to?" Paul asked. He lay naked beside her, still a little dazed from their lovemaking.

"You don't want to talk about it?"

"I just don't know what to say about it."

April didn't, either, but she felt the need to say something. She wanted to know what Paul actually thought. She placed a hand on his chest. "It was a *good word,* Paul," she said, mimicking the tone of the people in the congregation who had come up to him afterward. She giggled.

"Shut up," he said, laughing, but there was something in his smile that troubled April—she detected an edge of discomfort, as if he wasn't happy with her teasing.

So she pressed on. "Do you feel a new sense of direction now? A sense of the Lord's purpose? No more wandering in the desert for you?"

"Ha, ha," Paul said, sounding vaguely distracted. "I don't know. It's weird, but I sort of did feel ... *something* up there. I've never believed in God—never believed in *anything* like that—but I was thinking afterward, maybe I've been a little unfair. I've always thought of Christians as judgmental and closed-minded, but really, I'm just the same in the other direction. Who am I to say definitively there's no higher power somewhere out there in the cosmos?"

"Not to be a downer," April said, "but you really couldn't have picked a worse time to get converted."

He laughed, and again there was something strained about it. "Come on," he said, "obviously I'm not *converting*. I'm just saying maybe I shouldn't be so judgmental when it comes to other ways of thinking."

"Hmm," April murmured. She was remembering years ago, when, as new members of the congregation, she and Ray had been prophesied over. Most of their word focused on how the Lord had brought them together as a couple and how blessed their marriage would be and how far they would go together.

"I mean, *you* must believe it," Paul said, "or did at one point. Why else would you go there?"

"Yeah," she said almost to herself. "Why else would I?"

There was a long pause, and for the first time since they'd first slept together, the silence was uncomfortable. Finally, Paul said, "You know the Waids? Richard Waid came up to me after the service tonight, asked if I'd be open to giving DeShawn guitar lessons."

"What did you say?"

Lying down, Paul gave an understated version of his signature shrug. "I'm not much of a teacher. They could find someone who'd give him better lessons. But I said I'd try, because I don't think that kid would take lessons from just anybody, but he might from me. And I think learning guitar might be good for him. It definitely helped me when I was his age."

April nodded, but she couldn't help herself. "Maybe that's the 'big thing' the Lord is leading you to—guitar lessons for DeShawn."

This time, Paul didn't even recognize her joke. "No, but seriously, could you imagine being stuck in this town with no one who relates to you? I don't know, maybe I could actually be a good role model to a kid for once."

April looked at the boy beside her, staring up at the ceiling, completely oblivious. It was the same look she'd seen so many times on her ex-husband. It was the same look she'd seen on so many men at church, in town. They had no idea how they sounded. And although April was no prophet, lying on the bed in this Adirondack hotel, she had her own vision. Paul would give this boy guitar lessons. While mixing sound, Paul would start listening to what they said at Sunday service and during Wednesday-night prayer meetings. The clear, simple message of love and grace would have its appeal. People would invite him over to their houses for Sunday dinner, for touch football, for afternoon hiking trips. Paul would be struck by how *nice* everyone was. There would be a girl, someone Paul's age (April could think of a few), beautiful, gentle, Christian. When Paul "gave his heart to the Lord," he would quite genuinely be unable to separate his feelings for the girl and his feelings about religion and would conflate them as one and the same. Paul would find quitting such unsavory habits as drinking and smoking not so hard with such a vibrant and solid support group as the church. Really, there would be only one small snag standing between him and perfect happiness: April. His little secret, his dark spot. The woman twenty years older than he, whom he had slept with when he first came home a mess. Would he confess to the church, blaming it on his confusion, his vulnerability, or would he bury the secret down deep inside him and pray to God she did the same?

April sat up on the bed, letting the sheet fall away from her chest. "Let's go out," she said.

"Out?" he asked, not lifting his head from the pillow.

"We can get drinks."

This made Paul take her seriously. He sat up and tried to read her face. "Do you think that's the best idea, going out in public together?"

"Why not? Are you embarrassed to be seen with me?"

"No! It's just that … I know we're not in Grover Falls, but there's still the slim chance we'd run into someone we know."

April shrugged. "I'm willing to risk it." She got up off the bed, allowing Paul to see her in her full nakedness. "So I'm hopping in the shower, and then you're taking me out for my birthday."

IT WAS A WARM NIGHT, and after their air-conditioned room, April welcomed the heat against her body, her hair slightly damp from the shower. Though it was closing in on midnight, the streets were still filled with people, which only strengthened April's sense of deliberate recklessness—the more people, the greater the sense of anonymity, the more likely you were to be ignored. She and Paul walked down the cobbled sidewalk, past a few touristy stores selling things like "I ♥ NY" T-shirts, scented candles, locally made dream catchers, throw pillows featuring bull moose and black bears. A sad-looking Native American mannequin stood in the window of a gift shop—April didn't quite get what the sales pitch was. The sweet smell of cotton candy and fried dough floated on the air.

After a few minutes, April reached out and grabbed Paul's hand. He looked at her nervously, and she gave his hand a squeeze and pointed up the block, where a long line of people stood around an ice-cream shop. "Come on," she said, pulling him along. "Let's get soft serve."

The shop was called the Twist, and they had to stand in line a good ten minutes behind a dad and his two whining children. April wondered what sort of parent got the kids ice cream at midnight. She decided he was probably divorced and had visitation rights this week.

When they finally reached the window to order, a girl who didn't look much older than Laura, wearing heavy eyeliner and chewing her gum with fierce determination, greeted them. April smiled and asked for a chocolate and vanilla twist in a cone. The girl turned to Paul, nothing in her bored expression acknowledging anything strange about the two of them being together. Paul asked for the same.

"Paul," said April, "don't you know how this works? You're supposed to get a different flavor so we can sample each other's cones." She tousled his hair then turned back to the ice-cream girl. "He's taking me out for my birthday," she said, and as the girl's eyes grew wider, April put her arm around Paul's waist. "I'm turning forty."

"Happy birthday," the girl said, chewing her gum and not even trying to disguise the look of fascinated horror on her face.

Paul gave April a quizzical look, and she smiled back, daring him to say anything.

The girl handed them their cones. "On the house," she said.

As they walked on down the street with their ice cream, April thought about the couple she had seen while waiting in the parking lot of the inn, and drawing Paul close, she tucked her hand in the tight, warm hip pocket of his jeans. She tossed her half-eaten cone in the corner trash can and put her head on Paul's shoulder. She could smell his aftershave and a hint of sweat. People passing by for the most part ignored them, but every now and then they got a strange look.

"April, what are you doing?" Paul's voice sounded stuck somewhere between amusement and alarm.

"I'm just being your girlfriend. Isn't this what boyfriends and girlfriends do? I'm a little out of practice."

"It's just, before, you were worried about anyone finding out about us—understandably. Now, though, it's like you *want* people to know."

"Maybe I'm reassessing the situation. Maybe I don't care anymore."

"But what about your job?"

"We're not doing anything illegal. Besides, it's summer vacation."

"And your church?"

"I've been looking for an excuse to quit doing that Bible school anyway."

"And your kids?"

"They can deal with it. If not, they do have a dad in Buffalo."

"April, come on."

"What?"

"Just be serious for a second."

"I am. Does my new level of commitment to our relationship make you uncomfortable?"

"You're obviously not going to send your kids away for me."

"I'm just pointing out that they have other options if they find my life choices distasteful. Do you know I could never get a dog, because my daughter's allergic? I've *always* wanted a dog."

"So I'm a dog now?"

"Of course not. I'm just saying I'm tired of planning my life around what my kids do and do not approve of. And anyway, I think they'd come around to our side eventually. We'll just have to give them time to adjust. It might be good for them to have a father figure around. You know, a *role model*."

April let go of him and turned to smile at him. He looked utterly lost. She walked quickly on ahead, turning around at the end of the block to see him standing on the sidewalk, staring at her.

"Think about it, Paul—family movie nights, trips to the beach. It could be heaven."

She started laughing and quickly put her hand to her mouth. The warm breeze caressed her face. Paul was looking at her as if she were crazy. Maybe she was. But if the very idea of a future together struck them both as ridiculous, this was not likely to end well.

In that moment, she felt like crying. She looked around her. Down the street to the left, she detected the promising signs of a bar: laughter and boisterous chatter, and a neon sign advertising ice-cold Blue Moon.

"Let's go this way," she said.

A GAGGLE OF BIKERS held half the bar hostage—large men with long beards, clad in denim and leather and bandannas, some still wearing sunglasses despite the late hour. April couldn't help admiring their shamelessness, their complete lack of self-awareness. It was pretty adorable, really. She was grateful for the bikers because it meant she and Paul could sit at a small round table in the corner of the bar, more or less ignored by everyone else.

Paul stared at his glass of beer with a sad look on his face, not touching it, as if the drink held some secret he didn't want to learn.

"What's the matter?" April asked loudly over the music. She took a long sip of her Long Island iced tea.

Paul had balked when she asked him to order her one. "You know how much alcohol is in one of those?" he'd said.

April had assured him she was aware and that, believe it or not, there was a time when she hadn't confined her alcoholic intake to a couple of glasses of wine every other Saturday night. Putting down her drink, she felt it already beginning to work its magic.

Paul sighed. "I guess I just wasn't planning on drinking for a while."

"Really? Why's that?"

"I don't know. I'm not a good person when I drink. I make bad decisions." He took a large gulp of his beer.

It occurred to April that the reason they slept together in the first place was because Paul had been drinking, but she decided not to point this out.

Instead, she said, "My ex-husband, Ray—he never drank, either. A Pepsi man all the way—Mountain Dew if he really wanted to cut loose."

"What does Ray do?"

"He's a carpenter. Builds stuff, tears stuff down."

"I'm guessing he wasn't the best husband."

"Let's just say I have a bias against recently converted young women named Christina."

"Wow. So when did you two—"

"I actually don't feel like talking about my ex right now."

"Sorry, you brought him up."

"Well, now I'm shooing him away. Bye, Ray!" She waved at the window beside them, as if Ray's ghost had slipped through the glass and was now skipping down the dark street. She took another drink of her Long Island. Paul was staring at her with raised eyebrows. "What?" she asked.

"You've just been acting … very different tonight."

April put down her drink. "And you would prefer me another way, right? You would prefer this part of me to stay behind closed doors, in the bedroom, so you can sleep with me whenever you feel like it, but otherwise act like I'm just the annoying old woman from church who makes you run errands sometimes."

"That's not what I said."

"You thought you had things set for a minute, didn't you? You thought you had everything worked out—screwing the Bible school teacher in the morning, being a role model for the town's angry black kid in the afternoon."

"April, what are you *talking* about?"

She leaned forward in her seat and slowly stirred her drink. "Let me ask you this, Paul. Being completely honest, do you actually believe you're really going to help DeShawn by giving him a few guitar lessons, or is this just a quick, easy way to give yourself a little sense of fulfillment?"

The expression of utter confusion on Paul's face was almost comical. "Seriously, I'm lost. I don't know how we ended up talking about DeShawn."

"Well, try to keep up, then," April said, and took another long drink. She felt a stab of tenderness for the boy sitting across the table. He looked so bewildered and caught off guard. This whole thing would have been so much easier if she hadn't ended up liking him so much. If, when he left her alone in her bedroom last night, she hadn't felt a void open inside her. If she had managed to keep him from taking over her mind these past days. If she'd been able to look forward to seeing him just for the sex and hadn't begun to look forward to seeing his smile just as much.

Her vision earlier in their hotel room came back to her. Even if it wasn't likely, that version of Paul's future seemed possible in a way that a future for the two of them just wasn't. But there was a part of her, a very small part of her, that had meant everything she said earlier, on the street. Why *couldn't* they be open about each other? Why *couldn't* he move in? When she fantasized about a happy future with Paul, she didn't see them running away together and starting another life across the country. She saw them—all of them—together in the living room, watching a scary movie: Laura in the armchair, Jason sprawled out on the floor, and her and Paul sitting together on the sofa, the way they had that first night, his arm around her, her head against his shoulder. Why *couldn't* she, in the end, get what she wanted?

"April," Paul said as he swirled the suds around in his nearly empty glass, "do you think, if I'd been born earlier or you'd been born later, if we'd gone to high school together, or college, if we'd met somehow, do you think we'd …" He trailed off, never finishing his question, probably thinking it sounded stupid or pointless.

April sighed and said, "Who knows? It's possible." Then she reached across the table and took Paul's hands in her own and smiled. "But what would be the fun in that?"

The bartender's voice behind them rang out last call. April glanced up at the garish plastic Budweiser clock on the wall above her. She was now forty years old. It was past midnight, but the spell wasn't broken just yet. She would finish her drink in this bar full of bikers. She would take this boy back to the room she had paid for. They would drink the two bottles of wine Paul had brought with him. Then they would make love together drunkenly in the night, and the next morning … the next morning, she could afford to ignore until it was upon her.

# 15

## LAURA

At Camp Lone Eagle, the only place you could get cell phone service was down at the waterfront, by the docks. I wasn't sure why this particular spot was special—it was just as remote as the rest of the camp—but I didn't question it. It was the only balm for what was otherwise sure to be an ugly bruise of a weekend. On Friday, the first night at camp, I had set my alarm for 5 a.m. Usually, not even an earthquake could wake me up before seven, but under the combined annoyances of a thin mattress and Marcy Clemens' snoring, I hardly slept at all. When the alarm went off at dawn on Saturday, I shot right up, turned it off, and looked around me.

I hadn't woken anyone else. All nine girls and the other counselor were still sleeping in their bunks along the cabin walls. Turning onto my stomach so that my legs dangled over the side of the top bunk, I dropped as lightly as I could, my bare feet hitting the cold concrete of the cabin floor with barely a sound. I slipped into my flip-flops and grabbed my dad's old sweatshirt from where I'd hung it up on the post last night. I used to dread these camping trips because of the lack of privacy. Before seeing anyone besides my immediate family, I wanted time to assess the damage—the frizz level of my hair, check for any new zits. Just a few weeks ago, the only reason I would have forced myself to get up this early was so I would have the showers all to myself. But things were different now. I no longer cared whether people saw how I looked after just rolling out of bed—or, more accurately, I no longer cared whether *these* people saw me.

Outside, the sky was already brightening, the air already hinting at the heat to come. I heard birds singing and cicadas droning. Soon the air would be thick and heavy, and this now empty camp would be swarming with loud, wild kids. I wished I could freeze the day here and stay in perpetual early morning. I stepped outside the cabin door and looked around. To my right were two more cabins, where the rest of the girl campers were bunked. To my left, across a field of gravel, were the big rec hall and the bathrooms, and behind these, near the edge of the forest, the three boys' cabins. Across from the rec hall, in a grove of pines just before the ground began its descent toward the lake, stood the long, low structure of the dining hall, which also doubled as our sanctuary for the evening worship rallies. Last night, the campsite had been filled with the din of the worship band and kids screaming out their love for Jesus, the noise spilling out from the open dining hall windows and into the Adirondack night, no doubt striking fear in the heart of every woodland critter within a mile radius.

I walked toward the dining hall. The lights were on. They had already started prepping for breakfast. My mom was probably in there, too, getting a head start on her day. She was always the first one up. I could picture her sitting at a table with her notebook and a giant mug of coffee. I hurried past, not wanting to be seen. If I did run into anyone, I would merely say I was going down to the lake to check my phone before showering—which was, in fact, exactly what I was doing.

Past the rec hall, a dirt path led through the woods to the waterfront. I walked down it, barely noticing the birds chattering in the trees around me, or the deep, damp smells of pine and spruce, moss and mushrooms and fallen leaves. And when I got to the beach, I didn't really stop to admire the way the early sun glinted off the silvery surface of the water, creating thousands of little diamonds, or how the lake stretched out before me for what seemed like miles, finally stopping against the deep green of the pines on the far shore. I just sat down on the sandy beach, which was still a little damp, and pulled my phone from my pocket.

Even though I knew that it would be there waiting for me, I still felt a little tingle of excitement upon seeing I had a message from Martin on my mobile MatchUp app.

It was short, and I read through it quickly, then reread it, as I always did.

He asked me how things were going running the camp. He asked jokingly whether I was surviving. He asked how I was making out on *The Good Soldier,* a book he had recommended. He couldn't wait to talk to me about it in person. He told me he'd been thinking about me a lot—at work, at home, when he went to bed. He was counting the days until September. He couldn't wait to meet me. Reading these last words, I felt goose bumps rise on my arms.

As a postscript, he'd sent me a link to an article he was telling me about the other day, about how honeybees were disappearing, just vanishing inexplicably from hives all over the world. This might have seemed incompatible with the rest of the message, but for a while now Martin had been going on about climate change, saying young people shouldn't have kids or worry about the future, because within the next hundred years the planet was doomed. He sent me articles backing up this theory. These things scared me, and I told him so, but of course I didn't tell him it was because I was only fifteen and, thus, probably had more time left on this planet than he. So I said I worried about my kids.

The mosquitoes began to hover and whine around me, so I pulled my hood up as I wrote back. After every sentence, I paused to assess and keep track of my lies.

I told him that running the camping trip was one giant headache, as usual, and it was becoming harder and harder for me to remember why I ever agreed to do this in the first place. I was ready to stop for good. Because of camp, I hadn't really had time to read, but soon I would start the book. (In truth, I had borrowed *The Good Soldier* from the library more than a week ago, when Martin first recommended it, but the book had stumped me. It just seemed so slow and meandering. I'd decided I would read up on the SparkNotes before we met in person.) I told Martin I had been thinking about him a lot, too, that it was strange how close I felt to him given that we'd never met, and that I, too, was waiting impatiently for September.

It was strange, yes, how intimately we wrote to each other, but since about a week ago, when I told Martin I wanted to meet, things had quickly gotten heavier between us. He had given an enthusiastic yes—he was ready to meet anytime. I was the one who proposed the first of September, since that was the day the youth group would go down to Albany for the antiabortion rally.

So what was I thinking, going down in person to meet Martin, who thought I was a forty-year-old high school math teacher named Kim Moore, divorced with two kids? What, exactly, did I expect to happen when he saw a fifteen-year-old with frizzy red hair and freckles, who didn't even have a driver's license? How did I expect him to respond? The short answer was, I had no idea. I understood that when he found out the person he'd been corresponding with online for the past year was under eighteen, a host of legal ramifications would arise, and his first reaction might be simply to run—flee the scene, delete his account, and deny that anything had ever happened. Certainly, it was doubtful that after we met he would want to continue talking to me online, never mind seeing me in person ever again.

So why was I knowingly sabotaging a relationship (or whatever this was) that had become so important to me? I guess I knew I would have to at some point. It couldn't last forever. What was I supposed to do? Keep putting off meeting him till I really *was* forty?

But there was another reason, a deeper one—the one that I think had ultimately incited me to open my laptop that night and tell him we should meet. I wanted him to know me. *Me*, not some fake identity I had created online. I wanted to look Martin in the eyes and say, *this* is who you've been talking to all this time; *this* is the person you find so interesting, so incredible. But it wasn't as if I would be shedding Kim Moore the way you take off a disguise, throwing her away. No, I wanted to make Martin see that I *was* Kim Moore, that really, if he could understand it, in a way, I hadn't lied to him at all. I hadn't created a fake identity, so much as a *new* one. I was both Laura and Kim, if only he could see it. And I let myself hope in the possibility that he might, if he just sat across from me long enough to try.

Still, that was all abstract—what would *actually* happen when we met was something I couldn't begin to predict, and I didn't try. I was ready for anything.

THE NIGHT I TOLD MARTIN I wanted to meet, I was drunk, still reeling after my walk back from Ian's house. Immediately after typing the words, I had suddenly felt cold, though it was a warm night. Maybe I really was coming down with whatever my mom had. I got off my bed and went to my closet, looking for something to throw over my tank top. With a head full of bourbon, I had pulled out my dad's old sweatshirt advertising the construction company he used to work for. He had left it years earlier when he moved out, and I kept it in the back corner of my closet, for no particular reason I could name. Honestly, when I first took it out, it was only because, in my inebriated state, I thought it looked comfortable and warm. And that is about the last thing I recall doing before I fell drunkenly down on my bed, with the laptop still open in front of me.

The next morning, I had woken to a nasty headache and Martin's reply: *Yes, we should meet. When? Where?* I didn't regret what I'd done, but I waited till that evening to respond. After nailing down the date, Martin and I had chatted online until long after midnight, our words growing more and more intimate, laced with hidden meaning and things not explicitly said. After we finally said good night and I logged off my account, I felt warm and excited. My hangover was gone, and the bad feeling from what happened with Ian the night before had been replaced with thoughts of Martin. But I wasn't ready to sleep. I was restless. I remained on my bed, in gym shorts and hoodie, staring at my laptop screen. I opened Facebook, but all the photos and updates from the same old people seemed mind-numbingly dull, and I closed it. I checked my email, but there were no new messages. I thought about looking up some of the bands I'd seen on Ian's wall that awful evening, but I decided that if Ian listened to them, then I didn't want to. He was just a boy, and I was through with boys. I opened a new online search.

In the search bar, I typed in "Porn" and clicked ENTER.

I'd never searched for pornography online before. Of course I'd seen snippets of it, mostly old 1970s stuff full of sleazy saxophone music and unreasonably tan men and women. I knew that all guys watched porn online—probably even my little brother at this point—but I'd never actually looked for it, so I wasn't sure exactly what to expect.

My breath caught when I clicked on the first link. For a second, I thought I'd just clicked on a virus: the page was black and red, and words like "anal" and "titties" flashed across the screen. On one corner of the page, a flashing box invited me to "Meet Horny Singles in My Area," and I saw a girl who didn't look much older than I was, touching herself and pushing out her lips. But what really grabbed my attention was the penis. It was huge and hard and red and didn't seem to be attached to anything, as if it were its own entity, and it seemed to be coming out of the screen. Soon, it would burst through my computer and land on my lap, flopping around like a stranded fish. I reeled back, revolted, and a second later, without even closing the page, I slammed my laptop shut.

For a long time, I just sat on my bed, looking at my closed laptop, the image of the penis engraved in my vision, like one of those floaters in the eye that move around when you blink. Then I opened my laptop again. I went quickly back to the web and tried a different site at random. Again the flashing images, the ads, a GIF of a man fucking a woman in the ass. But I tried to ignore all of it and scrolled down the page to the videos, each one displaying a man and a woman (sometimes more), in various sexual positions. Just to avoid looking at the GIF on the sidebar, I clicked on a video and let it fill up the screen, blocking out all else.

It was filmed in the gym of what looked like someone's house, and the storyline was that this young, hot guy was feeling out of shape (ironically), and his best friend's shapely blond wife had come over to teach him some yoga positions. I knew people didn't watch porn for the story, but the ridiculousness of the dialogue and the artificiality of the acting still made me giggle. I was interested, though, curious to see how their flirting and not-so-subtle physical contact as they went about their yoga session would lead to all-out sex. There was no transition to speak of. I wasn't prepared. One moment she was showing him the downward dog, the next she had his dick in her mouth. Again with the penises! I shut my laptop.

Over the next few days, I had watched a lot of porn. Always at night. Always after I was done chatting with Martin. But it wasn't as if I were getting sexual pleasure out of it. No, I was watching the videos as a kind of research. I studied their faces as they did it, the way the men's features would grow coarse and red and ugly, as if they were lifting something really heavy or pushing something into the ground, the way the women would roll their eyes back or close them, and sometimes tear up, especially if they were getting fucked from behind. When they screamed and moaned, I listened for signs of faking, and generally detected it. I especially liked to watch the people's interactions leading up to the sex. It was strange, but in the short time it took them to take off their clothes before the fucking, they always seemed so awkward and nervous around each other, sometimes even frightened, as if looking into each other's eyes and talking were the scariest thing about this whole experience.

There was no arousal for me, though—at least, not while I watched. But afterward, when I had shut off my computer and lay back in bed, images from the videos would follow me, like ghosts, into my dreams. I would hear the moans and cries of pleasure and roll over onto my stomach and think about Martin.

SITTING THERE ON THE BEACH, I tried to read the article Martin had sent me about the vanishing bees, but I found it hard to concentrate, especially with the mosquitoes buzzing around my face, which also made it hard to sympathize with any insect, bees included, however dire the consequences.

I walked back to camp with Martin's words in my brain and headed to the showers. I didn't bother washing my hair—just stood under the hot water and sprayed off, using an old bar of soap. Last year, this would have been unthinkable, but now, since I no longer cared what any of these people thought of me, I didn't see the point in trying to keep myself looking any better than merely presentable while at this horrible camp. I just wanted to get out of these gross showers as fast as I possibly could.

By the time I stepped out of the bathrooms, the camp was stirring— kids emerging from their cabins and hiving off in different directions, some to the dining hall, others to the rec hall. Most of the girls headed straight to the showers, coming in twos and threes in their flip-flops, bath towels draped over their shoulders and shower caddies in hand. Standing outside the entrance, I could feel the sun beating down on me. Soon, the heat would settle down over everything like a vast steaming blanket. Even so, I pulled my sweatshirt on.

HALF AN HOUR LATER, everyone was gathered in the dining hall for breakfast. Long tables were set up in rows along either wall, stretching the length of the room. And at the front of the room, before the kitchen, two tables were set up buffet style, crammed with trays of food. Going up to get breakfast, I saw my mom sitting on a stool in a corner before the kitchen entrance, with a mug of coffee and her notebook, looking distracted, just as I had imagined. After giving the buffet the once-over, I put down my paper plate, poured myself a cup of orange juice, and took it back to an empty corner of a table at the far end of the room.

I watched kids load up their plates with mounds of rubbery yellow eggs, stubby brown sausage links, and giant pancakes doused in fake maple syrup. Ten-year-old Samantha Willard took a seat across from me. Watching her bite into a sausage link, I couldn't help thinking of a penis, and then of Samantha giving a blow job to the nearest one, which happened to belong to Ethan, sitting beside her. What was wrong with me? I tried to shake the image out of my head. The smell of eggs made me think of the article Martin had sent me a few days ago about factory farm conditions—how chickens got their wings clipped and their beaks cut off and were crammed together in tiny cages, so they couldn't even move, and were pumped with hormones. I felt sick. I took a drink of my orange juice and grimaced. It tasted sour and bitter, like vomit.

That's when Bethany appeared in front of me.

I had been pretty much ignoring Bethany since Ian told me about her. It started with her texts, which I didn't answer. And then, when she'd seen me in person at church and asked me why, I shrugged and told her I just hadn't felt like it and hadn't really thought she would notice anyway.

"What is *that* supposed to mean?" she asked.

When I shrugged in reply, something had crept across Bethany's face that made me want to slap her.

She said, "This is about Nola, isn't it?"

"It must be, since with you, *everything's* about Nola now."

"Laura, don't be so dramatic. You're still my best friend, and it's not my fault if you won't talk when she's around, that you avoid us and never want to do anything."

"Maybe I don't feel like being your third wheel. But then, since you never ask my opinion about anything, how would you know? With you, it's always *The Bethany Moyer Show*, written by, directed by, and starring Bethany Moyer."

I'd been proud of that one, which I made up on the spot, and it had made her angry. "Fine," she snapped. "Let me know when you're done being such a baby."

"Let me know when you're done being such a bitch," I had muttered back, but if she heard me, she didn't acknowledge it.

Now here she was, in the dining hall. "Hey," she said, "wanna come sit with us?" It was more of an accusation than a question, since she already knew I would decline.

"I'm fine here, thanks," I said.

She made her eyes big and looked at me imploringly. "How long are you gonna be like this, Laura? Let's stop now, okay?"

Standing there, I couldn't help noticing how beautiful she looked—even more than usual. The summer sun had tanned her skin a deep brown, and her hair was full and glossy. I could see the shape of her breasts under her black tank top. I examined her as if she were an interesting piece of modern art or a brightly colored bug and didn't answer.

Finally, she turned away, and the look she gave me—more hurt than angry—did make me feel guilty for a while.

I GOT OVER MY GUILT about two hours later, after morning devotion, when we all went down to the lakefront so the campers could swim or use the two Jet Skis the church had rented for the weekend. I stood back from the beach, in the shade of a few tall pines, and watched Bethany and Nola. They were in their bathing suits, walking into the water together, practically holding hands. Then, when they had inched their way in up to their waists, I watched Nola suddenly grab Bethany by the waist and pull her under the water with a splash. They came back up laughing, spitting out water and still clinging to each other.

I was relieved when Lydia Newman ended the spectacle by asking Bethany to man one of the Jet Skis and give the younger campers rides out on the lake. When Lydia approached me by the trees, I knew she was going to ask me to do the same. I shook my head. "I'd rather not."

Lydia frowned. "Well, Laura, you *are* a team leader, so it would be really great if you helped out here."

"It's against my beliefs," I said.

Lydia's wide face looked confused. "Against your beliefs? How?"

"Jet Skis are a first-world luxury that uses finite natural resources for no purpose other than pointless recreation. Therefore, they are inherently wasteful and harmful to the environment."

Lydia stared at me and I stared back, silently vowing that I would never let myself grow to look like her when I was her age. Then she sighed. "Fine, but will you at least take the younger kids out in one of the canoes? Those aren't powered by any resource but your arms." She smirked. She had outsmarted me, but I tried hard not to show it.

I feigned indifference. "Sure."

"Make sure the kids are wearing life jackets," she said as she walked away.

I hadn't wanted to spend the rest of my morning ferrying kids around the lake in an old canoe, but once I was out on the water, I couldn't deny that it was peaceful away from the screaming kids on the beach, and the Jet Skis roaring across the other end of the lake. My argument against them had been to get out of a job, but as I watched them speed across the water I did feel a sense of almost righteous indignation. Those things really were obnoxious: the noise they made, scaring away all the birds and wildlife, the stinky blue smoke, and all the gas they guzzled just so people could feel a brief sensation of speed. It was stupid. People were greedy and thoughtless.

After half an hour or so of giving kids lackluster canoe rides, my arms were aching and I was sweating hard. I rowed my last ten-year-old passenger back to shore, and there was Nola, standing on the dock as if she'd been waiting for me.

The boy took off his life jacket and wobbled out of the canoe and onto the dock, and she was still staring at me.

"What!" I snapped.

"Row me out to yon space of empty water, oh, ferrywoman?" she asked me, grinning.

I'd never seen Nola smile so wide. It almost scared me. She was wearing a T-shirt over her bathing suit, with "The Breeders" across the front. Probably another band I was clueless about. Her legs were bare and her dark hair was wet and gleamed in the sun.

"I'm done," I said. "You can have the canoe if you want."

"Nice try." She clambered aboard without tipping us over, and before I could do anything about it, she had pushed us off from the dock. "We're going sailing together."

Grudgingly I began to paddle. As we moved out into the water, I stayed silent and listened to the distant sounds of the Jet Ski motors, the kids laughing and screaming on the beach, and the gnats humming around our heads. Brushing them away from her face, Nola looked at me as if I were some puzzle she was trying to solve. A funny one, apparently, because a smile lurked around the corners of her mouth.

Finally, I couldn't take the silence and her strange looks any longer. "What?" I asked, pulling in my paddle and letting the canoe drift. By now we were far out in the water, where nobody on shore could hear us.

"Nothing," Nola said. "It's just … you don't *look* like a bitch, so that's puzzling."

"What are you talking about?"

"Well, what would *you* call someone who suddenly stops talking to their best friend for no reason?"

"Don't even," I said. "You don't know anything about us."

She shrugged. "Maybe I don't. But I do know that she's really upset. Bethany misses you a lot, Laura. You've really hurt her."

Again I felt that small stab of guilt. But counteracting it was the irritating way Nola talked about Bethany—so protective and possessive—

and the image of them laughing in each other's arms in the water earlier. Bethany hadn't looked so upset then.

"And I know why you won't talk to her," Nola continued, "even if Bethany won't admit it. It's because of me, because you don't like me."

"It's not because of you," I said.

"Of course it is. You don't like me, Laura, admit it. I rock the boat too much for you, don't I?"

"I don't even know what you're talking about."

Nola smiled and began to sway from side to side. "I rock the boat too much. That's it, isn't it?"

"Let's just go back to shore," I said, dipping the paddle back into the water.

But now Nola was moving rhythmically to and fro, getting some momentum and making the canoe tip more and more. She was singing now: "*Rock the boat, don't rock the boat, baby, rock the boat, don't tip the boat over ...*"

"Nola, stop it!" I snapped.

"*So I'd like to know where you got the notion ...*"

"Nola!" I shouted, as the canoe swayed more violently.

"*Said I'd like to know where you got the notion ...*"

I let go of the paddle and grabbed on to the sides of the canoe, trying to counter Nola's movements but actually making things worse.

"*To rock the boat, don't rock the boat baby, rock the boat, don't tip the boat over ...*"

And then it happened. She leaned too far to the left, and our canoe capsized. I screamed but stopped short when my open mouth filled with water. Cold hit me. For a second, I was sinking into blackness, my body slow to respond. Then my arms and legs started working together. I swam out from under the canoe and broke through the surface into the sunlight. Nola was hanging on to the overturned craft and laughing, her hair wet and dripping. I grabbed on beside her. "What the hell is wrong with you!" I shouted, spitting out lake water.

"I'm sorry," she laughed. "I tried to resist the temptation."

I didn't know what to do. I was so angry. I looked at her in disbelief.

But then she put a wet arm around my shoulder. "Come on, Laura," she said, giving me a squeeze. "Live a little."

Her touch made my arm hair stand on end, or maybe it was just the sudden cold of the water. Knowing what I knew about Nola, in that moment I couldn't help but wonder, did she find me at all attractive? But if Bethany was her type, then I couldn't possibly be. Still, with her arm around me, which she had not yet removed, I felt disoriented. We stayed like that for a moment, her arm around me, and me almost leaning into her, resting my body against hers, both of us bobbing in the open water. The sun beat against our faces, and I could hear the kids on the beach and a gull complaining as it flew overhead. Then I pushed away from her and swam for shore. I heard her calling after me to stop. I didn't.

After a few minutes, I felt my arms begin to tire. My breath came in short gasps, and the shore didn't look much closer.

"Laura," Nola called. "Come help me right this."

I kept swimming. I had a pain in my side, and I paddled with one arm, in a modified sidestroke, dipping beneath the surface and coming back up, spitting out water as I began to gasp for breath. *This is it,* I thought. *I'm gonna drown.* Land looked unattainable, and the water kept pulling me down.

At last, one of my scissor kicks hit sand and gravel. Panting and gasping, I waded onto the shore and collapsed onto the sand. A minute later, Nola pulled the canoe up onto the shore and then came and lay down beside me, as if we were friends, as if we'd just gone through something together.

"*Phew,*" she said, still breathing heavily. "Where's Jesus when you need him—when walking on water would actually have been helpful!"

I sat up, and for a second I almost smiled, almost replied amicably, but then I felt a weight in my pocket—a small rectangular weight. "I can't believe you," I muttered.

"Huh?" She hadn't a clue.

I stood up and pulled my soaked phone out of my pocket. "See this?" I shouted, waving it in her face. "See what you've done? See what you've ruined?"

Nola's mouth dropped open. "Laura, I'm sorry," she said. "I didn't know you had that with—"

I cut her off. I was nearly screaming now, not caring that everyone on the beach—all the kids and team leaders—were staring at us now. "Just stay away from me! You stupid, selfish, thoughtless ... *bitch*!" I ran up the beach toward the path and practically collided with Jon Newman.

AFTER I HAD CHANGED out of my soaked clothing and dried myself off, after I'd confirmed for certain that my phone was ruined, I went into the dining hall, to a small back room that served as an office. Jon had told me to come there when I was ready, and I had expected to find my mom there, too, sitting in one of the old armchairs, shock and disappointment on her face after hearing of my outburst. But when I came in, it was only Jon. He asked me to sit down.

I flopped down in the chair across from him and looked at the floor, ignoring his searching gaze.

"What's going on, Laura?" he asked at last. It was clear from how he put the question that he hoped I would open up to him, that he hoped he could become my confidant, guiding me through my adolescent angst. I tried not to laugh. "There's clearly something bothering you," he continued when I didn't answer. "Maybe you'll feel better if you get it off your chest."

I kept my eyes on the floor. I was thinking about how I would explain my lack of contact to Martin when I got home on Sunday afternoon. I decided I would tell him more or less the truth: a canoe I was on had capsized, and my phone was ruined. I just hoped that in the meantime he didn't grow too worried about me.

"Laura?" Jon leaned forward in his seat, trying to lock eyes with me.

I sighed and looked up at him. "Just tell me what my punishment is, okay?"

"I want to help you, Laura. But I can't if you don't tell me what's wrong."

"I'm fine," I said.

He leaned back in his seat, scratched at his chin, and gave me an assessing look. "How are you and Bethany doing? I couldn't help but notice you two haven't really been hanging out together the way you normally do."

*Of course you noticed,* I thought, *because you watch Bethany the way a dog watches over his bone.*

"Did you and Bethany have a fight?" he pressed.

"How is that any of your business?" I asked.

"I'm just trying to—"

"And how did this become about Bethany?" I interrupted. "Just because *you* want to screw her doesn't mean we're all equally obsessed with the pastor's daughter." The words were out of my mouth before I could swallow them. But seeing the shocked look on Jon's face, I didn't regret what I'd said. I felt a surge of heat roll through me and leaned forward. "Jon, I know the things you think about Bethany. It's right there in your eyes every time you look at her. But don't worry, your secret's safe with me."

I touched his hand, and he jerked it away as if I were possessed by a demon. I began to giggle uncontrollably and sank back in my seat. For a moment, Jon looked as if he was going to be sick. Then he stood up and walked out of the room.

"Where are you going?" I called after him, still laughing. "I thought you wanted to talk."

# 16

BEN

Nobody wanted to talk about what had happened during the worship rally on Saturday night. The second it was over, everybody rushed out of the dining hall to the back field, for the midnight game of capture the flag.

The game was a VBS tradition. We divided the giant field behind the rec hall in half—six tribes took one side and six took the other. Everyone played, even the team leaders. The game could go on for hours, way into the night.

I wasn't a fan. On my first year of camp, I'd been guarding the flag when a bunch of older kids charged our field and rushed me. They had taken our flag and brought it back to their side, winning the game before I could even yell out for help. Of course, I got blamed for losing the game, and ever since that year, I had a simple strategy: wander into the other team's territory as soon as possible and get caught. You got to spend the rest of the game sitting in the other team's "jail," a marked-off square at the back of the field near the woods, without any responsibilities, watching everybody else run around in the dark, shouting and acting like morons. It was almost relaxing, like how I imagined people on drugs must feel.

Tonight, Haley Thomas was the "jailer," which meant she had the job of guarding the prisoners. I was the only one who'd been caught. I could tell she really wanted to be up front, where the action was, not stuck in the back of the field with me.

So I did my best to annoy her. Haley was hot, and if she didn't want to be around me, I was going to make sure it was for an actual reason. That way, I could pretend it wasn't just because she thought I was totally lame. I turned up my phone as loud as it would go and rapped along with Eminem. It wasn't long before Haley groaned and shouted, "Okay, I'm *so* done with this. Somebody else has to be jailer now."

In the darkness, I could make out Ryan Fletcher, their team's captain, coming over. He was only a few years older than me but already had muscle definition in his arms and had even started shaving. I never liked him.

He checked his phone. "You're on duty for another ten minutes."

"Forget it," said Haley. "Aren't we supposed to be having *fun*?" She put her hand on her hip and leaned to her right, the way girls do when they want to look cute and dangerous at the same time. I could see Ryan trying to decide whether he should give in or try using his authority. (Which would a hot girl like better?) He looked at me and smirked. "I guess it wouldn't be such a major catastrophe if this one got away."

"Right?" said Haley. "I'm a wasted resource right now."

I was about to say that I could hear them, when a new voice chimed in. "I'll be jailer."

We looked over and saw my cousin Becca standing near, watching us. Even at camp, in the heat, she wore her ankle-length skirt and long-sleeved T-shirt.

"Great," Ryan said, not really looking at her. He and Haley both hurried away toward the front line, excited to be where everyone else was and away from both of us.

Becca came and stood by the edge of the jail, arms folded across her chest. I turned off Eminem.

"You got caught pretty early," she said.

"I guess my heart's not really in the game," I said.

My cousin flopped down on the grass across from me. "Me, either," she said. She started pulling up stalks of grass in front of her and breaking them in half.

There was a sudden commotion near the front line—laughing and shouting that died down again quickly. Someone must have tried to cross the line. I hesitated a second and then said in a rush, "It was really cool what you said before, during worship."

Becca looked up from the ground. "Really?"

I nodded.

I guess I shouldn't have been surprised about what had happened. For a while now, anytime I saw my cousin, she reminded me of a bomb ready to go off. It was all because of the protein-bar incident at VBS the other week. Ms. Swanson had been home sick that day, so it was Lydia Newman who discovered that Becca was selling the bars without permission during VBS. She'd called Becca's mother to investigate. My aunt had been furious—drove straight to the church and came storming across the field, searching for her daughter. It turned out those bars hadn't been Becca's to sell.

In the middle of the field, in front of everyone, my aunt had laid into Becca: "What are you thinking, taking things that don't belong to you? That's stealing, Becca! *Stealing!*"

Becca had already been close to tears. "But, Mom, it's for the orphans—"

My aunt had shaken her head. "I don't want to hear it! There's no excuse for what you did."

Becca was crying for real then. "I just wanted to feed the children. They don't have enough food and—"

"Did you ever think that maybe *we* don't have any food, Becca? Did you ever think your dad and I work so hard every day, and *this* is what you do? You're in big trouble. Wait till your father hears about this!"

She had grabbed Becca by the arm and marched her across the field to their car. Becca had her face in her hands, sobbing. It was not a good look. After they left, nobody knew what to say, so we all just pretended like it hadn't happened.

Later, the whole story came out: The protein bars were part of an online business venture my aunt was taking part in. The company that made the bars had shipped a ton of boxes to my aunt, and she sold them door-to-door, getting a cut of the profits. That was how Becca had been able to smuggle so many—there were boxes and boxes of them sitting in their kitchen. There was no actual connection to any Haitian charity. Becca had just been saving the small amount of money she'd raised so far in her sock drawer, planning on sending it to the charity when she'd raised enough. Of course, her parents seized the money.

It was all pretty dumb and sad, but I felt bad for Becca. When I saw her the next day at the VBS, her eyes were red and her face kind of wooden. I wanted to tell her something, but I didn't know what. Plus, if the guys saw me talking to her, the jokes would start up again. In some ways, she'd done me a favor—everyone had already forgotten about the fight between DeShawn and me and were now talking about the weird girl who stole protein bars from her mom. Nothing helps people forget your stupidity like someone else doing something stupider.

Eventually, people would have forgotten, but Becca didn't do herself any favors. Even though she didn't have anything to sell now, she kept talking about the Haitian orphans and giving people that Michael Keegan guy's flyer. Pretty soon, everyone was avoiding her.

So, in a way, what happened tonight had been building for a while. It had been near the end of the worship rally, when just Jon Newman was strumming softly on his guitar, and the rest of the band were sitting quietly on their stools or amps. We all knew what was coming next—it was the same every year—but the way Jon spoke, you'd think it had never happened before. He closed his eyes and told us he felt that the Lord was speaking to him, that there were kids who had words on their heart God wanted them to share, so if anyone felt God urging them to say something, just to raise your hand and Jon would pass the mike around.

This was always the worst part of the rally. It took forever, and you had to stand there, rocking back and forth on your aching feet. You could sit down with your head bowed and your eyes closed so it looked like you were praying privately, but that was risky. Somebody might come up and lay a hand on your shoulder, asking if you'd like them to pray for you. That's not like being asked if you want seconds at dinner—it's not something you can just turn down with a polite "No, thank you."

Last year, I had to sit there silently as Lydia Newman prayed over me for what felt like an hour. "Lord Jesus, we just thank you for Benjamin.

We just thank you that you've set his feet on a clear path, that you've prepared a way for him. Help him see your plan for his life, Lord Jesus."

I'd pressed my thumbs into my closed eyelids until my forehead throbbed. When Lydia began to run out of things to say, she stopped and asked me if I was sure there wasn't something specific I wanted prayer for. "Just like … being a good Christian and stuff," I'd mumbled.

So this year, I'd been wise enough to keep standing for the entire rally, near the back of the hall with the guys, ignoring my aching feet, sweating in the hot and stuffy room and silently cursing every time another kid decided God was telling them something everyone else needed to hear. Danielle Martin was first. She went on and on, teary-eyed, about how Jesus just wanted to tell everyone in the room how much he loved them, and if you weren't feeling the love of Christ right now, it wasn't because of him, it was because of *you*. Sin separated us from the love of Christ, and all we had to do to get back to his love was confess our sin to him, and he would forgive us. "Jesus," she sobbed, "just wants you to know that he loves you so-o-o-o much. All he wants to do is take you in his arms and show you how much he loves you, but you have to *let* him. You have to give in to *his* love."

Everyone clapped and shouted, "Amen!" and "Thank you, Jesus," and then Ryan raised his hand a little bashfully. When Jon handed him the mike, he cleared his throat and said in his low voice, "I just feel like God wants to tell us not to be afraid. We worry about so many things now, like our future, how we look to other people, what we're gonna do with our lives. And God just wants to say, 'Don't worry. Don't be afraid. I'm here, and I'm gonna take care of you. All you have to do is put your faith in me.'"

This was a cheap word, and I knew why Ryan had given it. As we got older, most of the girls at church got into boys that seemed really spiritual and gave public testimonies and prayers. It made them seem deep and mature or something. Ryan had probably made that little speech up a few seconds before raising his hand. I'd thought a few times about doing it, too. I imagined giving this amazing, spiritually convicting word that would have everyone on the floor, crying, and afterward they'd all look at me differently, including Bethany. But I knew I could never go through with it. Just the thought of speaking publicly into the microphone made my heart start pounding. I would have stood there stammering and sweating until I collapsed or threw up.

I looked around the room after Ryan gave his word. A lot of girls were nodding with tears in their eyes. *Seriously?* I couldn't believe they'd bought that BS. But there was one girl who didn't seem to care, or even notice, and that was Bethany. She was in the corner of the room, near the back, sitting next to Nola, who, at this point, I was pretty sure was her new best friend. They sat really close to each other on one of the benches, their shoulders practically touching. Nola had one hand on Bethany's knee. They weren't paying attention to anything else going on. I decided they must be praying on their own.

Somebody coughed into the mike. I turned and saw Becca standing with the microphone in her hand, with Jon Newman behind her, looking a little nervous. Of course, he couldn't refuse to let her speak, but since the protein-bar thing, even the team leaders were a little uneasy around her.

For a second, Becca just stood there, staring at all of us while we waited for her to say something. Then she spoke. "I just want to say, it's great what we're doing here tonight, praising Jesus, and everything. It's great that there are so many of us who want to follow him, serve him, use our lives for his glory. But I just want to say, if you're serious about all the things you've said, if you believe the words to all the songs we just sang, then maybe you should think about taking it one step further.

"There are so, so many people out there in the world who need our help. They aren't worried about where they'll go to college or getting the new iPhone. They're worried about if they'll be able to find anything to eat tomorrow, if they will have access to clean water. We all just ate a huge meal. You probably didn't even think twice about it; you probably didn't even think twice about taking a second hamburger or helping of baked beans. There are kids out there who've never even *seen* that much food in one place before."

Everyone was quiet as Becca talked. And it was weird, but somehow I could feel that it was a different kind of quiet from the one Danielle and Ryan had gotten. This one was uncomfortable. Jon looked like he wanted to step in and take the mike away, but since Becca wasn't saying anything *wrong* or *untrue,* he couldn't.

"My parents keep telling me I shouldn't make people feel guilty," Becca continued, "but now I'm thinking, why not? Why *shouldn't* we feel guilty? Did you know there's more commands in the Bible to feed the hungry than just about anything else? Did you? So yeah, maybe we should feel guilty. But the cool thing is, we can help. Instead of spending our money on another video game or pair of jeans, we can donate to charities that help these people in need. And when we turn eighteen, we can go *work* at these charities that help. We don't *have* to go to college; we don't *have* to live in America. We can do good in the world. We can serve Jesus, just like we promised we would in all those songs we sang."

Jon took a step toward her but didn't actually try to take the microphone away. It looked like he was hoping she'd just hand it to him. But Becca seemed to panic. She looked at Jon, then back at the rest of us, who were all watching her wide-eyed. And then her face got hard and angry.

"I know none of you will, though," she said. "I know none of you actually *believe* those songs, or if you do, you just think it's talking about being nice and happy and getting married and having kids and going to church, and maybe it is, but what's the point of that? What's the point? We just dance around to music while kids our age are starving. We just talk about love and grace while people die. Doesn't anybody *care?* Doesn't anybody want to *do something?* Doesn't anybody …" Becca was crying now. Tears were running down her red face. Jon was able to step in and gently take the mike out of her hands just as Lydia came over, took Becca by the shoulders, and slowly led her away. Becca was still crying as they passed by me and went into one of the back rooms and closed the door.

Jon did his best to smooth things over. He said at our age, it was normal to have questions, and easy to get confused about God's will for our lives. He said that some of us *were* called to go into the mission field and serve Christ that way, but it was just as important to serve God here, in our own country. Everyone's plan was different; the important thing was listening so we could hear it. The band played one final song, and then we all filed out of the building and into the night for capture the flag.

Now, sitting in the grass, after I had told her I thought what she'd said was cool, Becca's lips started quivering. "Thank you. I mean, I know you're just saying that. I know everyone thinks I'm crazy, but thanks anyway."

I didn't know what to say. I didn't want her to start crying again, but it wasn't true that I thought she was crazy. What she had said at worship made sense to me—sort of, at least. More sense than anybody else I'd heard at those rallies.

"So, you used to live in Haiti?" I asked finally.

Becca nodded and wiped her eyes. "As soon as I turn eighteen, I'm going back."

"You guys were missionaries there?"

"Yeah, we lived there four years before we moved back to the States. My sister kept getting sick, and my parents worried we weren't getting a good enough education. Plus, we were basically out of money."

I had more questions, but there was another commotion. I looked over the field. DeShawn was walking quickly our way. Devon Miller was following him. He was bouncing around behind DeShawn, shouting and pointing. "He's caught! I caught him! You're caught, DeShawn!"

DeShawn whirled around. "I *know* you caught me!" he snapped. "I don't *care*."

He turned back around and headed over to us, flopping down on the grass in the jail beside me. I looked at him, but he didn't say anything.

Ever since that day at the movie theater, when DeShawn had given up his seat so I could sit next to Bethany, I didn't know how to feel about him. I wanted to keep my anger, but I had a hard time remembering what it was I'd been angry with him for. Of course, there was the fight, but I had to admit that I'd pushed him first. There was the way Bethany treated him, but I'd been angry with him way before we'd started VBS. I'd been angry at him almost since he first moved in, when I discovered he wasn't going to be the funny, hip-hop-loving little brother I'd imagined he'd be. I hadn't known how to feel about him, so I just decided to dislike him, because it's easier to dislike someone than try to figure them out, I think. It was almost harder to be around him now that we weren't straight-up enemies. We were shy and awkward around each other. We didn't know what to say.

It was Becca who finally spoke. "Hi, DeShawn!"

"Hey." DeShawn cupped his head in his hands and looked down at the ground.

"You okay?" Becca asked.

"I'm fine," he said.

Becca and I looked at each other. He looked like he might have been crying. Something must have happened, but I wasn't brave enough to ask him what. Another bunch of shouts came from the front lines and then stopped. With DeShawn sitting next to me, I couldn't talk to Becca about her plans, or what it was like living in Haiti. Instead, we just sat there quietly, listening to the rest of the happy campers.

"It's a slow game this year," I said after a while. "Usually, there's more prisoners by now."

"Nobody wants to make the first move," Becca said.

DeShawn looked up. "Man, this is stupid," he said. "Let's get out of here."

I looked at him. "What do you mean?"

DeShawn spread out his arms. "Let's just *go.* I don't wanna play this lame-ass game anymore, do you?"

Becca smiled. "Do you want to?" she asked me.

It was weird, but I'd never thought about ditching the game before. I'd never thought I could just get up and walk away, that I didn't *have* to play. "What would we do instead?" I said.

"Something besides sitting for hours in the wet grass," Becca answered.

I smiled and stood up. "Sure, let's go. This game sucks, anyway."


"This is what the sky looks like every night in Haiti," Becca said. "You can always see the stars."

It had been Becca's idea to come down to the lake after we went to my cabin and I left my phone to charge. We weren't supposed to be out by the water this late without a chaperone, but Becca had said nobody would notice, because of the game. We'd walked down the dark pathway through the woods, to where the lake sat reflecting a sliver of crescent moon. Now we were sitting out on the edge of the dock, Becca on one side of me, DeShawn on the other. We'd taken off our shoes and had our feet dipped in the cool water. We could hear the laughter and shouts from back at camp. Closer, in the woods surrounding the lake, we could hear bullfrogs croaking and crickets chirping and the breeze rustling through the trees. Above us, in the clear sky, there were more stars than I had ever seen.

Becca looked over me at DeShawn. "You can't see stars like this in New York City, can you?"

DeShawn shook his head and craned his neck to look up. "Not like this."

"Wow, that's kind of sad."

DeShawn shrugged like this had never bothered him.

"Do you miss it a lot?" Becca asked.

"Soon as I turn eighteen, I'm moving back."

I suddenly felt left out. DeShawn had the city; Becca had Haiti. What did I have? Where was I moving when I turned eighteen?

"Can we visit you?" Becca asked. "In New York?"

DeShawn sat up, looking a little surprised. "I guess." Then he started pulling off his T-shirt.

"What are you doing?" I asked.

"Cooling off," he answered, and dropped off the dock and into the water, barely causing a ripple as he went under. Becca and I sat for a moment in silence. I thought of us all together in New York City, where I'd never been. All I knew were the pictures of Times Square and the Manhattan skyline. I pictured us walking down Broadway, or up on top of the Empire State Building. Somewhere, an owl called. Then, out in the lake, DeShawn's head burst up through the surface.

"How is it?" Becca called.

"Way nicer in here," DeShawn said. He ran his hands through his short, wet hair and spat out a stream of water. His head disappeared again as he went back under, and appeared again farther out, on his back, moving slowly away from us.

"Do you think he's gonna try to swim to the other side?" I asked, only half joking.

Becca laughed. "You'd miss him, wouldn't you?"

I could feel her eyes on me, but I didn't look at her. I kept watching DeShawn floating in the dark water.

Becca stretched her body back out on the dock. "When I was little," she said, "I used to lie on our couch with our cat and pretend that the couch was a raft and we were in Noah's flood and Smokey and I were the only survivors." She sighed. "I like it out here, better than in those stuffy cabins. I wish we could sleep out here tonight."

I didn't know who she meant by "we," and was trying to think of a way to ask her, when she sat up suddenly. "*Shh!* Listen," she hissed.

There were voices on the trail; it sounded like they were heading our way. Then we could see the glow of two flashlights bobbing through the trees, coming toward us. Then DeShawn's voice: "Get in the water, quick!"

I probably would have just sat there on the dock, wondering which was worse: getting caught out here by an adult, or jumping into that cold, dark water, if Becca hadn't grabbed me by my sleeve and pulled me with her off the dock.

The water wasn't as cold as I would have guessed—the day's hot sun must have warmed it some. Still, it was a shock. We didn't have enough time to swim out and around the beach, reaching the shore farther down and missing whoever was coming down the path. By the sound of their voices, they were already on the beach and heading straight for the dock. They would have spotted us. So instead, Becca and I hung against the side of the dock and, as quietly as we could, made our way to the very edge, where DeShawn was already treading water. The three of us hung in a row against the end of the dock. The only way we could be seen was if whoever was out there walked to the very edge and looked straight down.

We heard the boards creak as the two people walked out onto the dock and stopped short just at the edge. That's when I recognized the voices. It was Bethany and Nola. They'd been talking as they walked, and now, bobbing in the dark water, my hands gripping the slippery underside of the dock to keep from drifting too far out, I could listen to what they were saying.

"I still feel bad about earlier, though." That was Nola's voice. "I guess it really was a bitchy thing to do."

Bethany: "No, you were just trying to snap her out of it. Like, what else are we supposed to do if she won't hang out with us, won't even talk to us? And I don't know *what's* up with that horrible hoodie she's always wearing now. I've never seen that thing before in my life."

"You've got something against girls in hoodies?"

"Shut up. That thing needs to go. I don't think she's washed it in weeks."

"Well, anyway, I still feel bad."

There was a long stretch of silence. I wondered how long they were going to stay out here. Even though the water wasn't that cold in the beginning, now I was starting to shiver. I needed to sneeze.

"Oh, look," Nola's voice said. "Somebody's shirt and shoes."

I looked at DeShawn and then Becca. She had her eyes closed. I wondered if she was praying.

Then Bethany: "Gross. One of the kids must have left them out here earlier."

I heard Nola let out a loud sigh. "It's really pretty here. Wouldn't it be awesome to build a cabin on this lake and just live out here, cut off from society and everyone?"

"That sounds horrible, actually."

"What? You'd prefer to stay in good ol' Grover Falls?"

"I told you, I'm going to travel. Saving up for that plane ticket to London and then I—"

"I know, I know—backpacking across Europe, visiting all the essential cities: Paris, Florence, Rome, Athens, and then across the Mediterranean to Morocco. You'll see what there is to see in Africa, visit the pyramids. And then it's …?"

"India. I have to see the Taj Mahal. I want to see the Himalayas as well. Then I guess I'll go to China—the Great Wall would be cool—and then I'm off to Tokyo, catching a flight to Los Angeles, and then I'm driving across the country back to the East Coast. Australia will have to wait for another time."

"Well, I'm glad you're being realistic about this, at least."

"You laugh, but just you watch. I'm going to do it."

"And when is this little excursion taking place, again?"

"When I turn eighteen, before college."

"A trip around the world will take a while. You'll be gone a long time."

"That's the idea."

"Nice."

"I told you, you can come with me! But we'll be roughing it, sleeping out on the road and in hostels."

"The occasional brothel."

"Of course."

"Okay, but after our adventure, we come back here and build my cabin?"

"What about college?"

"Fuck college. Cabins are better."

"Okay, deal. But you're responsible for meals. I hate cooking."

"Ramen noodles it is."

There was a burst of laughter from both of them, trailing off into small chuckles, and then silence. But after a while, I could hear something, a new sound, and I knew what it was without looking—but I wanted to see.

So I turned in the water, reached up to grip the edge of the dock, and slowly pulled myself up out of the lake so that just the top of my head was above the dock—enough to see the girls where they stood, like giants, above me.

"You saw them? You actually *saw* them kissing?" Becca asked. We were standing on the beach, shivering in our soaked clothing.

I nodded. I felt sick.

"In the Bible, it says greet your brother with a friendly kiss. Was it that kind of kiss, or ..."

I shook my head. "It definitely wasn't that kind."

I thought of them in each other's arms, their lips pressed together and moving like they did in the movies, making little sounds, Nola's hands on Bethany's butt. It was like a fucking romantic comedy. Were stars shooting across the sky above them?

"So weird," said Becca. She shook her head and smiled.

DeShawn sneezed. "What do you think we should do?" I asked.

"I guess we'd better head back to camp," said Becca. "It's gotta be late now."

That wasn't what I meant. "But about what I saw?" I said lamely.

"Ben likes Bethany," DeShawn explained.

"Oh." Becca looked a little confused.

"It's not about that!" I said. "It's about ... I don't know, they're counselors, and Bethany's the pastor's daughter, and ..." I trailed off, not knowing what I wanted to say. If I'd seen Bethany kissing a boy, I would have been angry, jealous, but I wouldn't have felt like this, like that expression—the rug out from under me.

But Becca just looked annoyed with me. "I don't know," she said. "But I'm too cold and wet to stand here anymore." She turned and began heading back up the path toward the camp, and we followed.

When we got to the clearing, the game of capture the flag had ended. They had lit the bonfire down by the edge of the forest across the field. We could hear talking and laughing as everyone had hot chocolate and roasted marshmallows. Part of me wished I was down there stupidly making myself a s'more, and that I hadn't seen what I'd just seen. "Well ..." Becca stepped away from us. "I'm going to my cabin to change before anybody sees me." She looked at us both. "Guess I'll see you guys tomorrow?"

We nodded.

Becca turned to go, then stopped and looked at me. With her long hair wild and wet, her face a little red, she looked completely different. "You know her plan will never work, right?" she said. "There's no way she'll have enough saved to get all around the world like that. Not by the time she's eighteen, anyway." Then she turned and ran to her cabin before I could say anything.


I HAD A HARD TIME FALLING ASLEEP that night. It was hot and stuffy in the cabin. But only minutes after lights-out, almost everyone else was sleeping. Hearing other people sleep always made me more anxious to fall asleep myself, which made it even more difficult to drift off, because I was concentrating too hard. I tried lying very still in my sleeping bag and not thinking, but after an hour, I started tossing and turning. The thick cotton of my sweatpants itched against my skin, and I wondered if I was having an allergic reaction to the lake water. Jerking off usually helps when I can't sleep, but even with all the snores I couldn't be sure somebody else wasn't awake. There was that sound guy, Paul, lying on a single cot in the corner of the room. From my top bunk, I could see his back turned to the wall, not moving, but I got the feeling he wasn't a deep sleeper, either. Finally, I couldn't take the itching anymore and shucked off my sleeping bag, hiked up my knees, and pulled off the sweatpants and tossed them on the floor. I rolled onto my stomach and stuffed my face into my damp pillow.

For some reason, every time I closed my eyes, I saw that picture on the flyer Becca had given me weeks ago—of that man, Michael Keegan, and the Haitian orphans. And for some reason, it made me so angry I wanted to punch Michael Keegan in the face. I tried concentrating on something else— anything—but then I just saw Bethany and Nola kissing, and that was worse.

At some point, though, I must have drifted off, because I had a dream.

I dreamed that I was sitting at a campfire in the middle of a dark forest, and Becca was there with me. I had this feeling that I was supposed to tell her something important, something she had to know, but I couldn't remember what it was, and she was going on and on about Michael Keegan, so I couldn't think. While I hurt my brain from trying to come up with it, suddenly she turned to me and said, "You can kiss me." And in this dream, I suddenly really wanted to kiss my cousin, but maybe because it wasn't my cousin anymore.

When I looked again, it was Bethany, smiling at me with her brown eyes, and her long dark hair falling down past her shoulders. Here was my chance. I leaned forward to kiss her, but no matter how hard I tried, I couldn't get close enough. She was always just inches away from me, even though she didn't seem to move. It was like my ass was glued to my seat. I'd had dreams like this before, where I couldn't move, and sometimes, even after I'd woken up and opened my eyes, for a few seconds I would still feel paralyzed—this horrible feeling of my body frozen in my bed. I would have to concentrate really hard to finally be able to move. That's what I did now, in my dream: I concentrated and was able to lean forward enough to reach Bethany, but now I couldn't kiss her, because she was suddenly eating a marshmallow off a sharpened stick. Her lips were smacking, and her mouth was full of white goo.

She'd ruined it! I was so mad at her. Why did she have to eat a marshmallow *now*? I wanted to grab her shoulders and shake her. I almost wanted to hit her. But then her marshmallow fell off her stick and rolled into the dirt away from the fire. She looked so sad, I wanted to get it for her, but every time I reached down to grab the marshmallow, it rolled away from me. It was such an easy thing to do, but I couldn't do it. I was on my feet now, reaching out with Bethany's sharpened stick, trying to stab the marshmallow that was rolling away from me like it was alive.

Soon I was away from the campfire, following the ball of white into the dark trees. It led me through the woods and down to the river, where DeShawn was standing on the dock. The marshmallow rolled across the dock and was almost to the edge when I grabbed it, just before it fell in the water. I was relieved, but then there was another marshmallow rolling across the dock toward the other side, and I rushed to grab it, the first marshmallow still in my hands. Pretty soon, there were dozens of them rolling around on the dock, and I was trying to catch all of them before they fell into the water, while my arms were full of the ones I had saved. It was almost like a video game, but it wasn't any fun, just stressful. DeShawn wasn't any help. He just stood there with his hands in his pockets, watching me.

Finally, one of the marshmallows actually rolled off the edge of the dock, and when I tried to grab it, I lost the whole pile in my arms. All the marshmallows went spilling into the lake, so I had to jump in after them. They sank like rocks, and I dove down into the cold, black water, looking for them. I came back up, gasping for breath. I'd lost all the marshmallows.

"Got the whole thing on camera," somebody shouted. And I looked up at the dock to see DeShawn, grinning and holding up an iPhone, recording me. I panicked. For some reason, I didn't want anyone to see that video. I didn't want anyone to see that I had lost the marshmallows.

"Give me that, DeShawn!" I yelled, splashing in the water. DeShawn just smiled. And then suddenly, I couldn't swim. Even though I was still paddling, my body wouldn't stay afloat anymore, like the water was pulling me under. I called out to DeShawn for help, but he wasn't there. I was sinking. I couldn't breathe. Then I felt hands around me, somebody pulling me to shore. I was being dragged onto the sand. I looked up to see faces, faces of the Haitian orphans from Becca's flyer. They had saved me. They were looking down at me, waiting for me to do something, but I couldn't move. I still couldn't breathe.

"He needs mouth-to-mouth," someone said, and then Haley Thomas appeared, hovering over me. I had a great view of her breasts. She put her lips on mine. I opened my mouth and felt her tongue. And then her body was on top of mine, and she was rubbing against me. Her body felt so warm and real. I was getting hard, and I didn't care about the Haitian orphans watching, or the marshmallows I'd lost. It just felt so good. She was moaning and saying my name over and over: "Benjamin, Benjamin, Benjamin."

And then I woke up.

Before I even opened my eyes, I knew that I'd done it. Birds were singing, insects were buzzing, and lying on my stomach, I felt a wetness around my crotch and sticking to the front of my boxers.

I opened my eyes and looked around me. Everyone else in the cabin was still asleep. It must be early. I tore off my sleeping bag and swung down from my bunk onto the floor. I changed into new boxers and put my sweatpants back on, rolling my dirty boxers up into a ball and tossing them under the bunk in the corner—I didn't know what else to do with them. Then I put on my sandals and rushed out of the cabin.

I found Ms. Swanson where I thought she'd be: sitting in the dining hall at the back table, already showered and dressed, holding a cup of coffee. She looked up when I came in and blinked in surprise.

"Benjamin," she said, "you're up early."

"Ms. Swanson, I have to tell you something," I said in a rush.

She looked at me for a second. "Okay," she said, and gestured to the seat across the table.

I already felt a huge sense of relief, even before I'd told her anything. Here was an adult, a smart, trustworthy adult, an adult I'd known my whole life, who could take care of this problem for me, who could tell me what to do. She would sip her coffee and listen to me and make everything okay.

I sat down across from her. "I saw two people … kissing last night," I began.

Ms. Swanson's mouth twitched, and she looked around her quickly. "Benjamin, I …"

But I cut her off. "It was Bethany and Nola. They were making out down by the lake."

Ms. Swanson's eyes widened for just a moment; then her face returned to its calm expression. "Okay," she said. "Thanks for letting me know."

I waited, but there was no more. No asking for more details, no exclamations of alarm or questioning my truthfulness. She took a sip of coffee and then looked at me. "Anything else?"

"No," I said, "but aren't you going to do something?" This sounded rude and weird leaving my mouth, but I couldn't help it.

Ms. Swanson looked tired—tired, sad, and maybe even a little amused. "What would you like me to do, Ben?"

I felt confused. *I* wasn't the one who was supposed to know what to do. "I don't know. Talk to them? Tell their parents?"

"Are you going to tell their parents?" she asked.

"I don't think I should be the one to do that," I said.

She nodded. "Well, I think you're right about that, Ben."

Someone from the kitchen called out to her with a question about breakfast, and Ms. Swanson got up and left me there, sitting at the table in bewilderment. This didn't make any sense. How could she act like this? After a minute, I got up and followed Ms. Swanson into the kitchen, where she was talking to one of the cooks about when breakfast should be served. When she noticed me, she turned around and smiled sadly at me again. "It's our secret, Ben," she said. "Bottle it up tight."

I slumped out of the dining hall, stepped outside, and blinked into the already glaring sun. Nobody else was up yet, and I didn't know where to go or what to do.

# 17

When Paul woke up in the inn at Lake George on Friday morning, the first thing he saw was the note. It sat on the nightstand, directly in his line of vision. He stared at it for a long time, making no move to get up and read it. As long as he didn't, it could say any number of things: That she had stepped out into the hall for a moment to take a call from her kids and hadn't wanted to wake him. That she was downstairs in the lobby, asking the front desk for suggestions for breakfast. As long as he didn't read it, the note could say anything.

It was a full five minutes before he got up, naked and sweating, and stood over the table. Without actually touching the paper, he read April's small, neat handwriting:

Paul,

This probably isn't the right way to do this, but I think you'd agree our relationship has been pretty unconventional to begin with. I want you to know that none of it was your fault, but I don't think we can take this thing much further, so we should end it now, for both our sakes. I hope you can understand that.

We'll still have to see each other. This will be hard, but let's not make it any harder than it needs to be.

I'm sorry. I hope you understand.

April

P.S. Forget what I said about DeShawn last night. I think you should give him guitar lessons.

P.P.S. You need to be out of the room by eleven o'clock.

Paul had to resist the urge to take the thing and rip it into as many pieces as he could. He had to resist the urge to find a match and set it on fire, letting the flames spread across the room. He sat there on the end of the bed, his heart pounding. He ran his hands through his hair. It was becoming harder and harder to breathe. He got out of the bed, and only after rushing over to his overnight bag and ransacking it did he realize he'd forgotten to bring any of his pills.

The fact that marijuana was illegal had never really occurred to him until this moment, when he desperately needed some and had no idea where to get it. In high school, he'd never even had to pay for it, and in the city, it was easier to find than a good slice of pizza. But here, in this stupid tourist town, where he knew no one, at ten in the morning, for the first time in his life, Paul couldn't just walk out and score a bag of weed, and he didn't have time to mess around. Alcohol would have to do.

When he approached the front desk, the clerk did her absolute professional best not to acknowledge Paul's disheveled appearance, his breath, which must still smell of stale beer, his bloodshot eyes.

"May I help you, sir?"

"Yeah, can you tell me where the nearest liquor store is?"

COMING OUT OF THE LIQUOR STORE with a bottle of Jack Daniel's in a brown paper bag, he squinted at an ugly yellow sun. He looked around him. The parking lot was empty, but even if someone had been there, he wasn't sure that would have stopped him from unscrewing the cap and taking a drink even before he got in the church truck.

He put the bottle in the cup holder between the front seats, where it rattled as he sped down the empty street. He forced himself not to take another drink until he was well out of the town and making his way up a winding mountain road, leading him deep into thick woods. Nothing on either side but trees and the occasional giant boulder. With one hand on the steering wheel, he rounded a sharp curve and took a quick swig from the bottle. He glanced at the clock. 11:25. He had to get there as soon as possible so he could talk to her alone, before everyone else arrived. What time had she left? And how had she been able to leave the room without waking him? He was an insomniac, for Christ's sake! How the hell had she not woken him?

"Fuck you, April," he said out loud, flying around another hairpin turn. Every second, he expected to see a sign for the campsite, around the next bend, but all he got were trees and more trees. Cursing under his breath, he pressed down harder on the gas. Spread out on the empty passenger seat beside him were the directions he had scrawled down, showing the route from the town to the campsite, but reading them while driving this curvy, narrow road wasn't easy. And his head was pounding, and he couldn't think.

Her handwriting had been so neat. Nothing misspelled, and all the *i*'s dotted.

"Please, God," he muttered at eleven forty. "Please, please, God."

A side road appeared on his left. He screeched to a halt, checked his map, then made the turn. It was a dirt road filled with potholes and seemed to go on forever. After five minutes, he second-guessed himself and made a U-turn. Then, a mile or so back up the main road, he checked the map again, realized the side road had been right along, and, cursing a blue streak, turned back around.

It wasn't until five of noon, driving up the dirt road only a few minutes past where he had turned around, that Paul saw the big wooden sign for

Camp Lone Eagle. He sped down one final dirt road and pulled into a loose gravel lot that was completely empty except for one silver Honda. Trees surrounded the lot on three sides, and on the fourth, a large grassy field spread out. Paul could see behind it a collection of wooden buildings. But in the field, standing with her arms crossed around her chest, there she stood, completely put together, completely normal, as if by magic.

He heard the bang of the truck door as he slammed it behind him. He heard the gravel crunch under his feet as he strode across the lot, and the cicadas droning in the summer haze. But all he saw was her face, drawing steadily nearer as he walked, and her expression—not nervous, exactly, but tense, prepared, ready for his onslaught. She must have expected this.

When he reached her in the field, he stopped short. For a moment, she looked as though she was about to speak, but then she closed her mouth and waited.

"You didn't have to leave me like that," he said at last.

April cleared her throat. "I thought it might be easier."

"For you, maybe."

"I'm sorry, then."

Paul swallowed. "April, I don't understand why you're doing this."

Her voice was quiet. "What I said in my note was—"

"What? In *this*?" He pulled the piece of paper from his pocket and brandished it at her. "That 'none of it was my fault'? That 'we shouldn't make it any harder than it needs to be'? What the fuck *is* that, April?"

She stared at him, then looked down at the ground, as if embarrassed for him.

But Paul couldn't stop himself. "I think we should talk about this," he said. "We *need* to talk about it. We can make it work if we talk about it." He could hear the desperation in his voice, and even to him it sounded weak and flailing.

"This is what I didn't want to happen," she said quietly. "This is why I wrote the note and left."

He wanted to reach out and grab her by the shoulders, but then what? "How can you be like this?" he heard himself almost shouting. "Do you know how hard this is for me?"

"Oh, and it's easy for me?" April snapped. She looked up at him with hard eyes.

Before he could think of a response, he heard the sound of the vans pulling into the gravel lot behind him. He didn't turn around. He kept his eyes on April. The next moment, there were the sounds of doors sliding open and the voices and laughter of kids as they piled out of the vans. "April," he said.

"Please, Paul," she said, looking back down at the ground. "I'm trying to save you."

THE FIRST ACTIVITY OF THE TRIP, after everything had been unpacked and all the kids were assigned to their cabins, was a group hike. Everyone was required to go, April told all the campers, when they had gathered at the big fire pit in front of the rec hall, "unless you have a legitimate excuse. And no," she said with a wry grin, "'I don't feel like it' doesn't qualify."

*How about, "You broke my heart, April"? Does that qualify? Is that excuse legitimate enough for you?*

Standing there in the middle of the circle, with all the kids and team leaders gathered around her, she looked so put together, so there, it didn't seem possible that she'd slept with him last night, that she wasn't the always-perfect, always-virtuous VBS leader everyone thought her to be.

Paul, who never tried to come off as virtuous, had found an aluminum water bottle to put his whiskey in, and he took quick, furtive sips every time the kids laughed or cheered. He liked to think he understood women. He thought of himself as especially intuitive to female emotion—maybe too much so for his own good. Usually, when girls were angry or upset with him, he knew exactly why, and usually, he knew what words to say, what things to do, to make things right—even when he couldn't swallow his pride enough to actually say those words or do those things. More often than not, he feigned ignorance, acting like your typical clueless guy. *"I seriously don't understand why you're upset."* It was just easier that way. But with April, Paul's cluelessness was genuine. He didn't know what, exactly, was wrong, or what to do to fix it, although he was pretty sure drinking whiskey only somewhat covertly in front of a bunch of children probably wasn't a good start.

"This trip is always the highlight of our summer," April told the campers. "And we're going to have a lot of fun as long as we follow the rules and respect each other."

He remembered staggering out of the bar at two last night. April was laughing and clinging to his neck, their earlier argument forgotten. They stumbled their way back to the hotel, their bodies so close together they might as well have been fused.

"Remember that we're in the wild, so we should never be going anywhere alone. Use the buddy system. And I don't want to see anyone away from the campsite after dark without a counselor."

Back at the hotel, they had made the sort of stupid love you made when you were too drunk to do it properly. So they did it stoned, slow, and gorgeous. He remembered saying her name over and over as he kissed her face, her neck, her breasts. He remembered her teeth sinking into his right shoulder when she came.

"We're going to have a fun and safe trip this weekend, okay, gang?" April said, putting her hands together. "Jon, can you lead us in a prayer?"

IT WASN'T TECHNICALLY A MOUNTAIN, and it was less than five miles, but Paul's stomach was a mess of cheap liquor and runny scrambled eggs. He brought up the rear, and twice he had to retreat off the trail, into the trees. The first time was a false alarm, but the second, he vomited all over the moss and dead leaves.

A year ago, on a long weekend, Paul and Sasha had decided to go on a camping trip in the Catskills. Sasha's father had loaded them up with camping supplies—a top-of-the-line tent and backpacking equipment— and given Paul specific instructions on everything. The night before they were to head out, they'd gotten wasted at a friend's party in Williamsburg. The next morning, painfully hungover, Sasha had still been determined to make the trip, so she drove her parents' Jeep out of the city while Paul dozed in the passenger seat. Stuck in traffic on the George Washington

Bridge, they'd played My Bloody Valentine and fed each other Advils from behind dark sunglasses. At the campsite, they were too tired and hungover to figure out how to set up the tent. The humidity had been horrible, the mosquitoes even worse. It hadn't taken much effort for Paul to convince Sasha to ditch the idea, go get a hotel for the weekend, and never tell anyone. They had taken some pictures of themselves by the lake before they left, and a few in the woods for good measure, before packing up their belongings to retreat into an air-conditioned room and make love on two-hundred-thread-count sheets.

On the rocky summit, which, though only a hilltop, still afforded a decent view of the Adirondacks, Paul noted glumly his bottle's decrease in weight. Around him, kids rested together in clumps or goofed off near the precipice until a counselor shouted at them to stop. He could see April, standing by herself, apart from the group and as far away from him as possible.

"Pretty amazing, isn't it?"

Paul looked away from April to see Jon Newman standing beside him, looking out at the mountains stretching to the north in rolling tiers of green.

"What is?" Paul asked absently.

Jon held his hand out before them. "This! I mean, tell me there's no Creator, right?"

Paul took a long drink from his bottle and wiped his mouth. "They're just trees, man," he said.


PAUL GOT THROUGH THE REST OF FRIDAY and well into Saturday in a half-drunk haze and discovered he could do everything expected of him—helping clean up and tear down for meals, supervising kids, setting up the stage for the worship rally—just as well drunk as sober. By Saturday night, though, he had exhausted his supply. And as the rally started up, the kids jumping up and down in unison as Jon led the band in a familiar up-tempo number, Paul sat at his makeshift sound booth at the back of the dining hall like someone slowly waking from a bad dream to find reality even worse.

Ever since he began working at New Life, Paul had done his best to keep the whole worship thing at arm's length, but tonight, he couldn't help feeling a little bit drawn in by these kids and their misguided attempts to attain inner peace. The jumping up and down, the outstretched hands, the falling on the floor and weeping—tonight, it was almost moving. Even the lyrics to the songs, displayed by the projector in the front of the room, got to Paul. Their unaffected simplicity, their complete refusal to make any attempt at originality, was oddly affecting. *Jesus, I need you, Jesus, I love you, Jesus, please come and save me from myself.* All he had to do was substitute *April* for *Jesus*, and the songs made a lot of sense.

Halfway through the rally, the real April came out of her office in the back of the hall and sat on a bench in the back of the room, not far from him. Paul stiffened. For the past day and a half, she had gone out of her way to avoid him, and he had done his best to steer clear of her, but now she was sitting only a few feet away from him, staring in front of her with a sad but calm look on her face. She could have sat somewhere else; there were plenty of other places.

It was during the altar call, when Jon asked the kids if anyone had a word from the Lord, that April got up suddenly and walked out the front door. Paul counted to sixty before following.

Outside, the night air was warm and smelled of pine resin. Crickets chirped over the muffled keyboard tones and singing voices from inside. He saw her standing a few yards away, near the edge of the woods, arms crossed, looking out into the trees. She was wearing khaki shorts and a blue zip-up windbreaker. When she heard his footsteps, she turned and looked at him, then turned back to the woods. Paul approached her slowly.

"This is the part where, if I had any, I'd offer you a cigarette," he said when he reached her.

"And the part where I'd accept," said April, "if I hadn't quit almost twenty years ago."

Paul smiled and put his hands in his pockets. They stood side by side, looking out into the dark wall of pines.

April began to laugh softly. "You know, my daughter called somebody a bitch today, in front of everyone."

"Yeah," he said, "I heard something about that."

She shook her head. "I don't know what's gotten into her."

"She's probably just going through something."

April nodded and shivered. "Yeah."

He moved to touch her, and she drew back, as if his hand were hot iron. "Don't, Paul."

"Because someone might see us?"

"That's one of too many reasons."

"April, please, you have to at least tell me why."

She didn't say anything for a long time. Paul heard the wind stirring the top branches of the trees. Then, just when he thought she wasn't going to answer at all, she said, "You know, I was thinking about your question the other night, when you asked me whether we would have been together if we'd met another way, in different times or circumstances. And it got me thinking that if we had met in another life and gotten together, then somewhere along the way, in that life, we would be thinking the same thing, only the other way around: wondering what our lives would have been like if we *hadn't* gotten together, or hadn't met at all, if we'd met somebody else instead. And this might be really basic, teenager-smoking-pot-for-the-first-time talk, but it got me thinking, no matter what choices you make, no matter what you do, part of you will always be wondering what would have happened if you had made a different choice, done things differently. So in the end, it's probably best just not to dwell on it."

Paul waited a moment, then said, "Are you sure that's not just an elaborate excuse to justify the way you feel? I mean, if you're unhappy with your life, if you feel empty, don't you have the right to try and change things?"

She looked at him and smiled. "Do you feel empty, Paul?"

And he could say it with all sincerity, without a hint of irony, like the lyrics in those worship songs: "Without you, yes, I feel empty."

Paul didn't know how he had expected April to take these words, but he hadn't thought she'd find them funny. A smile spread across her face, and she looked up toward the tops of the trees, shook her head, and began to laugh. Paul felt a momentary flash of anger, but her laughter wasn't cruel or even condescending. It sounded genuine, as if he had told her a very funny joke. He thought about what he had just said, and then he, too, gave a nervous laugh.

April looked about her suddenly, scanning the area. No one was around. Inside, the altar call had ended and the closing song had begun. Paul could just make out the words: *"You're all I want, all I need. You're my everything."*

April turned to him and put his face in her hands, meeting his eyes. "Thank you, Paul Frazier," she said. "When you get back to Grover Falls, you need to try to move on with your life. Promise me you'll try."

At a loss, he met her gaze and nodded.

April took one more quick glance around. Then, still holding his face in her hands, she kissed him, quickly, forcefully, on the lips. Before he had time to return the kiss, before he had time to pull her closer, she let go of him, threw up the hood of her windbreaker, and walked swiftly away. Paul stood at the edge of the wood, watching her go. He expected to see her return to the rec hall, but at the last moment, she set off in the opposite direction, down toward the cabins. Paul wondered where she was going, but he knew he was not allowed to follow.

EVERYONE HAD GATHERED out on the front field for the midnight game of capture the flag, and the empty dining hall was quiet as a graveyard. Paul began tearing down the instruments and sound equipment. His heart was not beating fast; his breath came slow and steady; he felt an almost unnatural sense of calm.

He was kneeling to unplug the electric guitar from the amp when he heard footsteps behind him. He knew who it was without turning around.

In a weary voice, he said, "Shouldn't you be outside, DeShawn?"

"What kind of guitar is that?"

"It's a Yamaha."

"Is that good?"

"No," Paul said. He stood up and turned around to look at the boy. "It's a piece of shit."

DeShawn smiled, then scrunched up his forehead. "What's a good electric guitar, then, that's not, like, mad expensive?" His face lit up. "What did Hendrix play?"

Paul sighed. "Actually, DeShawn, I'm a little busy right now. I have to tear this all down tonight, so you should probably head back outside."

"I could help you."

"It's faster if I just do it myself." Paul took the guitar and walked past DeShawn, across the stage, to put it in its case.

For a second, DeShawn watched him silently. Then he said, a little uncertainly, "I just wanna get a guitar for our lessons. Mr. Waid gave me his old acoustic to use for now, but they say they'll help me out buying a new one. Mr. Waid thinks I should get a better acoustic because he says they're better to learn on, but I really want an electric, and they say it's my decision, so—"

"Yeah, I don't know about those lessons, DeShawn," Paul said, cutting him off.

"Huh?"

"I know I told your dad—I mean, Mr. Waid—that I would, but now I'm thinking it's probably not such a good idea."

"Why?"

"I just don't think guitar is a good thing for you to learn, especially from me. You should find another hobby. Don't you like basketball or something?"

DeShawn's eyes and voice were hard. "No. I wanna play guitar."

"Well, aren't you listening to the Stones by now, DeShawn? You can't always get what you want. You of all people should know that."

For a moment, DeShawn looked profoundly confused. Then this turned to anger. "Man, *fuck* you," he said.

Paul nodded and began coiling a mike cable—over, then under, over, under. "Yeah, okay." And he didn't look up again until he was sure the boy had walked across the hall and he heard the front door slam behind him.

Sunday afternoon, after following the vans of kids from the campsite back to Grover Falls, after parking at New Life and swapping the pickup for his own car, pulling out of the church parking lot, Paul wasn't certain about very many things, but one thing he knew without a shred of doubt: he would never go camping again. And glancing at the square brick building in his rearview mirror, he made himself another promise: he would never set foot in that church again for the rest of his life—or any church, for that matter. It would be easier now that he no longer worked there.

It had only been a few minutes ago. Paul had been in the parking lot unpacking the instruments and equipment from the truck and putting them on the asphalt to then take them into the church, when Jon approached him.

"Paul, can I talk to you for a second?"

Setting down the amp on the ground and mopping his brow, Paul made no effort to disguise his irritation at being interrupted in his work.

Jon looked around the crowded parking lot. Children were reuniting with their parents, who had just come out from the church. "Maybe we should go somewhere private," he said.

"Just say what you gotta say, man," said Paul.

Jon winced, and then his expression turned hard. "You were drinking this weekend, Paul."

Paul blinked. "Yeah?" Not quite a question, not quite an admission.

Jon nodded. He took the bag off his back, set it on the pavement, and unzipped it, pulling out Paul's aluminum bottle. He unscrewed the cap and took a quick whiff, scrunching up his nose, before offering it to Paul. "You were drinking out of this all weekend."

"Circumstantial evidence."

Jon sighed and dug into his bag again, this time pulling out the empty Jack Daniel's bottle.

"You went through my stuff," said Paul.

"I had to be sure. This is serious, Paul. I don't know how you could think it's okay to be drinking hard liquor while supervising children on a church camping trip."

"What else would you suggest?"

"I'm going to have to talk to Pastor Eric about this. I'm sorry, but this is just too serious to ignore. But I wanted you to know first."

"That's really big of you, Jon," Paul said, and began to walk away, leaving the instruments sitting on the pavement. "Oh," he said over his shoulder, "and when you talk to your pastor, give him a message from me, will you? Tell him I quit."

It was around two in the afternoon when Paul pulled into his mother's driveway, prepared to walk into that kitchen and field his mom's questions. She had just gotten home from church and would be extra chipper and interested in his life. He would dodge her words as best he could, walk up the stairs, go into the bathroom and down his medication, and stare into the mirror until he felt numb. Then he would go into his room, look slowly around at the physical manifestation of the waste that was his life—the dirty laundry, the unmade bed, the untouched guitars—before walking over to his bed and collapsing. He would lie on his back and stare up at the ceiling that he knew so well by now, all its stains and contours long since memorized, and wait while the sunlight through the slits in the shades slowly faded and the room went dark. If he was lucky, a few hours of sleep would come to him.

He sat in his car, working up the nerve, when something occurred to him. He pulled his wallet out of his pocket and opened it. A couple of crisp twenty-dollar bills looked back at him. At the bar in Lake George, he'd had to use the ATM, and this was all that remained. He put the wallet back in his pocket and pulled out of the driveway.

Fifteen minutes later, when Paul stood at the door of the apartment and knocked, he had taken it for granted that Nicki's little brother, Tommy, would be happy to see him. He'd taken it for granted that Tommy would invite him enthusiastically in. And he'd taken it for granted that when Paul told him why he had come, Tommy would be delighted to help him out. But when Tommy opened the door, his expression was one of surprise, quickly turning to hard mistrust.

"Hey," Paul said.

"Hey." The door did not open any wider.

Paul hesitated. "Can I come in for a minute?"

Without answering, Tommy turned around and walked into the apartment, leaving the door open. After a moment, Paul followed. The place was slightly cleaner than the last time he was there—at least, the empty beer bottles had been cleaned up.

Tommy stood in the middle of the room, hands in his pockets, glaring at him. Paul was a little surprised. He knew that Nicki was upset with him, but he hadn't expected that anger to extend to her little brother, certainly not to this degree.

Since small talk seemed pointless, Paul got straight to it. "So, I was wondering if you could hook me up with some of that stuff we had the other weekend—the pot, I mean."

Tommy blinked. "That's seriously why you're here? Weed?"

"Um ... yeah? Or if you could at least point me in the right direction? I have money."

Tommy stood looking at him for a moment, as if deciding something, then walked into the next room and came back with a small plastic bag of pot. He tossed it at Paul. "Now, get the fuck out of my apartment," he said.

Too taken aback to speak, Paul caught the bag, noting its pleasant heft, and turned to go. Tommy leaned against the door frame and watched him walk to his car. Paul opened the door, then looked back at Tommy. "You know, I'm sorry about your sister. I was an asshole, I know. But believe me, she's better off without me."

Tommy snorted. "That's about what any useless douchebag in your position would say."

"In my position? What's that supposed to mean?"

Tommy studied him, and the hard look on his face changed to wondering curiosity. "You don't know, do you?" he said. "She didn't tell you."

Paul felt something sinking inside him. "Didn't tell me what?"

"I guess it makes sense, seeing as I only found out by accident," Tommy said. He paused for a moment and then said, "My sister's pregnant, Paul. It's yours."

# PART III

# 18

It had been over a month since I called Nola Sternson a bitch in front of half the kids at VBS. But when I joined the rest of my church youth group for the trip to Albany, the first Saturday of September, I knew that nobody had forgotten my little outburst that day by the lake. On a cool, gray day threatening rain, sitting in one of two fifteen-passenger vans heading down the highway, I felt like a stranger even though I was surrounded by kids I had known all my life. Not that anybody was rude to me. Nobody ignored me or gave me dirty looks or said things under their breath—at New Life, no one would be so obvious. But no one went out of their way to include me in their conversations. No one offered to sit with me in the back seat or offered me a water bottle. They treated me as something precarious and dangerous, like some feral creature that might go off at any moment, biting and snarling and spitting out horrible obscenities into their wholesome ears.

If Bethany had been with me, I probably wouldn't have noticed. We would have been too caught up in talking to each other, trading jokes and comments, to bother with what was going on around us. Ultimately, these other kids had never really meant anything to us. Sure, as the pastor's daughter, Bethany was obliged to be nice to everyone, but what they thought about us mattered little. Bethany wasn't here, though. I hadn't seen her in weeks. It was just me in the back seat of the church van, alone.

As I sat with my head resting against the window—headphones in my ears to block out the chatter and laughter of everybody in front of me, watching cars in the opposite lane speed through the gray morning—I felt like the rope in a game of tug-of-war. At one end, the end this van was speeding toward, was Martin, waiting in Albany to meet me tonight. He had lately become my only real point of contact. These past weeks, we had spent hours talking online. And the fact that I would meet him in person in less than twenty-four hours still hadn't fully sunk in. On the other end, trying to pull me back the way I'd come, was Bethany—or, at least, my thoughts of Bethany, which, since earlier in the week, had become heavy and conflicted. I was annoyed with myself. On this day, all I should be thinking about was Martin, but I'd gotten the letter a few days ago, and since then I hadn't been able to keep Bethany out of my head.

When my mom came into the kitchen with the mail Wednesday morning and told me I had a letter, I was surprised. I never got mail—physical mail, anyway—unless it was my birthday. My first thought was that it was from Martin, and my heart lurched, but in that same moment I remembered that I'd never given him my address and he didn't know my real name, so there was no way he could know where I lived. Still, I didn't completely calm down until I took the envelope from my mom and saw that it was from Bethany. Her name and address were printed in her neat, pretty handwriting in the top left corner.

I took the letter up to my room, sat on my bed, and opened it.

Dearest Laura,

It feels so weird writing a letter like this, like with a pen and paper and everything, and I'm sure when you get this you're going to wonder if I've gone completely crazy. Has she lost her mind?? Sometimes these days, I feel like I have. But the reason I'm writing to you like this, in this long-forgotten form, is that I'm pretty sure my mom is checking my phone these days on the sly, and I don't want her to ever find this.

First, I want to say that I miss you. I miss you SO much,

Laura, I can't even say. You hurt me a lot when you stopped talking to me, but I think now I understand at least a little why you did. I wasn't being a good friend. I'd been keeping things from you, and we never keep things from each other. So I'm sorry. I'm really sorry. But my reasons weren't because I didn't want to share things with you. I was scared that if I did share this part of myself with you, I might lose you, and I didn't want that to happen. But seeing how things are now that we're not talking at all, I realize I should have told you from the beginning, that it wasn't fair not to trust you, that it was my fault.

SO here it goes … I like Nola. In a way that's different from friendship. You're my best friend, Laura. But the way I feel about Nola is the way you felt about Jeremy Walters in seventh grade. (Remember that, Laura? Remember how I used to be able to get you red in the face just by saying his name?) So yeah, I guess I should just say it: I'm in love with Nola, and I guess that makes me a lesbian. It feels so weird to write that, but it's true.

It started when I first sat next to her last year in Bio class. But at the time, I didn't know what was happening. I was fascinated by her, but I didn't know why. I remember thinking she was cool and really, really wanting her to like me. It was that night in June, the bath-salts night, when you went home and I slept over at her house, when I couldn't ignore the fact that I was attracted to her. Nothing happened, but we fell asleep together on the sofa, and I'd never felt anything like that before. Still, I tried to ignore it, or deny it. You know what the Bible says about it. You know what my dad says about it. I was really scared. I still am.

But the more I saw her, the more I got to know her, the harder it was to hide how I felt. I wanted to tell you, Laura! But you have to understand how scary and confusing it's been. Is there something wrong with me? Am I evil? It's weird because I've been so messed up about it, but also so happy whenever I'm around Nola, so it feels like there's a war in my mind, like I'm going crazy. Maybe I am.

Nola and I kissed for the first time at camp. We told each

other how we felt. Since then, things have been weird. I think my parents suspect something, although I'm not sure what. My mom's been acting strange. She doesn't like it when I go out, and seems not to want Nola around anymore. The other day, I caught her looking through my phone. My dad isn't as bad, but he's still quiet around me. I don't know what's going on.

I'm scared, Laura. If they found out, I think they would literally go crazy on me. I don't know what to do. And it's not something I can really talk to Nola about. You're the only one. I miss you, Laura. I know you're mad at me, but please try and understand why I felt I couldn't tell you. I need my friend.

I'm going to end now because my hand is killing me. (Seriously, how did people do this all the time?) Please call me, or just come over. I'm not leaving the house much these days.

> Your friend forever,
> Bethany

After I read it, I put the letter down, looked up at my ceiling for a moment, then picked it up and read it again.

Then I jumped up off my bed, ran down the stairs, threw on some shoes, and ran outside. I wanted to run all the way to Bethany's house, but I forced myself to stay at a fast walk. I had this crazy fear that the house wouldn't be there when I arrived, or that Bethany and her family wouldn't be in it, and I would never be able to apologize to my friend or talk to her again.

I'm used to irrational fears like that springing up inside me, and I'm used to having them very quickly put to rest whenever the crazy scenarios racing through my head turn out to be impossible. I'm not used to having those fears justified. I'm not used to having them come true.

Over the years, I had become accustomed to just walking right into the Moyers' house unannounced. But since I hadn't been there in so long, today I rang the doorbell. When nobody answered, I tried the door and found it locked. I walked around the porch and looked through the front windows. All the lights were off, and when I looked in the garage, I saw that one of the cars was gone.

Standing in their front lawn, I called Bethany, my heart beating fast. She didn't pick up. I called her again on the walk back home. Still no answer. I sent her a text: *Hey, got your letter. Where are you?* Somehow, I already knew I wouldn't get a response.

Every day for the next few days, I walked over to the Moyers' house, and it remained dark and empty. It seemed clear to me that the whole family must have gone somewhere. And if things had been normal, I might have known where. But I'd lost touch with everyone and with everything going on at church in the past month, because since the end of VBS, we hadn't been going to church.

It was my mother who stopped. In fact, she had stopped doing much of anything. Usually, during the last month of summer vacation, my mom was immersed in some project she wouldn't be able to do once school started—say, painting the porch or redoing the kitchen. But this year, she had mostly just sat around the house drinking unsweetened iced tea, watching old movies on TV, and going for long walks in the evening, which she would return from looking sad and forlorn. I was relieved when the school year drew closer and she had to start gearing up for work, attending meetings, and making up lesson plans. Things started to go back to normal, with one exception: she kept avoiding church, although she never said explicitly she wasn't going anymore. If I asked her, she came up with some lame excuse—she had a migraine that Sunday, or she was tired. But since I didn't feel like going to church, either, I hadn't pressed her about it.

Because of this, I hadn't even seen Bethany since July and had no idea where she and her family might have gone. Over the week, the sense of foreboding grew stronger, but I told myself I was being silly. Wherever they were, Bethany was sure to be back in time to go down to Albany on Saturday. I would see her then, talk to her then. But on Saturday morning, after my mom dropped me off in the church parking lot, I scanned the small crowd of kids waiting to depart and didn't see her. Quite a few kids looked surprised to see me, since I hadn't been to church in so long, but they quickly looked away, politely hiding their unease.

I waited around the parking lot for a few minutes, watching the dark clouds overhead. I hadn't dressed for rain and hoped it wouldn't start till we were on our way. I kept looking down the drive that led to the parking lot, waiting to see the Moyers' car pull in, but fifteen minutes went by and they still hadn't arrived.

I found Jon Newman by the vans, loading everyone's overnight luggage into the back. Even though it was only an hour's drive, we would be staying overnight at the church of the United Believers of Albany, who would also be protesting with us. It made the trip more exciting that way.

Jon stopped and looked at me warily when I approached him. I couldn't blame him after what I'd said to him at camp—which, from what I could tell, he hadn't told anyone about. He had every right to be a little afraid of me. I did my best to give him a reassuring smile of normality and asked whether he knew where Bethany was.

He started loading up the bags again, giving himself an excuse not to look at me. "Oh, she isn't coming. Pastor Eric called me and said that they'll be out of town this week—something about a family vacation."

I couldn't tell whether Jon was being vague because he didn't want to appear to know and care too much about Bethany's doings and whereabouts, or whether he really didn't know more than that. Either way, I decided not to press him. I didn't want him angry at me. I needed to be as agreeable as possible today. As casually as I could, I asked, "Oh, hey, my mom talked to you about this weekend, right?"

He thought for a second, then shook his head, still not looking at me.

"She must have forgot—she's always forgetting things before the first week of school. If it's okay with you, I'm going to meet my grandmother this evening, after the protest, to get dinner. She lives just outside the city and can pick me up at the church, then drive me back. It'll just be for an hour or so, while you guys eat."

"Okay ..." Jon sounded not completely sure of himself. "I guess that's fine."

And now for the big gamble: "Would you like me to call my mom to confirm it?"

Jon nodded. "We'd better."

I smiled, took out my phone, and called my own voice mail, held the phone to my ear for a few seconds, then looked at Jon, frustrated. "She's not picking up—probably still driving. I'll call her again in five minutes."

As if on cue, a rumble of thunder. Jon checked the clock on his phone. "That's okay, Laura, we should really get going. We can call later."

SITTING IN THE BACK OF THE VAN, I wondered what would have happened if Bethany were here. If we had talked and made up and become best friends again, would I have chickened out on the whole idea of meeting Martin? Would I have confessed everything to her the way she had confided in me? Maybe that was all I needed: someone to confess to. But she wasn't here, so I didn't know.

If I did this, I would never be normal again. Given enough time, people would forget about what I had called Nola. I could still slip back into my former safe and dull identity. But if word got out about what I was doing, people would never forget it. Some things stay with you forever—or at least, as long as you remain around those who know what you did. In our town, there was the Girl Who Got Caught with Cocaine in Her Locker, the Girl Who Ran Off with Her Boyfriend at Sixteen, the Girl Who Tried to Kill Herself. If I did this and people found out, I would no longer be Laura, I would be the Girl Who Seduced an Older Man Online … and Then Sneaked Away to Meet Him.

I wasn't completely stupid. I *had* taken some precautions. There was no way, in fact, that I could see how dinner with Martin could develop into anything more than just dinner, unless I wanted it to. We were meeting at a restaurant Martin had picked out in downtown Albany. I had told him I wanted to go somewhere casual for our first date. I was nervous enough about meeting him, I didn't need the added anxiety of finding something fancy to wear and worrying about mispronouncing the items on the menu. Martin seemed quick to comply with my request. And when I looked up the place he'd chosen as our rendezvous, it was even more casual than I'd been thinking. The Starving Artist looked more like a glorified coffee shop than a proper place to go to dinner. I felt almost insulted. But he said their food was organic and the coffee fair-trade.

I found out online that I could call a car to take me there right from the church, and then call another to take me back. It was expensive, and I would have to dip into my meager savings, but this way, Martin would never have the opportunity to be completely alone with me unless I let him.

Still, of course I was nervous; of course I was a little frightened. But I was also excited, full of a pulsing energy. It seemed to shoot through my body in an endless cycle, now and then manifesting itself in one spot or another, sending my hand into quivers, or my foot, or making my face warm and red.

I was so caught up thinking about meeting Martin, the incidental fact that between now and then I had to take part in an abortion protest rally didn't really hit me. Not while we drove down the highway. Not as we took the exit into Albany. It wasn't till we arrived at the United Believers church, parked the vans, and all piled out into their back parking lot that what we were about to do sank in.


New Life and United Believers of Albany had had a relationship for some time now. Pastor Eric and the pastor of UBA were friends, and we would come down here for big worship rallies, youth retreats, the occasional abortion protest. In some ways, I think UBA was everything New Life wanted to be. It was big, a giant modern building right in the heart of Albany, and it was hip and contemporary and active in the community.

When we all filed into the church's foyer, I noticed it had been redone since last time I was here, about a year ago. The floors were a new, sleek tile, and on the walls, giant flat-screen TVs advertised the week's church events in an endless loop.

Jared, a man I recognized as UBA's youth leader, greeted us in the foyer. He was a tall, thin guy about Jon's age, who laughed a lot and always clapped his hands together before saying anything. He had grown a beard since last I saw him and was wearing thick-rimmed glasses and shorts and sandals despite the gloomy weather.

"Hey, welcome, guys," he said, smiling and clapping his hands together. "It's great to see you." He gave much shorter Jon a side hug and we followed him into the sanctuary.

On one wall of the giant sanctuary, they had decked out some folding tables with pretzels and chips and two-liter bottles of soda. I didn't see how anyone could even think about eating right now, but everyone dived in like starving hyenas. It was as if we were about to go to a dance or a concert, not a protest outside an abortion clinic.

I was standing in the corner trying to swallow some too-fizzy ginger ale when I heard somebody call my name. I turned to see Liz Burchaw approaching me with a big smile on her face. Liz was the daughter of UBA's pastor. She was a little bit older than I, but over the years she had formed a lasting though intermittent friendship with Bethany, and with me by extension. Liz had come up with her parents to Grover Falls several times when her dad was the guest speaker at New Life. She was a nice person, but I always had a hard time knowing what to say around her.

"Laura!" she said when she reached me. "Hey, how are you?"

I nodded and gave as bright a smile as I could manage. "Hey, Liz!"

She looked around her and asked the question most kids who knew me asked whenever they found me alone: "Where's Bethany?"

"Oh," I said, "she's not here, actually. Um, she and her parents went on vacation."

"*Vacation?*" said Liz. "The week before school starts?"

"Um, yeah. I guess they're doing some family thing."

I heard somebody let out a snort next to me, and I turned. Tall, blond Haley Thomas saw me looking at her and feigned a look of surprise. "Oh, sorry. Yeah," she said, "vacation is exactly where they are." Then she turned and walked away.

I was startled and confused—what did Haley know about Bethany that I didn't?—but I did my best to smile at Liz, who smiled back dutifully. Usually, Bethany was the one to keep the conversation going in situations like these. But she wasn't here. She was on vacation. In September. Last minute. Not answering her phone.

"So," I said to Liz, but before I could continue, at the front of the room Jared cleared his throat loudly and clapped his hands together.

"Okay, guys, can we listen up?" The conversation died, and everyone turned to look in his direction.

"First off," Jared said, "I just wanna say how encouraging it is to see all of you young people here in this room, ready to serve God. I want to welcome our brothers and sisters from New Life and thank them for making the trip down. Everyone in this room is such a blessing to the Lord! I know you all have lives. You're teenagers, and there are so many other things you could be doing right now with your weekend—the last weekend before school starts, too! But you chose to come here today because you understand that *this* is more important.

"There's a genocide going on in America right now, people. A genocide nobody wants to talk about or even acknowledge. People don't want to hear, because they find it inconvenient or uncomfortable. But you know what? Sometimes, the truth *is* inconvenient; it *is* uncomfortable. So we're going out there to speak the truth in love. We're going out there, with the help of the Holy Spirit, to open hearts and minds to the truth. We know it's not easy. In the scripture, Jesus says, blessed are those who are persecuted and mocked for his name, for *theirs* is the kingdom of heaven. Let's pray."

ABORTION = MURDER!

PROTECT THE UNBORN!

IT'S A CHILD, NOT A CHOICE!

I read the signs, one by one, as Jon pulled them out of the back of the van and handed them to us kids, waiting in line in a public parking lot a block down from the clinic. It was drizzling slightly, but behind us I could see a break in the clouds, and sunlight filtering through. Soon the rain would end. As Jon pulled another sign out of the back of the van, Haley squeezed by me to the front of the line. "Oh, oh!" she said, raising her hand and jumping up and down. "That one's mine."

Jon handed Haley the sign, and she turned to me—maybe because I was the only one who didn't seem to be doing anything, maybe for some other reason. "I spent all yesterday afternoon making this," she said, holding the sign up for me to see.

It was a giant collage of photos of babies, and on closer inspection, I saw that she had written names under the pictures: *Martin Luther King Jr., Ronald Reagan, Oprah Winfrey, Taylor Swift.*

In the middle of the sign, in much larger letters, it read, *What if They Had Been Aborted?*

Haley was looking at me expectantly.

"You won't be able to tell who they are from far away," I said. "You have to be really close."

"So?" she said.

"So people passing by will just think they're random babies, not famous people, and your whole point is lost."

Haley looked at me with real hate in her eyes.

"Also," I said, enjoying myself a little, "I'm pretty sure Oprah is pro-choice."

"That's not the point," Haley snapped. "It's not about who they are. It's about opening people's eyes to the fact that all the unborn deserve the right to life."

I shrugged. "Okay." I thought of adding that Oprah would still probably object to her image being used for such a message, but held my tongue. I didn't want to start an argument. I needed to stay as under-the-radar as possible. So when Jon called me to come take a sign from the van, I obeyed, grabbing the most dispassionate, basic one available—OVERTURN ROE V. WADE—and followed the rest of the kids across the parking lot, toward the abortion clinic.

# *19*

APRIL

On Saturday evening, the last weekend of her summer vacation, April sat on the sofa in her living room and, as usual these days, couldn't think of anything to do.

This was a new experience in April's adult life—it must have been at least fifteen years since the last time she could remember feeling boredom in such an intense and enduring way. April always had things to do, more things than she could ever do, so being bored wasn't an option. And really, this hadn't changed—she still had plenty to do. It was just that the things she had to do no longer held her interest. In fact, they left her completely and excruciatingly bored.

When April ended things with Paul Frazier that night in July in the Adirondacks, when she told him to move on with his life, she had fully intended to move on with hers, as well—or, more precisely, return to her old life—the one she'd been perfectly happy with before Paul somehow crept in and shattered it.

But she hadn't really considered what going back to her old life would be like after, however briefly, living a different one. Suddenly, it was depressing to wake up in the morning without having Paul's face to look forward to seeing, although she had gone all these years perfectly fine without it. Things that used to motivate her—planning for the upcoming school year, working in her backyard, repainting a room—now seemed empty and pointless. She had little energy and less drive. Was it possible that a single week could so effectively and thoroughly render the rest of one's life void?

*So why did you end it with him, April?* asked the voice that was not quite her, not quite her sister, and not quite her mother. *Of course, you would have to eventually.* I know that. I'm not naive. *But why so soon? I mean, you had hardly even begun. There was so much more you could have gotten from each other! So much more you could have experienced! He was ready. He was game. And you know—I mean, you* know—*you'll never get that opportunity again. That was your last chance. And in the end, you really liked him, didn't you, April? That's the really sad part. Don't try to deny that you did.*

I did! I did! she would cry in her head. Can't you see that's why I had to end it? It was pointless to continue, pointless.

*Why do things have to have a point, April? What if there* is *no point? What does that word even mean: "point"?*

If a knife doesn't have a point, you can't cut anything. If a pencil doesn't have a point, you can't write anything down.

*So don't cut anything; don't write anything down. Just live. Just enjoy yourself for once, April. God damn it, why couldn't you, for once, let yourself get what you wanted?*

To drown out these arguments, halfway through the month of August, April had knocked on her daughter's bedroom door one afternoon and asked for some music to put on her phone.

Laura had been incredulous. "You want *my* music?"

April had nodded. "Please."

Sitting on the edge of Laura's bed, with Laura's laptop on her lap, scrolling through her iTunes, April had read through the band names. "The Cure," she said. "I think those guys were around when *I* was growing up."

"Yeah, Mom, they were."

She put an album by them called *Disintegration* on her phone—the title seemed appropriate.

She was just about to close out iTunes and unplug her phone from the computer when an album icon caught her eye. She clicked on the icon to enlarge it. There were four boys sitting against a bare brick wall, smoking cigarettes. One of them was Paul. He was younger—still in high school, she guessed. His hair was a little longer, and those circles under his eyes that she had come to find so captivating had not really sunk in yet. But even at this young age, there was something about him that looked older, tired, as if he knew something everyone else didn't. She read the name of his band: the Seizures. April had never once asked him about his band, his music. It simply hadn't occurred to her. There was so much she didn't know about him.

She became aware that her daughter was watching her. April cleared her throat. "That's Paul Frazier, right?"

Laura nodded. "He had this band in high school everybody was crazy about. Actually, I don't see what the big deal was."

April closed the icon and unplugged her phone. She sighed, looked around the room and then at her daughter. Laura was changing. Her freckles, once so prominent, were beginning to fade. Her body was beginning to grow into its adult form, the shape of her breasts now visible under her shirts. Since the weekend of camp, her volatile mood had begun to calm down. She was still quiet and withdrawn but no longer openly hostile, and at least, she had quit wearing her dad's horrible old sweatshirt. Still, something was bothering her, and April hadn't been able to break through her wall. "So," she said, "still not talking to Bethany?"

Laura shook her head. "I told you, I don't want to talk about that."

April nodded. "Okay, just curious."

Since Benjamin Waid told her a month ago about Bethany and Nola Sternson, April had put two and two together and determined that, at least on some level, this was why Laura and Bethany were no longer speaking. And while she no longer had any interest in the goings-on of anyone else's life, the idea that Bethany Moyer had feelings for another girl had struck a chord in April. She thought about it quite often these days, not as it pertained to the girl's life or anyone else's, but as if the girls were made-up characters in a made-up town and she wondered what they were doing, whether they were still together.

April got up off the bed. "Thanks for the music," she said, and bent down and gave her a kiss on the forehead, which her daughter tolerated graciously.

FOR THE REST OF THE SUMMER, April took very long walks. Early in the morning, before the rest of the town had woken up, or in the haze of the late-afternoon heat, she would walk, headphones in her ears. Best, though, was at night, after the sun went down and the crickets came out, stars dotting the sky, moths gathering in the glowing halos under the streetlamps. She would walk down the empty streets, listening to the Cure.

She did not expect to run into Paul on these walks, not when she went into the all-night Sunoco to grab a bottle of water, not when a car that, for a moment, she could mistake for a green Toyota cruised slowly past her on the street. She didn't expect it or even really hope for it, but every night, when she came back to the house and took off her sneakers and running clothes and changed into sweatpants and a long-sleeved T-shirt, she suffered a vague but palpable disappointment. It was the same disappointment she would feel, years ago in college, when she turned down an invitation to a party in favor of studying and then, sitting in her dorm hours later, regret it after it was much too late to change her mind. A sense that she was missing out on something but couldn't say what. A sort of all-encompassing loneliness.

And as the summer dragged to its end, this feeling grew stronger, more definite, nagging her not just at night but during the day as well—when she didn't see him at the grocery store, when she didn't see him on the way to the bank, and even, sometimes, when she got a message on her phone and saw, as always, that it wasn't from him. Of course, she didn't expect him to contact her, or maybe even want him to, but she couldn't help feeling disappointed and lonely when he didn't.

April wasn't going to church these days, but if she had been, she knew she wouldn't see him there, either. On the church newsletter email, she had read that they were looking to fill the position of sound person again.

It was as if Paul Frazier had disappeared, as if he'd never been quite real to begin with. She was even tempted to go to church one Sunday just to try to find out what had become of Sharon Frazier's son—discreetly, of course. But she wouldn't let herself stoop to that. *It's better this way*, she told herself. Every day after she once again didn't hear from him, every day that she didn't run into him by surprise in this small town, she told herself, *It's better this way.*

THE SWANSON HOUSE WAS QUIET THESE DAYS, with the children quite literally left to their own devices—Laura spending most of her time on her laptop and Jason on his gaming system. Other summers, April would force them to get off their electronics and drag them to the riverfront beach, the park—anywhere the sun was shining and people were out, determined to squeeze what little was left out of the summer. But this year, that was the last thing April felt like doing, so she let her children stay cooped up in their rooms if that was what they wanted. And there were hours, like now, when it felt almost as if she lived alone.

This evening was even quieter than usual, since Laura was away for the night. And as April wandered upstairs, she felt lonely for her daughter. She wished she could go to her room and annoy her, as she sometimes did, bursting into Laura's domain in a torrent of neediness cloaked in some mundane request.

When April eased open the door of Laura's bedroom, she found, to her disappointment but not surprise, that the room was clean and neat, with no dirty clothes for her to throw in the laundry, or empty dishes to clear away. This was probably for the best. If Laura noticed that her mother had been in her room without her permission, she'd be annoyed. Last year, for the first time, Laura had said to her, "Please don't go through my stuff without me there." April had at first been surprised, but soon saw it as a rite of passage for a teenage girl to express her need for privacy, and she respected her daughter's wish—mostly.

Standing in the bedroom, April admired her daughter's choice of posters on the walls: Kurt Cobain on one, the band Radiohead on the other, all of them staring listlessly past April with a forlorn look in their eyes.

She wondered what it meant when girls put up pictures of sad men on their walls, but she bet no teenage boy hung up pictures of girls looking similarly depressed. Marilyn Monroe—by no accounts a happy person in reality—always seemed to be having the time of her life in all the posters April had seen. And she'd be willing to bet that in the pictures of Britney Spears—or whoever was the current adolescent sex symbol, she'd stopped keeping track—they weren't looking off into the distance like the guys on her daughter's wall, ignoring you because of how sad they were.

Shutting the door of Laura's room and walking back down the hall, April heard Jason's voice. He was talking to someone in his bedroom, though she knew he was alone. Her son hardly ever talked on the phone. She knocked quietly on his door.

"Yeah?"

April opened the door and peeked inside. Jason was sitting on his bed, a video game controller in his hands, staring at the small box TV on his dresser. On his head was a pair of headphones with a mouthpiece.

"Oh, man, I just died again! I'm really sucking right now. That's the third time already."

Nowadays, to play with your friends, not only did you not have to go outside, you didn't even have to be in the same house.

Jason took off the headphones and looked at her expectantly when she came in.

"Hey," she said, smiling, "mind if come in?"

Jason looked doubtful. "Am I in trouble, or something?"

April walked into the room and perched on the end of her son's bed. "Do you have to be in trouble for me to come into your room?"

"I guess not."

"Whatcha doing? Shooting some people?"

"Yeah …"

"Okay, sorry." April moved to stand up. "I'll leave you alone."

"No, it's okay," Jason said quickly. "You can stay."

She sat for a moment and watched the TV screen. Jason was firing a machine gun with abandon. She wondered whether he would run out of bullets or whatever it was called for that kind of gun. Rounds?

"Excited to go back to school?" she asked after a while.

"Not really," said Jason. They both gave weak chuckles.

A second later, the screen image exploded in blood, and he said, "Mom, why don't we go to church anymore?"

April supposed she should have anticipated this question sooner or later. You couldn't bring your kids to church every Sunday of their lives, suddenly stop going for no apparent reason, and not expect some confusion. She should have been ready with an answer. "Well, we haven't *stopped* going, we just haven't gone for a while. I needed a break after VBS and before the school year. Some breathing time."

"Yeah, but it's been over a month now since the last time we went to church."

"Does it bother you that we haven't been going?" April asked, looking at her son.

He kept his eyes on the screen and shook his head. "No, not really. It's just a little weird, that's all."

Of her two children, Laura was the one usually up and ready for church early on Sunday mornings, while many times April would have to come into Jason's room and shake him repeatedly to get him out of bed. Once, she had even poured a glass of ice-cold water on his sleeping face, although that had mostly been for comic effect. But now she had to wonder whether not getting rousted out of bed anymore was secretly disconcerting for him.

His next question underscored the thought. "But you're still, like, a *Christian*, right?"

"Um, I …" But before April could continue, she heard the doorbell ringing. She gave her son a pat on the shoulder and said, "We'll talk about this later, okay?"

He nodded, feigning indifference and concentrating on his game, and April went downstairs to get the door.

It was Pastor Eric.

For a fleeting moment, she didn't even recognize him. Not that he was outwardly disheveled. His hair wasn't messy; his shoes weren't untied; he wasn't unshaven or wearing a mismatching outfit. But there was something in his face, in his eyes, that April had never seen in this man before: a look of worry, almost of desperation, that was fierce and uncontained.

The next instant, April collected herself. "Pastor Eric, how are you?"

Eric did his best to smile and said almost calmly, "April, hello. I'm okay. Listen, I'm really sorry to come over here like this, without calling, but I was wondering if I could come in for a minute."

"Of course. Come in." April opened the door wide and stepped aside.

"Backsliding"—that was the term used at New Life for members of the congregation who stopped coming to church for one reason or another. You were backsliding. She guessed she also should have expected this—if she stopped coming to church for an extended time, eventually her pastor would come over to find out what was wrong.

"Can I get you anything?" April asked, standing in the kitchen and offering Eric a seat at the table, feeling both nervous and irritated. "Water? Or I have iced tea."

Eric shook his head. "No, thanks. Listen, April, this is going to sound strange and out of the blue, but I have a very big favor to ask of you."

"Oh?"

"I'm sure you've heard about what happened to Bethany by now."

"No, I haven't." April felt a cold lump in her stomach. "What happened? Is she okay?"

Eric looked at her doubtfully. "Physically she's fine. It's okay if you know, April. I mean, I know word got around. And Laura's her closest friend, so it would make sense that you would know."

"Pastor Eric," she said, "I honestly don't know a thing." But now it was becoming clear where this was going. It was becoming clear that this must have something to do with what Benjamin had told her at camp—which she had not mentioned to anyone.

"We've discovered—Linda and I—that Bethany has been having a ... physical relationship with another girl. Nola Sternson, actually. We don't know exactly how long it's been going on or how ... far they've gone. It's been difficult talking to Bethany, and Linda and I—we're really at a loss." Eric's eyes filled with tears, and he put a hand to his eyes and pressed hard.

April came to the table and sat beside him, but she had no idea what to say. *I'm sorry? It'll be okay? There, there?* She had never been in a situation like this and had no basis for comparison. But she was suddenly reminded of a time, ages ago, when her marriage was quickly crumbling and she had gone to Eric to ask what to do. He had been so cool and calming. How things had changed.

"I'm sorry," Eric said, letting out a long breath and removing his fingers from his eyes after somehow magically pressing the tears back into their ducts. "It's just been really bad for us this week. Linda told a friend in confidence a few days ago, and I guess word got around the church. Apparently, that sermon on gossiping a few months back didn't really take." He forced a laugh, and April gave a faint smile. "Anyway, I was sure you must have heard by now."

"I haven't been to church in a few weeks," April said, "and Laura and Bethany haven't been hanging out for a while now."

Eric nodded. He didn't remark on April's absence from church of late. The only thing that concerned him now was his daughter. "Yeah, I wonder if Laura found out, and that's why she ..." He looked at April. "Bethany did tell us Nola was the first girl she'd ever ... been like that with. So you don't have to worry that anything happened with Laura."

April couldn't think of anything to say. This whole conversation was strange, but now Eric was acting as if his daughter had a virus or something and was assuring April that her own daughter hadn't caught it. Before, she had only felt pity for the man, but now she wasn't sure what to feel.

Eric didn't seem to notice the confused look she was giving him, though. "A few nights ago," he said, "we thought we might do better— talking to Bethany, I mean—if we went away somewhere. So we could really talk. We decided to drive upstate to Linda's parents' cabin on Lake Ontario—I don't know, we thought a change of scenery might help Bethany open up to us, get some perspective. I guess it was just wishful thinking. Things got even worse there. Linda and Bethany really went at it. They were screaming at each other. Linda even began to throw things— books, dishes. I've never seen my wife act like that before. And she was saying things. At one point, she said she thought Bethany had a demon inside her." Eric shook his head and picked up the saltshaker from the table, looked at it as if he didn't know what it was, then put it back down. "I don't know anymore. But I came here to ask you if you would come over and try to talk to Bethany."

April started. "*Me?*"

"She's in her room now. She won't come out. She won't talk to her mother or me. I'm really worried. At one point, at the lake, she talked about ... *doing* something to herself." He hesitated at April's confused look. "Suicide," he finally said, and then shook his head violently as if to get rid of the thought and, thus, the possibility. He looked at April. "Bethany always liked you, April. I don't think there's any adult in the church she respects more. And I thought if anyone could get through to her right now, it would be you."

"I don't know what I'd say to her. What you would want me to say."

He looked at her desperately. "I just need her to talk to someone. I can't let this get any worse than it already is. Please, just try."

THEY TOOK PASTOR ERIC'S CAR, and now that April had agreed to try, now that they were moving, his mood had changed. His desperation had morphed into a crazed and hopeful energy. As they drove through the town, and the clouds broke up to reveal a golden sky softening in twilight, Eric talked almost nonstop, every now and then glancing at April in the passenger seat for signs of agreement.

"I think she's really confused; that's what I think. I know, I *know* Bethany isn't that way, deep down. She's a girl who's going to grow up to do great things for the Lord—everyone can see that. It's just that, well, I think for girls it can be difficult to separate the emotional from the physical. Especially at her age, with all the hormones and the changes going on, I think it would be easy to get confused about it. You have this new friend, who you were trying to witness to, and you're sort of enamored with her. At that age, it would be easy to mistake that for love. I mean, it *is* love, even maybe, just not the sort of love Bethany thinks it is. With men, it's a little more cut-and-dried, but girls can get confused. Don't you think?"

"I … uh …" April shook her head. She was aware that the man beside her was rattling off some pretty insulting speculations, but she would have to go home and clear her head before she could properly take offense. "Did Bethany tell you she loves Nola?"

Eric nodded. "That's one of the only things she *will* tell us. Linda hasn't been helping, to be completely honest. This is very hard for her. I keep telling her we need to be patient, we need to show Christ's love here. That's the only way she'll respond. But Linda, well, she's just having a really hard time. She was the one who found them together. She opened Bethany's door without knocking, and there they were, on the bed, kissing. It was hard to see. I think deep down, Linda's blaming herself. I mean, I can't help thinking, how did I not see this coming at all? I've been so focused on the church, on my job, that I forgot about what's most important: my daughter, my family. If this has been going on for so long—at least, Bethany *feeling* this way—how did I not pick up on it?"

"It's not always easy to tell how your kids are feeling," April said, feeling for the first time that she had a useful tidbit of experience to offer. "They have ways of throwing us off the scent." She felt true compassion for the man beside her in the car. She had never seen him this way—so vulnerable, so desperate. Even at funerals, even in the wake of a national tragedy like when the World Trade Center collapsed, she had never seen him look like this. And yes, that might say something horrible about the man, but in a bizarre way, it also said something about how much he loved his daughter—whoever he thought she was.

"I'm just scared," Eric said when they had pulled up in front of his house and he turned off the car. "I'm scared that if we don't get her back now, I'll lose her forever."

Again the tears welled up in his eyes, and this time he couldn't hold them back. He began to cry, shaking silently there in the driver's seat. April still didn't know what to say, so she didn't say anything. She just put her hand on his shoulder and left it there.

Eventually, Eric wiped his eyes. "Okay," he said, "let's go inside."

# 20

## LAURA

"Abortion stops a beating heart! Abortion stops a beating heart!"

This was the chant decided upon—I'm not exactly sure how, since I didn't hear or see any of us discuss it. It was as if everyone had known ahead of time. Apparently, I'd missed the memo.

"Abortion stops a beating heart! Abortion stops a beating heart!"

My own heart was beating fast as I stood in the line with everyone, behind a tall chain-link fence that kept us from getting any nearer the clinic. By law, that was as close as we could get. On the other side of us, traffic passed on the road, and very often there would be honking horns—I was never sure whether those honks were expressions of affirmation or disapproval.

I had tried, unsuccessfully, to stay hidden in the back of the crowd. I had hoped just to stand there with my sign, like a statue, an inanimate object blending in with the others. But Jon and Jared had us spread out almost single file, so that we spanned the length of the fence. This way, I was in full view for all to see, completely exposed, and had to watch the people who came in and out of the clinic.

They kept their heads down and didn't look at us. I wondered what they must be thinking. I thought up crass jokes: *Of all the days to get an abortion, I had to pick today!*

Some of these women had people with them, but I was struck by how many I saw alone. Where were their boyfriends, their husbands, their friends, their parents? If I had to get an abortion, my mom would come with me. But, of course, I wouldn't get an abortion if I got pregnant, would I? That was the whole idea of me standing out here with this sign in my hands. I thought of that day with Ian, in his bedroom. What if we had gone all the way? What if he had impregnated me? What if part of Ian—a boy I hardly knew and, at this point, didn't want to know—what if a part of him had broken off and found its way inside me, shooting into my body and merging with a part of me, and then this new thing had grown and grown inside my body without my permission or control, and I, in turn, was supposed to feel love and protection for this thing? Suddenly, the whole idea of being pregnant seemed weird and frightening in a way I had never thought about before. And though I had no idea what I thought about abortion, I was secretly glad that none of the women who walked by us toward the clinic turned around.

We had been out here for about an hour, long enough that I'd begun to grow numb to the whole thing and now began to think about my aching feet and the beginnings of a headache. I kept looking up at the sky and hoping the clouds would open up and rain, forcing us to pack it in.

"Hey." Liz came up and offered me a water bottle. "How ya doing?"

I nodded, took the bottle, and began to open it. "Do you know how long we're going to stay out here?" I asked.

But before Liz could answer, we heard a screeching noise behind us. We turned to see a green Subaru pull out of the sluggish traffic and make a quick, sloppy job of parking on the curb right in front of us. A stocky woman with short, gel-spiked hair, wearing jeans and a brown sweater, got out of the car. Before I even had time to register my surprise that she was glaring at *me* as she approached, she was already on top of us, shouting. "You kids should be ashamed of yourselves! It's bad enough that you're doing this at all, but doing it *here*—that's just … Don't you have any decency? The last thing these women need right now are people like you waving a bunch of signs and shouting this nonsensical bullshit."

I opened my mouth, but it was dry. In that moment, I couldn't understand why this woman was so mad at me. What had *I* done? This had nothing to do with me. I was just standing here with my antiabortion sign, minding my own business. I glanced at Liz, but she also seemed to be paralyzed. A few feet away, Haley was watching the scene with interest. It was with relief that I watched Jared rush over to our aid. "Ma'am, do you have a minute to talk?" he said to the woman.

She turned her eyes from us to Jared, and you could almost see her rage transferring over to him, like a missile changing targets. "Did you bring these kids out here? You are just horrible, you know that? Brainwashing kids and then leading them here to do something like this."

"These kids have chosen to come here on their own," Jared said calmly, "speaking for those who do not have a voice. We're here because we believe life is a gift from God, and the unborn are part of—"

"What the hell would *you* know about the unborn?" she snapped. "Have you ever been pregnant, Birkenstocks? You know nothing about this, you understand me? *Nothing.*"

"I know that abortion is wrong. I know that God has a plan for each and every life he creates. I know that ..."

The woman ignored Jared and turned back to us. This time, she seemed to be almost pleading with us. "You don't have to listen to this crap, you know that, girls? Those are *your* bodies, *your* brains. Use them." And for a second, she looked as if she was about to cry. "I shouldn't have gotten out. This was a mistake," she said. Then she turned and ran back to her car.

Liz laughed nervously as her car disappeared back into the traffic. "Well, that was weird."

"She was probably a lesbian," said Haley, and glanced at me.

I tried not to look at her. My head was pounding almost as bad as my heart. I suddenly felt weak and stick to my stomach, the way I had the year before, almost as if I were about to faint, but I made myself stay on my feet. I couldn't faint. I couldn't attract any attention. *This is all for you, Martin,* I thought as I took a large gulp of water. *I'm doing all this for you.*


LATER THAT EVENING, I sat in a chair in the corner of the United Believers sanctuary, holding a cup of tea and watching everyone else carry on as if nothing had happened, as if we hadn't spent all afternoon screaming out for innocent lives and against the unseen genocide going on in our country. Half the chairs in the sanctuary had been put away, leaving the front end clear. There was a table set up with hot water for tea and hot chocolate. There were cookies and crackers, and later we'd be ordering pizza. Switchfoot was playing softly from the overhead speakers. Near the stage, I watched Haley flirt with a few of the boys of UBA, giving little jerks of her head so that her long blond hair made waves, placing her hand on one of the guys' shoulder.

Liz came over holding a handful of Oreos in a napkin. "Hey," she said, "want some?"

I shook my head. "No thanks, I'm good."

"Jared says after the pizza comes, he'll put *Lord of the Rings* on the projector. So excited."

I tried to smile. For a moment, I wished I could be like Liz, still content with the little things. I wished my heart weren't a gaping hole, wanting something I couldn't seem to find. I was fifteen, and why couldn't *I* be satisfied with hot chocolate and pizza and a movie?

One of the other girls from UBA called from across the room. "Liz, we're gonna play Twister. Come on!" A group of them were setting up the game.

Liz looked at me. "Wanna play?"

"Actually," I said, checking my phone, "I have to get ready to see my grandma. I'm meeting her in an hour." I stood up. "I'll see you later."

IT WAS ONLY WHEN I WAS ALONE, in an empty bathroom with the door locked, that I began to grow truly nervous about meeting him. Yes, a cloud of unease had been overshadowing me all day, keeping my stomach in knots and making it hard to eat, but now that unease had intensified and sharpened. I felt the way I did before I had to give a line in the school play or before taking a really difficult test I hadn't studied for—only much, much worse.

I opened up the duffel bag that I'd packed my clothes in and pulled out the brand-new pair of jeans and top I had bought and painstakingly folded so they wouldn't be creased or wrinkled. Because of where we were meeting, I had decided to dress casually, but that didn't mean I couldn't still look good.

The bathroom had a full-length mirror on the wall, and when I had finished getting dressed, I examined myself. They were the tightest-fitting jeans I'd ever worn. The fabric clung to my skin as if it wanted to fuse permanently with my body. The top I had brought was black and low-cut. I had chosen it because I thought it accentuated my breasts but also made me look thinner. Still, I was dissatisfied with the results. I didn't seem to look as good as I had when I tried it on in my room a few weeks ago.

I let my hair out of its ponytail and began to comb it. I hated my hair—its color, its frizz. It never did what I wanted it to do. It was always out to thwart my plans. Over the sink, I began putting on my makeup, trying not to overdo it. I had known I wouldn't have access to a shower or enough time to get ready properly, so the plan had been to look as if I hadn't put much time or thought into my appearance, like I had just crawled out of bed and thrown something on and still managed to look amazing. The only problem with this plan, when I examined myself again in the mirror, was that I didn't look amazing. My face was still too round, there was nothing the makeup could do about my freckles, and my hair was being a pain as usual. I turned around and looked over my shoulder into the mirror. I thought, with a mixture of pleasure and frustration, that I looked much better from this angle. Maybe it was just the jeans, but I couldn't deny that my ass looked good—almost a woman's ass, almost the kind of ass guys would turn and admire if you passed them on the street. But I wasn't sure how to feel about the idea that my butt was my best feature, that I didn't look as good from the front as I did from behind.

WHEN I CAME BACK INTO THE SANCTUARY, I prayed nobody would comment on my outfit or the fact that I was wearing makeup. But when nobody did, I felt a little worried. Did I look so ordinary that no one had even noticed? I spotted Jon over by the tables, opening the pizza boxes that had just arrived.

I made sure I was standing well in earshot of Jon when I pretended to get the phone call.

"Hello?" I spoke loudly into my phone. "Grandma? Grandma, I can't hear you." I plugged my other ear with my finger. "You're outside the church? Now? Okay, I'll be right there."

I put my phone in my pocket and turned to Jon. "That was my grandma. She's waiting out front."

Jon kept his eyes on the pizza. "Okay, Laura, have a nice time."

"Thanks." I turned and started away.

"Oh, Laura?"

I stopped; my heart stopped; I turned around.

Jon looked at me directly for the first time today. "How long will you be gone?" he asked.

"We're just getting dinner," I said. "No more than two hours."

He nodded. "All right. You've got my number, right?"

"Of course." I smiled and turned back around.

When I got outside, I saw that the clouds had cleared and the sky was a brilliant, beautiful yellow, though it was still drizzling slightly. What did they call that? A sun shower? I walked quickly down the sidewalk away from the church, and when I rounded the corner I saw the cab I had called for idling at the curb. I got in and gave the driver the address to the restaurant. As the car pulled out into traffic, I took out my phone and texted Martin to tell him I was almost there. Then I pulled my pocket mirror out of my bag and began applying a dark-red shade of lipstick.

# 21

BEN

In August my parents bought DeShawn a brand-new ten-speed bike for his birthday. I knew this wasn't what they originally had in mind. They'd been planning for weeks to get him a guitar. My dad had been doing research online—browsing user reviews and professional websites—and he'd even gone to a music store in Saratoga, to ask the owner there his opinion on what kind of guitar to buy. But when we came back from camp in July, DeShawn had changed his mind about guitar lessons.

"Why's that, DeShawn?" my dad asked him over dinner.

He shrugged. "Just don't feel like it anymore."

I watched my parents exchange looks, but they didn't press him. After two weeks went by, DeShawn still hadn't changed his mind, though he continued to blare my dad's old records in his room. My dad—though disappointed, I think—had thought of the bicycle instead. And maybe to make up for his disappointment, he got the nicest, most expensive bike in the store.

The first night DeShawn took it out, I followed on my old bike, which had stayed in the garage basically all summer. When I got on and started pedaling, it squealed in protest.

I could tell right away that DeShawn used to ride a bike a lot, and I wondered who had taught him. His mom? His dad? Riding on the sidewalk, he maneuvered quickly and easily around people or any other obstacle, never halting or changing his speed. He could ride on the grass and dart around trees and fire hydrants like it was second nature. And it was really only watching him on that bike that, for the first time, I could actually picture DeShawn back in Brooklyn, riding around his street on a New York summer night.

I didn't like taking walks, and I *hated* running, but there was something about a bike I enjoyed. Once you got some speed, you could just coast and not have to work too hard, and I liked feeling the breeze across my face, and the sense of freedom it gave us. On a bike, Grover Falls suddenly changed. I noticed things I hadn't when riding in a car, and we could go places we couldn't on foot. One Saturday in late August, DeShawn and I had ridden far outside town—over a mile, at least—down a back-country road. I'd been following his lead and was starting to get tired. I was just about to call to him that we should turn back, when he skidded to a sudden halt over a small bridge that passed over a creek running through the woods.

When I reached him, he was off his bike and peering over the edge, to the creek below.

"Yo!" he called.

I joined him and looked down. My cousin Becca was sitting on the bank of the creek, her feet in the water, a stick in her hand. When she looked up and saw us, her face blossomed in a smile. "Hey, guys!" she said. "What are you doing here?"

"What are *you* doing here?" I asked.

"Looking for crayfish," Becca said matter-of-factly. Then, sensing from our expression that this wasn't enough, she pointed left with the stick. "I live just up the road."

"What's a crayfish?" DeShawn asked.

"Come on down and hopefully, I can show you," said Becca.

We did. And when eventually Becca was able to show DeShawn, catching one under a stone and offering it to him clinging on the end of her stick, he shrieked so loud I almost didn't believe it was him. Then we all collapsed into giggles. He got her back later, though, when he found a frog and stuck it in her face.

"Wanna come back to my house?" Becca asked us later while we were putting our shoes back on.

DeShawn and I looked at each other.

"Come on," Becca said. "I'll make us grilled cheese sandwiches. My parents aren't home. It'll be fun."

Although nobody admitted it, I think it was her parents being gone that convinced us to come over. Why else would she have thought to mention it? Even though they were relatives, something about her parents, especially her dad, made me nervous.

"Where are your parents?" I asked as we followed Becca on the side of the road, pushing our bikes in front of us.

"They're both working," she answered. I hadn't planned on asking more, but she continued. "We're tight on money, so my mom had to take a weekend job, and my dad's putting in extra time at the plant. They've done this before. It costs money to travel, and we don't really have a good source of income while we're abroad."

I nodded, feeling a little embarrassed.

Their house was old and slightly run-down, set back a little way in a clearing in the woods. Although the inside wasn't dirty or anything, it was different from our house and most of my friends' houses, and I couldn't put my finger on how. It was only after we left that I realized the reason: their house focused on need, not comfort or looks. There wasn't too much in the way of decoration, and the things that were there seemed all mismatched, as if they'd hung that picture on the wall, or put that vase of flowers over there, not because they liked the way it looked, but because they knew that was what other people did in their homes. It was almost like they were just passing through, so they didn't see the point in really settling in.

Becca made us grilled cheese sandwiches and canned tomato soup, and when her older sister, Rachel, came down and saw all three of us sitting around the kitchen table eating, she looked surprised but didn't say anything—just told Becca to make sure she cleaned up after. I was surprised when DeShawn cleared the plates and helped Becca do the dishes, since he never lifted a finger at our house.

Next, Becca showed us her room. It was small, with not much more than a bed, a dresser, and a chest, though she did have a picture on her wall: a map of the world that was almost as big as I was. I had her show me where Haiti is. Sitting on her chest were a few books: a New King James Bible, a world atlas, and a book by that missionary Michael Keegan.

When we left, Becca told us we should come back again soon. And I would have liked to, but later that week Dylan came back from his family vacation, and when he and Jason started joining DeShawn and me on our evening bike rides, we never got the chance. I knew I couldn't bring Jason and Dylan.

So as the summer droned on, it was us four boys, riding around town almost every night, not really doing anything besides trying half-assed tricks on our bikes and sometimes stopping by the river in the park to skip stones. It was as if, now that the end of vacation was in sight, we wanted to be as aimless and lazy as we possibly could.

But the last weekend of vacation was gray and rainy, so on Saturday evening, DeShawn stayed in his room blaring his music, and I stayed in mine, watching TV.

I had gotten into this reality show called *Discernment*. It followed these real-life young guys around who were trying to decide whether they wanted to become Catholic priests. To be a priest, you had to be humble and selfless and devote your life to serving God. But the part the show focused on most of all was sex—Catholic priests had to give that up, too. And for much of the show, these young guys were put into situations where they were around superhot women who, for some reason, were always attracted to them. And then the camera would zero in on the guys' faces, as if asking, *Do you* really *want to give this up?* It was interesting, I thought.

I was watching a part where the potential priests had to go to Miami for some conference and ended up at this beach party where dozens of girls in bikinis flocked around them, offering them beers or martinis. The camera captured the guys' awkwardness and embarrassment as they politely turned down the drinks and tried to keep their eyes off all that cleavage.

That was when my mom walked in. "What are you watching, Ben?"

I quickly grabbed the remote and changed the channel, trying to answer casually. "Nothing, just flipping through."

My mom folded her arms across her chest and frowned. "I'm not sure I like the idea of you having a TV in here. That was meant just to be for your games."

"I wasn't even really watching," I said. "I'm just bored."

"Why don't you go outside?"

"It's raining."

My mom shook her head. "Not anymore. The sun's coming out. Go on, you and DeShawn should be outdoors. Soon, you'll be cooped up in school all day."

WHEN WE GOT OUTSIDE, I saw that my mom was right: the sun had come out, and the clouds were racing away across the sky, as if running from something. DeShawn and I walked wordlessly over to the garage and got out our bikes. By now, it was an unspoken assumption.

We rode down to the park and met Dylan by the river, where he had leaned his bike against a tree and was standing down by the shore, skipping stones across the water. We joined him. "Jason's on his way," Dylan said, and tossed a stone out. It skipped at least eight times before it sank. He was the best at skipping stones, but DeShawn was also getting pretty good now. I was terrible. I had a hard time getting even one skip out of my stone before it sank. So I just stood and watched as Dylan and DeShawn competed for the farthest-skipped stone, every now and then complimenting each other or arguing over whose rock had gone farther.

We heard Jason's bike skid to a halt behind us, and before we had even turned around, he was talking. "Oh, my god, guys, wait till you hear this. You're not even gonna believe me." He didn't even lean his bike against a tree. He just let it fall on the ground and ran over the sandy shore next to us.

"What?" said Dylan, bending down on the ground to find another stone. "Did your dick finally fall off from jerking off too many times?"

"Ha ha," said Jason. "This is serious, actually." But he had wide grin on his face. He looked at me. "Oh, man. This is gonna really kill *you*, Ben. I'm not even sure you should hear."

"What?" I said.

"Just promise me you won't have a heart attack or anything."

"What the hell are you talking about?"

"Just tell us, Jason," said Dylan.

"Okay, okay. So just before I left, Pastor Eric came over to our house to talk to my mom. I came downstairs to get a glass of water and heard what they were talking about. They didn't know I was there."

"And?" I said, feeling my heart speed up.

"*And* apparently, Bethany … she's been like, *hooking up* with that Nola girl."

"Hooking up?" Dylan repeated. "What do you mean?"

"Like *hooking up,* like … they're lesbians, I guess."

"*What?*" said Dylan.

Jason looked at me. "Ben, you're still standing. Did you hear what I said?"

I shook my head, pretending to be surprised. "Wow," I croaked. "Wow, that's crazy." I glanced at DeShawn for the first time. He was staring at me hard.

"Yeah," Jason was saying, "Pastor Eric seemed really upset. I've never heard him sound like that before—like he was about to cry, even. What do you think they're gonna do to her?"

"Ground her till she's eighteen?" said Dylan.

Jason snorted. "Try for life. I bet they lock her up in her room, only let her come out for meals and the bathroom. It'll be like in that stupid movie we watched in social studies last year, *Nell.*"

"That's different," said Dylan. "In that movie, the girl wasn't socialized at all, ever since she was a baby."

"You'd still be pretty weird if your parents locked you up for the rest of your life."

"Yeah, but Nell didn't know *anything.* She had to learn basic English."

"Her parents are really gonna be that mad?" DeShawn asked suddenly.

Jason looked surprised by the question, for a second, then nodded. "Oh, yeah. I mean, this is like the worst thing she could possibly do to them. I'll bet they'd be happier if they caught her with drugs, or even pregnant, because at least, that would mean she was doing it with a *boy.*"

His smile faded. "And I guess things aren't good. I thought I heard Pastor Eric say she was even threatening to, like, kill herself."

Nobody said anything for a moment, so I could feel my heart sinking.

"I wonder how they found out," said Dylan finally.

I swallowed. For a second, I wanted to say it: I was the one. It was me. I told your mom, Jason, and she must have gone to Pastor Eric about it even though she'd told me she wasn't going to. I was the reason Bethany's life was ruined.

"Man, that's sad," DeShawn said. "I liked Bethany." Speaking about her in the past tense, as if she was dead.

"You didn't really know her, DeShawn," I said.

"I knew her," he said defensively. "She always talked to me at Bible school. She liked me."

"That's just because you're black and from the city. That's the only reason people in this town like you." The words were out of my mouth before I even knew what I was saying. There was a horrible moment of dead silence. DeShawn was looking out at the river. Jason and Dylan were looking at me wide-eyed and openmouthed. Then, without a word, DeShawn turned and walked back up the bank onto the grass, where he got on his bike and rode away.

"Man, what the hell is *wrong* with you?" said Jason.

I didn't look at him. I began to hunt around for a smooth stone, keeping my eyes on the ground. I heard them get on their bikes and follow DeShawn.

After a minute of searching, I found the flattest stone I could, held it in my hand for a moment, then flung it out over the water, the way I had seen my friends do so many times. It sank without a single skip.

I sat down on the damp sand. Although I didn't think DeShawn would tell my parents, I wondered what they would say if they found out what I'd said. Usually, in my imaginary arguments with my parents—the ones that came before the actual arguments—I could come up with a pretty solid defense. But now I couldn't think of anything.

I remembered the day back in the summer, during VBS, when DeShawn argued with Jon Newman over that song "Amazing Grace." DeShawn had said there was no way he needed grace as much as the man who wrote the song, John Newton, the slave trader. And now I decided DeShawn was right. People like us, modern-day Americans who followed the rules, we'd never done anything even *close* to as bad as what that guy had done, and we never would. But that didn't make me feel better. Because it seemed to me that in the world there were really good people, like Michael Keegan, and really bad people, like slave traders and murderers and rapists and pedophiles, and Jesus had come for the really bad people. But what about the people in between? People like me, who would never do anything really horrible—just millions of little things, like being mean to our foster brothers for no reason, or sitting on our asses all day playing video games, or mouthing off to our parents, or just knowing there were people out in the world in trouble and still not giving a shit. I didn't think we deserved hell, but I didn't think we deserved heaven, either.

The sun was now setting over the river, making the sky bleed red. I thought that maybe we didn't deserve anything, so that's what we got.

# 22

## PAUL

Paul Frazier didn't have what it took to kill himself. He'd had the fantasies: a gun to the throat, the cold metal against his skin; a razor to the wrists, the warm blood vacating his arms and turning the bathwater a deep, dark scarlet. But these were only fantasies. He was jealous of those who could do more than fantasize. Suicide was the definitive life statement, the ultimate mike drop. One single act, and the way you were perceived changed forever. Were Paul to take his own life, he would no longer be a pathetic failure without a job, who lived with his mother, but a tragic artist who died too young. The problem, of course, was that he wouldn't be around to enjoy this reputation.

Despite everything, Paul still loved his life. No matter how empty or hopeless it had become, no matter how banal, he just couldn't bear to part with it. And he hated himself for this. He hated how it so thoroughly undermined the legitimacy of his depression. If his life was really that bad, he'd have no qualms about letting it go. Suicide gave you a way out, and if you didn't take it, could you really complain about where you were? Deep down, he was just a selfish, frightened kid, clinging to life like a child clinging to a security blanket, desperately and with sweaty palms.

So, since he couldn't actually be dead, for the rest of the summer he did the next best thing: he pretended to be. Again, the mornings spent in bed till well after noon, the shades pulled down over the windows. Again, he dodged his mother's questions and probing looks, her pleas for him to make an appointment with the doctor. He did his best to view his life trajectory as a forgone conclusion, something he had no power or control over. He did his best to block from his thoughts anything that triggered his anxiety: his jobless status, the unopened letters from Sallie Mae that kept coming, sustained reflection on just about every person he had ever cared about. He couldn't keep thoughts of April at bay, but he did his best to think of her in the past tense, as a person who had once existed but could no longer be attained. She was beyond his reach. This gave his extended fantasies a doomed, tragic mood.

Nicki's pregnancy was another matter.

On the Sunday when Paul returned from the VBS camp, when Tommy told him Nicki was pregnant it had taken him a moment to catch up to the words.

Paul had stood there confused. *Mine? It's not mine. I didn't ask for one. I don't want one.* Then rudimentary biology kicked in, and he felt a heavy weight pressing down on his chest. "Where is she?" he asked.

Five minutes later, Paul was in his car, speeding up the road to Saratoga, where Nicki worked at an Olive Garden. Barreling through the sunny afternoon, he concentrated on breathing as slowly and deeply as he could. The bag of weed Tommy had given him sat in the passenger seat like a dumb, happy-go-lucky companion, not taking his problems the least bit seriously. For a moment, he even considered pulling over to the side of the road and toking up.

When he reached the Olive Garden, he couldn't find a parking spot right away. It was Sunday afternoon, a time when many families chose to gorge themselves on their idea of Italian cuisine. Paul drove around the building twice before spotting a couple and their three kids making their way from the restaurant to a white Suburban. He tried to be patient, keeping his hands wrapped around the steering wheel so he wouldn't honk the horn. But these people were so slow, waddling their way across the parking lot like a herd of landlocked walruses. They had to see him there, waiting for their spot, yet they took their sweet-ass time. He gave his horn two quick beeps. The parents shot him fierce glares without quickening their glacial pace, and he had to wait another minute and a half before the spot was free.

In the restaurant foyer, he brushed past the line of people waiting to be seated, ignoring their indignant looks. "Can I help you, sir?" someone asked him, but Paul wasn't listening. He was scanning the restaurant, looking at all the waitresses. It occurred to him that she might not be a waitress—Tommy had said only that she worked here—she might be in the kitchen, for all he knew.

He spotted her in the corner, waiting on a family at a round table. Jesus Christ. Was it the same family from the parking lot, coming back for more? It *was* the same family! No, all these middle-American families just looked interchangeable: fat, dumb, and hungry. Nicki smiled widely at them and threw her head back to laugh at something the father had said. She was being a good waitress; she would make a decent tip. "Sir?" somebody said in his ear. Paul turned distractedly to see a towheaded kid with teenage acne still on his face, addressing him uncomfortably. His name tag said *Kevin*.

Paul pointed. "I just need to see ..."

Nicki turned her head. She caught Paul's eye. For a moment her smile faded, then she turned back to the family. In that moment, Paul hated her. She clearly knew what he was here for, yet she was ignoring him. This family's lunch was more important.

"Sir, you need to wait to be seated," Kevin said.

Paul shrugged him off. "No, I don't want to eat I just need to—"

"I think you'd better leave, sir."

Was he really about to get kicked out of an *Olive Garden*? Had his life come to this?

The next second, Nicki was in his face, eyes flaring. "What are you doing here?"

"We need to talk."

"Can't you see I'm working?"

"Your brother told me, Nicki," Paul said.

She opened her mouth, then closed it again. Kevin hadn't left. Paul kept Nicki's gaze and waited. "Meet me out back in ten minutes," she said, then walked away toward the kitchen.

THE FIRST THING NICKI did when she came out the back door of the restaurant, into the empty lot where the dumpsters sat, was to pull a pack of cigarettes out of her pocket and light up. "You don't have to say it," she said, taking a long drag. "I already know smoking's not good for the baby."

Paul had been standing out on the asphalt, baking in the hot sun and the rotting-vegetable smell of the dumpsters. He already felt a little sick, and when Nicki said the word "baby," he thought for a moment that he might vomit.

He coughed and cleared his throat. "How long have you known?"

Nicki thought for a moment. "Since Monday, so a week now, I guess."

"Were you planning on telling me?"

She studied him for a second, holding the cigarette just away from her lips. "I hadn't decided yet."

"Seriously? I have a right to know, Nicki."

She raised her eyebrows. "Yeah? Okay, so what are you gonna do, now that you have this knowledge that is rightfully yours?"

Paul hesitated. He had seized eagerly on the idea of Nicki's not telling him being some horrible injustice, but she had just called his bluff. She knew, even if he wouldn't admit it, that he would much rather never have found out. He ran his finger and thumb down the length of his nose. "I don't know," he mumbled. "I'm sort of in shock. I thought that night you told me you were on the pill."

"I *was* on the pill."

Paul nodded. "Okay."

Nicki let out a breath of disbelief and took another drag. "Wow, you don't believe me. That's great."

"No, I do. It's just … incredibly bad luck, I guess."

"Well, that's me: Nicki Chambers, the girl with incredibly bad luck."

Paul asked the question he'd been waiting to ask ever since Nicki confirmed she was pregnant. "So … have you thought about, you know, taking care of it?"

Nicki shook her head and chuckled. "Why can't guys ever say the word? It's like 'Voldemort' or something with you. *Abortion*—am I going to get an abortion?"

Paul sighed. "Yeah. Are you?"

Nicki paused. "I haven't decided yet."

Up until now, Paul had been anxious, but his anxiety had had an escape route, somewhere it was heading. He had fully expected Nicki to tell him yes, she was getting an abortion, and would he go with her to the clinic. Now all escape routes were quickly getting sealed off—a disaster zone inside his head.

"Nicki," he said, keeping his voice calm, "you can't really be thinking about keeping it."

"Last I checked, it was still legal in this country for a woman to keep her baby."

"Come on, think seriously about this. You're not ready to have a kid. You're not—"

She cut him off. "Oh, you don't think I've been 'thinking seriously' about this?" She tossed her cigarette on the pavement and ground it out. "That's all I've been doing for the past seven days. And you don't fucking know me, Paul, so don't tell me what I am and am not ready for. I've had an abortion before. Did you know that? I was sixteen, and my boyfriend convinced me not to tell anyone and brought me to the clinic. Two weeks later, he dumped me—said I was getting too emotional. I don't know if I want to do that again."

"It would be different this time," Paul said quickly, "I would—"

"You'd *what*, Paul?" Nicki snapped. "Hold my hand? Tell me everything's gonna be okay? You don't know what it's like, and you never will."

"Having a baby is a lot to go through, too."

"Oh, jeez, I didn't know that!"

Paul took a deep breath and looked up at a clean slate of blue sky.

"Look, I gotta get back in there," Nicki said after a moment. "Call me later if you want." She turned and went back into the restaurant.

Paul stood in the glaring sun, his breath coming fast and sharp. He knew he should wait, come up with a solid, reasoned argument, and call her later. He had logic on his side—history, statistics. He could create a PowerPoint, go through all the reasons with her, slide by slide. Use visual effects. But the prospect of driving back home with this lump in his chest, and sitting in his bedroom, his breath coming so heavy he couldn't even smoke the pot Tommy gave him, the idea of finally calling her, and her still unwilling to listen to reason—it was all too much to handle. Everything was narrowing to a pinpoint. He had to do something. Now.

So he charged through the doors, into the hot, stuffy kitchen. The clatter of dishes, fog from running water, people calling to each other. Before anyone even noticed him, he was already through another set of doors, back into the dining area. People eating their pasta and ziti and lasagna without a care. Sheryl Crow on the speakers, soaking up the sun, telling him to lighten up. His eyes scanned the room. Nicki was at a booth near the windows, asking an elderly couple if they were enjoying their meal.

He paused only a moment before marching straight over to the booth. He cleared his throat. Nicki turned from the couple, her smile disappearing. "Excuse me a second," she said without looking at them, and then grabbed him by his arm and yanked him roughly away.

"What are you doing?" she hissed, marching him across the room.

"We need to talk about this more. You didn't give me enough time to—"

Nicki stopped and let go of him just in front of the entrance. "Are you kidding me? I'm *working*, Paul. I told you to call me later."

"You don't understand what it is you're considering. You're not thinking straight. It's not like you can have the baby and then we just go back to our lives. It's not like that."

Nicki shook her head. "Paul, listen to my words. You … need … to … leave."

He knew he was babbling. He was aware that he was now hurting his cause, not helping it. But he couldn't stop himself. "Once you have a kid, that's it—your life's over. There's nothing else after that. And what are we supposed to do? We're not even dating. Why the fuck would we have a kid together? Why the fuck would you want to do that to yourself, to me? Is this just some sick, twisted way of getting back at me? Because it's not worth it, Nicki. I'm a bad person, I know I am, but that's all the more reason not to have my kid. Trust me, you don't want my kid, Nicki. You don't."

He heard Kevin's voice near his ear: "Sir, I'm going to have to ask you to leave. Right now."

"I'm not finished," Paul snapped. He saw Nicki turning away and took a step toward her. And when he felt Kevin's hand gingerly touch his shoulder, Paul would have liked to say that instinct kicked in, that it all happened so fast, he didn't know what he was doing. He would have liked to say that, but in reality, he was aware of everything he did. When he shoved Kevin roughly away, he knew what he was doing. And when Nicki shouted his name and grabbed him by the arm to stop him, and he spun around and pushed her with a swift and startling violence, in that instant he knew what he was doing.

It was only after he'd done it and she was sitting on the floor of the Olive Garden, holding her arm and looking up at him with eyes wide from astonishment more than pain—this pretty, frightened girl who was carrying their child—that he felt the shame and regret rising in him.

He left the restaurant without another word.

By the end of August, deep into Paul's withdrawal from the world of the living, it occurred to him, almost accidentally, that eight weeks had now passed since Nicki became pregnant. If she hadn't already made her decision, she would be making it soon. But of course, he hadn't heard from her, and of course, he hadn't dared to call.

So on the first Saturday of September, when his mother called up the stairs in the evening to tell him he had a phone call, Paul felt a little quiver in his chest. It had to be Nicki. But what would she say to him? And what could he possibly say to her? He knew that "sorry" wouldn't be enough this time—not that it ever had been. But he had nothing else to give.

When he came downstairs, his mom was sitting out on the front porch. Any opportunity she could find to get him out of the house, she seized. Paul stepped outside, blinking in the sunlight, and took the phone from his mom. Feeling suddenly queasy, he said, "Hello?"

It wasn't Nicki.

"Paul Frazier. Jesus Christ, you're a hard person to get hold of, you know that?"

It took Paul a few seconds to place the guy's voice. "Niles?" he asked hesitantly.

"Guilty as charged."

Niles, his old bandmate. Niles, who Paul had lived with in Brooklyn. Niles, who Paul had punched in the face once after he told a bartender to cut Paul off. Niles, who, very soon after that incident, had left the band, though he cited other reasons—namely that all of them were broke, the band was going nowhere, and, since Sasha had left Paul, Paul seemed to be going crazy. They hadn't parted on the best of terms.

"How'd you get this number?" Paul heard himself asking, glancing over at his mom, who was pretending to be absorbed in a book.

"It wasn't easy, man. If that's what you were going for, well done."

It had really been only a few months since Paul last saw Niles, but hearing his voice on the phone was still disconcerting. He felt as though Niles, Sasha, and all the other people he'd known in New York should have disappeared, existed in a parallel universe. Paul, who had deactivated his Facebook account months ago, who had gotten rid of his phone and never checked his email, found it strange that someone could still find him if they really wanted to.

Things only got stranger. Paul listened to Niles chatter away, surprised by his friendly, not-at-all-begrudging tone, and slowly he began to comprehend what Niles was telling him.

Paul remembered Mira Borsa, right? That Slavic chick who lived in Greenpoint and looked a lot like Nico? The Seizures had opened for her a couple of times, and she'd had that one song where she played nothing but a xylophone for fifteen minutes. Well, it turned out one of Mira's garage music videos had gone viral on YouTube a while back. While the Seizures were falling apart last winter, she had been signed by Rough Trade Records and went to London to cut an album. "Mira Mira" was her stage name.

She'd been on tour all summer in Europe and had really blown up over there. They were extending her tour into the States this fall. A major cell phone service provider was using her single for its new commercial. Niles was surprised Paul hadn't heard about this.

Paul was beginning to wonder why Niles felt the need to keep him informed of another musician's good fortune, when Niles finally got around to the point. A few days ago, Mira had contacted Niles online, out of the blue, and asked him to get lunch with her in Manhattan. Over Thai food on the Upper East Side, Niles, surprised that she had even thought to look him up, was even more surprised when she began to ask him about the Seizures. He'd told her they were taking a temporary hiatus. Then she had gone off on how much she loved the band, how much energy they had on stage, and how she had always admired their raw power.

"She asked about you a lot," Niles told him.

"Me?"

"Yeah. I covered for you, said you were visiting family upstate at the moment."

Mira had recorded her debut largely by herself, on her computer, and had found it difficult to translate to a live experience. Even though things were going really well for Mira Mira, she was dissatisfied with the tour. She wanted something heavier, more muscular and intense. She started talking about the confines of big record labels and how her art was suffering from it—she needed to do something brash and exciting to reignite the creative flame. And before Niles knew what was happening, she was offering the Seizures a gig as Mira Mira's band for the American leg of the tour, which kicked off in less than two weeks and wrapped up by Thanksgiving. Afterward, if things went well, she wanted to explore cutting an album with them—something raw and rough. She wanted to do it live in the studio.

"So, man," Niles said, "I've already talked to the other guys. I've spent over a day tracking you down. She needed a definite answer yesterday, but I'm willing to forgive you, provided you get your ass down here as fast as you can. I've got a couch you can crash on till the tour starts." Paul cleared his throat. "Wow, that's ..." He paused. "You think I could call you back tomorrow, take a night to think about it?"

"*Think about it?* What the hell is there to think about? What are you doing up there? Flipping burgers? Bagging groceries?"

"I'm unemployed, actually."

"Not anymore. You're going on a cross-country tour: Chicago, Seattle, Los Angeles, San Francisco. *California*, compadre! Are you listening? There's nothing to think about. This is our big break, the one we kept waiting for that never came. Here it is."

"Have you heard from Sasha at all?"

"Jesus Christ, Paul."

"I was just curious."

"Look, man, I need an answer. I mean, she wants our band, but not bad enough to delay her tour for you."

Paul let out a breath. "All right. Okay. Yeah."

"Yeah?"

"Yeah."

"Can you be down here by tomorrow?"

"I'm leaving now."


PACKING UP HIS CAR TOOK LONGER than he expected. His mother didn't offer to help; she just sat at the kitchen table, drinking seltzer and watching him as he traveled back and forth between his room upstairs and his car parked out front, quickly emptying the house of his belongings.

After a while, he didn't even bother trying to pack anything away in an orderly fashion—just grabbed armfuls of clothing or stacks of records and tossed them into the car. His guitars took up almost all the trunk, so most of the rest he piled haphazardly in the back seat. Soon, it was a jumble of boxes, records, loose clothing, and blankets. By the time he finished, it was dark. He shut the trunk and turned to go inside.

"You leaving?"

Paul turned back around to find DeShawn standing in the middle of the empty street, astride his bike.

There were a lot of things Paul could feel guilty about at this point, concerning his time in this town, quite a few people he would just as soon never see again. And DeShawn was right there at the top of the list. "Yeah," he said. "Going back to New York City ... *I do believe I've had enough*," he added in a bad Bob Dylan impression, and gave a weak smile.

DeShawn stared at him blankly.

Paul moved to go back into the house, then stopped and turned to look at DeShawn. "Not that you should listen to me, or anything," he said, "but here's a piece of advice: get out of this town as soon as you possibly can, DeShawn. Get out and don't come back."

DeShawn gave a snort—Paul couldn't tell whether it indicated agreement or contempt—then he put his feet on the bike pedals and rode away.

"So I'm heading out," Paul said, standing in the kitchen and facing his mother, who was still sitting at the table.

Sharon nodded without looking at him. "Uh-huh."

"If I go now, I'll get into the city late, avoid any traffic."

"Sure."

He looked around the room, scratched at the back of his neck. "Look ... thanks a lot, Mom, for everything."

"Anytime."

Paul flinched. Had she meant for that to sound as mean as it did? "You know, it's going to be different this time. This is something real. I have actual work."

Sharon nodded and finally looked at him with sad eyes. "So you told me."

"Okay, well, I guess I'm off."

His mom stood up and approached. When she hugged him, Paul was startled. She had never hugged him that way before, so tight, as if this were the last time they would ever see each other. "Take care of yourself," she said as she let go.

He nodded and turned to leave.

"Paul," she said, and he stopped. "What happened at the VBS? Why did you quit like that?"

She had asked him this question before, more than once, but the way she said it now was different, as though she already knew the answer. He opened his mouth but couldn't drag up his usual lies or excuses. He kept his face away from her so she couldn't see.

"Was there a girl, Paul?" he heard her ask. "Somebody at church?"

He forced himself to laugh. "No, Mom, there wasn't a girl. I just couldn't deal with it anymore."

"It's just … there were a few days near the end where you were different. For a second there, I thought you were actually happy."

Paul looked at his mother and smiled. "Yeah, for a second there, I thought I was, too."

PAUL WENT OUT TO HIS CAR. It was dark and there was a soft, cool breeze. Somewhere, a dog barked. He stood in the driveway for a moment, then got into his car, turned the key, backed out onto the street, and drove away.

# 23

LAURA

The hostess had long, shimmering dark hair and a perfect hourglass body, shown off in a black top and tight black jeans. She was beautiful. When she greeted me at the door, I wanted to strangle her.

"I'm meeting someone here," I said, surprised that my voice still worked. "Banner? Martin Banner?" It came out like a question—was I really meeting Martin here, beautiful hostess, the man I had stayed up so many nights talking to without ever actually hearing his voice? You tell me.

She smiled. "Right this way."

I followed her into the dimly lit restaurant, past an older woman drinking a latte alone, bent over a thick book; past a middle-aged couple, busy devouring their food so they wouldn't have to talk to each other. Looking at the hostess' butt made me much less confident in my own. I no longer wanted to strangle her. Now I just wanted to crawl inside her, keep my brain but inhabit her body, see how it felt to be treated when you looked like that. Why wasn't this scientifically and medically possible yet?

These were the crazy thoughts running through my mind as she brought me into the back room, which was larger than I expected, and gestured to a small table in the corner.

I saw him. He was sitting at the table, head down, scrolling through his phone. It was him. All those countless words I'd read on my laptop, this man had written. All those nights I had gone to bed and couldn't sleep, he'd been at the center of my restless dreams. I suddenly wanted to grab the hostess' hand and not let go, have her lead me to the table and make the introductions. But she had already disappeared, off to help the next online couple meet in person. I swallowed, touched my face randomly, then walked up to the table.

"Martin?" I said, and again my voice came out strong and clear. "Hello."

And I would remember for a long, long time the expression that spread across his face when he looked up at me. It came in a swift and violent evolution, like a sped-up blossoming of a flower on one of those TV nature programs. But later I would slow it down in my mind and parse it out, analyze what was going through his head with each change in his face.

First, simple confusion. When he looked up and saw me, his initial reaction was to wonder innocently what this teenage girl was doing standing in front of him. But a moment later, he realized I had just said his name, and the confusion deepened, and the creases in his forehead grew harder and seemed to freeze there. Then I saw him searching frantically though his mind for an explanation, cocking his head to the side just a bit, and when he couldn't come up with anything, that was when the horror came. The implications began to rise up out of the haze. Still, he didn't seem completely convinced that this was happening. He stared at me as if I were a ghost.

All this occurred in less than five seconds, and before he could do anything, I sat down across from him at the table. He actually flinched, as if surprised that I could move.

"Martin," I said, and smiled, "it's me, Kim."

His voice was a hoarse whisper. "What is this? What are you doing?"

"I'm here to meet you for dinner," I said, making my voice loud, as though he really didn't understand, as if I were talking to a small child or someone with a mental disability.

He shook himself. "I have to go," he said, and stood up.

And for a moment, I pictured him leaving me here alone. All those late-night chats, all that planning and conniving for nothing, just so I could sit here in a trendy restaurant in Albany, alone. I was so seized by horror at this prospect that my voice came to me unsummoned. "Wait!"

I cried loud enough that everyone around us could hear. "Dad, you can't leave me here! I have no way to get home!"

The tables around us fell silent. The middle-aged couple in the front room craned their necks back to see what was going on behind them. A group of teenage girls around my age, at a table at the other end of the room, looked up from their phones and iced coffees to stare. Martin was halfway out of his seat when he saw the attention we were getting. He paused for a moment, then sat back down. "I'm not leaving," he said, and laughed nervously. "No, I'm not leaving."

"Oh, good," I said, and smiled, shifting myself more comfortably in my seat.

I felt the eyes that had been on us go back to their own tables. Martin was about to say something when our waitress arrived. She wasn't nearly as attractive as the hostess, and I was grateful for that, at least. I didn't want Martin to be forced to compare. While she introduced herself as Mindy, I stared at Martin, who was looking intently at her so he didn't have to look at me.

As if to underscore the wrongness of what I had done, Martin was exactly as he'd presented himself in the few online photos I'd seen: a little scruffy but undeniably attractive for a middle-aged man. His hair was brown with gray streaks, and he had a small pair of glasses perched on the end of his nose. I liked the fact that he hadn't given in to contacts. I wanted to think that he looked smart and in control, but at the moment, he really didn't. Staring at the waitress and trying to ignore me, he looked terrified.

"Can I start you off with drinks?" Mindy asked.

It was a second before I realized she was looking at me. Surprised, I ordered coffee, though I didn't drink coffee. Martin muttered that he would stick with water.

When Mindy left, I cleared my throat to speak, but I had no words. Of course I had expected Martin to be surprised. I had expected him to be shocked and angry. But the way he looked at me, as if I were the grim reaper, as if I had ripped his heart out of his chest and were devouring it in front of him, made thinking difficult. I had expected to be the one nervous and a little frightened. Instead, I found that I was the one with all the power. I was the one who had to keep *him* calm. Still, there was something I liked about the power I seemed to have over him. He was legitimately terrified of me. When I kept him here just by raising my voice, I had felt dangerous and powerful.

It was Martin who spoke first. "So," he said, moving his napkin and silverware around on the table to avoid meeting my eyes, "the whole time, it was you?"

I nodded, feeling suddenly guilty. "Yeah, pretty much."

He looked up at me sharply. "'Pretty much?'" he repeated. "What does that mean?"

"No, sorry, it means yes. It was just me."

He looked back down. "Listen," he said, taking the napkin and beginning to tear it into shreds, "I don't know what, exactly, you were thinking here, but you have to know that this is illegal. I could get in a lot of trouble, but you could, too. I have all the evidence online. You led me to believe you were a woman—a woman my age—and ..." He looked up at me again. "How old are you?"

"Eighteen," I said.

He continued to look at me.

"Fifteen," I mumbled.

"Christ," he said. "Where are your parents?"

"My mom doesn't know I'm here. She doesn't know anything about this." I thought of Martin seeing my mother. All the pictures of Kim he'd seen online were of her. If only I could inhabit my mother's body the way I had wanted to inhabit the hostess', then Martin would have smiled when he saw me. Then he would have worked his hardest to impress me and make me laugh, tried to get me back to his place for drinks.

"Listen," Martin was saying, now looking desperate, a man pleading his innocence, "we can still get out of this. We just get up, go back to our homes, delete our accounts, and no one will ever know the difference. No one gets in trouble."

Although I didn't like what he was saying, I was glad to hear him treating me like a real person, like someone he was trying to convince. "Martin," I said, trying to make my voice warm and soothing, "we're just having dinner. That's all. There's nothing illegal about that." Out of the corner of my eye, I saw our waitress returning with our drinks. "I just want to spend some time with you, Dad," I said loudly, leaning forward across the table. "We never spend time together anymore."

Mindy smiled awkwardly as she placed our drinks on the table, probably wondering what sort of kid talked to her dad that way. "You guys ready to order?"

I looked at Martin pointedly. He sighed, picked up the menu, and pointed to the first thing he saw. I ordered the Caesar salad.

When we were alone again, I smiled and leaned forward. "Martin, relax. It's only dinner."

For a second, he looked at me with something that, although definitely not affection, was at least a sort of respectful wonder. I thought maybe I had him. I took a sip of my coffee. It was bitter and hot.

# 24

APRIL

It had been a long while since April last visited the Moyers' house, which by itself was a little telling, given that until recently, her daughter had spent basically every weekend and many a weeknight here. The times April came to pick Laura up, she had taken to parking out front and sending her daughter a text rather than going inside. She had never really considered why she started doing this. At the time, it had just seemed convenient. But now, as she followed Pastor Eric into the house and felt a little quake of nervousness, she wondered.

Of course, these weren't normal circumstances. Standing in his own living room, Eric looked around as if he didn't quite know where he was. April lingered near the doorway, waiting for instructions that he didn't give. Finally, she asked, "Is Linda here?"

"She's, uh …" Eric continued to look around the room distractedly. "She might be …" He trailed off when his wife appeared in the doorway from the kitchen.

Just passing this woman on the street, you wouldn't notice anything unusual. It was only here, in close proximity, that April could make out the sharp lines in the woman's face, the slightly bloodshot eyes, the clothes that looked slept in.

Linda smiled. "April! Nice to see you. How are you?"

April looked at Eric in confusion, but he was studying the sofa in the middle of the room, playing with a button that had come undone from the top lining.

"I'm well, Linda," April said. "How are you?"

Linda smiled and nodded and didn't answer.

Eric looked up from the sofa to his wife. "April's here to see if she can talk to Bethany. I've explained the situation already."

Linda nodded again. "Well, she's in her room," she said. And turning, she walked out of the room.

A moment later, April heard a door slam somewhere in the house.

She looked at Eric. "Linda doesn't want me here."

Eric continued to avoid her eyes. "We talked about it. She doesn't think it'll help, but I think it's worth trying. Like I said, Bethany respects you."

"Yeah, but I don't know if I'm comfortable—"

"April." Eric cut her short, looking her in the eyes. "Please."

As they went up the stairs, April felt herself growing more and more nervous, in a way she had no context for. This was her daughter's fifteen-year-old friend, who April was now scared to talk to. It was bizarre. But at the same time, a weird feeling of déjà vu kept flickering in the corners of her mind. She had been in this situation before, but for the life of her, she couldn't remember when.

At the top of the stairs, Eric pointed to the closed door of Bethany's room. Apparently, he didn't want even to announce April's presence to his daughter, as if the mere sound of his voice might ruin things.

April took a deep breath and tapped lightly on the door. No answer. *Suicide*, Eric had said, and for a second, April had the vision of Bethany lying naked in the bathtub, submerged in a pool of red. She could hear the muffled voices of doctors and nurses, hear the soft ding of elevator doors, smell the disinfectant odor of a hospital ward. Her stomach turned, and she had to take a deep breath. She turned to look at Eric, who was now standing halfway down the stairs, waiting. He gestured for her to knock again. She did, and this time, Bethany's muffled voice came from inside.

"What?"

April cleared her throat. "Bethany? Hey, it's April. April Swanson."

A long pause. "Ms. Swanson?"

"Yeah," she said. "Can I come in?"

"Okay."

She opened the door gently. Bethany was sitting up on her unmade bed, wiping her face. Her long dark hair was free and uncombed, and she was wearing gym shorts and an oversize Looney Tunes T-shirt that reached almost to her knees, Bugs Bunny munching on a carrot.

"Hey," April said, coming into the room. "Nice shirt."

Bethany looked down at it and sniffed. "Sorry, I'm not really dressed. I wasn't expecting anyone to come over." She looked up. "What are you doing here?" The question didn't come off as hostile or rude, just puzzled.

"Your dad asked me if I'd come over and talk to you."

"Why did he ask *you?*" Again only puzzlement.

April gave a half shrug. "Um, I guess he thought I might be able to help."

Bethany looked at her for a few seconds, as if realizing something for the first time. April soon guessed what she must be thinking. *No, Bethany, I'm not a closet lesbian,* she wanted to say. *I like boys—half my age and brooding, if possible.* She said, "Just 'cause, you know, I've known you for a long time and you and Laura are so close."

"Oh." Bethany nodded, looking slightly disappointed if not entirely convinced. "Well, Laura hates me now."

April came and sat down beside her on the bed. "Bethany, I'm sure Laura doesn't hate you. You know her—sometimes she holds on to things for a while." She paused. "Does she know …?"

Bethany shook her head. "I only just told her, in a letter." She ran her face through her hands and groaned. "Do you ever feel like you're going crazy?"

April smiled. "Only every day!" she said loudly, regretting it at once when Bethany gave her a confused look. "Sorry," she said. This whole situation seemed incredibly weird to her, but the feeling melted when she saw how Bethany looked: frightened and confused, unsure of anything. April looked around the room. The walls, painted a pale yellow, were completely bare. "You need some pictures or something to hang up in here," she said.

"My mom came and tore down all my band posters," Bethany said.

"She thinks they've been corrupting me. Like looking at rock bands all day turned me on to girls."

April nodded wisely. "That makes sense."

They both began to giggle. "I was planning on repainting my room soon anyway," said Bethany.

April hesitated a moment, then said, "Do you want to talk about it—like, how you're feeling?"

"What did my parents tell you?" Bethany asked, still looking at the wall.

"Your dad just said you were going through some—"

"My parents think I'm sinning," Bethany interrupted, "that my feelings for Nola are wrong and sinful. And I thought that, too, at first. I tried to stop them—my feelings, I mean. For weeks, I asked God to take them away, I prayed and prayed to him, but the feeling just got stronger. So what kind of sense does *that* make? If it's so wrong, why wouldn't God take it away if you asked him to? And I wanted him to do it, I really did." She wiped her eyes. "So finally, I just got sick of it. I told myself, if this is what being wrong feels like, what sinning feels like, then I don't care. If I go to hell, I go to hell. I'm in love with Nola, end of story." She looked at April. "Do you think that's crazy?"

After a second, April realized that Bethany hadn't meant the question to be rhetorical. She really wanted April to tell her whether she was crazy. The girl was only fifteen and already declaring that she was in love. Of course that was crazy, but maybe fifteen was the only time you could say you were in love, and really mean it, without any irony or strings attached.

"I think," April said, "that you're very young and allowed not to have everything figured out yet."

Bethany nodded but didn't look very satisfied with this answer.

"But whatever you do, you should take things slow," April continued. "You're only fifteen, and if you really like someone, you have plenty of time to share things with them. You don't want to rush anything." She paused, and for a moment she was tempted to leave it there, not to say what she knew she must say next. She took a breath. "And, Bethany, I need you to promise me that you'll never, *ever* try to hurt yourself, no matter how scary or confusing or sad it can be. If you feel that way and you feel you can't talk to your parents, you come to me, okay? I might not have all the answers, but we'll work it out or find someone who can help. But don't keep it inside. Don't keep it a secret. Promise me that. Promise that if you feel bad, you'll find me, or someone you trust, to talk to."

Bethany nodded. "Okay," she whispered. There was a space of silence. They both looked at the pale-yellow wall, and then Bethany turned to her and asked, "But do *you* think it's wrong how I feel about Nola? Do you think God will judge me for it?"

With everything that had happened over the course of the VBS—namely Paul—April had dropped the ball on a few things. One of those things had been remembering to take down all the pieces of paper that kids had nailed to the Cross of Repentance throughout the month and bring them with her in a garbage bag to Camp Lone Eagle. On these notes, the kids had been encouraged, whenever they felt the urge, to write down anything they felt guilty or ashamed about. Then, on Saturday night at the camp, the tradition was to dump the bag full of these notes into the bonfire and watch them burn to ash. But April had forgotten to bring the bag with her to the camp, so the notes remained unburned. The bag had sat in a corner of the garage for weeks until, one evening while putting away the gardening tools she hadn't used, she spied it and brought it into her room.

She emptied the bag on her bed and picked up some notes at random.

*I watched a scary movie the other night with my friends. I have bad dreams now. I don't want to tell my parents because they'll be mad at me.*

*Sometimes I get so angry with my sister I want to hit her.*

*I'm trying not to watch porn online anymore, but I can't stop.*

Some of them were surprising, some even amusing, but each one struck April as sad in some way.

She unfolded one last note. *I think I might be gay.*

That was all. No apology. No plea for forgiveness. Remembering it now, April wondered whether it had been Bethany. The Cross of Repentance wasn't meant for team leaders, and she remembered the handwriting looking younger, juvenile. That was part of what made it so sad.

The only gay person April knew well was Terry Moore from church, and, of course, he had renounced his homosexuality. April had always liked

Terry—he was kind and soft-spoken and always willing to help out with anything going on at church. But maybe that spoke less to his generosity than to his loneliness. Terry's boyfriend had died years ago, and he would never be able to open that part of his life up again, because he believed, right along with the rest of the church, that it was an abomination. April looked at Bethany and thought of her growing up that way, alone, never allowing herself the chance to fall in love or be with someone, because she believed that doing so would send her to hell. No wonder she wanted something more from April. No wonder she was desperate for a concrete answer. The thing was, April no longer felt she had anything useful to give. Recently, she felt as if she'd been floating in the middle of a vast ocean, with no land in sight. *God, sin, love*—all these words suddenly sounded like foreign concepts. She had no clue what any of them meant. *Don't ask me*, she wanted to say as she cleared her throat. *I'm just a math teacher.*

TWENTY MINUTES LATER, when April came back downstairs, Eric stood up from where he'd been waiting on the living room sofa. "How's she doing?" he asked, as if April were a doctor and Bethany her desperately ill patient, as if he couldn't go up the stairs and see for himself.

April stood in the middle of the room and wrapped her arms around herself. "I think she's confused," she said.

Eric nodded vigorously. "Yes, very confused."

"I told her she's allowed to be confused."

He looked at her blankly.

"I told her she's allowed to take her time figuring things out, that the important thing is, she keeps trying. She doesn't have to know anything for certain yet. I told her I'm forty, and I still don't have things remotely figured out. I mean, I thought I did. However I felt about my life, I thought it was how it was supposed to be, and it only just recently occurred to me that I could change it. I'm not good with metaphors, but it's as if my life were a stained-glass window or something—pretty to look at, but never changing—and then something came along to shatter my window, and now I'm trying to pick up the pieces. And I'm seeing that I don't have to put them back the way they were before. I could move stuff around, rearrange things, throw out and add stuff, even. Actually, that metaphor works pretty well, doesn't it? Go figure. Anyway, it's not like I'm suddenly happy now. Actually, I'm sad, really sad, but I don't mind being sad right now. It's better than what I felt before, I think, which was nothing."

April stopped talking. She hadn't meant to say any of that, hadn't even known she'd been thinking it; it had just tumbled out in a rush.

Eric stared at her. "You told Bethany that?"

"Well, no," said April, "just the first part. The rest of it I'm telling you, I guess. Because I had to tell someone, and you're still my pastor, right?" She gave Eric a smile that he did not return. "I know that's not what you wanted me to tell your daughter," she said, "but really, I'm not sure it makes a difference, either way, what you or I or anyone else tells her. Kids that age do what they feel they need to do, and to hell with whatever we tell them. That's just teenage nature," she added, remembering something someone had told her what felt like a long, long time ago.

Since Eric didn't seem as if he was going to respond anytime soon, April walked past him toward the door, then turned back around to say, "Oh, yeah, this is probably as good a time as any to tell you I won't be heading up the VBS next summer. I've decided to retire."

Outside, she was surprised to see that it was dark. It always took her by surprise how quickly the sun began to set at the end of summer. She stood out in the Moyers' driveway for a moment, looked around, and realized she didn't have a car. She would have to walk home or else go back inside and ask Eric for a ride. Her house was on the other side of town, and she wasn't wearing sneakers, but she hesitated only a moment before setting off across the driveway and down the street.

# 25

BEN

Something warm and rough and wet was scraping across my face. I opened my eyes with a start and lifted my head. Then I froze. I was looking straight into the eyes of a big black dog. It had stopped licking me and was now growling low, baring its long white teeth only inches away from my face.

I knew better than to make any sudden movements. The trouble was, I was allergic to dogs, and I felt a sneeze coming on.

Someone gave a whistle behind me. The dog's ears perked up, and a second later it had sprinted away, leaving me with my nose tickling and my heart pounding.

I winced as I sat up in the sand. My back hurt, and my neck was stiff. I couldn't believe I had fallen asleep here in the park. I never fell asleep in public places, especially outside. From how dark it had gotten, I guessed I must have been out for a while. My head felt fuzzy and disoriented. I pulled my phone out of my pocket and checked the time: ten after eight. I'd slept for over an hour. There was also a text from my mom, asking me where I was. My curfew was at eight. I had to get home fast to avoid a punishment. Groaning, I stood up and climbed back up the bank.

"Hey, kid."

I looked up. An old man sat on a bench a few yards away, staring at me. Beside him sat the dog, and he was stroking it gently with one hand. It had no leash or collar.

"You'd better get home," the man said. "There's some bad people come out here after dark. People with bad things on their minds."

It was too dark, and the man was too far away, for me to really see his face. His voice sounded familiar, and for a second I was sure I knew him, but I didn't know from where. I couldn't tell if he was joking. I'd never heard anyone talk like this in Grover Falls. I felt the hair on the back of my neck stand up. "Yeah," I said. "I'm going home now."

The man nodded and kept looking at me, stroking the dog's neck.

I went over to the big maple tree by the river, where I'd left my bike. It wasn't there. I looked around in the quickly fading light. Nothing. Someone had taken it while I was sleeping. I turned back to the man to ask him if he'd seen anyone with a bike around here, but when I did, the bench was empty. I looked around and didn't see him or the dog anywhere, but now it was getting too dark to see much. Cold, too. The hairs on my bare arms were standing on end. I shivered and started walking fast across the park.

If I knew what was good for me, I would have called my mom, told her I lost my bike and was on my way home, or asked her to come get me. But for some reason, I didn't. I'm not sure why, but I think maybe there was part of me that *wanted* to get in trouble for missing my curfew. Maybe that was why I fell asleep in the first place—I wanted to be punished for something.

Walking across town, I thought of Bethany. I wondered what she was doing right now, if her parents were yelling at her, if she felt guilty, or if she didn't care. I thought about that man Michael Keegan, and I wondered why I hated him so much. I thought of those guys on TV deciding whether to be priests, whether to give up sex for the rest of their lives to be closer to God. Maybe on the show it was all rigged, but it happened in real life, too, and I thought of the stories I'd seen on the news, of priests who'd secretly touched boys. I thought of what that weird man had said—*bad people with bad things on their minds*—and walked faster.

When I opened the door of the mudroom and walked into the kitchen, my mom came in from the office. As soon as I saw her, my desire to accept my punishment vanished, and I immediately felt defensive.

"There you are!" she practically yelled. "Where have you been? It's past eight."

"Somebody stole my bike," I muttered.

"What do you mean, somebody stole your bike?"

"It's like when somebody takes something of yours without permission."

"Don't take that tone with me, mister. *Who* took it?"

"I don't know!" I almost shouted. "I was …" I trailed off because I didn't want to admit that I had fallen asleep.

"Where's DeShawn?" my mom asked, looking past me to the mudroom. "He's not here?"

My mom looked at me hard. "What do you mean? He was with you."

"Yeah, but I thought he came back already."

My mom gave an annoyed groan—something she did to disguise real worry. "Oh jeez, it's past eight o'clock. When did you last see him?"

"We were at the park, and then he left. I thought he came back here," I said, beginning to feel a little nervous myself.

While my mom went into the other room to get my dad, I pulled out my phone and called Jason. As soon as he answered, I asked him if he knew where DeShawn was.

Jason said he didn't, that they'd all ridden around for a few minutes and then headed back home.

"Well, he's not here," I said.

"Honestly?" said Jason. "I don't blame him. After what you said to him, he probably doesn't want to be anywhere near you."

I didn't answer. I watched my parents come into the kitchen, my dad grabbing the car keys, my mom getting her purse.

"Anything?" she asked me, and I shook my head and ended the call.

"We're going out to look for him," she said, putting on her jacket.

"Wait, I wanna come."

My dad shook his head. "No, stay here in case he shows up. Call us if you find out anything."

Then they shut the door behind them and left me alone in the empty house.

# 26

## LAURA

I really needed to pee. Although I wasn't used to drinking coffee, I'd finished my first cup quickly, taking long, nervous gulps. As soon as I did, the waitress was back to refill it. Now, after three cups of black coffee, my bladder was crying out for relief. But I didn't want to leave the table. I didn't want to take my eyes off Martin for a second.

After he'd resigned himself to having dinner with me just to keep from starting a commotion in the restaurant, at first Martin had stayed silent, sulking like a child. No matter how hard I tried to make conversation, he wouldn't give in.

"Do you come to this place a lot?"

A facial shrug.

"So how long have you lived in Albany?"

"Can't remember."

I remembered asking him the same question online months ago, and he'd told me a few years.

I was beginning to despair. If all this night turned out to be was me forcing an unwilling man to have dinner with me in silence, then the whole thing had been a waste. But I didn't know why I ever thought the outcome could be different—he had been expecting a woman, and I tricked him. Of course he would be angry and upset. Why had I thought, even remotely, that some part of him already knew the truth, that when he saw me, a fifteen-year-old girl, his surprise would be only partly genuine, that deep down he had somehow known all along? I had lied to myself. Martin had every right to walk out then and there, but still I wanted to say, *I'm the same person you talked to for hours online. Everything I said then was true, truer than this dumb reality.* But I couldn't say that. It wouldn't have made any sense.

I was staring down at the table when Martin spoke. So far, his eyes had been around the room—anywhere but me—when they suddenly turned to me. "So," he said, "your real name isn't Kim Moore, is it?"

I hesitated a beat, then decided I had no reason to lie to him anymore. "No," I said. "My name's Laura." I didn't give him a last name and he didn't ask for it.

"Laura. That's a nice name."

"I've never really liked it, actually."

"Names are weird like that, aren't they?" he said, smiling a little. "They shape so much of our identity, and yet, they're something we have no control over. I always wondered what it would be like to live in a society where we chose our own names, when we felt ready. We might end up so different."

"Yeah!" I said. "I would love to choose my own name."

He took a sip of water. "Well, in a way, you did, Kim."

I smiled and blushed, suddenly happy. This was how we had spoken to each other online, chatting about random but interesting things, our conversation veering this way and that in unpredictable but never boring pathways, emotionally guarded but subtly flirtatious.

"So, Laura," Martin said, now leaning forward, "I was talking to you the entire time, yes?"

I nodded.

He leaned back and shook his head in disbelief, almost admiration. "How did you learn to talk like that?"

"Like what?"

"Well … like a *woman.* Like someone twice your age."

"I don't know," I said. "It just came to me."

He looked me in the eyes. "You're an old soul, I guess."

I nodded, hoping that was a compliment. Martin's eyes were watery blue, almost silver, like that thin space between ocean and horizon.

"And have you done this before, Laura?"

"Done what?"

"You know, created a fake identity, befriended an older man online, and then got him to meet you?"

"Oh, no!" I shook my head. "You're the first—I mean, the only."

He gave a dry chuckle. "Lucky me."

I smiled back, but uncertainly. Something about the way he was looking at me now was unnerving, but I wasn't sure I didn't like it.

"And what were you planning on us doing, now that we've finally met?"

"Um," I fumbled, "I don't know. I just wanted to meet you. I thought it was time."

"I mean, you had to be aware that it was going to come as a shock to me," he said. "That I would be … disappointed."

This, I thought, was some sort of come-on, a challenge, and I had to meet it. I gave a little jerk of my head, the way I had seen Haley do around boys, the way I'd seen Bethany do without even trying, and put my chin in my hands and looked in his eyes. "Are you disappointed?" I asked.

He paused for a long moment. "I don't know yet," he said at last.

That was when I really felt the need to pee, but I was scared that if I left the table, the fragile connection we were beginning to make would be broken, so I crossed my legs and, counterproductively, took another sip of coffee.

"And so who were those pictures of?" Martin asked.

"Huh? Oh. Um, just a random woman I found on Google." I didn't want him to know they were pictures of my mom.

"And do you really live in Grover Falls?"

"Yeah."

"With your mother?"

I nodded.

"And where does she think you are now?"

I didn't like the way he added a needless *and* before his questions, and I didn't like that the conversation kept coming back to my mom.

I couldn't tell him about the abortion protest—that would just open up another can of worms—so I lied. "At my friend's house."

"You're a very brave little girl," he said.

I uncrossed my legs and shifted in my seat. I had to pee so badly. "Why?" I asked.

He looked at me as though the answer was obvious, and maybe it was. "Because I could have been anybody. I could have been lying to you the way you were lying to me. I could have been a very bad person—I still could be; you don't know."

"But I do!" I said. "I already know who you are."

"Yeah?" His eyes narrowed. "And what am I?"

The question confused me—his use of "what" instead of "who." *What am I?* It seemed more philosophical, existential, than personal. "Um ..." I felt a little weak and dizzy. I hadn't eaten anything since morning and hoped our food would come soon. Martin was looking at me unwaveringly, with a thin smile on his lips. I wished he would stop. "You're ..." I said. How could I explain to him what I thought about our connection, that all the things I'd said online had been true, had been honest, despite being lies? That he knew me better than most because I had revealed a secret self in those late-night chats. But before I could come up with anything, Mindy arrived with our food, breaking the spell.

"Here you go, guys," she said, placing our plates in front of us. "Enjoy!"

I couldn't hold it any longer. I stood up and said I'd be back in a moment. I meant to go as quickly as possible, but once I was in the bathroom stall, sitting on the toilet, I found my heart was racing so fast it was hard to breathe, and I was sweating. I had to sit there a good few minutes, forcing myself to take long, slow breaths, before I could stand up again and leave the stall. I checked myself in the mirror after washing my hands, though at this point I didn't know to what end, and walked back into the dining room.

When I saw our empty table, for a moment I was able to tell myself he must have gone to the bathroom as well and would be right back, but then I saw the pile of cash tucked under his water glass.

He was gone. My mind raced, faced with a choice. I could just let him leave. After all, I had done what I planned on doing. I'd met him, and what more had I expected to happen, really? This might have been the best way it could end, if I was honest with myself. I couldn't deny that he had begun to make me feel nervous, even a little frightened. But something didn't feel right, and standing there in the middle of the restaurant, I realized that the flirting, the pointed questions, had all been an act, a ruse. Because really, the entire time, he'd been waiting for an opportunity to make a break for it, to leave me behind. He lulled me into a false sense of security just so I would give him the chance to run. And suddenly, I was no longer frightened of him, only furious.

I looked around the room wildly and saw that the group of teenage girls who had noticed us earlier were watching me curiously from their table. One of them pointed toward Martin's seat. "I think he left," she said. They waited for my reaction.

I gave them a pinched smile. "Thanks," I said. Then I turned and walked out of the back room, past the hostess' table, and out the front doors, into the street.

In front of me, cars went by in flashes of noise and light. I looked right, then left, but it was too dark to see very far ahead. I turned to my right and started down the street at a swift walk at first, but soon I was running, dodging anyone on the sidewalk who got in my way.

When I reached the next block, I saw him. He had his back to me, but I knew by the way he was walking—head down, as fast as he could without actually running—that it was him.

"Hey!" I shouted.

He looked over his shoulder and saw me. There was a moment's hesitation, and then he bolted.

I chased him.

We were halfway down the block and I was gaining on him when I saw him pull his keys from his pocket and wave them in front of him. The taillights of a silver Chevy parked at the end of the block flashed red. "Hey!" I shouted again, almost on top of him.

Without warning, he stopped and turned toward me. I skidded to a halt in front of him.

"Go home, Laura," he said calmly.

"You were just going to leave me there?" I shouted, panting.

"You need to go home." His voice was infuriatingly calm.

"No!" I shouted. I wasn't thinking when I reached out and grabbed his arm.

The instant I touched him, Martin changed. He wasn't the man I had come to know online, or even the one I'd met so briefly in the restaurant. He was something else. His face transformed; his skin seemed to burst into flame. His eyes emptied of everything except mingled terror and rage. He ripped his arm away from me as if my hand were a hot iron.

"Don't touch me, you little bitch!" he screamed. And then the look was gone. His face was drained, and he turned and walked out into the street to his car.

"You're an asshole," I yelled, and found myself sobbing.

He whirled around and looked at me. "Oh, I'm much more than that, Laura." He paused, decided something, and then he took a breath. "I'm a registered sex offender, all right? A very bad person. Still want to have dinner with me? I didn't think so."

His face was drawn, and I knew he was telling the truth, but I shook my head. "I don't believe you."

He looked up at the sky. "Unbelievable," he said, shaking his head. "Look, do yourself a favor: go home to your mom and forget this ever happened. Count yourself incredibly lucky."

I watched him walk over to the driver's side of his car. I watched him get in and slam the door. I watched the engine roar to life and the lights come on. If I'd had a baseball bat, I would have swung it into the taillights. If I'd had a rock, I would have chucked it through the back window. But I had nothing, so all I could do was raise my leg and kick the side of the car as hard as I could. It pulled out into the street without so much as a dent. My foot was throbbing.

I stood in the street for a long time, as if frozen. The lights from a store behind me were blinking on and off, off and on. I didn't know where to go now or what to do. It was only because nothing else occurred to me that I found myself walking back down the block to the Starving Artist. As if in a daze, I wandered into the restaurant, to the back room where we'd been sitting. No one stopped me. I half expected our food to still be on the table, my coffee waiting. But the table had been wiped clean, our plates cleared, the money gone. It was if our meeting had never happened. The disappointment was almost physical. I could feel it pulling on my stomach. I thought of *The Wizard of Oz*. How Dorothy went to such trouble to find the Wizard, only to discover that he was a fake, a pathetic hack. That movie had scared me so terribly when I was little. After I saw it the first time, I crawled into my parents' bed, between my mom and dad, for the next three nights. My mom still teased me about it sometimes. She could do a perfect Wicked Witch of the West imitation: *"I'll get you, my pretty!"*

"Hey." Someone was calling me, pulling me out of my daze. I turned. The girls were still here, watching me. "Did your dad really just *leave* you here?" asked the one who had told me he left.

"He wasn't my dad," I said, and walked over to their table. There was a free chair at the end, and I sat down. "He was my date." I was suddenly exhausted.

The girl gave a short laugh. "What?"

"I met him online," I said, looking down at the table and reciting as if from a script. "Told him I was older. Convinced him to meet me. Then he bailed."

"What were you planning on doing?" one of the other girls asked me.

I looked up to see them all staring at me with fascination. "I ... don't know. I guess I just wanted to see what would happen."

"Dude, that is so fucking weird," the first girl said, but the way she said it, "weird" wasn't a bad thing. There was admiration in her eyes. She was pretty, with long blond hair and glasses. They all were pretty. And they all were looking at me with wide-eyed respect.

"Yeah," I said, smiling a little, "it *was* kinda fun, actually, even though he turned out to be a tool." *I'm a registered sex offender.*

"What if he had been, you know, dangerous?" one of the others asked me. I felt as if I were giving an interview.

"Well, I didn't do it alone," I said. "My friend ... Kim—we planned it together, and she would have been there if anything happened. She's coming to pick me up now."

"I'm Jordan," the first girl said.

The three others said their names in turn, and they looked at me, expecting something. It was a second before I realized they were waiting for me to introduce myself. "Nola," I said at last.

"My older sister buses tables here," Jordan said. "We're just waiting for her to get off, then we're driving with her to a party in Latham. You should totally tell your friend to meet you there instead."

I heard all her words, but it was while before I could make any sense of them. "You're inviting me to a party?" I said at last.

"Yeah, we're taking my mom's van, so there's an extra seat. Lame, I know."

I pulled my phone from my pocket to check the time. I had a slew of unread texts and missed calls, but I ignored them. It was almost ten o'clock. I nodded slowly. "Sure, I'll go to a party," I said. I felt as though my night was finally turning around.

# 21

PAUL

It was inevitable, he supposed, that sooner or later he would go back to New York City. People never stayed away for good, did they, once they'd gotten a taste? The place had a sort of boomerang effect on the young and reckless—it might chew you up and spit you out, but you were only too happy to be swallowed up again.

Driving south on Route 87, for the first time Paul realized how much he had missed the city. The scents of lilac blossoms and grilling meat riding on the warm air of a Brooklyn summer night, the Manhattan skyline across the river, almost obnoxious in its grandeur. Why had he left in the first place? Suddenly, all the reasons that had felt so convincing now seemed stupid or irrelevant.

Before leaving the house, Paul had downloaded Mira Mira's album from iTunes and ripped it onto a blank CD. Now he was blaring it in the car, windows rolled down, the night air whipping his hair. The album was really good. Mira's voice was strong and soulful, the electronic production slick and immaculate, the hooks compelling. Paul was already starting to hate it. "You find an excuse to hate every young musician that isn't Robert Pollard or you," Sasha had once told him after he dismissed some new band as talentless and derivative. Paul decided it wouldn't help his case to point out that Mr. Pollard had been putting out music since the eighties.

But he liked to believe that his disdain for new artists wasn't rooted entirely in jealousy and selfish bitterness, that pop music really had been reduced to one giant exercise in reusing and recycling. Mira Mira's album might have been perfect, but it was *too* perfect, too clean. It didn't say anything to him. But it didn't really matter, did it? He couldn't really give a shit. For him, it wasn't about the music anymore. It was about the tour: a different city every night, a different club, a different drug, a different girl. An infinite number of bathroom stalls. In November, he'd be on the West Coast. Who cared what kind of music got him there? And then there was Mira.

Niles had said she asked about him *a lot*.

Paul remembered a night in Brooklyn, maybe two summers back, when it had almost happened between him and Mira. It was after a show, and they both had been drinking. She came on to him. At the time, Paul had been with Sasha and had been stupidly loyal. Now he had nothing to stop him. When he had downloaded Mira's album and seen her on the cover, done up in black eyeliner and makeup like some stunning European goddess, he'd thought about fucking her. And now, listening to her sing in his car, he thought about fucking her. He would fuck her because she had a record deal. He would fuck her because of her perfect album production. He would fuck her because what kind of name was *Mira Mira*? He would fuck her because he knew that as soon as this song was over, it would keep playing in his head. He would fuck her because, sooner or later, Sasha would hear about it.

But April wouldn't hear about it. April wouldn't know. Why would she? Even if Paul appeared on the cover of *Rolling Stone*, April might never notice. She was above all that. She didn't need it, just as she hadn't needed him. She would stay in Grover Falls, raising her kids, running the vacation Bible school, teaching high school algebra, immune to him, above him. And maybe, she'd still be teaching there years from now, when Nicki's child entered ninth grade. Maybe the kid would be in April's class, and April would sense something familiar about the kid, boy or girl, but never be quite sure what it was.

Nicki wasn't going to have an abortion, Paul knew. And not *despite* his having basically assaulted her in an Olive Garden, but *because* of it. She would have the baby just to get back at him. And in a year or so, she'd be after him for child support, just as Sallie Mae was after him for loan repayments.

What a cliché he had turned out to be. For all his subversive pretension, what a goddamn cliché. And as for Mira and the tour, it could last only so long before he found a way to screw that up, too. He would start using too much, become a drugged-out wreck onstage. Or he'd piss Mira off irrevocably by sleeping with one of her friends. Or he would simply decide that his talent wasn't being utilized to its full potential and become difficult. There were countless ways he could sabotage this opportunity and get himself dropped, though with any luck, by then he would at least be in California.

The idea that he was a shallow person did not surprise or even bother Paul that much, since it was something he had suspected for some time now. What he hadn't expected to discover, as the CD ended and immediately started over, was a complete lack of remorse after recognizing this shallowness. Yes, he had felt horrible for what he did to Nicki, hurting her, but part of him had also been relieved because he effectively and permanently ended the conversation. There was nothing more to say after that. If Nicki had the baby, there was no chance in hell that she'd want him around to help her take care of it. By being the absolute worst version of himself, Paul had dispelled any hope or expectation that he might improve. And this wasn't even what surprised him—no, what he found strange, as he sped down the highway, was that he couldn't make himself feel the least bit guilty about it.

A big sign appeared on the right, boasting gas and coffee and McDonald's. At the last second, Paul swerved into the exit lane, pulled into the parking lot, and shut off the engine. He sat there for a moment, breathing heavily in the silence.

He couldn't remember the last time he had cried. Even when Sasha left him, he had shouted and raged and drunk himself stupid, but he never once cried. He felt that if he could just get himself to let loose now and cry for Nicki, for the baby, for April, for himself—if he could just shed a few real tears—then he could let go and keep going. He needed to prove to himself that he wasn't completely empty, that he could still feel something, even if it was nothing more than guilt without follow-up, remorse without action. He even thought to pray to God—a God he was pretty sure he didn't believe in—just to let him cry.

But nothing came. His eyes remained dry. And in a sudden burst of frustration and rage, Paul brought his fist down hard on the dashboard, then again, and again, and again. After the fourth time, his hand was red and throbbing.

Paul was holding his right hand in his left, rubbing it gently, looking out at a gas mart parking lot busy with people and cars in the falling darkness, when he became aware of the presence. At first, he wasn't sure where the awareness had come from, but he was certain, beyond any doubt, that someone, or something, was here in the car with him. For one crazy moment, he thought of the lingo at New Life—the Holy Spirit washing over you. Then, after a moment of intense listening, he realized what it was: he could hear breathing—breathing that was not his own. Slowly, calmly, he opened the door and got out, loudly stretching his back and shoulders. As casually as he could, he looked in the back seat. Piled up almost to the car's headliner was everything he owned. In the middle of the seat, flanked on either side by boxes and bags, a blanket lay over a large and shapeless bulk.

Paul calmly opened the back seat door, then whisked the blanket out of the car. And although he had been expecting it, he still felt a jolt of surprise upon seeing DeShawn scrunched up on his side in the back seat. But before Paul could even say anything, DeShawn had slithered around a laundry bag of clothes and across the seat, opened the far door, and hopped out of the car. He streaked across the parking lot, toward a grassy hill and a dark wall of woods behind it.

"Hey!" was all Paul could think to say before he took off running in pursuit.

## APRIL

By the time April reached her house, it was full dark, and she was sweating and excited and determined not to identify what, exactly, she was excited about. She suspected that nailing it down might spoil the whole thing. Nothing in her immediate life had changed. She still lived in Grover Falls. She still taught the same subject at the same school she'd been teaching at for over ten years. The one romantic relationship she'd been in since her divorce had lasted barely a week, and it was a small miracle it had lasted even that long. Nothing had changed, and yet, April felt a rush of exhilaration, like a warm breeze against her back. The mysterious nature of this elation only made it more intoxicating, and she wondered, as she climbed the front steps to her porch, why she always felt compelled to give a cause for her feelings, whether good or bad. She could never simply be happy or simply be sad; there had to be a reason behind it. She decided that from now on she would let herself be however she felt, without looking for an explanation.

April lingered on the front porch. She didn't want to go inside just yet, even though the night had turned almost cold. Autumn was approaching. Maybe that was why memories of college kept coming back to her. Faces and scenes she hadn't thought about in years now flared up in her mind, briefly but clearly, and while she wouldn't linger on any single memory for too long, the thoughts added to her strange mood: excited, nostalgic, almost giddy. She wished she had a cigarette and, for a second, even considered jogging over to the store to buy a pack. But that would be silly. Cigarettes were expensive now, weren't they? She couldn't justify spending eight dollars on a silly whim.

She felt like talking to someone, and, of course, the first person who came to mind was Paul. A stab of sadness. She realized that she and Paul hadn't actually talked that much. With all the sneaking around and plans and fights, they'd barely had time for sex. If she could see him now, try to explain to him how she felt, would he listen? Would he understand? She didn't know, but she had a feeling he would at least try. She thought of that Stevie Nicks song, the one that had been playing in the bar. She wanted to hear it again. Okay, so she wouldn't buy a pack of cigarettes, but she would go in and download that song from iTunes.

It felt silly to stand out on her porch shivering slightly, without a cigarette and with no one to talk to, so at last, April turned and went into the house. She couldn't talk to Paul, and standing in her kitchen, the only other person she could think of was her sister, Sarah, in Florida. The clock on the stove told her it was a little late to be calling, but the beauty of cell phones was how easy they made rudeness. April could call her sister at almost any hour, and her sister could just ignore the call if she wanted, and neither would think less of the other for it.

First, she went upstairs to check on Jason, and as she did, she was thinking about Sarah and that they should go down to Florida to visit soon … maybe even do more than visit. She was thinking about her sister's long-standing job offer, but now she was getting ahead of herself. After hearing the reassuring sounds of Jason's video games, she went back downstairs to get her phone. But it wasn't on the kitchen table where she thought she had left it, and it wasn't in her bedroom, either. She finally found it in the living room, wedged between the sofa cushions, where it had ended up before.

When she pulled it out, she saw that she had three missed calls and a voice mail, all from Jon Newman. Listening to the message, April felt her chest tighten.

## LAURA

"Who the hell is *this*?" Jordan's sister pointed at me with her cigarette. I was standing with Jordan and the rest of the girls in a back lot behind the restaurant, about to get in the van.

"This is Nola," Jordan said to her sister, putting a hand on my shoulder. "We met her inside. She's coming with us."

"How old are you, kid?" Her sister stared intently at me.

"Seventeen," I said. I met the older girl's eyes, and this time I didn't blink.

"She's totally cool, Jen. She hunts down creepy old men online and gets them to meet her in person."

Jen took a drag of her cigarette. "Then what: you wait till they fall asleep, and chop their dicks off?"

I shrugged. "Usually, I just save time and slit their throats."

Everyone laughed.

Jen nodded. "Sort of a Buffy-the-Pervert-Slayer kind of thing." She sighed and tossed her cigarette to the pavement. "Okay, she can come, but remember, if Mom hears about this from *any* of you when she gets back, you're dead. I can't afford her taking the car away from me again."

The girls began piling into the van. I was about to follow them into the back when Jen called to me. "Hey, Buffy," she said, "you ride up front with me, where I can keep an eye on you." But she was smiling.

The van had the familiar scent of a family vehicle: stale and heavy from much use by many people. Sitting in the front passenger seat, I felt immediately at home. Jen must have been eighteen, but even the others still looked at least a year older than I. I wondered whether any of them believed I was really seventeen.

I watched Jen as she pulled out of the parking lot and onto the street. She had the same blond hair as her sister, but cut short. She turned on the radio, and a Top 40 pop hit blared from the speakers—a girl singing about partying in Hollywood, putting up her hands, moving her hips. It was just the sort of song Nola would have hated, the sort of song I wouldn't be caught dead listening to in front of anyone. But these girls began to sing along unabashedly, their voices filling up the van. Even Jen, who was older and cool, was belting out the words without any hint of self-consciousness.

She glanced at me. "Don't act like you don't know the words, Buffy!" she shouted over the music.

I leaned toward her. "Do you actually *like* this song?"

Jen shook her head violently. "It's god-awful. But that's not the fucking point!"

So when the chorus came, I joined in. We rolled down the windows and sang out into the night. I remembered the night back in June, riding in Paul Frazier's car, too embarrassed to ask him what he'd been listening to, because he might look down on me. Now here I was, singing a terrible pop song at the top of my lungs, and it felt good. I felt suddenly and strangely happy. How ridiculous that all the events of the day had finally brought me here, in a minivan with a bunch of girls I didn't know, going to a party. It was almost as if nothing leading up to this had happened. The abortion protest, Martin, chasing him to his car—all that was a dream I had woken up from, and this was reality, where I was supposed to be. I felt as though I belonged with these girls. I even liked my new name.

## BEN

I tried sitting outside on the front porch with my phone in my hands. I tried going into the living room and turning on the TV to distract myself. I tried going online. I even tried reading a book, but none of it worked. Finally, when I couldn't stand it any longer, I went into my mom's office, grabbed a piece of notebook paper, and went back into the kitchen to scribble out a note on the table. *DeShawn, if you come home please call me.* I was about to sign my name and thought better of it and wrote *Mom* instead, before realizing that wasn't right. I crumpled up the piece of paper, threw it in the trash, and wrote the note out again, this time singing my mom's name, *Deborah.*

It was only after I had rushed outside and into the garage that I realized I didn't have a bike anymore. I looked around. My dad's old mountain bike sat in the corner of the garage with a bunch of tools he never used. It was a little rusty and way too big for me, but I pulled it out anyway.

I wobbled a bit at first, but soon I was speeding down the dark and empty street. As soon as I felt the wind whipping across my face and through my hair, something in my head clicked, and suddenly I knew where to look for DeShawn. It wasn't anywhere my parents would think to look, but I felt sure it was where he had gone. I pedaled faster.

When I got to Becca's house, I was sweating and panting. It was farther away than I remembered. Even though it was a little late to be popping in, I rushed up to the door and knocked loud. Only after knocking did I realize that somebody besides Becca might answer, and I was suddenly scared it would be my uncle. *Please be Becca, please be Becca, please be Becca,* I whispered, but when the door opened it was my other cousin, Rachel.

"Hey," I gasped as she stared at me in surprise. "I'm looking for my foster brother, DeShawn. He's not here, is he?"

Rachel shook her head slowly.

Why had I been so sure? What had made me think he would be here? If he had been, they would have called my parents by now. I felt both disappointed and stupid standing there on the porch.

"Ben? What's wrong?"

Becca had come up behind her sister.

"We can't find DeShawn," I said, swallowing. "I don't know why, but I thought I'd check here." Becca stared at me for a moment. Then she said, "Hold on, let me grab my jacket."

"Rebecca," Rachel said as her sister went back into the house for her jacket, "it's way too late to be going out."

"Ben's brother is missing—our *cousin*," I heard Becca say as she put on her jacket and then grabbed something out of a drawer by the kitchen sink. "I have to help him look."

"Mom and Dad wouldn't want you—" Rachel began.

"Mom and Dad aren't here," Becca said, holding two flashlights and pushing past her sister to stand next to me on the front steps. "Come on, Ben," she said. "My bike's in the yard."

"Becca," Rachel called, still standing in the doorway as we headed across the yard, "if you leave, I'm telling Mom and Dad."

Becca hesitated for just a moment. "So tell them," she said, and grabbed her bike out of the grass. She handed me a flashlight. "Come on," she said. We jumped on our bikes and cranked out of the drive and onto the road, our flashlights making thin stabs into the darkness.

## PAUL

The kid was fast. Even before Paul had started smoking, drinking, and generally ignoring his physical health, he couldn't run like that. DeShawn had taken off and was well across the giant parking lot before Paul even registered what was happening.

Chasing after the boy seemed a ridiculous course of action. It also appeared to be the only logical and acceptable thing he could do.

Maybe twenty seconds after he began running after DeShawn, who was now nearing the end of the lot, it occurred to Paul how this sight might be easily and terribly misconstrued by anyone who might happen to witness it: an older white guy chasing a young black kid across a rest-stop parking lot well after dark. He remembered what April had said to him after the locker-room incident—*How was I to know what* you *were doing with him in there?* And even though he was still running, even though this was not remotely the time or place for it, even though DeShawn had now reached the end of the lot, Paul began laughing. He couldn't help it; the whole situation was just too ridiculous.

By the time he neared the end of the lot, Paul's laughter had turned to wheezing, and he had a stitch in his side. That wasn't supposed to happen. He wasn't even twenty-five, for God's sake! He should be able to run for two minutes without feeling on the brink of a heart attack.

DeShawn surely would have lost him, disappeared to who knows where in the darkness and the trees, if he hadn't tripped over something in the grass just outside the lot. He stumbled, fell, and had to get back up. Despite the pain in his side, Paul forced himself to run faster. The steep hill slowed him down, but DeShawn was slowing down, too. Both of them were scrambling up the hill now, almost on all fours. Paul gathered his last vestige of strength to lunge out and grab at DeShawn's legs, just catching his left heel.

"Get the fuck off me!" DeShawn cried, kicking out violently and shaking Paul's hand away.

Paul stumbled back onto the grass, catching himself with his hands. DeShawn was still moving up the hill, but only barely. He was trudging up the incline like an oxygen-starved climber nearing the summit.

Paul felt dizzy. His chest hurt. He could hear the traffic speeding by on 87, and the crickets chirring in the woods ahead. "DeShawn," Paul gasped between breaths, "where the hell are you going?"

DeShawn kept moving uphill toward the woods and didn't answer.

"DeShawn."

He whirled around, his face livid. "Just leave me alone! Okay?" he shouted. "All you people just leave me alone! None of you know me, so stop acting like you care! I don't need you. I don't want your help."

"Yeah, okay," Paul said, "but just tell me where you're going."

"I can't take it back there anymore. I'm going back to Brooklyn."

"DeShawn," said Paul, "you can't do that."

"Yeah? And why's that?"

All the obvious answers Paul could give—*you're too young; there's no one there to take care of you*—would only work the kid up. "Look," he said, "someday, yeah, you can go back to New York. Just not now, not tonight. The time's not right yet, that's all."

"You told me to leave," DeShawn said, quieter now, looking at the ground. "You told me to leave and never come back."

"Well, I'm not somebody you should listen to," Paul said. "I mean, *now* you should listen to me, but for the most part, my advice is shit." He paused. "I know it's hard, living up there, but sometimes you have to do the hard thing. That's part of growing up," he added, and immediately wished he hadn't, since it sounded dumb and insincere. But he had always imagined that was what fathers said at the end of some big talk with their sons—not that he would know.

DeShawn stood just above him on the hill, the forest a dark wall behind him. He was looking around. Paul waited, the night wind drying the sweat on his face, and wondered what the kid would do.

## LAURA

I hadn't brought a bathing suit. Normally, this would be enough of an excuse to keep me out of the water. Normally, even if I had come prepared, I would find some reason to stay out of the crowded pool. But tonight, I wasn't Laura. Tonight, I was someone else.

"Go Buffy! Kick her ass!" Jen was shouting underneath me. I was perched on her shoulders in the swimming pool, my arms locked with Jordan's, who was on the shoulders of a boy I hadn't met. Kids around us in the water were cheering and egging us on. I was already soaked from our first round of jousting and determined to redeem myself this time. But the boy Jordan was riding on was taller than Jen, and after a few seconds of mad pushing and tugging, I felt myself falling backward. But this time, I grabbed hold of Jordan's wrists and pulled her back with me. Then I was underwater. My mouth was full of chlorinated water, and the back of my head hit something hard.

Next thing I knew, Jordan was standing over me, asking if I was okay. I was laughing. "I'm *fine*," I said. I was sitting on a folding chair at the side of the pool, a towel wrapped around me. But as I watched kids doing cannonballs into the pool or standing around it talking and drinking beer, I realized I felt a little sick. The back of my head hurt, and my stomach was queasy.

"Okay." Jordan looked at me doubtfully. "You just whacked your head pretty hard."

"Where's my phone?" I asked.

"We left all our stuff inside, remember?" Jordan said. She offered her hand and pulled me to my feet. "Come on, Buffy, let's find something dry for you to wear."

I followed Jordan through the screen doors and back into the crowded house. The only sorts of parties I'd ever been to were alcohol-free get-togethers with other kids from church. Socially awkward Christmas parties where we drank fruit punch and played lame gift-exchange games. The girls sat stiff and awkward while the boys tried hopelessly to flirt with them. It was either that or evening worship rallies for the youth, where, under the influence of the rock music and the strobe lights, we fell down crying, confusing our feelings for our current crush with our feelings for Jesus.

Here in this big, adult-free house on the outskirts of Albany, I saw what a difference alcohol made. All the boys were funny, and all the girls were ready to laugh. They touched each other's arms in the kitchen; they danced without embarrassment to the hip-hop music blaring in the living room. But Jordan led me past all that, through the crowded downstairs to the stairwell, and upstairs into an empty bedroom, where my phone and bag were lying on the bed. The sudden quiet was welcome, though I could still feel the bass from downstairs pulsing through the floorboards. Jordan stripped out of her bathing suit and got dressed. Normally, I might have been a little surprised to have a girl I'd met only hours ago change clothes in front of me with no warning, but not a lot could surprise me tonight.

I sat down on the bed and picked up my phone—a bunch of missed calls and voice mails that I didn't bother to check—and opened my MatchUp app. He had already deleted his account. I blinked twice and shook my head. Then I opened Google.

*Find Sex Offenders in Your Area.* I clicked on the link and searched Albany, NY. It was scary how easy it was.

There were so many names, it made me dizzy. Each had a link to a picture and profile. I searched "Banner" and got nothing. Then I searched "Martin": three results. The second one was him. Sitting on the bed,

I stared openmouthed. He was younger and his hair was shorter, but it was him: Martin Sitwell, level 2, and underneath was his address.

Jordan had changed and was now going through our unwitting host's closet, searching for something for me to wear. I opened a new tab and searched Martin's real name. There was an article in a local newspaper, from 1999. Martin had been an English professor at a small private college outside Albany. He'd been caught having sex with one of his students. She was only sixteen. There were more details, but the online article cut off. Just a photo of him, looking angry and embarrassed. I wanted to see a picture of the girl, but that was it. I put down my phone, sat back on the bed, and closed my eyes, listening to Jordan pick out my clothing. I was suddenly tired. I just needed to sleep for a few minutes.

My new name was Buffy, but really it should have been Dorothy. I was Dorothy, sauntering down the Yellow Brick Road in my hot red shoes, looking for something, though I couldn't remember what. But I had bumped my head on the way, and now everything was confusing. The Wizard had been a major disappointment—a creep who couldn't keep his hands to himself—and the Witch? I had yet to find her, but she scared me. I could see her craggy green face and hear her mad cackle.

.

SOME BOY WAS STANDING IN FRONT of me, talking—talking to *me*, it appeared—holding a red plastic cup of beer in his hand. Looking down, I saw with surprise that I, too, was holding a cup, only half full. I brought it to my lips and took a long drink.

We were in the living room, and even though the music was loud and all around us kids were dancing, this boy was trying to have a conversation. "So you're a Mets fan?" he was asking me. He was tall and skinny, with eyes a little too big and just the beginnings of facial hair. "I'm a Yankees guy myself, but that's okay, we can still be friends." He tried for a charming grin, but I just stared blankly up at him. I didn't know what the hell he was talking about. "Your hat," he said.

I wasn't wearing a hat, but when I reached up to touch my hair,

I found, to my surprise, that I was wrong. I was wearing a hat—something I never did. A baseball cap, no less, I saw when I took it off. Bright blue. I'd been wearing it backward, apparently.

"So where are you from?" the boy said a little doubtfully as I, perplexed, continued to examine the baseball cap.

"Oz," I said without hesitation.

"Huh?"

Someone grabbed my shoulders from behind, and I turned to see Jordan. "She said she's from *Oz*, Dustin; deal with it." She looked at me. "Buffy, your assistance is required in the kitchen."

With her hands on my shoulder blades, she began to steer me through the crowded room. "I'd stay away from that one if I were you," she said in my ear. "He's sort of a creep."

"Jordan, where did I get this hat?" I asked. I still hadn't put it back on.

"Are you drunk already? I gave it to you upstairs when I basically had to force you to get up and get dressed. To hide that horrible bump you got in the pool."

I touched the back of my head. Beneath my wet hair, I could feel a large, soft bump that hurt when I touched it. I put the hat back on.

In the kitchen, a table stood in the middle of the room. On either side, plastic cups filled with beer were set up in a diamond pattern, in ridiculously perfect symmetry.

"Okay, ladies, I found her," Jordan said to the girls in the room. "Buffy's here to help me kick your collective ass."

"What do I have to do?" I asked as she handed me a Ping-Pong ball.

"Haven't you ever played beer pong before?"

I shook my head.

"Don't worry, it's not too complicated."

I tossed the Ping-Pong ball and missed every cup. Jordan laughed and told me it was okay and to chug my beer.

"Quick! Before it's our turn again! That's it!"

On an empty stomach, I found I could drink and drink without feeling sick, though my head got lighter and my skin felt warm. After a few games, I looked around the room but couldn't find Jordan. Then

I noticed with mild surprise that Dustin's arm was around me. He was laughing hysterically at something I had said. Although I hadn't heard my own joke, I started laughing, too, because everybody else was and it seemed like the thing to do. Then someone was passing out brownies, and I grabbed one because by then I was really hungry.

## APRIL

Phones only offered the illusion of control. You could call, you could text, you could leave as many messages as you wanted, but if the person on the other end of the line didn't want to contact you, there was nothing you could do about it. After April called Jon and learned that her daughter had left the church saying she was having dinner with her grandmother but didn't come back and hadn't returned any of Jon's calls or texts, April had hung up and called Laura. No answer. And after she called her own mother and confirmed that she had made no plans to have dinner with her granddaughter, April called Laura again. Her voice was tight and pinched when she left a message: "Laura, where are you? Call me."

Then April called the police.

And after ten minutes of pacing up and down the kitchen, rubbing her face, shaking her hands, waiting for a call from her daughter that didn't come, April knew she couldn't wait any longer.

When Jason came downstairs and asked her what was wrong, why she had shouted for him, why her face looked like that, she told him he had to stay at Dylan's for the night because she was going to Albany.

"What? Why?" Jason asked.

April could have lied to her son, found some excuse to keep him from worrying too much, but she was sick of lies, sick of sparing people from the truth. "Laura's missing, Jason. She left the church a few hours ago and they don't know where she went."

Jason's face was a portrayal of confusion that had not quite broken into fear yet.

She walked up and put a hand on his shoulder. "I'm going to go get her, okay? I'm going down to get her."

Jason nodded.

Fifteen minutes later, April was speeding south on 87, maybe faster than she had ever driven in her life.

## BEN

We ended up back at the park. We'd ridden all around the town, and my legs ached from so much pedaling, and my voice was hoarse from calling out his name so many times.

I skidded to a halt at the riverbank, the spot I had seen him last. The moon glistened over the surface of the river, its reflection dancing on the dark water like it was teasing me.

I felt around on the ground until my hand closed on a stone. I chucked it as hard as I could at the silver reflection. The stone ripped through the water and disappeared. I found another stone and threw it. And another and another.

"Ben," I heard Becca say quietly behind me.

Ignoring her, I felt around for another stone but couldn't find any more in the darkness. I sank down onto the sand and put my head in my hands.

"It's my fault he's gone," I said into my hands. "If we never find him, it'll be my fault."

"No, it's not." I felt Becca's hand on my shoulder. "And we're going to find him."

"What I said to him before he left … it was really terrible. What if that's the last thing I ever get to say to him?"

"It won't be."

I took my head out of my hands and looked at her. Strands of her long hair had fallen out of her ponytail from riding her bike and now fell across her forehead.

"How do you know?" I asked her.

"I'm praying to God right now, praying that we find DeShawn."

Her calmness angered me. How could she be this relaxed? "Well, pray harder," I heard myself snap, "because it's not working!" Seeing her surprised and hurt face, I felt ashamed. This girl had helped me look for DeShawn for over an hour now, even though it was late and she would be in trouble with her parents when she got home. "I'm sorry," I said. "I didn't mean that. You should go home. Your parents are probably gonna be mad if you're not back soon."

She shook her head and sat down next to me on the ground. "I don't care," she said.

I looked out at the water. "Do you think God always answers prayers?"

Becca nodded. "My dad says God always answers prayers, just maybe not in the way we hoped."

"That doesn't really make me feel better."

"I know."

We sat there together on the ground. I don't know if Becca was praying, but I was—or doing my best to try. I'd prayed for things before, of course, but the prayer had always been for me. I'd prayed that I had done okay on a math test, prayed that God would make me thinner, prayed that Bethany would like me. But this was the first time I ever prayed for somebody else, not myself, and it felt different, like maybe it actually meant something. I prayed DeShawn was okay. I prayed my parents would find him. I prayed he knew I hadn't meant what I said. I prayed God would make me a better person, prayed God would listen to my prayer, and while I was at it, I prayed God was even there at all.

## PAUL

Two Big Macs, two large fries, two sodas, and one McFlurry came to more than Paul had expected, and paying the McDonald's worker, he couldn't help joking that he remembered when fast food was unhealthy *and* cheap. The guy just gave him a blank look.

Waiting for the food, Paul looked around him, shivering in the too-strong air-conditioning. It was late, and the whole building was nearly empty, the gift shop was locked up, and a custodian was swishing a mop over the ugly brown tile floor. DeShawn was sitting in the McDonald's dining area, at a booth by himself. Paul had been a little worried the kid might bolt again if he left him there, but once he decided to take Paul up on his offer to come into the rest stop and get something to eat, he seemed pretty much resigned to his fate.

Besides, what eleven-year-old boy would run away when he'd been promised McDonald's? Paul brought over the loaded plastic tray and put it on the booth table, then sat down on the opposite bench. "Well, I called the Waids," he said, "so they know you're okay."

DeShawn looked up from unwrapping his burger. "They mad?"

Paul shook his head and grabbed a fry and popped it in his mouth. "More relieved, I'd say. I think they really care about you, DeShawn."

DeShawn took a bite of his Big Mac and nodded.

"You don't really hate them, do you?" Paul had to ask.

DeShawn, his mouth full, shook his head. When he swallowed, he said, "You still gonna go to New York?"

"I have to take you back to the Waids."

"Yeah, but after?"

A french fry stopped halfway to Paul's mouth.

After? Of course he was going back to New York—why wouldn't he? But it was late now. By the time he brought DeShawn back to Grover Falls, it would be past midnight. He might as well stay the night. He had a vision of himself getting up the next morning, driving to Nicki's apartment with a bouquet of flowers in hand, kneeling at her doorstep, begging forgiveness. It was a ridiculous thought, but still, it was funny to imagine her face melting in compassion and grace, her asking him to stay, and himself standing up and nodding. Embracing on the doorstep like at the end of a romantic comedy. He'd find a job somewhere close by—a different sort of job, where he worked with his hands, outside in the weather, his hands growing tough and calloused, his hair growing long. He didn't know how to do anything, but he could learn. He was a fast learner. He'd take care of Nicki through the pregnancy, bring her takeout after work to satisfy her pregnancy cravings, shovel the snow out of her driveway when winter hit. He'd be at her place so much, he'd practically live there, so it would make sense for him to move in. And when her water broke, he'd be there to drive her to the hospital, one hand on the steering wheel, the other holding hers. He'd be there in the delivery room to see the baby take its first breath.

Nicki would have to stay home to take care of the baby for a while, wouldn't she? Working with his hands, Paul would put in overtime at his job to keep them afloat. He imagined coming home after a long day, exhausted but content, to sit with the baby on the sofa, a record playing on the turntable. Something wonderfully dad-like—maybe Springsteen or the Beatles. If things went okay, it would make sense for him and Nicki to get married, just to simplify things. And in a couple of years, when the child was a little older and they'd managed to put away a little money, they could move. Somewhere new. Paul imagined a stone house on top of a hill, surrounded by rolling yellow fields and, beyond them, forests, red and gold in October hues. Somewhere in New England, it must be. They could raise animals. Collecting chicken eggs—a cow, even, grazing in the pasture. On weekends, Paul would take the kids (they would have two now) out on hikes in the woods. They would learn to distinguish birdsongs, one kid scrambling ahead, the other atop his shoulders. A dog barking at their heels.

But, of course, all that was fantasy—whether fairy tale or horror story, Paul couldn't say. He barely knew Nicki, and didn't even know for sure that she was keeping it. And even if she was, what made him think she could ever forgive him for what he had done to her? And what made him think he could get a job with his hands? He barely knew which end of a hammer to hold. And what made him think he'd be happy shoveling snow in January in upstate New York, when he could be drinking beer on a beach in California? He was going on tour across the country. Big things were going to happen. What was he supposed to do with his guitars if he moved back to Grover Falls? Let them sit in a corner with a blanket over them for the rest of his life? Or should he give them to this kid sitting across from him eating McDonald's, this kid who wanted to learn guitar more than anything? *What should I do, God? No—what should I do, April?* In the note, April said she had made a mistake, that she thought he should give DeShawn guitar lessons. But later, she had also told him to move on with his life. So.

DeShawn was looking at him strangely. But after?

Paul Frazier wondered. Maybe mediocrity wasn't as bad as it was cracked up to be. Maybe a life working a dead-end job, paying child support, seeing his kid on the weekends, could be better than anyone ever let on.

He let out a breath. "I don't know," he said, "but I guess I have a little while to decide." He bit into another french fry. They were already getting cold.

## LAURA

I needed to sleep. The sofa was so comfortable, all I wanted to do was curl up in a ball and shut my eyes. But all around me, kids were laughing, drinking, talking too loud over the music. Dustin had his arm around me, so I couldn't rest my head completely against the back of the sofa. Every now and then, he looked at me as if he wanted me to tell him something important or do something, but I didn't know what and was too tired to care, so I just looked down at my lap.

I had to keep my eyes shut or focused somewhere close, or else the room started spinning or things started to split apart and become two—faces, bodies, pictures on the wall—and I couldn't tell which version was real and which was in my head. I was afraid I'd be talking to somebody but actually be looking in the wrong direction, at their hallucinated twin, and they'd think me rude or just crazy. I didn't know why this idea filled me with so much anxiety, but it did.

I tried watching a few kids dance slow in the middle of the room. There was Jen, tall and beautiful, swaying in time with a dark-haired boy. They were barely touching, barely even looking at each other, but they moved in perfect synchronicity. It was beautiful. I watched Jen, and she didn't split apart.

The song changed to something soft and sad. Jen raised her long, pale arms over her head. "This song is pretty," I murmured.

Dustin's voice was suddenly in my ear. I'd forgotten he was there. "The Magnetic Fields. I prefer the Bright Eyes version myself, though."

Boys were always spoiling songs by naming them. Boys were always promising you a better version. "I didn't ask you," I said.

"Hey, calm down, kid." His laugh was fake and stupid. He squeezed my arm too tightly. I needed to sleep, but I didn't want to rest my head against Dustin. His hand was still on my arm. The room was beginning to spin. I tried to stand up.

"Whoa, where are you going?" he asked, holding my arm. I looked around. The room had gotten darker, and most of the kids were gone. The ones who were still there were locked in each other's arms, kissing. I realized that was what Dustin expected us to do.

"Let go of me," I said, jerking my arm away and hearing myself slur.

"Buffy, calm down. Come sit with me." He tried to pull me onto his lap, but I leaned forward and pulled my arm free of his grip.

For a second, he looked angry. I saw a face not too different from Martin's when I had touched him. I had a flash of clear thinking: this idiot would believe anything I said—I just had to smile prettily at him. I smiled and laid my hand on his shoulder. "I'm just going to the bathroom. I'll be right back." I let my hand reach up and touch his cheek for a moment, for good measure.

Then I stumbled through the room, past the bodies locked together on the couches and exchanging saliva, past boys leaning against the wall, holding bottles of beer and leering, past the few couples still standing in the middle of the room, dancing slowly to the music, looking like true lovers.

I found the stairwell and began to climb up, up, holding on to the railing for balance. It seemed as if the stairs never ended. My head hurt. I could barely keep my eyes open. I wondered suddenly where Jordan had gone. I wanted to apologize to her, tell her I didn't hate her for tipping over the boat that day back in July, that I was happy for her and Bethany and wanted to be friends again.

On the second floor, the first room I tried had a bed, but two bodies were in it, writhing under the sheets. I shut the door, ignoring their annoyed shouts, and tried the next room. This time, the bed was empty. I stood for a moment just looking at it, relieved. It was the most beautiful thing I'd ever seen. Then I heard Dustin's voice.

"Buffy, where'd you go?"

I shut the door and looked for a lock.

The knob began to turn. "Buffy?"

I slammed my body against the door and leaned all my weight into it. "Leave me alone," I said.

"Buffy, open the door. I need to show you something."

The door began to open, and I pressed harder, digging in my feet. At the same time, I felt around with my hands for the lock. I had the horrible fear that there wouldn't be one and eventually his weight and strength would win out over mine. Then my hands closed around a sliding bolt, and I latched the door shut.

"Come on!" Dustin sounded furious.

"You'll wake up the neighbors," I said in a loud voice.

With the boy still calling out my fake name and pounding on the door, I stumbled over to the bed, so spacious and cool and inviting. If I could just close my eyes for a moment, I thought, that moment would stretch on and on, forever. Suddenly, a conversation I had online with Martin at the beginning of summer came to me from far away. We'd been talking about death. I was afraid, but Martin told me it was okay because it would feel like nothing, be nothing. Now, though, that idea wasn't comforting; it was terrifying. What if I closed my eyes and never woke up? I didn't want to sleep, but I was so, so tired.

My head sank into the pillow. I rolled onto my stomach. Far, far away, the boy was still pounding on the door. What if the lock should break? What if he came charging in and tried to touch me? What if I fell asleep and never woke up? What if ... what if ... what if ... Something was pressing against my thigh, and I rolled over again and pulled the thing out of my pocket. It was my phone. I looked at it in amazement. I'd forgotten it was even there. Then I turned it over and realized someone was calling me—the sound was off—and when I saw who it was, I felt relief wash over me like a flood. I answered the call.

"Mom?"

# 28

On an early September Sunday morning in Albany, New York, the Johnsons were going to church. There were five of them—Mark and Lisa and three kids—and only one bathroom, so a Sunday morning was fraught with hassle and resentment. Mark complained that Lisa spent too much time on her hair with the bathroom door locked. Lisa shot back that if Mark would ever help with the kids' breakfast, she would have been done with her hair an hour ago. The kids had their own squabbles and feuds, most of which they saw fit to inform their parents of. By the time they emerged—all scrubbed and starched and shined—from the house and got into the car, everyone had resolved their various skirmishes or, at least, tamped them down so they didn't show until they began again the next Sunday morning.

The Grahams were going to church, too—even Chrissy, although she didn't want to. It was part of the deal she had made with her mother and new stepfather: she could move back in, but she had to quit using and she had to come to church. Since she wasn't entirely complying with the former condition, she felt that the least she could do was submit to the latter without complaining, though that didn't mean she had to look happy about it.

Greg Felix didn't like going to church, either, so he didn't. But his wife did. It saddened Mary Felix to no end that her husband had slowly but surely lost his once-vibrant faith, and she didn't shy away from telling him so. And no matter how many times Greg replied that he hadn't lost anything—he still believed in God, he just liked to sleep in and relax at home on the only day of the week he could—Mary wasn't convinced.

On that September Sunday morning in Albany, April Swanson didn't go to church—she woke up in one. Specifically, at United Believers of Albany, in an empty upstairs classroom, in a sleeping bag on a camp cot. Her daughter was sleeping beside her, her back spooned close against April on the narrow cot. Laura's hair smelled horrible—a mixture of perfume, cigarette smoke, pot, and who knew what else. But lying there with her head resting on the thin pillow, April breathed in deeply, and it was the most wonderful thing she had ever smelled. Here was her daughter, lying next to her. She could wrap her body in a hug; she could hold her tight; she could squeeze her arm.

Instead, April sat up and picked up her phone from where it lay on the floor. It was past nine, later than she usually slept, but that still meant they'd gotten only a few hours of sleep last night. By the time Laura had at last answered her phone and told April where she was, by the time April had gotten to the party house, by the time she had taken Laura to the emergency room for the bump on her head, by the time they were discharged from the hospital and they got back to the church, it had been too late to return home to Grover Falls. The easiest thing to do was just camp out in the church for the rest of the night.

And it was up here, as they lay together on the cot around three in the morning, that Laura told her mother the real story—or, more precisely, the part she had left out until everyone else was gone. Yes, she'd gone to a party, but that was not why she left the church group in the first place. For the first time, April learned about Martin. She learned that her daughter had been posing as a forty-year-old woman online for over a year. She learned that she'd met this man in a restaurant, and she learned what had happened after.

Hearing all this, any mother had the right to go ballistic. She had a right to lock her daughter up till she was eighteen. She had the right to scream and rage. But April didn't feel like doing any of that. In fact, she felt a surprising sense of calm. She didn't even doubt her own parenting skills. Instead, she felt, maybe for the first time since her daughter became a teenager, that Laura was opening up to her, revealing herself. And this only prompted a wave of relief and love for her daughter to wash over April. There was much more to talk about and resolve. She would have to think long and hard about this in the weeks and months to come. But drifting off to sleep together on the cot, it was enough that Laura had told her, and it was enough that she was here beside her, in this empty Sunday-school classroom in Albany.

April stood up and looked down at herself. In last night's rush to get down here, of course she hadn't thought to bring anything, certainly not pajamas. But Laura, who had packed for a night away from home, had let her borrow one of her T-shirts to sleep in. It was blue, and across the front were the words "Sonic Youth," just above her breasts, and below, four angry-looking kids. April rather liked it. She put back on the same jeans she had worn yesterday, and her sneakers. She dug into her purse for a pen and something to write on.

*Laura,* she wrote on a pink sticky note. *Went to get us something to eat.* DON'T GO ANYWHERE. *Mom.* April took the sticky note and stuck it on the screen of her daughter's cell phone, lying beside her on the bed.

April went down the stairs and walked down the hall, to the vestibule. The early churchgoers, the ambitious ones who attended Sunday school before the regular service, were filtering in through the open front doors, letting in the bright morning light. Worship music played softly through speakers somewhere above April's head. In a small room off the atrium, she could see people standing and chatting in groups around a table set up with coffee and juice and bagels. Standing in the middle of the room, she began to notice the curious glances she got as people made their way into the church. Was it the Sonic Youth shirt? Was it the slept-in hair and the un-made-up face? Was it simply that she was new here and they didn't recognize her? Or had word already spread about the crazy woman whose daughter ran away while attending a pro-life rally? Any one of these possibilities seemed plausible, but whatever the case, no one was rude. After the initial curious looks, they all smiled and said good morning, and April smiled and said good morning back to them, feeling that it really was good.

Jon Newman came rushing out of the next room with a Styrofoam cup of coffee in his hand. "April!" he said. "Great! Pastor Darren was wondering if you were up yet. He wants to say hi. There's coffee and stuff."

Jon looked at her expectantly. Last night, he had, of course, apologized profusely for what happened with Laura. But April had felt something lacking. Every apology had been laced with a subtle denial of responsibility. Sure, technically, losing Laura had been his fault, but really, it wasn't his fault. "*I know I should have confirmed with you, April, about her leaving for dinner. I'm so sorry. But it just didn't even occur to me that Laura would lie to me like that, you know?*" At the time, April had let it go—she had much more pressing matters on her mind—but now, seeing his wide, smiling face, free from any trace of remorse or contrition, she bristled inside. She did her best to let it go. After all, what did it matter? What was one more American boy living life in carefree, blameless denial? Instead, she nodded and pulled out her phone. "I'll be right there," she said. Looking at her phone as if at a compass, April turned and walked toward the church's big, open front doors. She didn't want to talk to Pastor Darren, who surely wanted to say more than just hi. She was done talking to pastors for a while. Besides, she knew that the coffee would be too weak.

Outside, the sky was dazzling blue, with not a trace of yesterday's clouds. She stood on the church's front steps and blinked and searched her phone for the nearest coffee shop.

April walked down the street. She was going to buy a cup of coffee for herself, an orange juice for her daughter, and two maple doughnuts. They were going to eat their breakfast up in their room, then they were going to gather Laura's things and go. No further explanation required. She found, with surprise and relief, that the strange sense of happiness she had felt walking home last night, before all this, had not abandoned her altogether as she had expected it to. Again she felt a new world making itself known, a hidden door cracking open. And again she felt the desire to talk to Paul, and for a moment, she felt a stab of regret—how nice it would be to walk down the street with him now, holding hands, laughing at some dumb joke between them. But the feeling lasted only a moment. She stopped at a crosswalk, waited for the signal, and stepped out into the street.

# EPILOGUE

It was the first week of summer vacation, a warm evening in June. I was sixteen. Bethany and Nola and I were sitting out on the abandoned bridge overlooking the river, passing a joint around. Or really, they were passing it back and forth while I sat between them, every now and then taking a sip from an old water bottle I had brought along, filled with cranberry juice and vodka—my current favorite drink. I still didn't like getting high, but drinking was a different matter.

We had gone to see a movie—the latest *Twilight* installment. None of us had seen the earlier films, so we just ate popcorn and heckled the screen loudly until others in the audience got annoyed and told us to be quiet. We left early.

After last summer and "the Albany incident," as it came to be known in our house, for a while I was afraid that my mom would never let me go out unattended again. I would have deserved it. But nothing like that happened. "I'm hoping," she had told me, a few months into the school year, "in my clichéd, naive way, that you learned something from all of it, and that you grew." Moreover, she had reasoned, the whole thing had started online, without me even leaving my room. That's where most of it had taken place, so what good would grounding me do?

Not that she let me roam free, or anything. I had a strict curfew and had to check in with her every hour. Really, though, it hardly mattered, since I didn't have much of a desire to go anywhere. My only friends were Bethany and Nola, and they liked to come to my house anyway, probably because it was one of the only places they could see each other. We hung out a lot in my room over the winter, doing our homework together and watching stupid movies. My mom was okay with it because I was there, a natural impediment to my friends getting overly intimate with each other, and I didn't much mind being the third wheel. In some ways, it gave me a strange sense of superiority—I wasn't dumb and in love like my two idiot friends.

Now, as we sat on the bridge, my idiot friends leaned out in front of me to share a quick peck on the lips. "Ugh," I said in mock revulsion, "why do you two always pick the most inopportune moment for displays of affection?"

"Ah!" Bethany cried, grabbing my shoulder. "Is Laura feeling left out?" She kissed me on the cheek. "Laura, please don't be mad! And please don't go! P-p-p-please!"

"Bethany, you promised," I said.

"No, you're not going. I won't let you." Bethany put her head on my shoulder. "It's just not going to happen."

But we both knew it was. I was moving to Florida. My mom had taken a job at the nonprofit my aunt Sarah worked for. By next month, we would be saying goodbye to Grover Falls. My mom had told me she was going to wait—not think about moving until I finished high school. But after she'd talked with me about it, I told that she shouldn't wait, that I wouldn't mind moving somewhere new, starting in a new town at a new school. Of course, I would miss Bethany, miss her more than anything. And I realized, over the winter, that I would miss Nola, too.

"You'll come visit," I said to Bethany. Though I wasn't sure she'd be able to—things weren't going well with her parents, and they didn't give her a lot of leeway. The only way she even got to go to my house was in the aftermath of a horrible fight where she screamed and even threatened to kill herself if she couldn't. I don't think it was an entirely empty threat. They had given in, but they wouldn't have if they knew she met Nola there. Mostly, Bethany lived these days in a constant state of tension with her parents—tension that often erupted into outright war. A lot of days, she looked tired and sad. Sometimes, I caught her looking off into the distance with a vague expression on her face.

"It's up to you to take care of her now," I said to Nola, patting her on the back, and we both knew I was only half joking. Bethany loved Nola. No matter what her parents put her through or what she had to give up, that wasn't going to change.

"Are you kidding?" said Nola, taking a long drag. "We're hitchhiking down to Florida to live with you. We'll hide in the U-Haul van."

"If only," said Bethany after a moment, sounding very serious, "if only there was a way we could all be rich and famous and never have to leave each other."

We laughed.

"We could start a band," Nola suggested. "Sometimes that works."

"Hey, yeah!" said Bethany. "The three of us on tour forever, traveling across the world!"

"What would we call ourselves?" I asked.

"I always thought a great name for a band would be Everlasting Gobstopper," said Nola, looking dreamily off into the dark.

"Seriously," said Bethany, "that's the stupidest name I've ever heard."

"Well, what's your amazing suggestion, then?"

"I don't know, something cool and classic. Something with 'the,' you know? Like … 'the Royal Bitches' or something."

"The Royal Bitches?"

"It's better than Everlasting Gobstopper."

"You say that with such certainty."

"Anything's better than Everlasting Gobstopper."

As my friends argued beside me, I suddenly thought of something. "Hey," I said, "can any of us even play an instrument?"

Bethany and Nola stopped arguing and looked at me. They shook their heads. Then we all burst out in hysterics.

"Who cares? We'll learn," Bethany said, but she was shaking so hard with laughter, she could hardly get the words out. We all were. I tried to take a drink from my bottle, and cranberry juice and liquor spilled down my chin. I was tearing up, and my side hurt from shaking so hard.

I don't know what got into us; it really wasn't that funny. But I swear, no matter how hard we tried, we just couldn't stop laughing.

# ACKNOWLEDGMENTS

I am deeply grateful—

To my wonderful agent, Nell Pierce, who took a chance on me. To Michael Carr, whose patience and sharp eye were invaluable during the editing process. To Haila Williams, Lauren Maturo, Jeff Yamaguchi, and all the fantastic people at Blackstone Publishing.

To all the teachers who have encouraged me through the years, especially James Allen Hall, who gave me the courage to take the plunge; Luis Jaramillo and everyone at the New School; Helen Schulman, whose keen insights and advice helped me hit the ground running; and Darcey Steinke, whose continual guidance and unfailing generosity leaves me stunned.

To all my friends who have supported and put up with me, especially those who read this book in its early stages: Paul Florez, who reassured me so many times I'm sure I drove him nuts; my sister Leslie Ann, who probably didn't realize how relieved I was when she told me she liked it; Kyle Lucia Wu, who never let me give up, who let me complain her ear off, and ask her question after question, and send her draft after draft. I don't know how I got so lucky.

To my family. To my parents, who built me. To my wife, Alissa, who supports but never indulges me, keeps me driven, and makes me better. I owe you big.